# REX

They watched as the flames soared, crackled and then found a steady rhythm. From where she sat in the crimson shadows, Hailey could see the city lights against the midnight blue sky. She had the eerie sensation that no life before had ever existed for her. She shouldn't get too carried away with the moment, she told herself again. She was just vulnerable and she should never let herself think that she was anything special to him. He must have had hundreds of women, and most of them far more sophisticated than she. She must and she *would* keep her guard up.

Her eyes were locked on the fire ballet when she felt him watching her . . .

*Other Avon Books by*
**Catherine Lanigan**

Bound by Love

# ADMIT DESIRE

## CATHERINE LANIGAN

AVON
PUBLISHERS OF BARD, CAMELOT, DISCUS AND FLARE BOOKS

ADMIT DESIRE is an original publication of Avon Books. This work has never before appeared in book form.

AVON BOOKS
A division of
The Hearst Corporation
959 Eighth Avenue
New York, New York 10019

Copyright © 1983 by Catherine Lanigan
Published by arrangement with the author
Library of Congress Catalog Card Number: 82-90484
ISBN: 0-380-81810-8

First Avon Printing, January, 1983

AVON TRADEMARK REG. U. S. PAT. OFF. AND IN OTHER COUNTRIES, MARCA REGISTRADA, HECHO EN U. S. A.

Printed in the U. S. A.

WFH 10 9 8 7 6 5 4 3 2 1

*For Rene, my husband, my love.*
*For Ryan, my son, for being patient.*
*And for you . . . wherever you are.*

# BOOK I

*Hailey*

# Chapter One

HAILEY glanced at her ultraslim gold watch, a long-ago Christmas gift from her father, and realized it was too late to beat the rush-hour traffic. Once again, she'd been lost in her daydreams. That was another bad habit, she thought. Considerable effort had gone into finding a baby-sitter for the afternoon's shopping; she'd needed some time to herself to relax and think. Instead she found herself knotted and tense.

She signed the sales slip and accepted her receipt, credit card and parcels from the overtired saleswoman. She dashed out of Neiman-Marcus and raced across the white tile floor of the Galleria. As her blond hair, in a post-"Farrah" stage, flew in a sparkling silvery veil over her shoulders, Hailey was unaware of the admiring, if not lecherous, looks she received. She'd parked in Lord & Taylor's lot and now scolded herself for not having paid attention to where she was. Suddenly she slowed her pace and heaved an exasperated sigh.

"It's just like Mike says, I can't do anything right. Now dinner will be late and it's my fault."

Hailey's attitude of late had been puzzling even to herself. She spent the majority of her days convincing herself with a litany of overused phrases that she was happy. The mental ploy wasn't working anymore, for everything about her life was out of kilter.

After leaving the opulent shopping center, she scrambled through her wine-colored leather purse searching for her keys, cursing under her breath. She finally located them and unlocked the door to her four-year-old Thunderbird. As her car bobbed over the speed bumps on the down ramp, her immediate options posed a dilemma. If she went west on Westheimer, she'd encounter stop-and-go traffic and long lights, and if she took the loop, it was bumper-to-bumper. She chose the latter.

To anyone who ever visited Houston the traffic was always a shock; the only solace one could take was that no matter how bad it was today, tomorrow would be worse.

As she took the exit to Interstate 10 and crept along at twenty miles an hour, she remembered how she and her husband, Mike Asher, had been transferred to this southern mecca by his new employer, Texaco.

Mike had been employed by a small oil firm in Chicago until he'd flown to Acapulco last fall on business and met a group from Texaco. They were impressed with Mike, which was not hard to imagine, and whisked him away from the Illinois firm in a matter of weeks. Hailey did not mind moving; she was used to it. Mike was a corporate genius of sorts. He could scan company P&L sheets and instantly discover where losses could be cut and profit margins increased, and then proceed to rectify the problems. She was proud of his ability, and sometimes envious. He had what he wanted, and she only wished she could say the same.

Two days after moving into her new house, Hailey went next door and introduced herself to Alice Blakeman, who in turn was kind enough to introduce her to the other neighbors. Swiftly, Hailey found herself volunteering as block chairman and room mother for the PTO, jobs no one else had time for. It was Hailey who gave the first in what became a series of neighborhood barbecues.

Alice often called for Hailey's advice on decorating or a certain recipe. The others, Martha, Helen and Joy, seemed content with their roles as homemakers and easily accepted Hailey into their group. Even though their lives were similar, Hailey felt like an outsider. Alice, Martha and the rest were sincerely happy. They were all intelligent women with diversified interests and accomplishments

4

they were proud of. But Hailey knew she could not be easily categorized as "just a housewife" even though she had done nothing outstanding to disprove that, even to herself.

Hailey had continued to build upon the intellectual nurturing her parents had begun. She was a voracious reader and when exposed to ideas that she heard Mike discussing with his clients, she would listen attentively, taking it all down in mental shorthand. She wanted to show Mike that she had a brain, though she doubted that he took her seriously. The problem was that Mike couldn't see beyond her physical attributes, which were better than average, but hardly superior. He felt it was sufficient that she be a good mother and an asset to him and his career, and nothing else was necessary or expected.

"But I do expect more of myself!" she mumbled and was suddenly angry. "Stop that, Hailey. You should be grateful for the life you lead."

She did keep trying to improve herself, and she could remember that once even Mike had been pleased. Leaning upon her background and love of art, she expressly watched the value of prized art escalate over the years and had managed to persuade Mike to invest in a few minor works. Reluctantly, he had agreed that the decision had been profitable. Not only was art a stimulus to her aesthetic eye, but also Mike had reveled in the boost it had given to his personal balance sheet.

Hailey possessed a need for contact with the art world ever since she left college. She instilled in her children an appreciation for art, music and literature. For years, she had taken them to every art exhibit she could find, explaining different techniques, shading, composition and subject matter. But through it all she was reluctant to express her buried desires for a career in art, for she was well aware of her lack of talent. Hailey rationalized that she was realistic and logical, for she had very little training. She dabbled in an occasional acrylic on canvas, some charcoal sketches, a watercolor ballerina for Kim or an oil of a horse for Joey. She had, at times, found it impossible to accomplish even these things in her own home. Once she had painted a mural of farm animals on the walls of Joey's room. Mike had hated it, saying it would give Joey nightmares. Hailey suspected he was fearful of her ability to stand without him. Their problems went much deeper and rather than root them out, she avoided the confrontation and angrily painted over the mural with a bland and noncommittal designer blue.

How many times had she sketched portraits of the children and sent them to her mother as a Christmas gift? How many hundreds of watercolors had she painted with or for the children that had only found their way into a packing box when they transferred yet one more time? Why hadn't she taken her art seriously? Would rejection be all that terrible? It was she who had handed Mike the key to her prison and he had gladly kept her locked in. She smiled sarcastically at the image of herself, finally possessing the tenacity to approach a gallery owner with her work. The fantasy was ludicrous!

She turned up the radio and hoped it would clear her mind, or fill it up. One or the other, it didn't matter, just as long as she would stop dwelling on the impossible. However, that was an improbability for her, just as it had always been. Even as a small child, her vivid fantasies conquered many a lazy summer afternoon. Her mother had been sympathetic, but there always came the inevitable lambasting from her father for fabricating wild stories.

Her father, Austin James, had been her hero. A tall, handsome dark-haired man with flashing, intense blue eyes, he was the most highly intelligent and literate man Hailey knew.

For over twenty years Austin had prided himself upon his superior and unreproachable reputation for molding, cajoling, inspiring and oftentimes browbeating his somewhat reluctant students into becoming the most sought-after graduates of Harvard Law School. They all had high ambitions but he was demanding of them, so much so that the majority hated him with fierce, aggressive explosions at times. But every semester his classes were full, for to graduate from Austin James' strenuous senior-year ordeal meant a job with a top Manhattan or Boston law firm.

When Hailey was five years old, Austin spoke to her as if she were one of his graduate law students. He had no concept of the workings of a child's mind. His attitude had always been, "If she can't understand me, that's her problem. She'll just have to raise herself up to my level."

Thus, Hailey had spent entire evenings under the covers in her blue-and-white gingham-wallpapered bedroom with a flashlight looking up the meanings of her father's words in a dictionary. Half the time, even the definitions sounded foreign to her and she became more confused than ever. At an early age she'd known frustration and what she perceived as rejection. But she was Austin's daughter and it was his stalwart determination and unswerving conviction to rules and principles that drove her to better herself throughout her life. He expected more than the best from her. He pushed her to become a scholar in the true sense of the word. To him, her excellent grades were requisite. He wanted her to be an intellectual, not a "flighty artist." Each time he caught her so much as sketching, he flew into a rage. She was wasting valuable time on child's play, he'd said, and he would not tolerate it! How could she expect to accomplish anything significant if she degenerated into an artist? Hailey always felt that nothing less than winning the Nobel Prize would satisfy him. She knew she could never live up to his expectations, even though she spent her life trying.

For years, Austin had planned that his daughter would attend either Vassar, Smith or Radcliffe. When eighteen-year-old Hailey, jubilant over her newly acclaimed status of valedictorian, proclaimed that she had been accepted at all three universities and also at the two midwestern universities she'd applied to, he was proud.

Unabashedly, Hailey informed her parents that she didn't care to enter any of their chosen schools, but had selected DePauw University, a small coed school in Greencastle, Indiana. It was highly competitive and she thought it would surely meet with her father's approval. She had been dead wrong.

It was the first time in years that he had truly lashed out at her. His heated words singed the edges of her conviction and she was utterly stunned at how she had disappointed him.

This model daughter, her deportment, personality and temperament; the envy of his peers who wrestled daily with their anti-establishment offspring who balked at all authority; his fair-haired, exquisitely beautiful Hailey had taken it upon herself, without his approval, to enroll in some godforsaken midwestern school. He demanded she accept Vassar and put an end to her ridiculous plans.

Hailey attacked with the stealth of a lioness. If he would not accept her decision, she would then not attend any college. She wanted to do this one thing on her own. It was her decision and she had made it intelligently, she thought. Once she presented him with the proof of her alternative plan, an interview with TWA as a stewardess, he relinquished his order. In her frame of mind at that point, Hailey was bound to do as she threatened. Above all things, Austin would not allow her to forgo her education to become a stewardess. That was worse than becoming an artist! He decided that if he continued with a more subtle approach, perhaps Hailey would change her mind once she found how dreary and unchallenging that university was and would move back East.

Before the furor abated, Austin suffered a massive heart attack and died. Sonja, her mother, had attended the funeral in a state of shock, against the doctor's advice. She had cried and mourned the loss of her husband and through the weeks afterward her grieving had followed a natural course. Hailey's had not.

Hailey was angry with her father for not warning them, abandoning her and her mother and, in her mind, for not loving them enough to stay alive. Her actions were defiant and rebellious. She deliberately pursued her plans to enter DePauw, childishly believing she could infuriate Austin enough to come back to life.

Though distressed over leaving her mother alone in Boston, Hailey had been self-absorbed at the time and wrongly thought only of the end of her relationship with her father. He hadn't stayed alive long enough for her to have the chance to prove herself to him. How obsessed she had been! He had demanded much of her, and then before she could accomplish the goals he had set for her, he had removed himself from her life. She was floundering and directionless. It wasn't until she accepted the finality of his death almost a year later that she consciously discerned the motivations behind her actions.

Hailey remembered the torrent of tears that finally came, and she admonished herself for holding them back so long. By then, the university and her friends were a real part of her life and she knew she did not want to transfer back East. This time the decision was for the right reasons.

If anything, she was flooded with remorse over the conflict she had created during Austin's last year of his life. To rectify the situation, she struggled at every turn to do all the things that would have pleased him.

However, in the past few years, Hailey knew that her mother was concerned with her daughter's inability to dream anymore. Sonja was a poet and a romanticist. Her Russian ancestry had left her with a respect for superstition and an almost religious belief in fairy tales and folklore. The underlying themes in her poetry recounted glorious tales of maidens and ruggedly handsome noblemen who captured these female hearts and conquered over all evils in the name of love.

Within the context of Hailey's innocence and nourished by a childlike search for the truth and reality, Sonja's poems and tales had combined to weave a tapestry of unflinching idealism, blind hope and an acceptance of what both parents instilled in her. That she had never seriously challenged their convictions never occurred to her. They had no reason to tell her anything but the absolute truth.

Unfortunately for Hailey, until this day she had never questioned the fact that most times in life, there were no absolutes. Only change; change was inevitable.

Those years after Austin's death had been difficult for Hailey, but now she could see they had been even worse for Sonja. Sonja had lost her love to death and her daughter to college. How lonely Sonja must have been as she rattled around in that house! No wonder Sonja's tendencies to romantic fantasies had grown through those years!

Mother and daughter had always been close. Hailey's phone bills were testimony to that. But over the past few years, when Hailey had asked for Sonja's advice about various things, Sonja's answer was: "What do you think you should do, Hailey? It is your decision."

"My decision," mused Hailey. On the surface, she believed she had handled her life fairly well, but now she could see that she had relied too heavily on Sonja's experience and her father's advice.

Sonja had never pushed Hailey to grow up. She needed Hailey's dependence on her to fill the void Austin's death had caused. Fearful that she had somehow caused Austin's heart attack, Hailey through guilt had bonded herself too closely to her mother. Perhaps now they were both maturing.

Putting herself back in time, she knew her innate need for achievement had propelled her through college. She thrust her energy into her courses, wanting to know everything about every subject she studied. There was no room for mediocrity. That had been her philosophy of life back then, a decade ago, and now she continually settled for little snippets of hope. Oh, how she wanted to believe that happiness was more than just another Russian fairy tale!

One of her regrets was that she had left her best friend in Chicago when they transferred to Houston. Janet Brownlee Spencer was much like Hailey in both personality and looks. They had met on one of those autumn days of rustling dried crimson and gold leaves over a decade ago. Hailey had arrived on campus two days early, but was already engulfed in the throes of rush week. She had been late for a tea at the Chi Omega house and was stealthily easing herself through the doorway when she literally bumped into a startled Janet Brownlee. They had gaped at each other, noting their physical similarities. Janet was slightly shorter and her hair more golden than Hailey's but her round doe eyes were filled with friendliness. As Hailey peered into their almost black depths, it was as if she had found a sister.

Janet's effervescent outlook on all the banal aspects of sorority life, strenuous class loads and meaningless though inevitable dating of fraternity playboys and football jocks enabled Hailey to retain a humorous perspective on the situation.

Janet had the ability to stumble into the most unbelievable situations. Even a simple shopping spree would turn into an adventure in some way or another. Janet was always the first to be locked in a bathroom, get stuck on an elevator or find that all her tires were flat in the midst of a rainstorm.

Throughout her freshman and sophomore years Hailey's mind was crowded with unresolved decisions. Even though she felt as productive at an easel, she had discovered that she was more suited to scholastic pursuits. She abandoned the idea of attending art school after graduation and entered the elementary-education program. She adored children, and not having any brothers or sisters, she had felt she had missed some segment of life and she wanted to grasp it now.

For the majority of the time, she was undaunted, fully believing she could conquer the world and that should she find an opportunity other than teaching that she might enjoy, she would pursue it, too. She just might find she was the best kindergarten teacher Boston had ever seen! She was armed with new open-classroom procedures and was crammed with innovative ideas even her "methods" professor hadn't dreamed of. She would set the public-school system on its stuffy conservative ear.

She had her future ahead of her and she could explore any one of a hundred careers and life-styles. It was the challenge she sought. *She* would be important.

Throughout Hailey's college years Sonja continually pressed her to transfer to Vassar. Not that Sonja was unduly lonely, for she was active in numerous community charities and kept a full social calendar. Sonja was acutely aware that the best prospects for a proper marital match for Hailey were to be found in the East. Hailey realized that her mother harbored anxieties due to her father's death. Sonja felt stranded in life without Austin and longed for a protector and in her grief she projected her fears onto Hailey and pushed for the girl to marry. If Hailey could find a man with a real future—a professional man, perhaps—Sonja's misgivings would abate and she would feel secure once more.

The summer before her senior year, Hailey met Mike Asher at a poolside barbecue. Mike, looking as bored as she did, had been standing next to a portable bar in a pair of cutoff jeans and a blue-and-white-striped rugby shirt. As soon as Hailey arrived he made a beeline for her. He was easy to talk to and she was impressed with his charming smile and easy manners. He dominated her time for the rest of that day and the remainder of the summer. They became friends quickly and enjoyed sailing, picnicking and water skiing.

Sonja had been thrilled, for she knew of his family and could see that Mike would have a brilliant business career. Looking back on it now, it had been Sonja who had relentlessly pressed the relationship.

Mike had been continually invited to dinners and various outings with both the James'. Hailey hadn't been particularly drawn to him, she thought now in recollection, but they shared many of the same interests at the time. He had just graduated from Harvard Business School with honors. Hailey knew Austin would have been pleased with that.

During Hailey's senior year, Mike drove to Greencastle as often as possible from Chicago, where he worked for an oil company. Most times they did nothing special, simply enjoying a quiet companionship. When he proposed at Christmas, Hailey had not answered him immediately but had asked for time to think it over. Sonja had been both baffled and annoyed at Hailey's reluctance to marry a man with such a promising future. Here was the white knight and her daughter was hesitant!

Hailey relented, knowing Sonja knew what was best for

her. After all, wasn't that the next logical step for every girl to take? First college and then marriage?

To this day the church ceremony and small reception were still an unfocused flash of memory to Hailey, as if they had happened to someone else. She did remember that after three days of her supposedly week-long honeymoon in Jamaica, she wanted desperately to come home. It had been more important to be with Sonja than with Mike. Hailey had felt an overwhelming need to reassure Sonja that she was not being abandoned. At least that's what Hailey told herself at the time. Now she realized that she had felt no passion for Mike, and the honeymoon was immaterial to her. The revelation was startling! How could she have been so blind?

Two weeks after the honeymoon she had packed all her personal possessions, said good-bye to her mother and moved to Chicago to join Mike. Their address, north of the Watertower, was impressive, but the building was old and Hailey had painted the interior herself. Like most newlyweds, Mike and Hailey began discovering each other. Mike revealed an acquisitive side to his nature she hadn't seen before. What bothered her was the selfishness he displayed when he contemplated his purchases. Their income was good but by no means grand, even though Mike spent money as if it were. Appearances were uppermost to Mike. He never discussed his material desires with Hailey until after the items were delivered. She'd put on blinders when the color TV and elaborate stereo arrived. Next came a solid wood Tudor bedroom set, two pieces of which would not fit in their bedroom. But when he purchased a four-thousand-dollar red Oriental rug, Hailey flew into a rage.

"Why is it that you never consult me about these things? We can't afford luxuries like this!"

"Never mind that. I'll make enough money to buy a dozen rugs. And there's no reason to consult you. I work hard and I'm entitled to spend my money as I please!" With that he left the room.

Hailey cut corners everywhere to pay the bills and keep their credit in line. Her resentment grew every time he

13

bought a new suit from Brooks Brothers and she was still wearing her Villager outfits she'd had since college. But Mike did get good raises and somehow they did manage to pay the bills.

During that time in Chicago, Janet telephoned her one night at three in the morning to inform her that she had just eloped. As Hailey remembered it now, she couldn't help saying with a laugh, "Just like Janet, too!" She had met Dan Spencer while covering a story for the *Chicago Tribune* about two weeks previously. It had actually been only nine days, but Janet thought that rounding it off to two weeks sounded better. It was love at first sight and she knew she couldn't live without him.

Janet remained in Chicago while Hailey and Mike transferred to Atlanta. Hailey was seven months pregnant with Kim when they left. Once there, they were able to scrape up the small down payment on a forty-year-old bungalow in a respectable and safe neighborhood. Mike's hours were long and he was expected to travel extensively. Hailey managed the move, the household and the yard single-handedly. She spent the last months of her pregnancy sewing curtains and slipcovers on a portable sewing machine her mother had given her, and she taught herself to put up preserves, freeze vegetables and hang wallpaper.

The night Kim was born, Mike was in New York, but he sent flowers and called her long distance the following morning to say he would fly home in four days to take her and the baby home from the hospital. Hailey was joyous over this tiny, wonderful creation who cooed and smiled at her.

Hailey, like most new mothers, found herself besieged with laundry and barely any time to herself. Mike was now called upon to assume much of the entertaining for his company when he was not on the road. During the week he could be found at Atlanta's most exclusive restaurants, and on the weekends he played golf.

When Mike did take Hailey out, it was always connected with business. He wanted the perfect ornament for his arm and she made him look good. As the years passed he began purchasing her clothes for these occasions. Never mind that the price tags were extravagant, Hailey had no say in the matter. He bought the perfect Adolfo theater suit, the Bill Blass sweater and silk taffeta pants and the Calvin Klein rose silk organza party dress. Her wardrobe was now an odd mixture of unusable party clothes and ten-year-old blue jeans. Mike did have better taste than she did, but she resented his dictating even her clothing, which reflected his personality and not hers.

They lived in Atlanta just over a year when Mike announced that he'd been promoted and they were to move to Minneapolis. Hailey was happy for him and agreed to help all she could. As the movers placed the last of their furniture on the van, she lamented the tree she had planted two months earlier, the wood floors she had just refinished and the Montessori day care school where Kim had just been enrolled.

For the following seven years, the pattern was the same. Another promotion, another city, another house with twice the mortgage. Mike traveled across the continent, stopping at home long enough for her to conceive Joey.

Hailey had been thrilled with the news she gave to Mike about the baby, but he apparently did not share her joy.

"I thought you were taking the Pill," was his first comment.

"I told you the last time you were home the doctor was worried about side effects. It isn't all that safe."

"It's safer than having a baby!"

"Mike, don't you want the baby?"

"My God, Hailey. The timing is all wrong. We can't afford it!"

"Oh, sure, but we can afford a two-thousand-dollar grandfather clock and silk suits for you!"

He had tried to console her then, telling her she had just gotten him at a bad moment. He assured her he was happy about the baby. Hailey wanted to believe that he meant it, but she felt more alone than ever.

"I'm just being selfish, Hailey. I'm sorry. Everything

will be fine. I'm just taken aback by all this. We hadn't talked of another baby. I just wasn't prepared . . . I'm sorry."

"It's okay, Mike. I understand. We'll manage. We always do."

"That's right, honey. I'll take care of you."

And the next day he left again on business.

As the years passed, Hailey lived like a single parent. It was she who sought out the new pediatrician, dentist and schools for the children in each city. She never remained in one area long enough to form friendships, enroll in graduate classes or see her roses and tulips bloom in the spring. Hailey thought she would never become used to the tension that surrounded her. How long would they live in this city? How many people would she meet and never see again? How many projects would she start and never finish?

It wasn't an easy life for Mike, either. There were plenty of lonely hotel rooms, cold hamburgers and constant telephone calls home, his only contact with his wife and children. He blessed his good fortune to have married a girl who seldom complained about the transfers and who supported his struggle for a top-management position. They had both sacrificed a great deal, but he continually promised Hailey that he would make up to her for the lost time. When he finally made it, he would buy her the best of everything. He would employ a housekeeper to alleviate her household duties and he would buy his dream house that would be the envy of all his friends. That these things did not matter to Hailey did not occur to him.

When they moved to Houston, he had done as he said he would. Even though the house was more than he could reasonably afford, he had bought it anyway, flinging Hailey's protests aside. It was a contemporary architect's dream become reality in glass, wood and stone. It had overwhelmed Hailey, but he had wanted her ensconced in the kind of luxury that befitted and enhanced his position. What baffled him was her rejection, subdued as it was, to the elaborate house. He couldn't comprehend her refusal to understand the importance of appearances in the corporate world.

Mike was married to his career, and Hailey knew he would continue to spend more money on material things to compensate for his lack of interest and his presence in family affairs. They were at cross-purposes. It was no longer a matter of Hailey's complaints about the manner in which he spent money. It went deeper than that, and now that he was home more often he, too, could sense that the valley between them had grown.

As Hailey drove home today she realized that the foundation of her life had developed thin, weblike cracks that, though minute in scale and depth, were enough to crumble the tower of her life. As if it had been a slap on the face, she realized that her parents, the once authoritative Austin and the romantic Sonja, had been wrong. Nothing was absolute and there were no fairy tales.

## Chapter Two

HAILEY'S head was pounding the next morning when she awoke. She had slept through the alarm and not only did the children nearly miss the bus, but also Mike was late for an early appointment and had been quick to chastise her for the oversight. As she finished putting the breakfast dishes in the dishwasher, she decided that he was probably just under a lot of pressure at work the past few days, and if she made the first effort, she just might be able to rectify this whole situation.

She was just about to reach for the phone when it rang. Her voice was low-pitched and too abrupt, revealing a good deal of tension, and then she realized who the caller was.

"Janet? Is that you?" Hailey asked delightedly.

"Of course it is. Didn't you recognize my voice?" Janet said and laughed.

"My mind was elsewhere. You'll never believe this, but I've been thinking a lot about you lately. How are you?"

"Wonderful. I really am, though I miss you a lot. Say, how is the weather in Houston?" Janet asked, suppressing a giggle.

"It's lovely here, since you ask, but I can't believe you called to talk about the weather. What's new with you?"

"Plenty. How would you like a visit from me?"

"What? You must be kidding. I'd love it! Is this a vacation?"

"Nope. Better than that. Dan is being transferred to Houston! Can you believe it? After all these years, we're actually moving!"

"And to Houston, of all places! Lucky for me! It's like a dream come true. When?" Hailey asked, her anticipation ringing through her voice.

"As soon as we find a house. Ours is already sold up here. I'm flying down in the morning. I've got three days with a realtor and one day with you. How does that sound?"

"Janet! This is all happening so fast!"

"You're telling me! The details are about to drive me wild!"

"I guess I've been through it so often, I had forgotten how exciting the first time can be."

"Yeah, you'll have to show me the ropes," Janet teased. "When does your flight arrive?"

"Ten o'clock at Intercontinental Airport," Janet informed her. "Will you be able to pick me up?"

"Of course! I'll be the one with the roses!" Hailey joked.

"Just as long as you're there, that's all that matters. Well, I have to cut this short if I want to leave here at the crack of dawn."

"Okay. See you tomorrow, Janet. Bye."

"Bye, sweetie. Take care," was Janet's answer and she hung up.

Hailey replaced the receiver and then let out a whoop. Janet! Here! It was too good to be true. Instantly Hailey began formulating the next day's activities. She wondered how Mike would take the news. Not well, she knew. He had always been jealous of her relationship with Janet. There were numerous times in Chicago when Hailey spent more of her time with Janet than with Mike. For Hailey, it had been right, because with Janet she could be herself. Now Hailey wondered just how she would survive the hours until Janet's plane touched ground tomorrow.

When Janet walked off the exit ramp from the plane, Hailey was there waving a half-dozen roses and a bottle of champagne. She flew into Janet's arms and they hugged each other fiercely. It was all Hailey could do to choke back the tears.

"Don't you dare, Hailey," Janet warned her, "or I'll start, too, and there'll be no stopping us!" Janet sighed. "Gosh, it seems like centuries since I've seen you."

"I know," Hailey said, swallowing the lump in her throat as she beamed at her friend. Instantly Hailey felt wonderfully at peace. It was a feeling she hadn't experienced in a long time.

"This is such a great welcome and I love it!" Janet exclaimed.

"Come on. Let's get your bags and then we'll go to lunch."

As they walked down the corridor to the escalator to the baggage-claim area, Janet said, "Hey! It's only a little before eleven. Don't you think it's early for lunch?"

"Are you kidding? By the time we get there, we'll be lucky to get fed before one."

Janet looked at the wine and her brows raised. "Yeah, and I'll be smashed."

"Oh, no you won't," Hailey replied with conviction.

They located Janet's luggage and tossed it into the trunk of Hailey's car. As they drove out of the airport parking lot, Janet asked, "What did Mike have to say about our moving down here? Was he as excited as you are?"

Hailey evaded giving her a direct answer until they were almost to the North Belt exchange. "I didn't tell him." Hailey glanced over at Janet's concerned face and smiled blandly. "You haven't seen me in over a year and I don't want to get serious your first few minutes in town."

"Are you sure?" Janet asked. "Hailey, I think you've forgotten that I know you too well. If you can't tell me about it, well . . ."

"Oh, Janet," she replied with a heavy sigh. "Something is dreadfully wrong, and I can't figure out what it is." Hailey could give her only fragments of the problem, for that was all she knew.

"I think I can. You're married to Mike Asher!" Janet burst out without thinking and then, wild-eyed, threw her hand over her mouth. Before she could make an apology, Hailey interrupted her.

"Why do you say that?" Hailey was flabbergasted by Janet's remark.

"Hailey, for God's sake . . ." Janet scrambled for the right words.

"I'm not being facetious. I really want to know. What do you see that I don't?"

"You wouldn't like what I have to say and it's not my place. Why don't you tell me what you think it is and we'll go from there?"

At the stoplight, Hailey looked directly into Janet's brown eyes and said quite flatly, "I think I'm going insane."

At first, Janet almost roared with laughter but checked her response. Hailey was dead serious. "I don't believe that for one minute," Janet said resolutely.

"It's true. I spend half my time in a fantasy world. It's like regression of some sort."

"I see . . ." Janet mused. "If it's not too bold of me to ask, what are you trying to escape from?"

Hailey had never thought of it that way. "Everything," she said bluntly and then abruptly stopped, letting her own words sink into her head.

"Would you describe 'everything' to me?" Janet probed.

"I feel there is this enormous void in my life and no matter how hard I try, I can't find out what it is. Ha! Just listen to me! I don't feel like I even have a life!"

"Hailey, are you listening to yourself?" Janet asked, more concerned than ever.

"Yes, I have, and that's what scares me," she said, her eyes revealing a pained expression grown out of fear and confusion.

"I can see how you would be. I wish I could say something to make it less painful, something to ease your mind."

"You don't understand. I have no reason to feel this way."

"But your feelings are real, and if they're that strong maybe you should pay more attention to your emotions."

"Maybe I should. About all I know is that I love my children, and if it weren't for them, I'd have nothing."

Janet pondered Hailey's awesome words. "I gathered as much. When you wrote to me, I've sensed for some time that you weren't happy. So I don't want you to think that this comes as a total shock to me. Have you thought about what you want to do about this?"

"Well, I do need something, that's for sure. Something I can be proud of, besides taking care of Joey and Kim."

"We need to find something that will make you feel better about yourself. Let's see . . ."

"I've been thinking about getting a job," Hailey said in tones so low Janet almost didn't hear her.

Janet grasped the idea and took it a step farther. "I think that's a great idea," Janet said, knowing full well that that was only part of the problem. She watched Hailey sort through the confusion in her mind.

"But Janet, I've never had to work, not really. I can't do anything but run a household."

"That's absurd! There're a million things you could do. What's the one thing that interests you more than anything else?"

"Art!" Hailey said quickly. After a long pause she asked, "Now, why did I say that?"

"Because it's what you truly want. You were so good at your artwork in college, I've always wondered why you've neglected it so."

"There just didn't seem to be enough time, what with the children and always moving—"

"Bullshit!" Janet interrupted. "We make time for the things we really desire. You're just making excuses."

"I can never pull any punches with you, can I?"

"Nope. So don't even try."

"Well, at any rate, I'm not ready to plunge into that yet. I was thinking I could get a secretarial position," Hailey mused.

"Yes, you could do that." Janet waited.

"Ah, but I can see that you still think I should paint."

23

"I most certainly do! I always liked your work—loved it, in fact. Especially your portraits, because they were always curiously happy and sad at the same time."

"Must be my subconscious view of life, I guess," Hailey said absentmindedly as she chewed her bottom lip. Janet's words were striking home. She had needed someone to help her find the truth.

"Hailey, listen to me. You've always been an optimist. I swear, I don't know anyone who can look into the face of adversity and pretend it was a rainbow as much as you can."

"Am I really that naïve?"

"Yes, you are. Happy-go-lucky or just resilient, I can't tell which. Perhaps that's the one quality that makes you more of a survivor than any of us. Nothing can get you down when you don't want it to. That's why all this about going insane is such a crock."

"You think I'm normal, then?" Hailey asked hopefully.

"Ha! You've never been normal a day in your life. I hope you never are!" She glanced at Hailey's crushed expression. "I'm just teasing. What I meant was that you are too talented, beautiful and kind to be normal. You're the very best and don't *you* forget it."

"Janet, I wasn't fishing for compliments. This isn't boost-Hailey's-ego week."

"Maybe it should be," Janet said softly.

Hailey's mind was full as they entered South Post Oak Road. "You know, I think it's time I started being resilient, like you said. I'm going to find a job. This town is screaming for office help and I'm sure I'll find something."

"I'm sure you will, too," Janet replied. "If that's what you want, go get it. I personally would like to see you paint again. I know! How about a painting of me for over my fireplace in my new house, which I haven't even found yet!"

"Janet! I'm sorry! We've spent all this time talking about me and here you must have a thousand questions you want to ask about the city."

"That's all right. This was your turn. When mine comes

up, I know you'll be there for me. That's what friends are for."

Hailey pulled the car under the portico at Tony's and waited for the valet to open the door. She reached over and squeezed Janet's hand. "I don't know what I would do without you. I'm so glad you're going to be living here."

"Me, too," Janet said and smiled.

"This is the most fantastic city in the world as far as I'm concerned," Hailey said emphatically, and with a wistful twinkle in her eyes, she added, "I hope I can find what I'm looking for here."

"I know you will," Janet said confidently and then they entered the restaurant.

# Chapter Three

ONCE Hailey had made the decision to find a job, she was convinced that all she needed in her life was a sense of accomplishment, and she refused to listen to Mike's unsupportive gibes.

She spent two weeks combing the help-wanted ads in the newspapers, honing her typing skills and refreshing her memory of filing, bookkeeping and shorthand. She hadn't held a secretarial position since college, when she'd worked in the dean's office, but her determination boosted her energy level to the point that she was already accomplishing more tasks in a given day than ever before.

She filled out an application from a personnel agency and in a few days she had her first interview, with a small, established advertising agency located in Pennzoil Plaza in downtown Houston. Hailey's knowledge of that part of town was next to nil and it took her twenty minutes to find a parking garage that wasn't full.

When she had walked between the double doors to the suite occupied by Design Media Company she found she was precisely on time. The secretary, April, announced her. Mr. Stockton, a strikingly handsome man, interviewed her and was impressed with her credentials. After a short interview he informed Hailey that he would hire her on a sixty-day trial basis. He was in need of a girl Friday who would run ad copy and veloxes to his clients and free April's time for the major office work. He implied to Hailey that many avenues were open to her in his

27

company. Hailey was so thrilled with the results of her first interview, she agreed to take the job and told him she would report at nine the following morning.

That evening Hailey wanted to celebrate getting her new job and so she set the dining-room table with her very best linens, china and crystal. She chilled a bottle of champagne and placed a sirloin tip roast in the oven.

By six o'clock Mike was home and in a pleasant mood. He swirled a glass rod in a tall pitcher of dry martinis while extolling his productive if not almost adventurous day in the corporate world. He was on his second martini when she called the children to dinner. Nine-year-old Kim, her silver hair in pigtails, sat across from her seven-year-old brother, Joey. They were carbon copies of Hailey, slim, long-legged and blue-eyed. They sat in the dining room conversing with their father when Hailey entered with the bottle of champagne.

"What's that for, Mom? Is it somebody's birthday?" Joey asked and she could tell he was racking his limited memory for an accounting for her unscheduled overture.

"No birthday, but a celebration all the same," Hailey said, pouring the wine and noting their confused faces.

"Hailey?" Mike said. "What's going on?"

"As of today, I am a career woman!" she said proudly with her head cocked confidently to one side.

Mike's eyes narrowed as he peered at her across the table. "You aren't saying what I think you're saying . . ."

"Oh, yes I am!" she replied firmly. "Tomorrow morning I start work at Design Media."

Kim was first to react. "Hey! That's neat, Mom! Will I ever be able to come visit you?"

"Of course you can, honey. Not right at first, but soon."

"Boy, Mom," Joey said. "What do Design Media people do?"

"Well, I'll just be doing light office work for a while. But later I can advance to other departments. Maybe even the art department."

"How much?" Mike asked tersely.

"How much what?"

"Money! How much do you get paid?"

"Oh," Hailey said lightly, "a thousand a month."

"Is that all? Hailey, when you first started all this nonsense I just humored you because I didn't think you'd get the job."

"What is that supposed to mean?"

"Be realistic! Who would want to hire an inexperienced housewife?"

"Plenty of people would. I'm not dumb! I learn quickly. I should think you'd be proud of me, that I got the job on my first interview. Doesn't that say something about me right there?"

"This whole thing is ridiculous. And did it ever occur to you what this will do to our taxes?"

"Taxes? What's that got to do with me trying to accomplish something?"

"We'll get pushed into a higher bracket and be eaten alive. See, that's what I mean. You never think of all these things. I'll turn this over to my accountant and let him decide."

Hailey couldn't believe her ears. She wondered if he could see the steam that was surely rising from the sides of her eyes. He was trying to beat her down again, as if she were some sort of embarrassment to him, or nothing more than a tax shelter that wasn't going to pan out. "Don't you dare, Mike Asher! The decision was mine and I've already committed myself. We're talking about my credibility, which would be questioned if I were to quit now." Hailey was incensed by his attack and vowed she would stand her ground.

The children sat mute, watching the interplay as though it were a tennis match. Joey was rapidly chewing his roast beef and stared at his mother with wide eyes.

"Hailey, not once did I ever tell you it was all right to get a job," Mike said. "For Christ's sake, you have everything you need. We don't need the money."

Hailey was unbelieving at his insensitivity. "Screw the money! I didn't decide to go to work for that reason."

"Then why did you?" he demanded.

"For my own sense of accomplishment! And I can tell you this, I do not for one second intend to remain a

29

receptionist. That's just manual labor as far as I'm concerned. I want to learn, I need to have some sense of self-importance. There's more to me than just being your wife." She was dangerously close to tears.

"And since when did your being my wife not give you what you need? Don't I make you feel important? Don't you think I need you?"

His question was a little too direct and ill-timed. Hailey hesitated and in those split seconds realized for the first time that she didn't need him. Like a flash of lightning she knew that she didn't want him, either. Why was she thinking such things? She finally admitted that she had purposefully pushed them out of her brain for years. She had made excuses, asked for very little for herself and, therefore, got nothing from Mike in return. That way she couldn't be disappointed. Maybe she should have demanded more. She was frightened by these thoughts. She wished her stomach would quit churning and she could find some courage somewhere.

"Hailey! Answer me!" Mike stormed, his eyes full of fear, too.

She lost her strength with the force of his outburst. She was wrong to upset them all so much. She avoided his eyes and the issue. The time was not right for such direct confrontation. "Of course I know you need me." She felt ill with the blatant lie between them.

She saw Mike relax. "Since this is so important to you, I'll let you do this." He had decided he had won the argument.

He and the children finished their meal in silence. Hailey felt as if she were being unduly pressured almost to the point of punishment, as if Mike were her father, not her husband. He was and always had been too domineering and she'd let him go on with it. Of course, no vital issues had ever arisen, for they had not once in all these years truly communicated. The only goals they had were his corporate ones of a vice-presidency. It was her own fault she had no dreams.

The very thought that she could have allowed herself to become this complacent was ludicrous. She had always been an intelligent, innovative girl, eager to shoot for the stars. What happened to the Hailey James she had once been?

Buried! she thought. She knew she must assume the blame for that, and now was the time to make her own decisions. This simpleminded job was only a start, but it was a beginning. The only person who could stop her now was herself.

# Chapter Four

FOR two months Hailey felt alive. She was the force behind her dreams becoming reality. She found, much to her delight, that she now spent over half her workday involved with the art department. It hadn't taken long to learn the terrain of the central business district, for she had progressed from answering the phones to running ad copy, contracts and proofs from the office to various clients and back again. She met more people, saw more places than she had in her whole life. It was exhilarating and she loved it; but Mike was only tolerating the situation.

It was her association with Stephen Ainsley, senior art coordinator for the firm, that prompted her to reconsider her lost interest in her painting. Stephen liked her, she thought. He was an intelligent low-key person who fascinated her with his knowledge of history and foreign cities. He knew absolutely everyone who was anybody in Houston. Talking to Stephen was like reading the gossip columns in the *Post* and the *Chronicle*.

Twice in just this past week they'd had lunch together, once at a gothically romantic deli near the office, and once they simply shared a glass of wine on the patio at Cody's, high above Montrose. Hailey loved Cody's because she could view both skylines at the same time. But most of all, she valued Stephen's friendship and honesty. He was the only person she knew who was as much of an optimist as she was. He told her he woke up every day knowing it was going to be a good one. And these days, that's just how Hailey approached her life.

Once the trial period was over, Hailey found herself even more nervous than she had been when she was first interviewed. To reassure her, April promised to treat her to a celebration drink after work at the Spindletop in the Hyatt Regency Hotel.

Hailey finished her assignments in record time and when Mr. Stockton buzzed her on the intercom, she took a deep breath to steady herself. When she opened the door to his office she was surprised to see him standing at what she thought was an enclosed bookshelf area but in reality was a hidden bar. He was mixing a drink.

"Hi!" he smiled. "Please close the door, won't you?"

"Oh!" Hailey did as she was asked.

"Scotch?" he asked with a raised eyebrow and a flashing smile.

"Pardon me, sir?"

"Scotch or bourbon?"

"Oh," she said, chiding herself for her stupidity. "I don't care for anything, but thank you." She started to sit in the armchair near the desk.

"No, Hailey. Over there," he said, pointing to the love seat against the wall.

Hailey sat down but was very uncomfortable. She didn't like what was happening, but she told herself it was better not to make snap judgments.

"Now, Hailey, I realize you've been with us for only two months, but even in that short while I'm impressed. The office has been running more efficiently and you've made a favorable impression on some of our clients. That's very good for our business."

"Thank you, sir," Hailey said, elated with the good report.

"No need to thank me. You've earned it. Tell me, Hailey, do you like working here at Design Media?"

"Oh, yes!" she said but then thought she shouldn't be too enthusiastic. She wanted to keep her cool, but it was wonderful being appreciated for her hard work.

"Hailey," he said, his tone becoming more familiar, "one thing I've realized is that the full extent of your talents and capabilities has not been tested yet. This job isn't for you."

"It's not?" Her eyes grew wide. Here it comes, she thought, the ax.

"No. Any kid out of high school could do as well. And don't take that as a put-down, it wasn't meant that way," he said, noting her suddenly rigid posture. "What I would like to do is advance you—immediately." He stressed the last word.

Hailey's expression brightened and her hopes rose again. "Are you serious?" She couldn't believe it! This was too good to be true!

"Of course I am. You should be in public relations. You aren't the kind of person who should be stuck behind a desk all day. You do best with people contact. Don't you agree?"

"I must admit I do enjoy dealing with the clients and discussing various programs with them."

"Precisely. I think you should do more of that and I would feel responsible for wasting your capabilities if I didn't do just that."

"Thank you, sir. You can't possibly know how much that means to me."

He finished his drink, took his hand out of his pants pocket and asked, "You're sure you don't want a drink?"

"Yes, I'm sure."

He nodded, went back to the bar and mixed himself a stiff Scotch and water. He took two sips and then sat on the edge of the desk, dangling the drink with one hand between his legs. "I want you to become more involved in the management end of this company. I've noticed your gravitation toward the art and design area . . ." He waited for her comment, which was quick in coming.

"I've always enjoyed painting, though I'm not talented. But this practical application is intriguing."

He interrupted her. "That type of job would put you right back there behind a desk, I mean. Take some good advice. You would do fantastically well in public relations. It's the best thing for your career—not to mention the financial rewards."

"I see what you mean."

"Naturally, at first you would go about your duties as always—that is, until I can find someone to replace you," he said and sipped his drink nonchalantly.

That wasn't exactly what Hailey wanted to hear, but it was what she expected. "I understand."

"Not for long, though. I intend to introduce you to our major accounts. Some you've met here in the office, but as any adman worth his salt knows, the best impression you can give is during social situations, where the major amount of our business takes place. We'll take it slow for now; a lunch here and there, a few dinners and see how you do. I for one have no doubt as to the answer to all this."

"I—I—" she stuttered, but he spoke before she could voice her objections.

"You'll do famously."

"Mr. Stockton," she said and took a deep breath, "this is more than I had been prepared for. I have two children and I wouldn't get to see them much if I had to work after hours, too."

"Hailey, use your common sense. This is your career we're discussing. And besides, it wouldn't be all that much. Surely one night a week . . ."

"Well." Something told her not to agree to anything. But she couldn't understand why not, since the picture he painted looked positively glorious to her.

"I promise you, we won't put any more demands upon you than you can handle." It was at this point that he put his drink down on the desk and before she knew it, he was sitting next to her on the love seat. "Hailey, just think about it. We'll be going to the finest, most exclusive restaurants and clubs in town. You'll meet intelligent, well-traveled businessmen and -women. Many times we take them to the theater, symphony and ballet. One of your duties will be to coordinate these evenings according to the personality and taste of the client."

Hailey listened intently. Even she was surprised when

he finished at how wide her eyes had become. "It sounds too good to be true," she said more warily.

"I think you need a little wining and dining." His smile was so carefully practiced, he looked like a toothpaste commercial on television.

Hailey's head snapped back with the impression and she gazed at him with a frown. "Why would you say that?"

He picked up her hand and held it between both of his. "I just could. There's something about you that screams, 'I need attention!' I saw that look, I hesitate to refer to it as neglected, but when I first laid eyes on you, that was my impression."

Hailey slowly eased her hand away from his grasp. "I think you were mistaken," she said flatly and looked away from him.

"Perhaps I'm not stating myself clearly. All I wanted to tell you is that I have confidence in you. I earnestly believe that with a career with this company your future looks quite exciting."

Hailey didn't hear a word he said. Her mind told her not to believe him. "Thank you," was all she could say.

"Think of the broad scope of things. Eventually there will be some travel involved, if you're interested."

"Travel? What kind of travel?"

"We do have clients in New York, San Francisco, Chicago, Denver and Miami, to name a few. I usually handle those accounts on my own. But I'd like you to meet some of these people," he said, putting his hand on her knee.

Hailey looked him square in the eyes. How dare he? She didn't consider herself worldly, but she wasn't stupid, either. "And you'd like me to accompany you on these trips, is that right?" she said, prodding him.

"That's what I had in mind, yes." He flashed another wide grin at her, thinking she was in full assent to his proposal.

Hailey let her words roll out of her mouth like honey. "And we could see all kinds of exciting places, couldn't we?"

"Of course!" he answered enthusiastically and gazed into her gorgeous blue eyes.

Hailey stood slowly, all the while smiling affectionately at him. "I think this sounds just too, too marvelous," she cooed. She took a step backward. "But you see, I don't need a job that badly. And I really don't want to go to dinner with you, much less to New York. So I guess, Mr. Stockton," she purred, "what I'm trying to say is, I quit!" she nearly screamed. Then she turned around and was out the doorway before he had a chance to blink.

Hailey flew to her desk, grabbed her purse and raced to the elevators. She pressed the down button. Luckily, the elevator doors opened in a matter of seconds. As they closed behind her, she could hear his footsteps in the hallway as he called after her in a low but direct tone. Hailey let out a deep breath and felt her cheeks flush. Brother! She should have known!

"Men! What creeps! What nerve! To build me up like that and then . . . to think . . . Why on earth would he think I'd agree to something like that?"

By the time the elevator reached the lobby, she was depressed. She hadn't even said good-bye to April. But then Hailey remembered they were to meet for drinks. She left Pennzoil Plaza behind as she walked toward the Hyatt.

# Chapter Five

HAILEY sat near the window at a table for two twirling a glass of Chablis between her fingers. Her chin rested on her hand as she stared at the cityscape below. The last rays of sunlight died for the day and one by one lights were flicked on, creating an impression of a Christmas tree. But at this moment Hailey felt anything but merry. She fought back her tears, thinking it was not quite the "thing to do" at the Spindletop, when she sensed someone standing over her. She refused to turn around, fearing it might be Mr. Stockton.

"Hailey?" a familiar mellow voice asked.

She brightened and turned her head to see Stephen smiling down at her. She returned a smile of her own and asked, "Stephen, what are you doing here?"

"I come here every night, didn't you know?" he joked as he sat down across from her.

"No, I didn't. And you just saw me sitting here?" she asked, not comprehending his statement.

He chuckled and shook his head. "I asked April why you didn't leave with her at five. She said you had quit your job and then I talked her into letting me fill her shoes as your companion for the evening."

"Oh," Hailey said with a sigh. "Then you know what happened. It must be all over the tower by now!" she said and took a sip of her wine.

"I don't know any of the particulars. I thought you might need to talk about it. Could you use a friend?"

"I can use all the friends I can get," Hailey said as a tear fell.

"Hey, hey," he said, reaching in his pocket and pulling out a handkerchief. "Don't do that. It can't be as bad as all that. Is it?"

"You don't have to cheer me up, Stephen. I'm sure there are lots of people who would be much better company than I," she said as she wiped away her tears and handed the handkerchief back to him.

"Do you want to be alone?"

Hailey, thinking she'd surmised his intentions correctly, said, "Yes . . ."

He looked into her eyes and smiled. "Liar," he said.

Her chin quivered slightly and she looked away. "I'm really stupid. Did you know that, Stephen?" she asked, looking back at him.

"There you go again, lying to me." His voice was cheering and yet genuinely sympathetic. Hailey smiled.

The waitress came, lit the candle in the center of the table and took Stephen's order for Chivas and water. Stephen's light brown hair glistened with golden hues in the flickering candleglow. He looked like some dashing hero out of a novel, she thought. He was quite handsome and she admired him for not being conceited, and if he was, she'd certainly never seen it. He was a good deal older than she, but his thoughts and actions were young. He looked to be in his late thirties, but something told her he was a decade older. Perhaps it was simply his ease about himself. He was never in a hurry, though he managed to accomplish a great deal in a given day. Strangely, Hailey felt as if she'd known him all her life.

The waitress returned with his drink. He had the unusual ability to make Hailey feel as if she were the most important person in the world without saying a single word. He was oblivious to the ever-increasing number of people in the bar and to the spectacular view. Hailey felt as if she had moved, ever so slowly, into another sphere and she, too, could hear and see only Stephen. Amid the crowd they were uncannily alone. It was comfortable and she liked it.

"I'm not intentionally lying to you," she said finally.

"I know that. But I don't want there ever to be any lies between us. Friends just don't do that. Why don't you tell me what happened?"

"When I went in to see Mr. Stockton he started telling me how he was going to advance me to public relations and how wonderful that job would be. And then . . ."

"And then he told you what it would cost. Am I correct?" he interrupted her and then lit a cigarette.

"Exactly. Brother! I can't believe how dumb I was! Two months thrown away. All that work for nothing," she said, incensed at herself.

"Oh, I wouldn't say that," he replied. "And I don't think you were dumb at all. I think you are probably the smartest girl I've met in a long time."

"You can't be serious!" She decided that Stephen must have a bolt loose somewhere.

"Yes, I am. You knew in only a few moments exactly what the score was. Now, an ignorant person wouldn't have realized what was going on for weeks, maybe even years. It happens all the time. So many women fall into that trap, and they don't have to. No job is that important."

"I agree. Not when the price is so high. I won't sacrifice my self-respect for a promise."

"Very wise of you, my dear. Promises can be broken," he said and quickly broke off.

"I know," she replied sadly and looked away. Stephen recognized that often-seen melancholy expression. She said no more but when she turned, he caught her glance and brought her back to him. "Regardless of the ethics of the situation, I've still managed to be in and out of work in only two months," she said. "Mike's going to have a heyday with this!"

"I'm sure he'll understand," he said, trying to console her.

"He didn't want me to work in the beginning, and when he discovered I'd taken this job, he was livid."

"Why?" Stephen guessed the answer before she replied.

"A blow to his male ego." She smiled at Stephen and

*41*

then laughed. "No offense intended." It was strange, she thought, how Stephen seemed almost sexless to her; just a friend, someone whom she could confide in. She had to make a conscious effort to remember that he was a male.

"None taken."

"I hope now I can live through the 'I told you so's!'" she said jokingly, but she could see that Stephen knew exactly what she meant. It was curious, she thought as she watched him light another cigarette, how Stephen sensed her every mood. It was as if he anticipated her needs and thoughts, and she wondered just how he did that.

He put his elbows on the table and cradled his chin in his palm as the cigarette smoke curled up and over his head. He peered at her so intently that Hailey shook visibly. "You cold?" he asked.

"Yes, just a little. It must be a draft or something," she said, wishing he would quit staring at her so.

"Would you like my jacket?"

"Goodness, no. I'll be fine, but thanks, anyway."

Just then he dropped his gaze, grabbed the edge of the table with his hands and leaned forward. His eyes were bright with excitement. "Hailey, I've got it!"

"What? What are you talking about?" she asked, startled at his abrupt change in mood.

"Another job, of course. We've got to find you suitable employment, lady."

"Is that right? Listen, the last thing I want now is to have to go through all this again."

"You won't have to. I also think I can find you something that will finally convince you to pursue your interest in art."

She tossed her reluctance aside and picked up on his enthusiasm. "Do you have something in mind?"

"I certainly do. It may take a week or so to set this up, but I think you'd be perfect for it."

"Stephen! I'm dying of curiosity. What is this job you have in mind?"

"Be patient, my dear, and I'll tell you. I have two friends who own a successful art gallery in Montrose. They've been dealing in art for years and have managed to acquire some fabulous pieces. However, what I find most interesting is their ability to spot new talent. They handle a number of local artists who now are doing well. Their gallery is well run—businesswise, I mean. They have impeccable taste in everything from wine to food, to art and decor. That's why I know you'd be perfect."

She was baffled. Hailey hadn't known Stephen all that long, but she did know that he loved creating a mysterious aura about certain things. Even when they went to lunch he never told her where they were going. He adored the element of surprise. She decided to humor him. "Perfect?" she asked.

"Yes. You're impeccable." His words were delivered with such a soothing conviction that, with a start, Hailey realized he was serious.

"That's a difficult description to live up to. Nobody is perfect," she replied, wondering why he would say such a thing as her vast array of faults and inadequacies flashed across her mind.

"You are, especially when you find your niche. Which is in your art."

"Stephen, you keep reiterating this one point. Why, you have no idea of my talent or lack of it, as the case most assuredly is. How can you be so positive when you've never seen my work?"

"How can you be so negative when you've never even tried?" Stephen knew that statement was harsh, but he also knew there was something behind her reluctance and he swore to himself he would find out what it was.

"I did try, damn it!" she snapped back and was astonished at her reaction. "I'm sorry," she said quietly. "Stephen, it's a long story . . ."

"That's all right, I want to hear it anyway," he said, leaning back in his chair.

"Are you sure?"

"Yes, I'm sure."

She sensed that he wouldn't relent. She'd never told anyone since college, but as he sat in attentive anticipation she felt he should know.

"When I was studying art in college I had managed, in

my freshman year, to take a senior seminar course. It was a small class, but a professor I'd had for a color and design course recommended me."

"It must have been a hell of a sell job," he broke in. "I'm sorry, go on."

"I never thought of that. Well, anyway, we were all to bring in a piece of work, whatever we did best, and then the class and the professor would critique it. All projects had to be turned in three days prior to the seminar meeting on Monday night. On Sunday, my instructor called and said he wanted to see me in his office that night about the portrait I'd painted. I was scared to death and I had no idea what to expect. He was a mountain of a man, complete with beard, pipe and leather patches on the elbows of his herringbone tweed jacket."

"I know the type."

"Me, too," she said and laughed. "I went to his office and he had my portrait sitting on his desk. He told me to sit down. I felt like a dwarf; his presence was so overpowering because he always bellowed rather than spoke. He leaned back in his chair and said, 'Frankly, Miss James, this work stinks!'"

Stephen made no comment, nor did his expression change.

"Then," she went on, "he shoved my painting at me so that it fell into my lap. He told me that he was aware of my GPA and knew that I wanted a good grade out of his class. So then he said he'd strike a bargain with me. He said that if I promised to quit painting, go into something I was better suited for, he would give me a 'B' in the class. I was almost in tears. I asked him if my work was really that bad. He said I had a good eye for detail, but that was all. He knew I was out of my league and why I'd been suggested for his class, he couldn't understand. So he convinced me. And I took the 'B.'"

"And never painted again?" he asked.

"Not seriously. There were always watercolors and sketches for the children but nothing important. It wasn't worth the time and effort." Hailey waited for Stephen's reaction. Surely now he would understand—she had it on good authority that she had no talent.

"Hmmm." He took a deep breath and sat up straight. "I want to see your work." His statement was flat, but the look in his eye was stern.

Hailey's shoulders slumped with an exasperated sigh. "I just told you, it's no good."

"Hailey, after all this time don't you know what happened that day?"

"I most definitely do! You're the one who doesn't," she shot back at him.

"Hailey, listen to me. He saw something. Something he, in his own frustrated career efforts, could never attain. Didn't it occur to you that if someone reacts to the point of hostility, like shoving the painting back to you, that something was odd?"

"Well, yes, but I was just too afraid of him that I didn't . . ." She couldn't finish, Stephen was so eager with his explanation.

"Hailey, he was jealous."

She began laughing and checked herself abruptly. "Stephen, that's insane. He was a college professor. He knew so much more than . . ."

"Maybe he did know more, but he didn't have talent. There's nothing more frustrating than desiring to paint only to find you don't possess that uniqueness that sets the true artist apart from the rest of humanity. And he was jealous, I'm telling you!"

"That's ludicrous!"

"Bunk! What's ludicrous is you believed him all this time!"

"But," he raised his index finger into the air, "alas! There is still plenty of time."

"Now, what are you talking about?"

"I want to see your work. I want to see what caused that man to so intimidate you that he was able to extract such a promise from you. And the most curious part is why you were so loyal to that promise."

"I am loyal to the end," she said and chuckled, but her

expression was stoic. She had trusted more in her professor's authority and opinion than in herself. Could that be the reason? Had the professor been a surrogate paternal authority while she lived on campus? How much did all this play along with the scheme of things in her life? Could it be possible that Stephen was right and she did have talent?

"You'll let me see something, won't you?"

"All I have are a few sketches I've done for the children. Not a serious piece of work in the bunch."

"That's easy enough to correct. You'll just have to get busy. What do you like to do?"

"Portraits mostly . . ." Her thoughts skipped over themselves as her enthusiasm was rekindled. "You know, I have this friend, Janet, who's moving here from Chicago and she asked me to paint her. She wants to hang it in her new house . . ."

"Has she ever seen your work, Hailey?"

"Of course."

"And she wants you to do a portrait—"

"She's my best friend," Hailey interrupted.

"She may be your best friend, my love, but I doubt if she'd hang a dreadful painting in the center of a room."

Hailey smiled. "I see what you mean. I'll get to work on it."

"Good," Stephen said. "That will be your next project. While you get busy on that, I'll see what I can do about an interview with Leonard and Barrett."

"Leonard and Barrett?" She raised a curious eyebrow.

"My friends, I told you . . ." He noted her amused smirk. "What are you looking like that for?"

"Really, Stephen. Leonard and Barrett?" She laughed. "They almost sound . . ." She didn't finish.

"Gay? They are. I'll bet you've never known anyone who was homosexual."

"Only a couple of hairdressers," she said airily. "No wonder you weren't worried about my being harassed anymore!"

"Stick with me, kid. I'll take care of you," he teased, but then he quickly cleared his throat and downed the drink.

"Listen," he decided to change the subject, "I mean it about the portrait of your friend. Use this time of unemployment wisely. If it were me, I'd start tomorrow."

"But Janet's not even here yet!"

"Terrific," he said with disappointment.

"But I've got a lot of photographs of her, and besides, she's been after me to paint again, too. Although, I must admit, you're far more persistent."

"Thanks a lot," he said and groaned good-naturedly. "But I know what I'm talking about."

"Well, anyway, it'll be great fun to be able to surprise her with a finished portrait for a housewarming gift."

"You know, you really *are* something else," he said, nodding his head.

"To tell the truth, I'm almost afraid for you to see it when I am finished."

"Why?"

"I already feel like the world's biggest dumb cluck. What if you are right? I have no one to blame but my own stupidity. Gosh!" she gasped suddenly. "Stephen, what if I'd never told you the story? What if I'd never met you?"

"It was meant to be. You had no choice in the matter. At this point it's all conjecture to be realistic. But I'm convinced that you possess something. I can sense it."

Hailey's emotions were stumbling over themselves. Her adrenaline raced through her body, charging her with a need to discover herself. She was torn between hope and dread over the wasted years. But more than anything, she wanted to know the truth. She was determined that nothing was going to stand in her way.

Stephen winked at her. "I want to be there when it all happens."

"When what happens?" she asked, still lost in her reverie. She prayed this wasn't another daydream.

"When you discover what you have. The world will discover *you,* no doubt in my mind. And I'll be there for that, too."

As Hailey sipped her wine, she wondered how he could always be so sure.

# Chapter Six

WHEN Hailey reached home it was well past eight o'clock. At first, she wondered if anyone were home. Only a light in the kitchen burned. It seemed early for the children to be in bed, but it wasn't all that unusual.

She unlocked the front door and immediately ran her palm upward over the four switches in the foyer. The downstairs was once again bathed in light, the way she liked it. The house was very still. No radio, no television. Just then she heard pots and pans clattering in the kitchen.

"Mike?" she called as she walked toward the noise.

He was bending over a pile of stainless-steel bowls and pans that had obviously fallen out of the cabinet. He didn't look up.

"Mike?" she said hesitantly. He made no answer as she walked closer. "Can I help?"

"Where have you been, Hailey?" he asked very quietly as he shoved the bowls back onto the shelf and carefully shut the door. Finally he stood up and looked at her.

"I stopped to have a drink with a friend after work."

"Oh, I see," he replied and turned around and finished sprinkling cleanser into the sink and then scrubbed it out. As he used the sprayer to rinse it, he asked, "Male or female?" His back was rigid and she noticed that his movements were unusually slow and deliberate. She stared at his wide shoulders and expansive back. He looked like a brick wall.

"It was just Stephen, from work. I've told you about him," she answered, attaching no importance to the sex of her companion. She expected Mike to be upset over her neglecting to phone him. She was confused by his reaction.

"I fed the kids. They're asleep now." His hands rested on the edge of the counter and it looked as if he were holding himself up. "I was going to surprise you and take everybody out to dinner."

"Oh, Mike, I'm sorry! I know I should have called, and I meant to. I just didn't get the chance."

He turned and looked at her and for the first time, Hailey could see fear in his eyes and that he was pasty white. She thought he was physically ill. "Mike, are you all right?"

"I didn't know. I thought you'd been in an accident or something. Hailey, please, be more considerate."

Hailey felt as if she'd failed them all terribly. "I didn't know." She wanted to say more but couldn't. It had been the one time she'd allowed herself to dwell more on her problems than on the family. She vowed to herself never to let it happen again. Then Mike appeared to gather his bearings and he leaned his hip against the counter and crossed his arms over his chest.

"What's this guy, Stephen, like?"

"I told you before. He's lots older and quite nice. Very interesting," she answered nonchalantly as she stepped out of her shoes, picked them up and held them by the back straps in her hand. When she looked at him, his entire body seemed to radiate hot anger. "Mike, you . . . you should see your face. What's the matter?"

"I don't like some guy taking my wife out to a bar!" His voice was possessive and his words seemed to hiss at her through his clenched teeth.

"It wasn't like that at all, Mike. And it wasn't just some bar, either," she explained, placing her hand on her hip.

"Then what was it?"

"The Spindletop."

"What? That's even worse. Now he's trying to impress you!"

"It wasn't like that at all. I'd never been there and I'd heard you talk about it so I wanted to see for myself. I had no idea Stephen would show up there. It was just a coincidence. We got to talking and I lost track of time, and that's all there was to it."

Mike grumbled and eyed her suspiciously. "Just don't let it happen again, Hailey."

"Next time I'll call and tell you where I am. I promise," she said, remembering her vow.

"No, Hailey. You didn't hear what I said. There won't be a next time," he said thunderously.

She could see that he'd mustered every ounce of self-control he possessed and he was just as angry at himself for this outburst as he was at her. She had her own views on the matter and though the timing was bad, she would not surrender. "You can't tell me what I can and cannot do," she stated coldly.

"You're my wife!" he shot back at her.

"Exactly. Your wife. Not your dog or your toy; not a possession," she said, fuming. "I'm a person. I think and breathe and feel. You can't own me, even though you try . . ."

"I do not!" he retorted.

"Mike," she heaved a sigh, "please, I don't want to get into this. I'm tired. I had a rotten day and I can't take any more hassle. I just want to go to bed and get some rest." All she could think of was escape . . . she didn't want to hurt him. He was a good person and yet he wanted to keep her from attaining her goals. He would push and push until one time she would turn and retaliate. She had to squelch her anger and resentment one more time. She wasn't ready for this confrontation, for then the truth would come out.

She turned and walked toward the stairs. She was surprised that he wasn't calling after her. She mounted the stairs as quickly as possible, hoping he would prefer to remain downstairs and watch television. Then she could relax in a hot tub. She was still undecided as to whether she would tell him about her "resignation" or not. That was a good term, she thought. It gave the unsavory incident some respectability. But then she was only lying to herself, and that was even worse than lying to somebody else.

She unbuttoned her silk print dress and hung it up in the closet. She turned around quickly and there was Mike just standing in the doorway staring at her. She jumped with a start.

"My God! You scared me half to death! I didn't hear you come up the stairs."

"What's wrong, Hailey?" he asked, his temper under control now.

"Nothing. I'm just dead tired. And I'm sorry about what happened downstairs."

"Yeah, me too," he replied. "Maybe you should get some rest. It's not as easy as you thought it would be, is it?"

"What?"

"Working. That's just what it all is, you know. Plain old toil."

She let him have his say. The last thing she needed tonight was an argument. "You're right about that."

"Well, I've got some paperwork to finish up and then I'll be up to bed." He turned and left the room.

Hailey grasped the closet rod with both hands and hung her head between her arms. "God, Hailey, where's your courage?" She stood there for an inordinately long period of time and then proceeded to bathe and dress for bed.

It was over an hour and a half before Mike came upstairs. She remained ever so still under the covers, listening as he brushed his teeth and undressed. He sat on the edge of the bed, depressed the alarm button on the digital clock radio and then stretched out next to her.

"Hailey," he whispered as he slowly ran his hand up and down her thigh. She made no move and feigned sleep. He nudged her gently and she continued the ruse. "Hailey," he said again, and then he rolled onto his side and drifted off to sleep.

Hailey stared at the ceiling and felt a steady stream of tears trickle down her temples and into her hairline. Why did she keep taunting herself with hopes for something better? She *was* a coward and she believed she would never have the kind of strength it took to pursue her ideals. She was a dreamer and that was all. It wasn't Mike's fault that she was so miserable. None of it was. He couldn't help her when she couldn't help herself, and it was wrong of her to take out her frustrations on him. He hadn't changed. She had, and it was time she dealt with it. Mike was right, though. There would be no next time. Why fight it? She would just lose the battle in the end. With that thought sleep overcame her and gifted her with the escape she had sought.

The following morning, Mike dashed out of the house at six-thirty to make an early appointment. Hailey packed a lunch for Joey because the school menu was not up to his usual incomparable standards.

"Their hamburgers are rotten! Not like McDonald's at all!" he complained as he poured milk over his cereal and then proceeded to fish out the treasured plastic puzzle which Hailey knew was the reason behind his discriminating purchase of that brand.

Kim was still tying pink piquot ribbons around her braids. She had gone through four colors before making her final decision. She tightened her belt on her designer jeans and buttoned the cuffs of her pink and lavender plaid western shirt.

"Kim, there's toast and juice on the table for you," Hailey said as she poured herself another cup of coffee.

"I'm not very hungry," her daughter replied.

"You have to eat something," Hailey implored.

"But Mom . . ."

Hailey glared at her the way she knew all mothers did to reinforce an order, praying all the while that it would work. "No 'buts' . . . . eat!"

"All right." Kim slumped into her chair, downed her juice and reluctantly ate half a piece of toast.

Joey was shoveling cereal into his mouth so fast Hailey doubted he even chewed it. He threw his spoon down, ran to her, kissed her quickly on the cheek, grabbed his lunch and backpack and was through the front doorway before Hailey swallowed her coffee.

"I wonder why he never moves that fast when I want him to clean up his room?" she said aloud.

Kim walked up and looked at her mother. "Motivation, Mom. You know how boys are. No motivation for what's important."

Hailey laughed at Kim's serious expression, picked up one of her braids and said, "Thank you, Sigmund Freud!"

Kim's face screwed up and she said, "Who's that?"

"Just someone else who thought he had all the answers."

Kim shrugged her shoulders, whisked her satchel off the counter and kissed her mother. "Have a good day at work, Mom."

"Thanks, honey. Be sweet." Hailey waved at her as she dashed out of the kitchen.

The door slammed shut and once again Hailey felt as if no one were at home. She was just about to clear away the breakfast dishes when the telephone rang.

"Hello," she said and paused.

"Good morning, Hailey," Janet said.

'Where are you calling from?" Hailey asked.

"Houston! Where else would I be?"

"You weren't due for another four days."

"I know! But everything went so smoothly. The van is here unloading now. You wouldn't believe this place!"

"Could you use some help?"

"Boy! Could I ever . . . wait a minute, don't you have to work today? Gees! I haven't had a chance to really talk to you since you started at the agency. How is the career woman?"

"I'm just fine," Hailey said, hoping to evade a direct answer just yet. "Listen, I don't have to go in today. Tell you what, I'll get dressed and be right over. What's the address again?"

"It's 5670 Pines Hollow. Just take Memorial out to the subdivision. Second left."

"Don't worry, I'll find it," Hailey assured her.

"I really appreciate this," Janet said.

"Don't mention it. For me, it's a godsend. Just give me an hour."

"Okay. See you soon."

"Bye," Hailey answered and hung up.

She finished cleaning up the dishes, dashed up the stairs and donned a pair of jeans and a brown-and-white-striped cotton blouse. She stood before the mirror brushing out her hair and then tied it up in a ponytail. It was going to be a good day. She applied a light smudge of eyeshadow and a whisk of blusher, then inspected herself.

"Damn!" she swore as she noted how tightly her jeans fit. "Now I need to diet too. I wonder how the movie stars find the time to keep this flab under control?" she asked herself as she sucked in her stomach. "Tomorrow I'll start an overhaul program. That sounds positive. Think positive, Hailey, and thirty sit-ups a day. Hmmmm. Make it a hundred." Pleased with her new promise to herself, she left the house.

It was not far to Janet's house, and Hailey was glad that they lived nearby. Janet had told her little about it, only that the note on it was easily equal to the national debt.

Hailey stopped at the grocery store and purchased a Boston fern in a hanging basket, some fresh Danish, a carton of orange juice and two six-packs of Dan's favorite beer.

As Hailey turned onto Pines Hollow, she immediately spied the moving van. She parked the car and locked it. Just as she reached the door of the house, parcels in hand, two young and brawny men came bounding down the stairs on their way to the van for the next item. Hailey walked through the open doorway.

"Janet!" she called. "I'm here!"

Janet came running down the curved staircase. "Hailey! Am I glad to see you!" she exclaimed. Hailey set the grocery bag on the Italian marble floor and hugged her.

"Hey, what's all this?" Janet asked.

"This," Hailey said, holding up the plant, "is for you. And the rest is for Dan. Where is he, anyway?"

"Right here, sweetie," Dan said, walking into the foyer

from the dining room. He grabbed her playfully and kissed her. "You look terrific. I'd say Houston has been good for you."

"I look terrible. I must have gained ten pounds," she lamented.

"I wouldn't worry about it," he said and slapped her behind lightly "I always did think you were too thin."

"Is that so?"

Dan pushed his wire-rimmed glasses back up to the bridge of his nose and smiled. "Well, what do you think of the house? We did good, huh?"

Hailey looked around at the traditional French home with its appealing sense of intimacy. Her own house was sleek, sophisticated, impeccably decorated and stark. Hailey couldn't help comparing the two. This was a home, not a showplace for clients. Her mother's patchwork quilt would fit in nicely here, she mused, instead of being stored away. Hailey was wistful when she said, "Yes, you certainly did well, Dan."

"Listen, I'd love to stand here and chat with you ladies, but I'd better make sure these men know where to put everything. So if you'll excuse me . . ."

"No problem, Dan. I came here to help out anyway. Where do we start?" she asked Janet.

"Where we're needed the most. This way," Janet said, and Hailey followed her to the kitchen. Hailey poured two cups of coffee while Janet opened a carton of dishes. Janet took the porcelain mug from Hailey, who appeared to be on the verge of tears.

"I seem to be forever asking this, but here goes again. What's wrong?"

"You probably aren't going to believe this, but I quit my job." Hailey's voice was strained.

Janet nearly choked on her coffee. "You've got to be kidding! You were doing so well and wanted a job, *this* one so much . . ." Janet's mind was racing. "Why, Hailey?"

"It turned out not to be what I thought it was. I was led astray, if you will." Hailey caught Janet's piercing look. "The boss wanted to sleep with me," she said bitterly.

"I don't blame him," Janet joked as she watched Hailey's face change from disgust to surprise.

"Janet!" Hailey cried in shock.

"Don't take it so seriously. Hailey, you've got to have a sense of humor about the whole thing. And, ordinarily, you would have. I think there's something else, and I'm right, aren't I?"

Hailey glanced surreptitiously at her friend but knew Janet had only her best interests in mind. "Yes, you're right. I still haven't been able to get up the nerve to tell Mike . . ."

"Hailey, no . . . ." Janet's tone was worried and Hailey knew that she couldn't fool her. "You can't go on keeping things from him. What are you so afraid of?"

"Confrontation," Hailey replied too quickly and halted. Why was she always so surprised with her own answers to Janet's questions? Perhaps Hailey was relieved finally to be able to tell someone how she felt.

"Why?"

"Oh, I've finally figured that out: Once I got started, too much truth would come out."

"Too much?"

"Yes, and the odd part is that even I don't know what is actually wrong. But I do have this abnormal fear of any arguments with Mike."

"Perhaps you're right. I think you could use some time to think, don't you? However, you'll have to tell him, and you should do it tonight. Only take my advice and don't tell him this happened yesterday. Let him think he's the first to know."

"I see your point," Hailey agreed. "You'll be glad to know there is a bright side to all this," she said with a smile that lifted her face and brought back the sparkle in her eyes.

"Oh, really? What's that?"

"I've decided to start painting again," she replied with her old self-assurance, which of late had been lost to her.

Janet looked at her aghast. "I couldn't be more thrilled for you. Now, *that* was a wise decision."

"I knew sooner or later you'd bug me about it so much that I'd probably do it just from the mental duress alone!" Hailey bantered airily.

"I'm not that bad!" Janet said and laughed.

"I know, and I love you for being so concerned about me."

"Must be some strange motherly instinct or something," Janet replied, laughing again. "Now, here," she said, handing Hailey a stack of cookbooks. "We've settled all the earth-shattering problems of the day. Now, down to the more mundane matters."

"Yes, ma'am!" Hailey replied and stacked them on an open rack on the counter.

Hailey spent the bulk of the day helping Janet get settled. By three o'clock the kitchen was in order and all appliances were functioning. From there on, Janet said she could handle the rest. Hailey wanted to stop at an art supply house and purchase the equipment she would need. She told Janet she would call her in a day or two.

As Hailey drove away she wondered why she hadn't told Janet about Stephen or about the prospect of working in a gallery. Perhaps she just didn't believe it herself.

That night, after she finished loading the dishwasher, Hailey gathered her resolve and went into the living room, where Mike was reading *The Wall Street Journal*. She picked up a novel she'd been reading and sat on the banquette next to him. He was engrossed in an article and took no notice of her presence.

"Mike, I hate to interrupt you," she started.

"Hmmm," he grumbled but did not look at her. "I'm almost finished." He read the last paragraph and folded the newspaper and smiled at her. "What's up?"

"Well, I really don't know how to say this. But I thought you should know that I . . . I . . . quit my job." She waited, for he barely moved.

Mike was momentarily taken aback, blinking his eyes as if an alien light were piercing them. Then he flung the newspaper onto the coffee table and threw his arms around her. "That's great! I'm so glad you finally came to your senses," and he slowly released her.

"My . . . my senses?" she asked, his last statement pricking at her ears.

"Hailey, that job was too much for you. Ever since you started, you've been . . . well . . . cranky, and I think it's too much strain on you. You're better off here at home." He patted her shoulder.

"Mike, I think you've got this all wrong," she said and then quickly stopped herself. Perhaps it was wise to let him believe whatever he wanted. As far as she was concerned, the gallery idea might never come to pass. She wished she hadn't said anything. In the past weeks, it was obvious that Mike felt alienated by her "new" desires. Even Hailey feared they were simply flights of fantasy. She was trying to break free, to discover, and Mike was restraining her, keeping her pinned to the ground.

Mike's back straightened and he edged his way back into the dove-gray Ultrasuede banquette that lined the perimeter of the immense room. He looked more like her father then, especially when he was about to lay down the rules. "And just how am I supposed to take it?"

"I didn't think I was 'cranky,' but maybe I was. The most important thing was that I was accomplishing something and learning. Even if I did get tired, I loved working."

"I see. So then why the hell did you quit if you 'loved' it so much?"

"Because . . ." she started, then lost her courage again. This time the truth was not called for. "I don't know how you're going to feel about this, but I've decided to take up my painting again."

"Painting? When did all this come about?"

"I thought I'd at least give it a try," she said lightly.

He put his hand on her knee. "You know, that sounds like a good idea, now that I think about it. You could work right here at home and be here for the children . . . and me." He added the last thought as a test, she thought.

She sensed that he needed reassurance. Suddenly she realized that she couldn't give it to him, and she was

59

overwhelmed by guilt. All she could do was dodge the issue. "I thought you might be pleased."

"I am. And I'm behind you all the way. Whatever you need, I'll help you. We could take the extra bedroom upstairs and fix it up as a studio for you. You'll need supplies . . ." Mike was rambling but his enthusiasm was genuine.

"I picked up a few things today, so that tomorrow I could start sketching," she said, hoping it would please him.

"You certainly haven't wasted any time, have you? That's good. What do you plan for your first project?"

"I thought I'd paint Janet and then give it to her as a gift."

"Good idea. How are Janet and Dan, anyway? Shouldn't they be moving fairly soon?" he asked, obviously more at ease as he rested his hand on the back of the banquette.

"They're already here! Their house is lovely. I liked it a lot."

"When did you see them?"

"Just today. She called first thing this morning and I went over to help her unpack."

"Then you didn't go to work today."

"No . . ." Hailey knew he'd caught her.

"Exactly when did you quit your job?" he asked tersely, his mood drastically altered.

"Yesterday," she told him the truth.

He stood up instantly. "Am I always going to be the last one to find out what you're doing and what's going on?"

"Mike, I . . ." she tried to explain. He was hurt once again. It didn't matter what she did, she seemed to bungle everything. She was close to despising herself. Why was something so simple as wanting to paint or getting a job so unreasonably disrupting to their lives?

"You don't need to explain. It's apparent where I fit into your life, Hailey. Last on the list. And I've got news! I don't like it one stinking bit," he exploded, and before she could say anything he stalked out of the room and pounded up the stairs.

Hailey sat on the banquette listening to the rising beat of Ravel's *Bolero* on the stereo.

"Building to a climax," she said aloud without thinking. She was astonished when she listened to her words echo back to her. She felt dizzy as she surveyed her stylish prison. She was trapped. Her question now was the most puzzling one to date. Who was the warden? Mike? Or her own lack of confidence?

## Chapter Seven

JANET'S portrait became Hailey's refuge. Mike's silences now spanned both day and night. Initially, Hailey thought he would be thrilled with her presence at home, but he wasn't. All she was asking was that he learn to share responsibility with her and let her be equal with him. She didn't want to usurp any mystical male power he felt he had; she only wanted to extend herself and become more of a person.

She wondered what had happened to sharing, equality, loving and touching. Odd how those words pressed most viciously on her brain. She hadn't thought much about them but they were important words. She doubted she would ever find their definitions in her old dictionary.

She dipped the camel-hair brush into the cleaner and methodically wiped the handle clean as she thought about Stephen. She hadn't heard from him in over two weeks and therefore had abandoned all hope for the job at the gallery. Now that she was so involved in her project, her mind could not handle anything more anyway. Over a dozen charcoal sketches of Janet were fastened by clamps to a piece of clothesline she'd hung across the room. She found her old easel from college in the attic and once her canvas was stretched, she delved into work with a fury. Already she could see it taking shape. She worked until late at night after everyone had gone to bed, and last night she had actually fallen asleep on the floor beside the easel. She had even lost interest in food, and with a cynical chuckle she thought it was as if she were possessed. It was only to be a gift for Janet, and yet she believed that somehow it would eventually become more important than that. She had no basis for that assumption, but she had to believe in something. She wanted this work to be the best she had ever done.

She was in the process of mixing colors when the telephone rang. She was surprised when she recognized Stephen's voice. "Stephen! I was beginning to think I'd never hear from you again."

"Oh, ye of little faith," he quipped, but his voice was a welcome respite. "What are you doing for lunch today?"

"Probably skipping it," she answered.

"Not today, fair lady. How about meeting me at Rudi's?"

"Well, I suppose I could . . ." She was trying to think of excuses not to go, lest her concentration be lost.

"Great! I'll get reservations for twelve-thirty if you're agreeable to that."

"Okay. That's fine. I'll see you then." She hung up the receiver. She looked at her watch. An hour and a half! It would take her that long just to drive there! She'd been so involved in painting that she hadn't washed her hair in three days, and her hands and cuticles were splotched with paint. "I'd better move fast!"


Stephen was talking to the headwaiter when Hailey, her mass of silver hair flowing down her back, swished into the restaurant dressed in a long-sleeved apricot silk dress. He turned when she spoke his name. His approval shone in his expression.

She was radiant and her blue eyes snapped with an electricity he'd never seen in any woman before. The color of the dress matched the peach blush of her cheeks, one he knew was natural, for she wore very little makeup. He inhaled her expensive perfume. Marvelous was not nearly a strong enough word to describe her that day. Every male eye in the restaurant was focused on her, and though she did not notice, Stephen saw their gestures of approval toward him.

"My, but you look fetching," he complimented her, and

she responded with a smile that showered him with a million unspoken words of appreciation.

"I've been cooped up in that house for two weeks and I'd forgotten how wonderful it is to be out."

"Good! I'm glad I was the one to rescue you," he said, smiling. "I intend to alter this cloistered life you're leading."

Hailey stared at him curiously and was about to pursue the subject when the waiter signaled that their table was ready. Hailey sat in the red upholstered banquette, and Stephen sat opposite her. He ordered two glasses of white wine.

"Stephen," Hailey began, "would you mind telling me what is going on? I know we aren't having lunch just because you wanted to see me."

"You don't have much faith in your charm. Shame on you!" he said and laughed. "Of course I wanted to see you, but you're most correct, my dear. I do have an ulterior motive."

"Ah-ha! I knew I detected a note of mystery to all this."

"All right, I give up. What tipped you off!"

"Well, Stephen . . ." She glanced around at the ornate brass chandeliers and red fabric walls studded with fine oils. Each table was exquisitely set, and the waiters served their patrons with a minimum of fuss and a maximum of attention and crisp professionalism. She leaned closer to him and whispered, "This isn't exactly the deli, you know."

"Curses!" He chuckled merrily. "I was enjoying the intrigue and you had to go and spoil it."

"Sorry about that. Now, out with it," she demanded lightheartedly.

"Goodness, aren't we impatient," he foiled with her. The waiter brought the wine, and Stephen ordered for them both. When the waiter left, Stephen lifted his glass of wine and touched the rim of her glass. "A toast. Here's to unlocking the door to your prison."

"What?" she replied, thinking it a strange thing to say. How could he know what she had been thinking? Or was he merely guessing? Then he spoke again.

"After lunch we're taking a short ride."

"Stephen, I can't . . ." she said quickly.

"To an interview," he said and noted a concerned if not hesitant expression cross her face. "Don't worry. It's in the bag. I talked to my friends I told you about. They're most anxious to meet you."

"But today! I haven't thought about it . . . haven't prepared!" And then her annoyance at his presumptuousness rose. "Stephen, I didn't hear from you at all. In fact, I had given up the idea altogether. It never dawned on me that this would happen, that you would follow through—" She was interrupted.

"You're being negative again." Then he eased off a bit and his tone lightened. "Now that you've been duly chastised . . . Hailey, I'm not about to let you lock yourself away from the world anymore. You belong out where it's all happening. The least you can do is listen to what they have to say and then make your own judgments."

Hailey nodded her head. "You're right. I know you are."

"Of course I am and I think you're going to like what you hear."

"You're keeping secrets again." She smiled sweetly, but the look in her eyes was skeptical.

"Indeed I am. However, it's not my place to disclose any more details. You'll just have to wait."

Hailey sighed deeply but agreed. "At least it's not that long a wait." Hailey was glad to get the interview over with. It was such a nerve-racking invention—interviews.

"True, true," he was saying in answer to her statement, and then he leaned back as the waiter placed his entree in front of him.

Hailey was growing more nervous every minute and found she could hardly swallow her food. Her dry mouth felt as if it were stuffed with cotton. She wanted to order another glass of wine to bolster her courage, but she realized it would make a bad first impression if she were intoxicated. She had a problem stumbling over words as it was! She listened intently as Stephen told her throughout the rest of lunch and the short ride to the Galleria about the latest projects at Design Media.

He parked his car and aided Hailey with her door. As they were walking between the glass doors, she looked at him and said, "It just dawned on me! I thought you said the gallery was in Montrose. What are we doing here?"

"Hailey, you really must do something about your lack of patience. It must be your only fault."

Hailey quickly glanced away, thinking of at least a thousand faults she had, but she masked her thoughts with a bright expression. "Definitely my Achilles' heel," she said as they entered the lobby of the Houston Oaks.

Stephen approached two conservatively dressed businessmen. He shook hands with the taller man and exchanged greetings. "Hailey, this is Leonard Sims, and this is Barrett Anderson."

"I'm pleased to meet you," she said to the bearded Leonard and she shook hands with Barrett, who was seated in a chair.

"We've heard quite a lot about you, Hailey," Barrett said, flashing her a most charming smile. He was slender and so unbelievably handsome, Hailey believed the word "beautiful" was a more accurate description of him.

"We wanted to meet you here in order to show you the location of the new gallery we will be opening in a few weeks," Leonard was explaining. He was quite tall and very thin, and thankfully his quiet self-assurance put Hailey instantly at ease. She liked him almost immediately.

"I have no idea what Stephen has told you—" Leonard was saying.

"Not much," Stephen piped in and winked at Hailey.

"I suppose we will have to go over a few preliminaries, then. Barrett and I have recently joined in partnership and have made the decision to expand. The only reason we have hesitated is that we were afraid we would be spread too thin. We can't afford to remain in the stores when we have so many outside appointments."

"And," Barrett pushed in, "once Stephen told us about you we were most anxious to meet you and discuss your managing this store in the Galleria." He flashed her another smile.

Barrett seemed a bit too smooth and suave to her, but she let her apprehension die in her excitement over what they were saying. "Maybe I'm just a little slow, but you both seem certain that I'm the right person for the job."

"Well, you are!" Stephen said adamantly.

Leonard crossed his arms over his chest and smiled at her. "It's very simple, Hailey. Stephen has always had nothing but the best advice for me. After what he told me about you, I knew you were what I was looking for. First, I knew I wanted a woman and she had to be bright, personable—and the fact that you are attractive was a real bonus. It was when Stephen told me about your interest in painting that I was adamant about meeting you."

"I'm very flattered by all this, but I need more specifics. Just exactly what does the job entail?"

"Let's walk over to the store and we'll discuss it more," Barrett said as he rose and led the way.

They took the stairs and turned the corner. The area had been vacated recently, Barrett said as he unlocked the door. They entered the expansive area and he flicked on the newly installed track lights. There was ample room for displays, Hailey could see. Off to the right was a glassed-in office with a contemporary glass-and-brushed-steel desk.

Hailey loved it immediately. As Barrett described their plans and the layout of the store, she was able to visualize the complete picture.

"Your duties will be supervised by one of us, at first. We'll show you what paperwork you'll need to do, but most of it will be handled at the main gallery, so you needn't worry about that. You'll be given portfolios on the artists we wish to feature. These you'll have to study and I'd like you to meet some of the local artists in person. It will broaden your perspective and help you to sell if you know them as individuals and perhaps some of the things they are hoping to accomplish through their work. You'll have some technical memorization and we'll teach you about shipping procedures. We won't leave you alone here until we feel you are ready, but that's our goal. We need you to manage this store so that we can make our contacts and business appointments. Later, you'll progress and we'd like you to become involved in larger projects."

"May I ask what kind of projects?"

"Certainly. Many large corporations phone us every day to coordinate with their designers concerning art and its placement in their offices."

"I think I'd really enjoy that!" Hailey said enthusiastically, not afraid to let her feelings show.

"Sure you would. It's great fun," Leonard replied. "It's not difficult, but we do need someone who wants to sell and not merely to show. This isn't a museum. It is a business. I can't stress that enough."

"I understand, and I believe I would be very good for your company," she assured him.

"I'm certain of it," Barrett said, grinning. "So, what's your answer?"

Hailey looked at each one of their eager faces. They were almost breathless with anticipation. She secretly thought this kind of power was wonderfully delicious. "I'll do it, of course!" she said. She was so excited she could barely stand it. She wanted to hug all three of them in her exuberance, but she strove to remain calm and appear businesslike. "When do I start?"

"We've planned a grand opening complete with champagne which, if it goes as planned, is only a month away. We haven't sent out the invitations yet. I'd like it to be in three weeks, but the carpenters aren't finished yet and all the stock hasn't arrived from New York. You'll be open from ten in the morning until five in the afternoon. But I'm afraid there's no lunch hour, because most times there won't be anyone here to relieve you."

"That's fine with me," she replied.

"We'll pay you thirteen hundred a month plus commissions on what you sell," Barrett said, anticipating her next question.

Hailey thought it a generous offer but merely said, "That's acceptable to me. Do you need help with any arrangements now before the opening?"

"I'm glad you brought that up. We would like you to see the main gallery, get acquainted with our procedures, that sort of thing. I may need you to stay there while I run over here to supervise the workmen. If it's at all possible, I'd like you to start on Monday."

Hailey's eyes lit up. "Monday it is! At the Montrose location?"

"Right," Leonard said. "Well, Hailey, I think I've covered as much as we can today. I'll see you Monday at ten." He shook her hand and smiled. "Welcome to L'Artiste du Monde."

"Thank you, Leonard. And let me assure you, I'll do my very best."

Stephen, who had stood off to the side during the conversation, stepped up and gently grasped Hailey's elbow. "I think it best that I take you back to your car. I've got an appointment I need to keep."

"Stephen, I'm sorry I've kept you. Leonard, Barrett, please excuse us. I'll see you both Monday," she said and turned and left with Stephen.

As they drove back to the restaurant where Hailey's car was parked, she could not control her eagerness nor her soaring aspirations for what this job could mean to her. Stephen chuckled silently as he caught a glimpse of her out of the corner of his eye. As she rambled on about the integral part he'd played that day, she detected a smug look on his face. She could tell he was just as excited as she was, but he refused to show it. She thanked him again as he pulled up next to her car.

"I'll call you soon, Hailey. And listen, just because you're a working woman again doesn't mean you are allowed to abandon your portrait."

"Stephen, how will I ever find the time now?" she asked skeptically.

"I have total confidence in you. You'll think of something. That portrait must be finished. It's imperative," he said, as if he were issuing a military order.

"That's a pretty strong word."

"I meant it to be. Imperative for you and your sense of yourself. Hailey, I know one thing: You're not a one-dimensional person. Just having a job will never be enough for you."

She peered directly into his eyes. He was truly concerned about her and she was totally baffled as to why she and her talent and her life should so suddenly become important to him. "Stephen," she asked softly, "why do you do this?"

He glanced away but only momentarily. "Because I like you. And I want to see you happy."

"And I'm not happy?" She couldn't decide if it were a question or a statement, even in her own mind. She smiled and nodded. "Bye, Stephen." She got out of the car and closed the door and then unlocked the door to her Thunderbird.

"Until next time, Hailey," he waved as he drove off.

Hailey started the engine and thought it was all too good to be true. Stephen was right. She did have to finish that portrait, if nothing else; just for Janet. But in the back of her mind she knew she was doing it for herself and that was why she felt so positive about it. It was good work and contained much emotion. For the first time in so very long, she felt wonderful and . . . yes . . . free.

# Chapter Eight

HAILEY despised weekends. The children were off to swimming team and soccer practice or playing with their friends, and that left her vulnerable to more arguments with Mike.

To escape, she'd gone next door to Alice's and discussed her new job prospect, but as usual, Alice couldn't understand why she would want the hassle of commuting, deadlines and sitter problems.

Hailey had seen Martha at the grocery store over a week ago and even Martha seemed almost delighted that Hailey was back to being a housewife. Hailey couldn't decide if they were jealous, or if she was missing some special satisfaction in staying at home. Even though she was frustrated and confused, she was more determined than ever to take on this job at the gallery.

She spent the majority of the weekend in the "studio," as she now referred to the empty bedroom, but even here there was no security and no peace, for the room was crowded with her anxieties. She struggled to block out everything but her painting.

Mike had been on the rampage about her late hours and the time she spent away from him. What bewildered her most was that up until she'd had that first job, Mike seemingly had paid little attention to the fact that she existed, so caught up was he in his own career. Now suddenly it was as if he were obsessed with her every breath.

There were times she would catch him standing just outside the door, watching her. She sensed that his silence was only a mask for his anger, which was about to explode once again. She believed he was afraid of her newly discovered self-esteem. In essence, she was a threat to him and the past patterns of their life. She was coming into her own, and his reactions vacillated from one extreme to the other. He was hanging onto unrealistic hopes that she would give up her art and the pursuit of a career. Though she tried to understand him, her anger at being kept in a glass cage collided with his insecurities. It was like living in a battle zone.

Now that it was Sunday, she had to tell him about her new job at the gallery. Her stomach cramped with the thought, for she still couldn't decide how to approach him on the subject.

The portrait was nearly finished now and an odd sense of loss engulfed her as she stared at it. She dreaded its completion; it had become part of her.

A light tapping on the door disrupted her thoughts. "Come in," she said and turned to see Mike cautiously enter the room.

"Are you going to take a break and help me with dinner?"

She glanced at her watch. "I had no idea it was so late. Just let me clean up and I'll be right down."

"I've got steaks ready to grill," he said and watched as she put her brushes away. "It looks good, Hailey. It's almost finished, isn't it?"

"Yes, it is," she answered. She watched his features as he observed her work. His eyes crinkled in the corners as he smiled at her. It was a look she'd almost forgotten. The first time she had seen it was eleven years ago, when they had gone sailing near Hyannis Port on a blustery summer day. Mike loved the sea and the relaxation, the escape it afforded him. It had been a peaceful day, with the flapping sails slicing a jagged pattern across a brilliant horizon. Mike had been so enthusiastic about his future then. The sparkling blue of his eyes now was the same as it was then. Hailey's heart whimpered painfully as she listened to him.

"I'm glad it's finished. Maybe now you'll be able to remember you have a family to consider."

Hailey's thoughts crashed and sank. He still didn't understand her and she knew he never would. "I've never forgotten my family," she said softly but couldn't pull herself to look at him. There was no use defending herself, but she had to fight for her future. "There's something else I'd like to talk to you about."

"What's that?"

She straightened her shoulders and looked at him. "Tomorrow morning I start a new job." She'd finally said it, and she could see it was like waving a red flag at him. Her heart was beating rapidly. Why did they have to be like this? Why wouldn't he relent? She braced as she watched his face flush.

"I thought we had been through this!"

She tried to be gentle. "No, Mike. You've stated what you want me to be. I can't go on living vicariously through you. I can't accept that life anymore."

"Oh, yes you can! You just won't, that's all. Hailey, what's wrong with you lately? I feel like I'm living with a stranger. I can't stand the tension in this house and you never bother to consult me on anything anymore."

"Would it do any good, Mike? You don't want me to work or to paint. You've certainly made that clear enough. You're treating me like a child!"

"But you've been happy up till now, and all of a sudden everything is topsy-turvy. I feel like I'm walking on eggshells and I don't understand why. What has happened to change things so much? Your life is easy and you've got everything you need . . ."

"I guess I just don't know any better," she said sarcastically. She immediately saw the error in using that tone and dropped it, but it was so hard to control her anger. "I like working *and* painting. I'm not the best in the world at either one, but I'm trying. For once, I feel like I'm accomplishing something just for myself. Maybe I am being selfish . . ." Her misgivings were flooding her head again.

"Why isn't what we had good enough anymore?" he demanded.

"It just isn't!" she cried, exhausted at this perpetual bickering. She wondered how much longer she could go on. "Why must we argue so much about it? I've got this wonderful opportunity and I don't want to pass it up."

"What if I said you couldn't do it?" he asked, folding his arms across his chest.

She stared at him, fighting the impulse to scream. "You wouldn't," she replied in a whisper.

"Don't be so sure," he said, smirking, but she could hear the strain in his voice. She was challenging him and he was quite unsure of the rules, something she didn't understand either.

"Mike, don't press me on this. Please, don't insist on keeping me chained up," she begged. "What you don't realize is that I'm a person. I have some dreams of my own and this is my chance to try my wings. I can't live anymore without having freedom of choice. I'm asking you to give me that. Why is that so much to ask?"

"It pushes me out of your life," he answered, his voice quaking.

Hailey's mouth dropped. She hadn't realized that was what she was doing. She knew now that he was not a part of her life the way a husband should be to a woman. Her anger faded and was replaced by pity. Mike had done nothing but try to hang on, to save himself. She was the one who was being cruel by her lack of understanding, and she was devastated by the knowledge. What sort of horrible person was she? All these years, he could have had so much more. She had to acknowledge that she was keeping him from finding happiness.

He was waiting for her to refute his words, to tell him everything was fine, that she loved him and her life with him. And she couldn't do it. It would be a lie and so she said nothing.

"Hailey," he said, "for God's sake, say something!"

"I don't know what to say, Mike. I can't . . . I mean . . . I won't quit my job. This is mine! Don't you understand that? I've given all my time to you and the children. Now it's my turn. I don't understand why you feel threatened. You do, don't you?" she asked him pointedly.

"Yes, I do. I don't know why. I would tell you if I did. I'm confused, too." His eyes were pleading with her, tearing her apart.

"I know, but you shouldn't be," she reassured him. "Couldn't you just give me some time to find out for myself if I like it or not?"

"I suppose I could," he said, but Hailey could see that he was hoping this wouldn't last.

"Come on," she said with a lighter tone, grasping at the upturn in their thoughts. She prayed she wasn't being cruel by running from their difficulties. "Let's grill those steaks, what do you say?" she asked as she finished cleaning the paint off her hands and walked toward him.

He seemed pleased, almost eager, to drop the matter and so he kissed her cheek, flicked off the light and followed her downstairs.

The following morning was one of those almost subtropical days Hailey loved. The blue sky was mounded with huge white clouds. A gentle, moist breeze fanned the tops of palm trees that stood in front of L'Artiste du Monde as Hailey entered through the front doorway. Surprisingly, the main gallery was not as large as the Galleria offshoot, though it did contain the business offices and a large reception area where a woman sat frantically organizing the morning's correspondence before the mailman arrived.

"Good morning!" she said with a cheery smile when she noticed Hailey. The woman stood and stretched out a hand to welcome her. "You can be none other than Hailey! My dear, the place is bubbling about you. Yes, yes, indeed. Ever since Stephen . . ."

"Stephen?" Hailey interrupted her. "Do you know Stephen?"

"Goodness, yes, I do!" She beamed like a Cheshire cat.

Hailey looked at the red-haired woman and noted that

she had no wedding band, though her chubby fingers were nearly all adorned with rings, running the gamut from exquisite to gaudy. Her silver-framed glasses were suspended around her neck by a gold chain studded with tiny imitation pearls that were scratched, and most had lost their thin film of coating. Hailey wondered if it were prized for its sentimental value. Paradoxically, the beige linen suit she wore was well tailored and of designer quality. The mischievous sparkle in her eye led Hailey to believe that this woman had led an adventurous life, and it wouldn't surprise her to learn that she had a multitude of lovers sprinkled through her life like bawdy poems.

Hailey found herself smiling at this effervescent creature and totally unable to answer quickly enough to the questions posed to her, so the woman continued with a stream of nonsensical chatter until Hailey interrupted her.

"I'm sorry, I didn't catch your name," Hailey said.

"I never said!" was her answer. "It's Agatha Smythe. Isn't that an absolutely abominable label to stick someone with all their life?"

"Why, no, not at all," Hailey said but couldn't finish.

"You're just being sweet. I've always thought about changing it to something more dramatic. But," she said and laughed, "I was never able to find the right combination." Her look was distant as she crossed her forearms over her thick waist.

Hailey felt criminal taking Agatha's thoughts back to business. "I don't suppose Leonard is in yet."

"What?" Agatha shook her head and blinked. "Oh, yes, yes, he certainly is. As a matter of fact, he's gathering up some portfolios for you to study."

"Wonderful! I can hardly wait!"

Agatha looked at Hailey. "It's exciting, isn't it?"

"What is?"

"A new job, of course! Anything new is an adventure. I just adore adventures, don't you? But don't you worry. I personally can guarantee that you'll always find something new here."

"I'm glad to hear that," Hailey said and then heard a

door open behind her and turned to see Leonard stroll in with a folder in his hand.

"Hailey! Good to see you! You're certainly prompt," he said. "All set to dig in?"

"I sure am!"

"Good. I want to go over the architect's plans for the Galleria store and then have you supervise for me. I've got so many appointments I don't know how I'll finish before midnight," he lamented.

"I'll help in any way I can."

"That's what I like to hear. Now come into my office," he said, and Hailey followed him into an impeccably furnished room. Brass miniblinds had been lifted, and the morning light streamed in.

Leonard reviewed the floor plan and the placement of displays and lighting with Hailey. Since Hailey's knowledge of commercial design was not anywhere near expert, she felt uncomfortable offering suggestions, though she did inquire about traffic flow and location of office equipment. Mostly she absorbed every word Leonard said and every detail of the sketches. He spent the morning and most of the lunch hour explaining billing procedures and the arrangements for deliveries. Leonard informed her that Barrett had flown to New York that morning and she would need to assume his duties until he got back.

Their meeting over, Hailey left for the Galleria. When she arrived, she was amazed at the activity she saw. There were easily a dozen different carpenters and electricians and painters working furiously to meet the deadline Leonard had set. She had been prepared for a few half-hearted laborers, like the kind she had employed at her own house, but this was mind-boggling. She skirted the perimeter of the room so as not to disturb anyone, all the while keeping her eyes on the three men on the scaffolding above, who were installing the last of the lights. Directly behind them followed another man, who was shooting nails into the ceiling substructure with a high-powered nailgun.

Hailey went to the office and was met by the telephone installer, who immediately began asking questions about the placement of the phones. She found to her dismay that she would need to rearrange the furnishings to accommodate the installer's needs. She also decided to have an extension placed in the file rooms and hoped Leonard would approve. It would be just like her to botch it up completely before she had a chance to get started.

Throughout the afternoon she was barraged with questions from the construction crew, and without phones until the very end of the day she had no way of contacting Loenard or Agatha. She constantly referred to the blueprints for information, but with a joint pooling of minds, the carpenters and she were able to keep the work on schedule. By the time five o'clock arrived, Hailey was exhausted but they had accomplished a great deal. After the last workman filed through the doorway, she turned the key in the lock, pleased with herself.

# Chapter Nine

FOR the following three weeks, Hailey was caught in a whirlwind of activity. The store was nearly finished and the shipments of paintings poured in. With Barrett's help, she tried her hand at positioning and categorizing the display area. Together they worked diligently and with great precision. To her it seemed as if they had rearranged the gallery a thousand times, and she was surprised when Barrett informed her there had been only one major and two minor revisions. Hailey was pleased both with her work and with herself these past weeks.

She and Agatha had painstakingly planned the arrangements for the opening. The caterer had proposed a mediocre fare with an open bar. Hailey immediately canceled him and his menu and pushed for a more sophisticated array of food and champagne. Leonard approved of her decision, for this was an elegant, invitation-only affair. "Just pretend your only daughter was getting married to Prince Andrew. What would you do?" he had asked her. Hailey needed no further encouragement. But once she received the bill for the beluga caviar, she wondered if her overhead costs would warrant the extravagance. However, no one batted an eye.

The two afternoons she spent with the floral designer had been her most frustrating. Hailey had nearly thrown up her hands twice over the man's inability to understand her ideas. He had not a grain of good taste and kept insisting on gladiolus. Hailey sweetly yet firmly endeavored to explain she was planning a gala and not a funeral. Finally he relented and placed an order for a dozen enormous glass bowls of white calla lilies and pink rubellum lilies to blend with the mauve and gray and stainless-steel decor. It was obvious the words "art deco" were unknown to the florist.

When she started to walk out of his shop, she was most surprised when he stopped her. "Mrs. Asher, let me assure you that I would never let you down. I always do my best to please a beautiful woman."

Hailey had blushed at the compliment and mumbled an awkward good-bye. This was not an everyday occurrence for her and she was even more puzzled when she realized that she liked it. That man had actually thought she was pretty!

But as she drove back to work, the florist's words vanished as she reflected on her problems. There were two things she was naggingly aware of: Mike's insensitivity and Stephen's absence. The tension at home was now so intense that she and Mike rarely spoke, and when they did, it was explosive. Mike was totally unable to cope with her need for a paying job and her drive to paint.

She was plagued with guilt over the hours she spent working when she used to be at home with the children. Her only consolation was that there were thousands of women like her. Mike was pushing her farther toward the decision. Once again she felt as if she were waiting, but this time she knew what was in store for her. Just when it would happen, she was unsure. Daily she became stronger, and with every step forward she took, Mike took three backward. It was a living hell for them both. Mike could sense that she did not love him, and Hailey was tormented by her inability to give him what he so desperately needed.

By this time, Hailey was becoming used to Stephen's prolonged disappearances and sudden resurrections in her life. When he came blithely strolling into the gallery that afternoon, she was surprised not by his unannounced appearance but by her own feelings of irritation at him.

"And how are you today, fair lady?" he asked airily,

stubbing out his cigarette in a black onyx ashtray on her desk.

"Just fine," she said coolly.

"Hmmm. Doesn't sound like it to me. What's wrong?"

"Why, nothing at all. I've been pretty busy," she replied, nodding toward the display area, which was now complete.

"I can see that. An admirable job, I must say!" He answered her with such flippancy that when he spun around and plunked his palms on the desk and leaned so close to her that their noses almost touched, she jumped back.

"Now, where the hell is it?" he demanded with a sardonic scowl.

"God! What is the matter with you, Stephen? What *are* you talking about?"

"The portrait, of course! I've given you enough time to finish it. I want to see it."

"Well, it's not here, if that's what you mean," she retorted.

"Why not? This *is* an art gallery!"

"I know that."

"Have it here tomorrow so I can see it, okay? I have an appointment I've got to make in twenty minutes and it's at least an hour's drive from here. Bring it tomorrow and I'll take you to lunch."

"I can't leave for lunch," she said. "There's no one here to cover for me."

"Then I'll bring the mountain to Mohammed . . ." His voice trailed off and he breezed through the doorway before Hailey could catch her breath.

She stared after him and then burst into laughter. "Stephen! What am I going to do with you?"


Hailey placed Janet's portrait on an easel in the office. Her back was to the door as she inspected it. With a groan of despair she wondered if she would ever produce anything of real quality. Surrounded by work that was truly inspiring, her portrait paled. Hailey braced when she thought about anyone actually viewing it!

83

So immersed in thought was she that she was unaware of anyone else. When she turned around, her heart leaped to her throat in surprise, for not only did she see Stephen, but Leonard and Barrett, too.

None of them noticed her; their eyes were on the portrait. Leonard moved behind Stephen and quickly shot his arm up the wall and flipped off all the lights save for the two overhead spots. Hailey stared in amazement at them and felt her heart sink. Stephen looked white and his eyes were clouded. He hated it, she could tell. She had disappointed him so much she wondered if she would ever win him back to her side. Barrett's lips were pressed together tightly; she thought he would burst in outrage at any second. He knew every piece of work in the gallery, and this portrait was an intruder.

"Where did that come from?" Barrett demanded.

"I . . . I brought it from home . . ." Hailey could barely get out the words.

"It's unsigned," Leonard murmured. "Was it a gift from someone?"

Finally, Stephen broke through his mesmerized state. "Gentlemen, this is what I wanted you to see, and Hailey is the artist."

Odd, Hailey thought. He appeared to be pleased and yet had not committed himself in words.

"Hailey, is that true? You painted this?" Leonard asked.

"Yes. I really didn't mean any harm. You see, Stephen wanted me to bring it in to show him and I just put in on the stand . . ." She was rambling and her thoughts were whizzing about her. She edged closer to the painting, as if to protect it from criticism. She put her hands on the frame and was about to take it down.

"Don't touch it!" Leonard said, making Hailey jump.

"I was going to put it away," she said apologetically.

"No! It belongs here," Leonard said emphatically.

"What?" Hailey was stunned and confused.

"It's damn good, Hailey. Just as I suspected," Stephen said.

Hailey was caught in his look. He meant it! She pulled herself out of his gaze and studied the portrait. What was it that appealed to him? All she could see were shortcomings.

Leonard spoke. "It's not something you can move away from. She seems to be drawing us toward her, as if she were alive. What I find unbelievable is that I hate portraits. But this is different!"

Hailey was flabbergasted by what she was hearing. They couldn't be talking about her work! Finally, Leonard turned to her.

"Hailey, I want to show this painting at the opening."

"But all the displays are finished and we really don't have the room . . ." She was flustered by Leonard's pronouncement and hadn't had time to digest all he was saying.

"Don't worry about it, we'll find space, even if it's here in the office. With the spots on it, it makes a perfect showplace. There's no time to print any literature about it, but I can think of a few clients who might be interested in it."

Hailey didn't say a word. All she could think about was not being able to give the painting to Janet. She felt a pain of loss. "It's not for sale," she blurted out.

Stephen sympathized with her and said, "Of course, this particular painting isn't, but you can do more like it. No one said it was for sale, did they, Leonard?"

"Uh, why . . ." Leonard read Stephen's implication. "No. Did you have special plans for this piece?"

"Yes, I did."

"Well, the important thing is that we give you exposure, not so much for this painting, but your abilities. I hope that will ease your mind."

Hailey sighed deeply and relaxed. "Thank you." She was stunned by the situation and felt as if everything were moving in slow motion. Their words began to sink into her brain in garbled phrases, as if a stereo needle were dragging on a record. Finally their conversation broke through the barriers in her head. They thought she had talent! The recognition wasn't the most important thing, she thought. The discovery of her innate ability was like finding a chest of pirate gold. She had done this all by herself! The accomplishment was a new realm, far removed from her employment. Whether it was a success or a failure, it was hers alone, and that thrilled her. The best part was that she loved the work; the painting and the success were merely sidelights, but wonderful ones. Judging from the admiring expressions of these men, she had been successful, and she smiled with satisfaction.

Stephen was watching her, for she could feel his eyes on her back. For the first time she wondered if he were a sorcerer with magical powers. She turned to him but said nothing. She knew he was reading her thoughts.

Leonard and Barrett were discussing the placement of the portrait, and their voices seemed like the buzzing of summer flies in her ears.

"Is it time for me to say 'I told you so'?" Stephen asked and grinned.

"I think so," she said quietly.

"You know what I want you to do now?"

"No. What?"

"Believe in yourself."

"It sounds so easy, but that's a big request for me."

"I know. But you'll do it, won't you?"

"Yes," she said, and her eyes sparkled. "I'm working on it already."


The morning of the gallery opening was hectic at the Asher house. Hailey hadn't slept all night, but she was cheery as sunlight splashed through the kitchen windows.

She raced through the breakfast preparations, intermittently snatching a quick moment to apply her makeup. She hurriedly laundered the children's dress clothes and laid them out. She prayed they would get the message. It meant a lot to her for them to be present at the opening. They would come early and no doubt leave early, but she wanted them to see where she worked. And, too, if Mike saw it, perhaps then he would understand her better. She didn't know how much longer she could live with this choking apprehension.

These days, at quitting time, she dreaded coming home. Joey had been daydreaming in class lately, and his teacher had telephoned Hailey about it. Kim was not doing much better and seemed just as apathetic toward her schoolwork. It was uncharacteristic of them both. She knew it all stemmed from the situation between herself and Mike. She vowed she would not let her children suffer any longer. She placed all her hopes on this opening. Yes, Mike would understand, he would encourage her. Everything was going to be fine.

Joey came bustling into the kitchen and flung his arms around her waist. "Good morning, Mom," he said as she bent over to kiss him.

"Good morning, big time," she said as he squeezed her quickly and then snatched a strip of bacon off the platter and ran to the table giggling.

"I saw that, you rascal," she teased. "You didn't think you'd get away with that, did you?"

"Naw," he snickered playfully. "But maybe I thought so. Girls are all alike. They always fall for that mushy stuff."

"Is that so? And since when have you become a Casanova?"

"Casa who?" he asked quickly, stuffing the bacon into his mouth.

"Never mind. You can't fool me. Boys like to be hugged just as much as girls do."

"I like to hug you," he replied and then curiously looked away and out the window.

Hailey sensed that something was bothering him. "I like to hug you, too," she said. When he turned back to face her, his smile was in place, masking his real feelings, and she worried about him even more.

Mike and Kim walked into the kitchen and seated themselves at the table without saying a word. Hailey, conscious of their pregnant silences, served the waffles and fresh strawberries. Joey and Kim talked about the opening and asked every question imaginable while Mike drank his coffee. It was apparent he wanted Hailey to think he was totally uninterested in this "excursion," as he referred to it. Just once she wished he would get excited about something. Anything. He seemed not to be a part of the family at all, but an onlooker. And for that she felt sorry for him, because it was his own fault that he was missing out.

Hailey finished her meal hurriedly and dashed upstairs to change. She needed to be at the gallery in an hour to check on the florist and the caterer. Mike and the children would arrive at one o'clock, when the crowd would be light. She chose a simple black nubby linen skirt that buttoned up the front and a matching jacket with padded shoulders and which fit snugly at her waist. The cuffs and the waistband were knitted and she loved the blousy yet fitted definition it gave to her figure. She wore a simple gold rope around her neck and plain gold buttons at her ears. Her black patent tuxedo pumps were just the right touch. She bent over, brushed out her hair and then flipped her head back. With another four strokes of the hairbrush and a light misting of hair spray she was ready to go.

When she rushed into the kitchen, the children were putting the dishes in the dishwasher, though they were playing more than working.

"Well, I'm off! I'll see you all later," she said, walking over to Mike, who was still sitting at the table. She gave him a quick kiss.

"We'll be there, don't worry. We wouldn't miss it for the world," he said, but his tone lacked sincerity.

"Great!" she said, trying to keep everything on an up note. "You two behave and I'll see you later," she said to the children.

"Okay, Mom," they sang together, and as Hailey walked through the doorway, Joey squirted his sister with the sprayer and then ran out of the kitchen with Kim after him in hot pursuit.

As Hailey stood back and inspected the florist's handiwork, she marveled at what he'd accomplished. Every lily was strategically placed in its container; it was like a still life. They were magnificent. She told Barrett jokingly the man must have imported help; she would never have thought him capable of this.

The slender silver floor urns of lush areca palms were an

added touch that enhanced the entire room but did not detract from the displays. At the entrance, the caterer and the florist had combined forces to create a reception area. Two round, fully skirted tables in mauve taffeta topped with snowy squares of linen were placed on either side of the doorway. Clusters of palms and ligustrums created a living wall of greenery as a backdrop. The table to the left was centered with a tall, clear cylinder of rubellum lilies and was surrounded by candleholders shaped in round crystal balls, holding tall mauve tapers. Square silver trays held champagne flutes. The hors d'oeuvres table was to the right, with a matching floral arrangement and array of candles. Duplicate silver trays held crab shells filled with crab salad, lobster-stuffed artichokes and marinated mushrooms. A tiered server held *pâté de foie gras,* wedges of Brie and a wealth of caviar. Smaller glass plates with assorted finger sandwiches had been prepared to be passed among the guests.

Leonard and Barrett had arrived only a few minutes ago, and though they hadn't finished their inspections, she could tell from their faces that they approved. Right now, the topics of lighting and security were more pressing.

When the first guests arrived, Leonard greeted them and then he introduced them to Hailey. She passed out what literature she could and answered questions. Two of their featured artists, native Houstonians, arrived, and Hailey was thrilled to meet them. Both dealt in abstracts and she was intrigued by their work. She couldn't ask enough questions, but she did not want to monopolize their time; all the guests wanted the opportunity to speak with the talented ones.

Hailey spied Janet out of the corner of her eye and eased her way through the crowd.

"Hailey! This is marvelous! No wonder you've been so excited. Your hard work has paid off."

"I'm glad you like it. You just can't imagine how good I feel about all this."

"Oh, yes I can," Janet said and squeezed her hand and glanced around. "Where are Mike and the children?"

"I don't know. It's after two and they should have been here long ago. I'm getting worried."

"They'll be here soon," Janet reassured her. "Listen, I'm going to look around a bit. I'll talk to you later."

"Okay," Hailey replied. Just then she heard Leonard and Barrett arguing behind her.

"I just forgot all about it! So crucify me!" Barrett was saying.

"Lucky for you it's not too late," Leonard said angrily and went into the office. He turned on the spotlights and dimmed the lighting in the main room until it approximated candleglow. The effect was overwhelming.

Hailey thought she'd been transported into a celestial sphere. All conversation ceased and every head turned toward the lights in the office. Through the wall of glass, Janet's portrait was bathed in filtered light. For the first time, Hailey could see its worth. The eyes beckoned to every onlooker for they were friendly, vulnerable and haunting. Hailey felt a warm pair of hands on her shoulders, and she knew they were Stephen's. She didn't turn around, for she was spellbound.

"She has the face of an angel and eyes like yours," he whispered.

Hailey could only nod slightly, for her tongue was like lead. She was caught somewhere inside that portrait. She could hear faint, reverent voices of praise. It was so strange; it was hard to believe she had painted that portrait herself! Why all these people were so interested didn't make sense to her because portraits were not the "in" thing to buy. This was a sophisticated and knowledge-able group who were more in need of abstracts and sculptures for commercial offices than for something to hang in a cozy library at home. Why they even stopped their cocktail chatter to look was beyond her comprehension.

Janet eased her way to Hailey's side. "You didn't tell me!" she said breathlessly, but Hailey could see the pleasure in her eyes. "It's so very good. You've got real talent, Hailey."

"Yes, she does," Stephen said.

Just then, Hailey remembered Stephen standing behind her. "Janet, meet Stephen Ainsley. Stephen, this is my good friend Janet Spencer."

"I've heard about you ever since Hailey started your portrait. I feel as if I know you," he said, shaking her hand.

"I don't mind telling you that suddenly I feel as if everyone knows me, the way they are inspecting that painting!" she said and laughed. "I've tried to get Hailey to paint for years. I'm grateful to you, Stephen, for accomplishing the mission."

"I think she would have done it sooner or later," he said.

"Maybe. I'm just glad it was now. Well, if you'll excuse me I'm going to take a closer look."

"Janet," Hailey said, "I'm glad you like the painting. It's a gift for you."

"I'm so proud of you, Hailey. I'll cherish it." She hugged Hailey. "It was nice meeting you, Stephen," she said and worked her way into the office.

Stephen bent his head to Hailey's ear. "Just look at Leonard over there. He's reveling in all this attention. He knows as well as I that you might become the most valuable artist his gallery has ever seen."

"Stephen, don't exaggerate!" she protested.

"I know how his mind works. Just look at these people, Hailey. I've been listening to their comments. There aren't any portfolios on you, and so right away they've assumed Leonard has an exclusive property on his hands."

Hailey was whispering her protests to him, but he didn't hear them, for he had caught Barrett watching Hailey with a strange intensity. Then he watched as a sly smile curved Barrett's impeccably chiseled mouth. Barrett nodded at Stephen, as though he had read Stephen's mind. Stephen got the distinct impression that Barrett had anything but Hailey's best interests in mind.

Hailey stood stock-still as the patrons slipped past her and moved toward the portrait. True, some ambled off to view other works, but the majority were interested in her work. She turned her head just slightly to reply to Stephen's statement, when out of the corner of her eye she saw Mike standing in the doorway.

His eyes were icy and his facial muscles were constricted and tense. It was an expression that was now familiar to her. She struggled to smile at him as he stalked angrily toward her.

"Mike! Hi! I was wondering when you would get here!" She promised herself she would keep hoping.

"Really? I'm rather surprised at that, Hailey."

She felt Stephen's hands slip from her shoulders. "You must be Mike. Hailey has told me so many good things about you. I'm Stephen Ainsley," he said, thrusting his hand forward in greeting.

"So I gathered," Mike replied virulently, not accepting Stephen's hand.

Just then Joey and Kim came rushing up.

"Boy! Mom! This is fantastic!" Joey squealed.

"Yeah! No wonder you like working here so much," Kim said with delight as her eyes scanned the room. "That's your painting those people are all staring at, isn't it?"

"It sure is, honey. What do you think of it?"

Joey studied it for a second and said, "Janet's hair is longer."

Hailey forced herself to stifle a chuckle. "Do you really think so?"

"Yeah, but otherwise it's okay, I guess. I like the one in the back better. You know, the block with the blue triangle. Could I have it for my bedroom?"

"Joey, I don't think so. It's rather expensive for your bedroom. Why do you like that one so much?"

"'Cuz my bedspread is blue."

"Joey," Stephen said, "that was spoken like a true art critic."

Hailey laughed aloud this time. Kim was obviously undone by her brother's lack of sophistication. "Joey, for Pete's sake, you don't choose art because it matches your bedspread!"

"Oh, yeah? Well, I still like it," he taunted his sister.

"You're supposed to feel it," she said as if she'd been

schooled in art appreciation all her life. "It should mean something to you."

"Well, it does!" he retorted. "It looks like my collection of flags. And I like it!"

"That's all the reason anyone needs to buy art, Joey," Stephen said. "Kim, don't you think that's the same thing as feeling it?"

"I suppose so . . ." She was pondering his words.

Hailey spoke up then. "Children, I want to introduce you to a friend of mine. This is Stephen Ainsley."

"Hi," Joey said, shaking his hand timidly at first and then was won over by Stephen's warm smile.

"Your mother speaks of you all the time. That's how I knew your names. So, what do you think of a gallery opening?"

"Far out!" Joey said, putting his hands in his pockets and assuming a mature stance.

Hailey glanced at Mike. He'd turned away from the four of them and was downing a glass of champagne. His lips were pressed tightly together and he looked as if he would rather be anywhere but here. She walked over to him.

"What do you think? It's a beautiful gallery, isn't it?" Her smile was cheerful and she was looking for his approval. Please, she thought, say you like it. Say you accept me. But as soon as he looked at her, she knew they had passed some fragile, definitive point.

"It's quite nice." He looked away toward Janet's portrait. "I don't know much about these things but it looks to me as if your painting has caused quite a stir." There was not so much resentment in his voice as pain and sadness.

"Thank you," was all she could say.

"You don't need to thank me. It's true. You worked hard on it and your talent does show. I think you're very good at what you do. Keep it up." He tried to give her an encouraging smile, but he couldn't somehow. His mouth fell and Hailey felt her insides crumple and twist in a knot.

"I . . . I . . ." She was at a loss for reassuring words. "I couldn't have done it without you," she said, hoping it would mend their rift.

"No, Hailey. That's just it," he whispered. "Don't you see? You can do all this without me, and you did. You don't need me at all. That spotlight isn't meant for Janet. It's for you and not for anyone else to share with you."

"I didn't mean for it to be that way. Is it a bad thing for me to have done?"

"No. Just very solitary. Because you see . . . there's no room in it for me." He peeled his eyes off her and she could see he was shaking.

"Mike . . ." Hailey's eyes darted around the room. She felt as if the floor would open up and swallow her whole. In those few split seconds, they both knew there was no turning back. He had dreaded this moment and battled against it. He wanted to make everything the way it used to be for him; the Hailey he had always known was gone. He had tried to stop her and couldn't, and he would never understand why he hadn't been enough for her. "Mike, I really don't think we should be discussing this. It's not the time or the place."

"No. You're right. Let the kids look around and then I'll take them home. You go back to your friends and I'll see you later."

"Mike . . ." She wanted to stop him, but then Barrett came rushing up to her and grasped her elbow.

"I want you to meet these people, Hailey. They're singing your praises! They all want to meet the lady who is behind the painting. Strike while the iron is hot, I always say," he said as he pulled her arm.

All Hailey could see was Mike's back as he walked the children around.

In moments she was surrounded by a dozen clients who were drilling her with questions. Stephen was nowhere to be found, but somehow she knew he was still there. Mike was leaving now and she forced herself to smile at these people, who were wondrously begging her for sittings of their own.

Their mouths were moving excitedly, and their noises seemed to ebb as the groaning of her guilt overtook her senses. Her past was walking between the glass doors. Someone, one of the customers, was shaking her hand, pulling her to the center of the crowd, of the present. She wished she could run after Mike and tell him that she *could* go back to being just his wife, but that was a lie, too. It would be the greatest cruelty if she offered him false hope. There was no joy in her triumph that day. She was learning, oh so swiftly, the intensity of the pain when one grows up.

# Chapter Ten

IT was after nine o'clock when she parked her car in the garage. She shut off the ignition and sat for a moment clutching the steering wheel. She felt disoriented and it took a conscious effort to gather her bearings. God! She felt tired. Every muscle in her body ached from the tension. How good it would be just to come home and relax—soak in a tub, read a book and fall asleep. At this moment, she foolishly wished she would never have to answer to anyone ever again. Inexplicable tears welled in her eyes as she stared into blank space.

Her guilt was corrosive. It was all her fault, the way she was feeling. She kept trying to feel good about her success, but the effort was a sham. She told herself she wasn't a bad person, but the pleadings with her heart were to no avail. She was beginning to hate herself.

She opened the door, got out of the car and hit the automatic garage-door opener as she left. When she entered the house through the back kitchen door, Mike was waiting for her.

"It's about time you got home," he said. His rage was seething just below the surface.

"It's not all that late," she replied, trying to reason with him. "I was just at the gallery. You could have called me there if you needed me for anything."

"I thought this thing was supposed to end at six." His voice was deep and graveled.

"At seven, but there were still a lot of people who hadn't left and I had to supervise the cleanup for a while." She hated accounting to him for every second of her time. Even though she understood it, living it was nearly impossible.

"Hailey, that's not the point. No matter what needed to be done, I'm sure you would have volunteered to help."

"Of course I would have. What's the matter with that?"

"The point is that you'll do anything to keep from coming home."

"That's not true!" She stopped herself. She wasn't going to do this. She promised herself she wouldn't fight with him. She wanted to cry and run away from the truth, but it kept rolling after her like an avalanche.

"Think about it, Hailey. Anyplace, anywhere and with anybody but me." His eyes were burning into her. He was not confused at all and he could see everything more clearly than she.

"Just what are you implying, Mike?"

"I saw you with that . . . Stephen."

"Stephen? That's ludicrous. What's he got to do with anything?"

"Everything, that's what." Mike's eyes were stormy.

"Now, that *is* crazy! He's a friend and that's all." Hailey had to stop his unreasonable thinking. This was getting out of hand.

"Sure. And that Barrett seems pretty interested in you, too. I saw him putting his arm around you."

"Mike, you really have gone too far. You don't know what you're talking about, believe me. I think you had better get your jealousy under control."

"I'm not jealous! I never have been."

"Until now," she said quietly and looked down at the floor. Her head felt so heavy on her shoulders. His emotions were so intense they heated the very air about them. She couldn't blame him because she would have done the same thing—fought with every ounce of strength in her body, and no tactic would have been left untried.

"No, Hailey, not even now," he said defensively as she raised her eyes to his face and steadied her gaze.

She had to make him understand some realities before he misconstrued every deed and thought she had. "Yes, you are. Mike . . . I've never given you reason to worry about me and I never will. You've never been put in a situation to test your emotions and reactions before. I've always been the dutiful corporate wife. I've been home all these years, while you were out working on the road and entertaining. Now it's different. There are people out in the world and maybe some of them will be attracted to me, but that doesn't mean I'm looking for anything."

"You are looking for something, Hailey. I can see that much. I'm not blind."

"What are you accusing me of, Mike?" Hailey's voice cracked quietly. Her eyes were filled with tears that refused to fall, only blurred her vision.

His voice took a decided turn and became more sympathetic. "You are searching, don't you see? All these things you're doing—the job, your painting, the long hours. It all adds up."

Hailey was completely baffled. "You're getting everything all mixed up. I just don't understand anything you're saying."

"You know what? I believe you. Everything is happening so fast and you're caught in the middle of it. But I've been watching you. It didn't start just recently. It started a long time ago. I've taken the wrong approach with you, I know that now." He looked at her and knew instantly that she was in total agreement with him.

"You keep trying to cage me in more each day," she whispered.

"I know, and I can't stop. I don't want a career woman for a wife. And I know that I can't change. At least I've discovered that much about myself."

"But you could try . . ."

"I have tried, Hailey. Maybe you can't see that I have, but it's the truth."

"And I can't go back to the way I used to be. I like myself now. You want me to be your appendage, but I could never do it."

"That's what I've been trying to tell you. You've been

more independent than you, yourself, have ever realized. When I used to travel, you took care of everything and everybody all by yourself. You've never needed me."

"Is that so wrong?"

"Obviously, not for you."

"That's all you want then? Somebody to need you? Mike, for God's sake! A thousand women could need you, and all for different reasons."

"Yes, but you don't even have one reason to need me. Now that you've got a good job, something I've always dreaded, you don't need me for money or security. You've certainly never needed me for anything else. The security is the only reason I've kept you."

Hailey was stunned by this bitter statement. His description of her was nearly inhuman, and she despised herself even more. "Have I been that cold and callous toward you?"

"No, but I have been toward you, and I can't let myself become even more so. It's not good for me or for you."

"I agree. But what are you saying?"

"When I saw you at the gallery today, I knew it was over. You're strong now. Maybe you always were and we both just avoided it. There's never been any real communication between us. Half is my fault and half is yours."

"Mike, I didn't know I was doing this to you." She felt weak and sick to her stomach.

"You weren't doing anything. That's just the point. I don't think if we had a chance to start over it would be any different." He stopped and looked at her, but she couldn't return his look. Her eyes fell. She felt trapped and yet set free. Maybe this was what dying was like, or birth; this pain and relief. She felt secure and insecure all at once. He just watched her and she felt a cold pall envelop her, so she hugged her arms over her chest. She could feel goose bumps spread over her body.

"Hailey, can't you even look at me?"

"Please, Mike . . ." she begged, but she looked off to the side, still shivering.

"Hailey! Look at me!" he stormed.

Her tears were now streaming down her cheeks in thick

100

rivers and her vision cleared. She held her breath but could hear her heart slamming against her chest wall.

"Can you look me in the eye and tell me you love me?" he demanded.

"Mike," she said, searching his face. She wanted to die. She wished she could faint, but she couldn't say it. This would be the biggest, ugliest lie she had ever told. She was suspended there between the lie that would save her marriage and the truth that would give her freedom and peace of mind. It was such a high price. She thought of Kim, of Joey, and what she would be doing to them. The disruption in their lives could be devastating. She wanted to save them, herself and Mike. She was strong and she had to remain strong. She said nothing, only stood there, letting her tears burn like lava. She shivered again.

"That's what I thought," he said and stepped to the side, walked past her and out of the kitchen.

Hailey sank to her knees and let her sobs go. What was going to happen to her now? The future loomed before her, filled with the only promise it could make: more uncertainty. She had to control herself. Where was her composure? Why were she and Mike arguing? Why had she hurt him? Why couldn't he accept her career? What were the rules of the game? Mike must have forgotten to read them to her off the top of the box. Had she lost? Or just defaulted? Maybe Austin knew the rules. He had always known the rules. She wasn't supposed to forget the rules.

She fought her way back to reality and found herself alone in the kitchen. Frantically, she looked around. Where had she been? What was Mike doing? He must have made plans. She knew she should find out what they were. Yes . . . That's what she should do. She wiped away her tears and found the strength to stand.

She was about to mount the stairs when she saw Mike coming toward her, suitcase in hand. "Where are you going?" she asked, her voice quivering and her stamina all but drained from her body.

"I can't stay here, I'm sure you can understand that. I'll call you tomorrow. I just need some time to think. Okay?" he said so calmly as if nothing had happened.

"Sure . . ." she said, not quite certain what all this meant. Maybe she didn't want to know.

"Tell Joey and Kim that I had to go out of town or something."

"How long will you be gone?"

"I don't know yet." He just looked at her and she tried to read his thoughts, something she hadn't done very well. And this time she could see nothing. "Good-bye, Hailey."

"Bye," she said and let him pass.

The door closed quietly behind him. She walked over and turned the lock. At that moment, the oddest sense of peace fell over her. It was a reaction she never dreamed would happen. It was as if all her fears had been neutralized. How could that be possible? Didn't she want him to come back? Why wasn't she running after him? It was what he wanted her to do. Her thoughts were disjointed and nothing made sense anymore. Where were the answers?

It was quiet in the house and finally her mind was silent, not answering but not questioning either.


As Hailey unlocked the door to the gallery the next morning, she could hear the telephone ringing. She flipped on the lights and raced to answer it. "Good morning, L'Artiste du Monde."

"Must you always be so disgustingly prompt, Hailey?" Barrett teased her.

"Would you have it any other way?"

"Never," he said and laughed. "How's everything with you today?" he asked casually.

She paused long enough to sweep the vision of last night from her mind. "Fine," she said noncommittally and offered no further explanation. She would keep her mind on business and take each hour as it came and not ask for anything more. She could survive another sixty minutes. Then she would go on from there.

"Well, my dear, the telephone has been ringing off the hook down here all morning and Agatha is about to go mad."

"What's wrong?"

"Nothing! Everything is very right. I just wanted to call you with the good news before Leonard had a chance to take all the glory."

"Barrett, would you please tell me what you are talking about? I swear, you beat around the bush more than Stephen."

"Nobody is that bad! Anyway, so far we have five orders for portraits by Hailey Asher!" He waited for the reaction.

"James," she corrected him.

"Hailey James, then. It's not earth shattering, but it's a tremendous start."

"I should say so. I can hardly believe all this!"

"It's true. Now, my only problem is the mechanics of handling it. We need to discuss your price per portrait. For your own sake and ours we should have an attorney draw up a contract. Or we can handle you the same as we do our other artists."

"But this is different. I don't have a finished product to sell to you on consignment."

"Well, don't you worry about it. I'll work it out and present several different methods of payment. Just leave it all to me."

"All right. I'll talk to you later."

"Right!" Barrett answered and hung up.

"Orders! I've actually sold my talent!" she said aloud, fearing that if she didn't, she wouldn't believe it. This must be a dream!

Barrett had said he would handle the money problems for her. That was a load off her mind. She leaned back in her chair and stared at the paintings in the gallery. So many artists. Some had struggled for years to get to this point. Some were famous, others were not, and some were celebrities, some deceased. There were many more out there who were unknown and whose pictures would never be inside a gallery. Her mind was swarming with the possibilities.

She picked up the telephone and placed a call to her attorney. The secretary patched her through immediately.

"Gerald," she said, "I'd like to see you about handling some business matters of mine. Hmmm. Yes. Well, I'm about to sell some of my artwork and I want you to do some investigating for me. Yes. Next week will be fine. See you then." She hung up. It was imperative she begin to think as logically as possible. She needed to protect herself, her children, all her assets. She would have to steel herself against the world. She wondered if strength was cold to the touch.

# Chapter Eleven

A MONTH, Hailey thought. An entire month had passed since Mike had moved out of the house, and now she was doing what he asked. Torrents of rain splashed against the windshield, almost immobilizing the wipers as she drove toward downtown Houston, where Gerald Harrison's law offices were located. Gerald was a longtime friend of her family's; his father had gone to school with Austin. Gerald had guided her through her monetary negotiations with Barrett and she trusted him implicitly. She needed to depend on someone now, and she was certain Gerald would act in her best interests.

With these assurances she entered the reception area of his office. The young secretary announced her immediately and Gerald came out to greet her.

"Hailey! How lovely you look today!" he said, taking her hand and patting her arm. Gerald was not an overly handsome man, but compassion and sincerity flashed in his eyes and gave him a gentle magnetism. Gerald was the kind of man my father would have wanted for a son, she thought. He was soft-spoken yet always direct, and he possessed an insight into human nature that had served him well. He had won numerous awards for his community and charity work, but what pleased Hailey most was that she knew she was more than just a client to Gerald; she was his friend as well.

He opened the door to his office, and Hailey entered and sat in one of two Chippendale wing chairs. Their crewel upholstery was worked in soft blues and yellows, and though his burl-wood desk was massive, the room was relaxing and Hailey felt her tension dissipate.

Gerald sat behind his desk, dressed in dark gray slacks with white shirt, tie and pearl-gray sweater vest. His suit jacket hung on a brass coat tree in the corner. His hazel eyes smiled at her.

"From our conversations on the telephone, I understand most of the situation. You and Mike are agreed on all this?"

"Yes, we are. We both feel there is no other answer. Mike requested that I file all the necessary papers, but I have zero understanding about the logistics of it all."

"I hope I can clarify some points for you. In the state of Texas there is no legal separation until you formally file for divorce. The waiting period is sixty days. In that time, Mike's attorney and I will go over the property settlement. It's a community-property state, so the majority of the division is cut-and-dried."

"I see. I suppose I should tell you that Mike says he wants the house."

"Can you agree to that, Hailey? It's a big request."

"Yes. I don't want it. I never did. Is it unusual for him to stay there?" Her eyebrows were raised and though he could detect uncertainty and fear in her eyes, he felt she was bolstered by an inner conviction. He knew that she had made the right decision in filing for this divorce; he could only hope it wouldn't take long before her confusion would lift and she could see all the good things that were soon to be hers.

"It's a little unusual. What happens is that he would have to buy out your portion of the equity."

"I see." Hailey couldn't think of anything intelligent to ask. Her eyes darted about the room and came to rest on the window where the rain had washed the dirt away. The sun stretched its arms through the clouds and pushed them to the north.

"Hailey, don't worry over all the details. That's my job. Once we get something concrete on paper, I'll phone you.

You'll have general custody of the children and all Mike's visitation rights are more or less according to the laws of the state. Is there anything else that's bothering you at the moment?"

"I dread telling the children . . . and my mother," she said ruefully.

"Hailey, the children will be fine. They may even surprise you. Just give them a chance. Your mother, on the other hand, may prove to be a different matter. She hasn't seen you for a long time. Whereas the children have sensed your tension and the situation, your mother lives very far away. I don't want to cause you any unnecessary worry, but she'll be in shock. You'll have to understand that. It's going to be difficult, to say the least. I want to prepare you for her first reaction, which will be denial of even the thought of divorce, regardless of your feelings. She'll try to talk you out of it. Then there will be anger. Luckily, that won't happen until you leave and are back in Houston. I'm assuming, of course, that you will fly to Boston to tell her in person."

"Yes, of course. She deserves that much. I think it would be the worst thing I ever did if I were just to phone her with something like this. But Gerald, how can you be so sure that she will react like that? It sounds so dreadful. I can't imagine Mother being like that. I love her and she loves me, I'm sure of that."

"She does, but I've been through these things before with a number of people. You have always been dependent on both your parents' approval. Austin's opinion of you was nearly sacred. You told me that yourself. You are now finally breaking the apron strings and struggling to build a life for yourself. There will be growing pains for both of you." He wanted to soothe her, but he knew the more he explained to her, the more upset she was becoming.

"I'm sorry, Gerald. It's just that I feel so burdened. Sometimes I feel like I don't know where to turn. I have a hard time connecting all these details about settlements and taxes. God! I don't even have a place to live yet!" she said, floundering for some coherency to her thoughts.

"I may be able to help you out in that respect. I'll have a realtor friend contact you very soon. I'll give him an idea about what to look for. How does that sound?"

"It sounds wonderful, but how could you possibly know what I want?" she asked skeptically.

"Hailey, trust me," he said, standing up. His smile was genuine and friendly, and she believed him.

As they walked to the door they chatted briefly about Hailey's painting. But when she entered the elevator, she was slightly more secure in her destination than she had been the day before. Tomorrow she would strive to gain more ground. She would take each day as it came. There were so many things she would have to do by herself, things she had never done, not because she couldn't, only because she had never tried.


Hailey flipped the three hamburger patties over in the skillet while Kim sliced tomatoes and placed them on a large platter next to some lettuce.

Joey was setting the table and, as usual, had the silverware in the wrong place, but he was so methodical about his task, carefully folding the napkins in perfect triangles, that Hailey said nothing.

Joey went to the refrigerator and withdrew the mustard and catsup.

"Boy! I'm glad we're having kid food for a change!" he said as he checked the progress of the french fries on his way back to the table.

"Joey," Hailey said as she smiled at him, "all the food I serve is child-oriented."

"Huh?"

"Everything I make is for you kids. Even down to the cauliflower."

"Oh, Mom. I mean food we like."

Hailey was trying to keep her mind off the fact that this was the night she had to tell them. Mike had left the task to her, and now that her trip to Gerald's office was reality, this was the first of many hurdles she would have to conquer. She had prepared herself for the inevitable deluge of questions and recriminations.

She stared at the hamburgers. They were so ordinary, so mundane, so American. And this night was the most explosive one she might ever meet; almost like a head-on collision. Everything seemed so normal. She could see Joey's hair glisten in the incandescent light; a light which was put to shame by her daughter's smile.

Her babies! She was about to mark them for eternity as if she were heating the branding iron this instant, and then she would thrust it against their foreheads, searing it into their brains.

*Divorce* . . . "Hi, I'm Joey Asher and I'm from a broken home." The vignette reeled off in her mind. "Hi, I'm Kim Asher and I live with my single parent." New clichés were always coined to replace the old. Times were changing. The family unit was disintegrating and Hailey felt as if it were her divorce statistics that would topple the scales. *Divorced* . . . No matter what they ever did or accomplished in their lives they would come back to this night. They would blame her, hate her, ridicule her. Ultimately, they would leave her and she knew she deserved it. Would they turn away from her? Would they fall into the wrong circle of friends? Take drugs? Drink? Lose their ambitions and dreams? Would all their failures be magnified because they would not love themselves enough to dream and keep hoping and praying? God! How could she do this to them?

They sat down and as Kim placed a tomato slice on her hamburger, without a word of warning to Hailey she said, "Are you and Dad going to get a divorce?"

Hailey's throat constricted and she feared she would be unable to answer. Should she tell the truth, she knew she had to, but . . . "Why . . . why do you ask that?"

Joey sneaked a conspiratorial look at his sister. Then he looked directly at his mother. There was only trust in his eyes. "Kim and I have talked about it, Mom. Dad hasn't been home for a long time. So we thought that might be the reason."

"You aren't happy, are you, Mom?" Kim asked and Hailey thought it quite strange that her young voice could possess so much concern and yet no trace of fear.

"No, Kim. I haven't been for a long time, but I guess you

both already know that." Hailey glanced at Joey and then came back to Kim.

"Yeah, we did. Joey and I would stay up after you went to bed and talk. Lots of times you thought we were asleep, but we could hear you and Dad arguing."

"Why didn't you tell me?" Hailey asked, but she knew why. For the same reason she hadn't said anything to them. No one wanted to admit there was trouble in the Asher house. At that moment she felt as much a child as the two persons sitting next to her. She was supposed to be comforting them and yet at this moment they existed as a team. Joey was quiet. Hailey thought she would always worry more about him than she would about Kim. Kim was strong; Hailey could already see the woman Kim would be and her pride swelled.

A flicker of a smile caressed Hailey's lips. "I had all kinds of speeches prepared about how to tell you. I really don't know how to explain any of it to you. Your father and I don't hate each other, we just can't live together anymore. He still loves you both and I love you, too. You do know that, don't you?"

"Sure we do, Mom. But are you gonna be all right?" Kim's eyes were wet, but she didn't cry.

"Of course, I am," Hailey assured her.

"Mom?" Joey's voice was low, almost as if he hadn't spoken. "We are gonna stay with you, aren't we?"

"Of course you are, honey." When she saw relief cross his face, Hailey thought that through this whole ordeal, nothing would ever be so reassuring to her as that look. They didn't blame her, and suddenly the future looked green again. She edged out of the chair and knelt next to him. She took his face in her hands and kissed his cheeks over and over. Then she hugged him. "I love you, Joey, and I always will. Don't ever, ever forget that."

"I won't, Mom," he said and then gulped hard.

Kim came around and knelt beside her mother. She put her arm around Hailey's shoulder. Hailey turned to her and picked up a long silver curl, twisted it in her fingers and then gently let it fall onto Kim's shoulder.

"I love you, too, my little princess, and you know what?"

"What's that, Mom?" Kim asked, her eyes full of innocent faith.

"As long as we have each other and all the love that's here, we can make it. I just know it."

Kim and Joey nodded and hugged their mother in unison. Hailey's smile rose up from the underside of her heart. She'd never felt so positive and so loved in all her life. They would support each other in the days ahead. She vowed to protect them from whatever evils it was in her power to do so. And the shield she would use was love, the strongest weapon on earth.

Families, Hailey believed, should be one's port in a storm. She knew she had been successful in instilling this axiom in her children, as her parents had done with her. Perhaps that was the reason Hailey had placed the wants and needs of everyone else before her own. With Joey's and Kim's acceptance of her decision, she was encouraged and strengthened for this next trial of informing her mother. Bolstered by innocent childhood remembrances, she was confident Sonja would take her in and comfort her.

It would have been easier for her if there had been some horrendous explosion between herself and Mike. When two people divorced, one always expected to hear gory details, make judgments and finally place blame. Unfortunately for her, there was no blame to place.

For a very long time Hailey had sheltered everyone—the children, her mother and Mike—from her inner conflicts and she had borne the brunt of the turmoil within herself. That Sonja had no inkling of trouble made Hailey's task even more difficult.

As she buckled her seat belt and braced for the landing, she prayed that Sonja would be able to accept the reality of the situation.

"Courage," she told herself as the wheels of the 747 hit the paved runway and the flaps broke the jet's speed. As they taxied to the terminal, a swarm of butterflies swooped and fluttered inside her. Already she wished the weekend were over.

Sonja stood off to the side behind a cluster of excited people who were jubilantly welcoming their family members from on board. Hailey smiled and waved.

Sonja rushed up and kissed Hailey on the cheek.

"I missed you so much," Hailey said. Though it was the truth, she could only think of a thousand places she would rather be than here.

"I missed you, too, dear," her mother said, taking her flight bag and then carrying it as they walked through the terminal.

"I do wish the children could have come with you," Sonja said ruefully. "It seems that I never get to see them anymore. I'll bet they've grown so much. Did you bring some pictures with you?"

"Yes, I did, Mother. I know you want to see them, but they're almost finished with the school year and need to stay in Houston right now. Perhaps I could fly them both up for a few weeks this summer. Would you like that?"

Sonja's eyes brightened at the thought. "Oh, yes! That would be wonderful! Let's do plan on it!"

Hailey was thankful for the diversion in conversation. They talked about the children until they were driving away from the airport. Hailey sat in the front seat and was commenting on the weather when Sonja abruptly turned and faced her.

"Hailey, please tell me what is going on. You didn't explain anything over the phone and I've been so worried. It's just hard for me to imagine. You wouldn't fly up here for no reason . . ."

"I'll tell you what you want to know." Hailey took a deep breath. She felt sick. She looked away and then caught her mother looking at her with clear and pleading eyes. She swallowed deeply and decided there was no evading the situation any longer.

"It's like I said, Mother. Mike and I have been having some serious problems."

"Well, everything is all right now, isn't it?" Hailey could see hope in Sonja's eyes as she waited for her daughter's response.

"No, Mother, I've filed for divorce," she replied bluntly.

Sonja's head nodded up and down, but Hailey could see that she didn't understand.

"That's the most idiotic thing I've ever heard! I don't believe it for a second. Michael has been good to you."

"Yes, Mother, he has. I just haven't been good for him."

"What do you mean? You've been a good wife, a wonderful housekeeper and the children couldn't ask for a better mother."

"I'm not what Mike needs. He doesn't want a career woman, he says," Hailey explained.

"Then quit your job!"

"I can't! I want it! Maybe not as much as my painting, I have to admit that. Don't you remember I wrote and told you that I was working on a portrait of Janet . . ."

"Yes, yes, I remember," Sonja replied exasperatedly.

"Well, that portrait was well received at the gallery opening. It's not earth shattering, but for me, it was important. I've received over half a dozen requests to paint portraits. For the first time I've got something that makes me feel like a person. A real person, not just a nonentity who wears a label instead of a name. I'm Hailey! Not Mike Asher's shadow, not his ornament!" Hailey stormed and then abruptly stopped herself. Her face was flushed and her head pounded. Her neck ached. She was hungry, or maybe she was tired. She was frightened, but she couldn't run away, so she folded her hands in her lap and retrieved her control.

"I apologize for that outburst," she said and Sonja nodded slightly. "Mike wants everything the way it used to be and I can't do that. The tension in that house was so unbearable, I couldn't stand to go home after work. Once Mike moved out, it's been so much better."

"Mike doesn't live with you and the children anymore?" Sonja was incredulous that this whim of Hailey's had gone so far.

"Yes, he's been gone for several weeks," Hailey said.

"Hailey," Sonja was struggling to retain her serenity through this farcical conversation, "answer me one question."

"Sure," Hailey replied and clutched her fingers.

"Don't you feel a lift at the end of the day when he comes home?"

"No, Mother, I never have," Hailey answered and wondered why on earth her mother would ask such a senseless question.

"Then I need to ask you something else." Sonja was disturbingly cool and Hailey was confused about the sudden alteration in her mother's approach. "Do you love him, Hailey?"

"No . . . I wonder if I ever did." It was a simple statement of fact.

Hailey didn't see anything wrong with that. She cared about him, she had been friends with Mike. She had once thought that a good basis for a marriage and now she wasn't so sure.

"It's worse than I thought," Sonja muttered, but Hailey heard her.

It was as if all discussion on the matter had ceased. Hailey's mind was a blank, though she still could not calm herself. She couldn't think of anything to say. She was determined not to let Sonja change her mind. She could do it, she knew; she had the power, if Hailey would allow it. No matter how much Sonja closed her mind to it, the truth was slowly erecting a stony barrier between parent and child.

Curious, Hailey thought. Just days ago she had been playing the role of parent herself and now she was a child again. Sonja still represented authority to her. It was a shock to realize she was still bound to the values of others. She needed to form her own opinions and revere those and let them guide her decisions. She could no longer burn incense to parental authority.

"The children are well, Mother. But they do need you. It's not their fault that Mike and I can't resolve our differences. I know it's nearly impossible for you to understand me, right now especially, and I don't blame you for any of that. I don't see how you could react any other way. But Joey and Kim are your only grandchildren. They love you and they need your support and understanding."

"It seems to me that if you were so overly concerned

with the children and their welfare, you would stop all this nonsense."

"Mother," she choked back her tears, "I've thought of no one else for almost ten years. I want them to remember good things about their father. They've heard us argue and fight as it is, when I thought Mike and I were being very discreet. I don't want every moment of their lives shredded into unconnecting pieces because they live with tension seething under some god-awful veneer of cordiality. That's what it has been. What kind of life is that for any of us?"

"But . . ." Sonja started to say.

"Did it ever occur to you that I might be trying to save us all?" Hailey said defensively. Her words froze in the air like icicles, sharp on the ends, but crystal clear. Hailey watched Sonja stare at the highway as it snaked around the bend. Sonja wasn't listening anymore.

Hailey felt completely shut off from her. She knew in her heart her mother was only trying to adjust and that she wanted to understand. But if they remained inaccessible to each other like this, their relationship would be destroyed.

As the weekend passed, Hailey was able to read Sonja's dilemma more clearly. It was strange how Hailey felt like an outsider observing the crisis. Sonja was angry at Hailey for ruining the ending of the fairy tale. Sonja had only wanted the best for Hailey but had failed to include human frailties and needs in her fantasy. Sonja had forgotten the struggles that made her own marriage strong, and for some reason had believed or hoped that Hailey would never experience pain or sorrow or loss. As long as Hailey perpetuated a storybook life-style, then Sonja would support her.

More importantly, Sonja had to come to grips with the fact that Hailey was growing up. She hadn't flown to Boston to ask for advice at all. Hailey was here to state the facts. Ironically, Sonja had been the one who had pushed Hailey for years to make her own decisions, and now Hailey was doing just that. Sonja wanted Hailey to command her own life, and yet she reinforced her own need of her daughter's dependence by making Hailey feel guilty about the decision she'd made. Hailey understood and was willing to be patient.

Sonja was still reverberating from the shock and treating her coolly, but Hailey knew that time would restore communication between them. Sonja felt as if Hailey's news were a personal blow to her. Above all, Hailey trusted and loved her mother and vowed she would bring Sonja back to her. It wouldn't be easy. It was already more painful than she'd thought this confrontation could be. She had shed plenty of tears over the weekend and there would surely be more. This time, though, Hailey knew her vow was not simply an optimistic dream. She just hoped Sonja was wise enough not to waste their tomorrows on bitterness and disappointment.

# Chapter Twelve

IT had been over a decade since Hailey had lived in an apartment, and even then, it had been Mike's, not hers. This task of locating a new home was unbelievably frustrating. For Hailey, it was twice as difficult now, because she had two children. She was not a swinging single, nor did she intend to become one. Most of the apartment complexes advertised tennis courts, saunas, spas, recreation rooms, swimming pools and racquetball courts. Hailey's priorities were in direct opposition to that life-style. She needed good schools for the children, security, quiet streets, and ample space.

With Janet's help at scouting these uncharted waters, within a matter of two weeks they had rejected over fifty different complexes. Amenities such as fireplaces, two baths, garden view and washer/dryer connections were tossed aside in lieu of the greatest of all barriers: no pets/no children.

Janet was just as angry as Hailey at the outright discrimination they faced and was near to screaming on that Sunday afternoon as they sat on the floor at Janet's house, both clad in cutoffs and T-shirts. Dan was playing golf, and the two of them had used the opportunity to formulate a new attack on the situation.

Sections of the newspaper were scattered around them as Hailey kept fishing through the apartment section praying that this time she'd find one apartment to set her free from this aggravation.

"Hailey," Janet said, sticking a pencil in the knotted coil of blond hair on top of her head, "I've got the answer!"

Hailey looked up and rubbed her eyes. She'd been reading fine newsprint all afternoon and her vision was bleary. "What?"

"All you have to do to get one of these neat places is lie! Don't tell them you have two kids!"

"You must have pulled the plug on your brain! You can't be serious!"

"Well, how do people find a place to live in this town? I mean, this city is full of single-parent families. Where are they?"

"In rented apartments, dummy. That's why there are no vacancies," Hailey said and sighed. "I don't want to live in a dump, either. I want it to be nice and something I can afford."

Janet's look was compassionate. She couldn't help placing herself in Hailey's situation. People were divorcing every day. Did they all have to go through this? And this was only one of the tasks the trio of Ashers now faced. With every corner Hailey turned, Janet had watched her grow stronger. Hailey had not made any decision impulsively. She'd meticulously thought everything through. Janet thought her friend still idealistic, but she could see now it was a mask to hide her fears. Janet did all she could to encourage Hailey and to bolster her fragile ego. And Hailey had fed on it at times, but to a large degree it was Hailey's newfound belief in herself that sustained her.

Hailey looked up to see Janet watching her intently. "Anything wrong?" she asked, noting the curiosity in Janet's eyes. "I know you're dying to ask me something, so go ahead."

"I have been wondering . . . well . . . all these years I thought you were like one of the chosen few. You seemed to have everything and now . . ."

"Go on," Hailey urged her gently.

"Why has it taken you so long to become your own person?"

"I've asked myself that same question a million times. I only know part of the answer, I think. I've been so busy living a life my father had planned and marrying the man my mother chose. I had never defied them. I accepted everything they told me. Authority has always been supreme to me, because they had taught me that."

"What made you stop and turn everything around even long enough to investigate the problem?"

"I'm not really sure. Perhaps it's just age. I'm over thirty now; maybe it was just a phase. But I did want to paint even though my father thought it loathsome. The biggest reason was that once Mike was home more often I realized I had never been in love with him. I kept telling myself I was crazy, that I *was* happy, but my anger kept growing until it seemed that everything was out of control."

"I'm so lucky to be in love with Dan. I hadn't realized what repercussions could happen if you don't have love in your life. I always assumed you had the same kind of relationship."

"When you moved here and I saw you with Dan, I knew I was missing something tremendously important in life. Maybe I'll never find it, but I can't settle for second best anymore. I was willing to settle for half the pie if Mike would have approved of my painting and work at the gallery, but he couldn't. So it all fell apart."

Janet remained silent; there was no need for a comment. Hailey listened to the children playing on the deck outside. Their laughter slipped through the walls and filled the room. Hailey's eyes burned and she fought to stem the tears.

"Hailey, don't . . . you can't go on feeling guilty about something that isn't your fault."

"How do you know how I feel?"

"I know you. Your guilt is all over your face every time you look at Kim and Joey. They're going to have some tough days ahead readjusting, but they understand a lot more than you realize. They're proud of you and love you. They don't blame you *or* Mike. There will be times you'll have to be superstrong for them, but take my advice: Give them some credit. They'll stick by you. You've raised them both almost single-handedly. They'll probably see more of Mike than ever before now that you're divorcing. They're smart, beautiful and loving individuals and there is something you keep forgetting."

"What's that?"

"They can't be happy unless you are."

"You really think that's true?"

"Yep," Janet said, nodding her head. "I wouldn't say so if I didn't believe it."

Hailey scooted over to Janet and hugged her. "Thanks." She wanted to say more, but Janet knew what she felt.

The jangling telephone halted Hailey from speaking just then.

"Sit tight, I'll get it," Janet said, jumping up and then sprinting into the kitchen. Hailey went back to the apartment selector guide.

"Hailey, it's for you. It's your attorney," Janet reported.

Hailey's heart sank. What could it be? She picked up the receiver. "Gerald?" Her voice was frantic. She was imagining all kinds of things—custody suits, court battles over property. "What's wrong? What is it? How did you find me?"

"Hailey, would you calm down? I can answer only one question at a time. Nothing is wrong and if you didn't want any calls you shouldn't have left Janet's name and number on your answering machine."

"Oh, gosh! I'm sorry, Gerald, I forgot I did that. But . . . if it's not an emergency . . ."

"Hailey, attorneys don't always carry bad news."

He was trying to ease her tension and she wasn't listening to him. "I'm sorry."

"You should be. The reason I called is because I have something you might want to hear. Or see, rather."

"What?"

"Remember I told you about my realtor friend?"

"Yes, I do! What happened to him? Did he die?"

"Nope. He's alive and very definitely breathing. Do you have some time today to look at a town house?"

"I sure do! When? Where?" she sputtered excitedly.

"In one hour. I think it's just what you need."

"If they take kids and pets, I'll love it!" she quipped.

"Hailey, I'm surprised at you. You're more discerning than that, I hope!" She could hear him clucking his tongue as if he were a disapproving uncle.

"Beggars can't be choosers."

"Be choosy, Hailey, you'll get farther. That's my advice for the day," he replied in his sternest tones.

"Okay. I'll take the advice."

She wrote down the directions and the address and promised Gerald she would meet the agent, Mr. Bridley. Then she hung up.

"Janet! Manna from heaven!"

"What did he say?" Janet asked as Hailey came rushing into the room.

"He's found me a town house!"

Janet was instantly skeptical. "A town house? Those are awfully expensive."

"Well, it's worth a shot. What have I got to lose?"

"Not a thing!" Janet exclaimed. "Why don't you take the children and give it the full inspection?"

"Done!"


Tucked away in a quiet corner of the Memorial area beneath spreading hundred-year-old oak trees rested a double row of town houses, five units to each side. Meticulously groomed azaleas and pittosporums were arranged in formal borders alongside each walkway. Each town house had a different façade, ranging from French to Colonial to New Orleans style. Rather than appearing helter-skelter, the construction and attention to detail was exquisite and presented a sense of planned unity and flow. The interior courtyard area was spectacularly landscaped beneath tall oaks and pines.

The moment Hailey laid eyes on them, she knew. "They look just like the town houses in Boston!" It was a good omen.

Three doors down to the left a young, well-dressed man stood and waved at them. The children bolted out of the car and inspected every nook and cranny of the area. Hailey walked up to him and shook his hand.

"You must be Mr. Bridley. I'm Hailey Asher."

"Pleased to meet you. I hope I've used Gerald's information about you effectively in finding this house."

"I've had such rotten luck on my own that I now see why these things are better left to the professionals."

"Thanks for the vote of confidence. Now, what do you say we go inside and see if I've been able to strike the golden chord here."

He unlocked the newly painted white door and stood aside as Hailey entered an unexpectedly large foyer.

Hailey's mouth dropped in pleasant surprise at the soaring though narrow Georgian staircase. The banister and spindles were painted in a glossy white and extended down the upper hall. The stairs were carpeted in a soft green that blended with the trellis-patterned green-and-white wallpaper. To the immediate right, a pair of louvered doors opened into a sunny breakfast nook. A curved bay window looked out onto the courtyard, and white ruffled curtains were pulled back to reveal a deep window seat. The compact kitchen was well equipped and housed not only a pantry, but a small laundry room as well. The main room of the house was good-sized, with white french doors leading onto a fenced-in patio in back. The formal dining area was mirrored and in its center hung an inexpensive brass chandelier.

Upstairs the master suite, carpeted in sunny yellow with yellow-and-silver-foil oriental-motif wallpaper, was enormous. It was almost as large as Hailey's present bedroom, minus the plush accessories. Two large walk-in closets, a marble vanity in the dressing area and full adjoining bath completed the suite. Down the hall were two adequately sized bedrooms with connecting bath for the children.

Hailey appeared hesitant as they roamed the house, for somehow she felt this was too wonderful and that she might not be able to afford it.

"I feel like I've finally come home, Mr. Bridley. I hesitate to ask this, but what's the tariff? Be gentle . . ." She squeezed her eyes shut in mock self-defense.

"That's the best part. It's five hundred a month and the landlord pays the maintenance fee for the grounds."

Hailey's eyes flew open. "You can't be serious! Why? What's the catch?" she asked, immediately suspicious. "I thought it would be higher."

"Obviously you don't know how difficult it is to find good renters. I do emphasize the 'good' in that statement. It normally rents for about six hundred, which isn't all that much higher, actually. But if you'll notice, all the carpet, paint and papers are brand-new, and the reason for that is because the last couple that was here just tore it up. You wouldn't have believed it. The owners live in Colorado and don't have the time nor the inclination to worry about it. Gerald called them directly and assured them that you would not only maintain the property but would undoubtedly improve it. It's worth it to them just to get it rented and have some peace of mind. It's a tax write-off for them to begin with, but still . . ."

"I can see your point. I can promise that I'll take very good care of the property. How soon can I sign the lease?" she asked impatiently.

"I can meet you at Gerald's office early tomorrow and we can handle everything there. He wanted to read the lease agreement before you signed. I assume that's agreeable with you."

"Yes," she replied. Just then Joey and Kim came running up the stairs.

"Hey, Mom! You should see! There's a big carport in back and we met the kids next door and they showed us the mailboxes and the bus stop for school and . . ." Joey was more out of breath from talking than from running.

"Whoa, slow down, Joey." Hailey laughed, for he mirrored her own enthusiasm. This was like a glorious holiday for them all.

"Are we gonna live here?" Kim asked, peeking past her mother into the bedroom. "Say! Which one is mine?" she asked but didn't wait for an answer. "I want this one," she said, slipping past Hailey and claiming the yellow-painted room similar to the master.

"Great! I'll take the other one!" Joey said. "My closet is bigger than yours!" he yelled through the bathroom doorway.

"Maybe so, but my window looks out into the treetops!" Kim shouted back to him and then she investigated the closet and began planning where to place her furniture.

"I guess that confirms it for me, Mr. Bridley. The children love it and so do I. My search is over."

# Chapter Thirteen

DURING the next two months Hailey grew tired of self-pity and regret. If she couldn't make herself happy, then no one could. There always came a time to move ahead. Her steps were in forward motion now, and she vowed they always would be. Flashes of guilt, failure and regret would invade her world, but she fought them. It was a time for accomplishment and joyous moments with her children, and through it all she was alone. But she was constructively alone, and that made her feel good; not wonderful, just plain good.

Since she had been transferred from city to city so many times in the past, moving posed no dilemma. She had always handled the family finances, and with Gerald's advice she set up a personal accounting system, arranged for her own safety deposit box and spoke to an investment counselor.

Since Mike was to retain the house, the majority of the furnishings were to remain in his possession, save for the children's things. Mike agreed to pay Hailey in cash for half the household goods. The list of dividable goods was three pages long and there was enough china and kitchen-ware for three households, let alone two.

Hailey was delighted with the opportunity to furnish her town house. She watched her purchases carefully, guarding every penny. Her needs were not great, but they *did* have to live. Knowing from past experience that she could do as well as any interior decorator, a luxury she definitely couldn't afford, she plotted the colors, arrangements and lighting with a scrupulous eye.

For the breakfast nook she chose a white-painted rattan set of oriental-design chairs and covered the seats with fabric to match the wallpaper. The round tabletop was glass and above it hung a white wrought-iron chandelier. In the foyer, a matching rattan *étagère* held favorite china pieces and a multitude of healthy green plants.

For the formal dining area, a heavy country french rectangular table and four cane-back chairs were placed beneath the chandelier. The table's carvings were few and the lines simple and didn't detract from the parquet top. A dark cherry lighted china cabinet with grilled doors housed Hailey's collection of Waterford crystal and assorted family heirlooms. For the living area she had a Chippendale camel-back sofa and wing chair upholstered in a vibrant peach and yellow floral chintz. The coffee table had Chippendale legs supporting a glass top with a wide fluted edge of solid brass. This was her only truly extravagant purchase, but she just couldn't resist it. Two brass-plated apothecary lamps provided the necessary lighting. Until she could afford other chairs and tables she intended to fill the room with plants and throw pillows.

For her bedroom she allowed her romantic sentiments to take flight. She couldn't afford a canopied bed, as she wanted, so she retrieved her old sewing machine and went to work. She hemmed mountains of India gauze and stapled the material to thin slats of balsa wood, then nailed them to the ceiling, creating her own exotic though not plush canopy bed. Versailles it was not, but maybe a plantation house in the Bahamas.

Between the two narrow white-shuttered windows in her room was a tall highboy whose intricate brass Chippendale drawer pulls reflected the sunlight that danced about the room. Once all the major pieces were delivered, the first thing Hailey did was retrieve her mother's patchwork quilt from the depths of an antique trunk and drape the quilt over the bed.

The overall effect of the house was airy, tasteful and welcoming. She needed a retreat from the outside pressures of the world as much as anyone else did. Her room was large enough to accommodate her easel and supplies. She knew it wouldn't be difficult to paint amid such tranquillity.

To her great surprise she had coped remarkably well with the changes in her life. The things that had frightened her the most—struggling to support the family on her small salary, even if it were combined with Mike's child support, beginning her new career and her obligation to her talent—she accepted and welcomed. Things like installing Joey's miniblinds, changing her tire on the 610 loop at rush hour and developing her sales skills at work were now routine. A year ago she would have thought herself incapable of handling these things. She had progressed far in her sense of herself, and woven into this was the awareness that she possessed real artistic talent! It was a blessing and she did not for one moment take it lightly or abuse it, for it carried its own responsibilities.

Tomorrow she had scheduled an appointment with her first client; she was excited and apprehensive. She had never painted a stranger before, and after consummate deliberation she concluded the best approach was to change the status of the client to that of a friend. She knew her best work came from feelings about people; therefore, she would interview her client in her own surroundings, learn her likes and dislikes, hobbies and ambitions.

Should this strategy fail, she purchased a 35mm camera and a notebook to aid her. It seemed best to work on only one portrait at a time, at least until she was more secure in her work and the approach she was taking. With the addition of these commissioned works into her life her time would now be even more valuable than before. However, she needed the money, for her monthly budget was being stretched to the limit considering day-care costs, the price of dry cleaning and all the regular bills. If she only had more time to do the household chores!

Hailey's conflict with her mother was at a stalemate. The only consolation she had was that Sonja had requested that the children visit her for four weeks in July. As Hailey had suspected, Sonja had heeded her pleas about the children's needs. She hoped that her mother would unbend once she saw the children and realized that they were all right.

Kim and Joey were anxiously awaiting their first unchaperoned plane flight. Since the day school let out, Kim had altered at least a dozen times the list of clothing she planned to take. Joey was still arguing with Hailey over the number of games and toys to take. He saw no use for clothes or shoes beyond a pair of swim trunks, sneakers, one pair of Levi's and a short-sleeved shirt. He relented when Hailey threatened to do all of his packing for him.

It was hard for Hailey to realize that they would be leaving in only a week. She would miss them terribly but she also knew she would be so busy that the time would pass rapidly. She wondered how she would get it all done. She packed her hopes in her children and prayed they would be the solder that would keep the family links together. Nothing she'd done—the calls, the explanations, the pleadings—accomplished anything significant with Sonja. She was polite and coolly pleasant but she made no attempt to conceal her hurt. To maintain her own strength, Hailey buried herself in anesthetizing work.

The next day, when Hailey finally located the River Oaks address of Gwendolyn and Arthur Farrell, she circled the block twice in a state of disbelief. Perhaps she had written the address down incorrectly. But no, the huge brass numerals on the massive wrought-iron gate proclaimed it. It wasn't a house but a mansion, like something out of *Gone with the Wind*. Hailey steadied herself and drove up the circular drive through lush tropical plants, canopied overhead by centuries-old oak trees. Two gardeners, their backs gleaming with sweat in the noonday sun, were bent over liriope, trimming it to perfection.

Hailey parked her car in front of the stately Greek Revival mansion whose four white columns soared to the pitched roof and supported the semicircular roof of the portico. She walked up the brick steps feeling as if she had entered another century. She lifted the brass knocker and let it fall twice. The white Georgian door opened and a butler's stoic face greeted her.

"Yes," he said impatiently.

"I'm Hailey James and I have an appointment with Mrs. Farrell."

"Won't you step inside and I'll announce you, Miss James," he said, then turned and vanished from the vestibule.

Hailey thought him odd, for his tight lips barely moved when he spoke and his mechanical movements rendered him somehow less human. While she puzzled over the butler's demeanor, her eyes scanned the room for clues to her client's personality.

The pale yellow silk-covered walls and gleaming white woodwork instantly set Hailey at ease. Though the furnishings were formal Louis XVI, the owners' use of contemporary art and floral fabrics of the upholstered pieces in the vestibule and adjoining living room imparted a relaxed and convivial air. Scores of fresh flowers were randomly placed throughout the main rooms, and Hailey felt as if she were walking in a garden. To the right of the vestibule was an unusually large dining room. A fabulously ornate crystal chandelier was suspended above an oval glass table with a solid brass pedestal. It was surrounded by gold gilt Louis XVI chairs upholstered to match the walls. A profusion of summer blooms rested on the table. As in the living room, the dining-room windows were not draped but open to view the side gardens and terraces. The interior white plantation shutters had been moved back and sunlight streamed throughout the entire house.

Hailey stepped back into the foyer when she heard the click of approaching footsteps against the parquet floor. Mrs. Farrell entered through the living room. She wore a blue-green silk blouse that accentuated the unusual color of her eyes. Her skirt was fine light linen in a soft beige and she wore dressy sandals to match. Her silver hair was expertly coiffed and she appeared the essence of the well-tended wife of an oil baron. Her jewels were mounted in good taste, and the diamonds were typically Texan in size.

"Miss James! It's so nice to see you." Mrs. Farrell greeted her warmly and took Hailey's hand in both of hers. "I do hope it wasn't presumptuous of me to take you away from your family on a Sunday. But it's just about the only time I have to myself these days."

"That's quite all right, Mrs. Farrell. In fact, my own schedule is rather hectic, too. I'm pleased it worked out so well for both of us," Hailey said with an eager smile.

"Well, Miss James," Mrs. Farrell said with a sigh and clasping her hands in front of her, "I've never sat for a portrait before. Just how and where do we begin?" she asked while her eyes searched Hailey's hands for signs of artist's utensils. Hailey noted the disappointed look on her face.

"I'm afraid my approach is quite unusual, Mrs. Farrell. I'm not going to have you sit at all."

"You aren't?" She looked at Hailey quizzically.

"No. I'm not. However, what I would like is to talk with you for a while and become better acquainted."

"Why, that is interesting," she replied uncertainly.

"What's your favorite room or place in the house? The one you drift to whenever you feel the need to be alone?" Hailey asked, watching Mrs. Farrell and mentally recording her mannerisms.

"Why, that's easy," she said with delight. "The garden. I just adore flowers, as you no doubt could tell," she said, gesturing to her bouquets in the four corners of the vestibule. "If I'm happy, depressed, angry or just need to meditate, I nearly always feel the need to be outdoors."

"I know just how you feel," Hailey replied.

"I'll have some iced tea sent out to the terrace. How would that be?" Mrs. Farrell asked, leading Hailey through the living room and between the french doors to a wonderland of subtropical foliage.

Hailey had been totally unprepared for such splendor. She felt as if she were confronting a smorgasbord of showy natural color, and the sultry air was heavily scented by gardenias and jasmine. A roofed terrace provided ample shade, but if it hadn't been for a breeze created by two white ceiling fans, Hailey thought she would have suffocated in the dense, humid heat.

They sat on white wrought-iron furniture, made luxuriously comfortable by striped-cotton-covered seat and back cushions. A uniformed maid approached them carrying a round silver tray bearing tall icy glasses of tea decorated with sprigs of mint and lemon slices. Hailey sipped her tea and asked Mrs. Farrell questions regarding the garden and its upkeep, and the conversation flowed easily.

Hailey withdrew her camera and took photos of Mrs. Farrell as she pointed out favorite plants as they walked through the maze of japonicas, azaleas and ferns. Hailey caught her pouring tea, instructing the servants and conferring with her secretary. The afternoon sun cut a path through the tall oaks and pines and spread a filtered golden web over this intelligent, witty and proud woman. She was both gutsy and elegant, the epitome of the landed Texan family. She had breeding, a zest for life and an unswerving devotion to Texas, and when Hailey left, she knew she had made a friend.

## Chapter Fourteen

TWO silver heads bobbed up and down like sea gulls diving for dinner in an ocean of business suits, summer dresses and carry-on luggage moving toward the American Airlines jet bound for Boston. Hailey waved to her children long after the plane taxied away from the terminal. She could still feel the pressure on her neck where they had hugged her before boarding. They'd been all smiles and shining eyes in anticipation of frolicking summer days to come with Sonja. For the first time Hailey realized how interminably long four weeks was, rather like a prison sentence. How would she react to these days without Joey and Kim, her appendages, her shadows, these living parts of herself? Right now she wasn't faring too well, she thought as she resisted the impulse to race to the ticket counter to book a flight on the next plane to Boston. She missed them already and as she drove home from Intercontinental Airport, she kept glancing behind her to the back seat to see why they were being so still, only to realize once again that they weren't there.

"Hailey, you've got to stop this! You weren't this bad when they started kindergarten!" she rebuked herself for being so childish, so overly protective, so motherly. Joey and Kim weren't having half the problems in maturing that she was! She wondered just how she would get through the days ahead without them. Maybe these weeks of privacy would be good for her. She would have the opportunity to delve into herself and make necessary repairs. It was a time to discover just who Hailey was.

It was the last day of her marriage to Mike, for at nine the next morning she was to meet Gerald on the second floor of the Family District Court building on Congress Street. He'd telephoned her with directions and last-minute instructions. Gerald had informed her that Mike was to be represented by his attorney and would not appear in court. For that she was grateful. Whether Mike had arranged this out of compassion or bitterness, she didn't know. But she did know she couldn't face him. She knew she would have to eventually, but mercifully he wouldn't be there tomorrow. God! How she hoped he didn't hate her too much. She did enough of that for both of them. She felt like a fragile wax doll who'd been placed too near the fire, and her face burned with tears that sliced into her cheeks.

The sun withdrew the last of its amber rays from the branches of the moss- and mistletoe-covered oaks as Hailey drove to her town house. After turning the key in the lock and opening the door, she realized there was no one to greet her. No children . . . no husband . . . no one but herself.

Hailey sat on the edge of a pewlike bench, feeling anything but reverent as she watched a parade of attorneys pass back and forth. The only individuality she could see in them was in their pace. Some shuffled, some ambled and some whizzed by her, coattails flying. Her back was ramrod straight and her hands were folded in her lap; she knew the smile she wore fooled no one. Everyone who walked past her knew. It was as if she'd been Hester Prynne quietly bearing the scarlet "A." Except in her case, a "D" perhaps, or an "F" for "flunk," for "failure." If her father could have graded her, she'd get an "F." Yes, that's what he would have done. But Sonja—would she, because she was a woman—could she ever understand?

Gerald walked up to her. "Hailey," he addressed her in fluid, cool tones and watched as her breath returned to her and she relaxed somewhat.

"Oh, Gerald, there you are, I was beginning to wonder . . ." Her eyes snatched a quick reference to her watch. "It's . . . it's almost time."

"Don't be so nervous, Hailey." He patted her forearm. "There are a few things I want to go over with you before we go into the courtroom. The judge will direct me to ask you a few technical questions, which you will answer. These are all things we've discussed, mostly about properties and custody. You needn't worry about the judge, or Mike's attorney. Just look at me. The judge will state that the divorce has been granted and then you can leave. I'll have a few points to discuss with Mike's attorney, so wait for me out here."

"Are you sure that's all there is to it?" she asked. She had expected—and feared—more. She guessed she just hadn't thought much about things like this.

"That's all. And I know what you're thinking. No, this isn't the Nuremberg trials any more than you're a criminal. Now get rid of those ridiculous thoughts. I have to go. Find a seat and I'll talk to you afterward. Okay?"

"Okay," she said, wishing that her forced smile would stop trembling.

The courtroom was not overly large, rather like a small chapel. Directly ahead beneath the American flag on the right and the Texas state flag on the left sat a black-robed judge. Gerald and Mike's attorney, looking official and somber, were told to approach the bench.

The middle-aged judge, his hair gone to gray and his wrinkled face flattered by an expensively acquired vacation tan, spoke a few words into a microphone, which she thought was unnecessary since she was the only person in the room who wasn't a court official. Then Gerald motioned for her to step forward.

Hailey walked up the aisle and stood before the judge, next to Gerald. He told her to answer "I will" or "I have" to his questions. Even as they were posed to her, she couldn't remember them, for she was struck with the eerie thought of how startlingly similar this ceremony was to that of a wedding. It all began and ended in the same manner, and for too many people, in a place much like this.

She had a sensation of shrinking as if she'd eaten poisoned mushrooms in that fairy tale . . . oh, yes—Alice. And was this Wonderland? No, this was real.

The judge's gavel resembled a sledgehammer as it pounded against his desk. It was done, the gavel proclaimed. Hailey miraculously resumed her adult height and nodded to Gerald, who whispered something to her about meeting him outside the doors. What doors? The doors to the left? Didn't they lead to the sacristy? Or to the right? No. No. The ones at the end of the room. The two big ones.

Hailey marched down the aisle, alone and not on the arm of a bridegroom. She sat once again on the bench-pew. She had no bouquet, there was no reception line; no kisses. It was a beginning, but there was no rice.

When Gerald saw her in the corridor, she looked like a pile of rumpled clothes. This strong woman . . . this friend . . . But he had been prepared for this.

"Hailey, let's go downstairs to the lobby, where we can talk more freely."

Her eyes were saucers spilling over with dread. "What's wrong? Did I do something wrong?"

"No, nothing like that. I'd like to have a cigarette and talk. I have another case in half an hour, so we can't go back to my office. That's all."

"Oh, I thought . . ." The truth was, she didn't know what she thought.

"I know," he said, taking her arm as they turned the corner and dashed to make the elevator just as its doors shut.

The lobby was deluged with sunshine and she could almost see the mammoth tropical plants generating chlorophyll. She sat on a surprisingly comfortable beige Naugahyde sofa with Gerald next to her.

"This is something I don't usually do, but I feel I should this time. You're more than just a client to me and I want you always to know you can call me for advice or anything." He looked at her with that brand of sincerity that was not taught by years of theatrics in a courtroom but rather sprang from his deep compassion.

"I will, I promise," she assured him hesitantly, for she also wanted him to know she would not do so unless it was truly urgent.

"You've made the right decision. I knew that long before you consciously approached the matter. It's a difficult thing to do at your age. Your children are young, for one thing. You must see how brave, and I don't use that word lightly, you are to do this before bitterness overtook you. It's easy to divorce when all you do is live and breathe hatred for each other. It's another to come to this decision when there is no animosity. You've borne a lot of pain and guilt and those are more difficult to shed. In my opinion, there was no other answer for you, Hailey," he said, looking away momentarily as she whisked away a silent tear. "You're going to be fine. You're a worthy person and I just hope you can believe that soon."

"It's so hard not to look back, Gerald." Her voice skipped a beat.

"I know, but it will get better. Give yourself some time. I think I've gotten to know you pretty well. You have needs that haven't beeen met."

"Needs? I don't need anything," she answered defensively.

"Oh, yes, you do. You don't know it yet, but you will and that will take time, too. But someday you're going to meet somebody and fall in love—and when you do, it'll be like a ton of bricks."

"Gerald," her eyes wore an incredulous expression and were shadowed with doubt, "is that some platitude you hand all divorcees?"

"No, Hailey, I don't. I don't want to see you get down on yourself and drown this emerging person who is, beyond a doubt, someone extraordinary."

"But, love?" She laughed one of those high-strung, taut laughs that belong to the deranged, she thought. "I don't need that . . ."

"How do you know? You've never tried it," he said, his eyebrows raised as if to say, "Don't contradict me, I know best."

Hailey scanned his face. He was serious! Gerald really

believed what he was telling her. How could he know so much?

"In two weeks I should have the last of the papers. I'll have Susan call you and set an appointment."

"All right," she said, "I'll wait to hear from you then." She rose and he took her hand and shook it.

"Take care, Hailey," he said and then turned and walked toward the open elevator doors.

Hailey's feet took her toward the glass doors, awash with sunshine, and she emerged into the world outside. "You've made the right decision," Gerald's voice told her. She wanted to believe him.

# Chapter Fifteen

MECHANICALLY, Hailey drove to the Galleria and then remembered she didn't have to work that day. It was probably just as well; she wasn't thinking too clearly and wouldn't be of much use to anyone. She drove toward Rice University. It was so beautiful, these winding streets rimmed with oaks so huge their branches interlaced above the street, creating a green tunnel of shade. She slowed the car and parked near the Warwick Hotel. As she walked across the street, the splashing sounds of a trio of fountains made her feel cooler, even though it was nearing ninety degrees. Befriended by a cool breeze, she sat near the largest fountain and plucked a wild flower from the grass. She twirled the flower between her finger and thumb, and then quite suddenly she ripped it to shreds. The mutilated pieces tumbled to the grass as if in slow motion. Her fingers were shaking as she stared at the life she had destroyed.

She wondered what other people did on the day their divorce was granted. Some threw extravagant parties. Certainly they couldn't be celebrating; maybe it was just a form of Welsh wake. Getting drunk or stoned, according to personal preference, might not be all that bad. It was an understandable course of action. Some might fall into the arms of a secret lover. If only she had one! She wondered fleetingly what Mike was doing. Working? She couldn't concentrate on work, she didn't have the energy. It was all she could do to raise her eyes to the sky. Robin's-egg blue it was. An appropriate color covering the shell of new life. She wondered how long until her future would seem bright again. She nearly allowed her tears to flow.

"Damn it!" she cursed herself. "I won't become one of those teary-eyed, depressed zombies! I just won't do it! I've got to do this myself—and I will! Nobody can live my life for me. I've done that for too long." She snapped another wild flower from its base and held it gently, then rose and tossed it into the fountain. It swirled, was battered to the bottom from the force of the cascading water and then miraculously surfaced, intact, like Neptune's daughter. She would be like that, she vowed.

She stood, brushed off her skirt and as she walked to her car, there was a noticeable spring to her step. As she unlocked the door she happened to glance up at the elegant entrance to the Warwick and there, tipping the valet, was Stephen!

She couldn't believe it! She had barely heard from him in two months. Except for one of his unannounced forays into the gallery, he'd nearly disappeared from her life. She was tempted to go on about her business, but then he spied her. Now he was sprinting toward her, waving his arm, motioning for her to wait. She had half a mind to get in the car and peel away from the curb, but she didn't. She waved and waited. He was out of breath when he reached her.

"Brother!" he said, wiping the beads of sweat from his forehead. "I should quit smoking or take up jogging! I must be more out of shape than I thought!"

"You could do both, you know."

"What are you doing here?"

"Uh, just passing by . . ." She couldn't think of an answer without divulging too many details.

"Do you have to go back to work right now?"

"No. Actually I have the day off."

"Great! We'll spend it together. Did you have lunch yet?"

"No, I haven't," she started to explain when he grasped her hand, put her arm through his and walked her toward the hotel.

"Good. You can break bread with me. I've got an 'in' with the proprietor," he said, holding the door for her.

As they walked through the extravagantly decorated corridor to the main dining area, Hailey's eyes couldn't flick from side to side fast enough. They passed one priceless antique after another and the chandeliers looked like honeycombs of tiny crystals and appeared nearly as large as the lobby in which they hung. The oils on the walls were exquisite originals.

The oval dining room was surrounded by glass walls soaring over twenty feet high. The opulent carpeting, walls and upholstery were coordinated in turquoise, gold and cream.

They sat at a table near the window up two levels from the main floor. She glanced out at the fountain and strained her eyes to see if the wild flower was still there, but it was too far away.

"See, isn't this better than a peanut butter and jelly sandwich in that stuffy gallery?" Stephen said, trying to break her silence.

"Huh? Oh, yes, it is!" She smiled but then a scowl altered the sparkle in her eyes. "Stephen, just out of curiosity—have you ever noticed how you never ask me anything? I mean, you just take it for granted that I'll go along with anything you want to do. You have a way of putting things so that there's no room for argument on my part."

"Pretty cagey of me, don't you think?" He smiled. "I can't stand rejection. Besides, it worked, didn't it? You're here," he teased as he lit a cigarette. "Anyway, I'm not chaining you to the table leg. You can leave if you want." His eyes narrowed, but he was only baiting her and she knew it.

"Oh, forget it," she said and laughed. "I wonder why I let you do that to me."

"Yeah, I wonder, too." He looked away but she could see the shadow that veiled his eyes. The corners of his mouth turned up before he looked back at her. "What were you doing here today, anyway?" he asked, changing the subject.

"I had some business downtown . . ." He knew she was separated, but she hadn't told him when the divorce was to be final. How could she? She hadn't seen him in weeks. And yet when he was with her she sensed something about him and his feelings for her. Magnetism? Infatuation? No, it couldn't be either of those; otherwise she'd never get him off her doorstep, and he seemed to rush in and out of her life like a roaring train.

"What kind of business?"

He wasn't going to let go. She might as well tell him; he would find out sooner or later, anyway. "My final decree was granted today, so I had to go to court."

"You're divorced now?" He seemed unduly tense.

"Yes. Why? Don't you want to be seen in public with me now?" She couldn't help taunting him.

"On the contrary! Just to prove it, since this is your first day of freedom, I'd like to take you out tonight. You don't have any plans, do you?" He stopped, but only for a second. "See, I'm getting better. This is your chance. You can rebuff me if you want. Go ahead. I can take it," and he squeezed his eyes shut and leaned back as if to shield himself from her words.

Hailey, caught in his attempt at lightheartedness, said, "No, Stephen, I don't have any plans for tonight. And I'd love to go to . . . Where are we going?"

"Oh, just a party at some friends' home. I think you might enjoy it."

"I hate asking this typically feminine question, but–"

"I know: What will you wear," he interrupted, rolling his eyes in his head. "It's a cocktail party. Need I say more?"

"Nope. Gotcha," Hailey said just as the waiter arrived with a bottle of wine.

After lunch Stephen walked her to her car and told her he would pick her up at eight o'clock. As she drove home, she silently thanked Stephen for being her friend.

As Hailey bathed, her first bubble bath in weeks—what an extravagance that was now, to spend costly moments on herself—she realized that for the first time in over ten years she was, to put it accurately, going on a date! Quite suddenly, her relationship with Stephen acquired a new perspective. Was it simply because the divorce was final now that her meetings with Stephen were technically different from the lunches they'd shared while she was at Design Media, or was it that she saw herself differently? It was the first time he—or anyone else, for that matter—had come to call for her at her own home, and the cover of evening gave it an almost clandestine aura. But, she thought, shrugging her shoulders, she was glad she wouldn't be forced to sit alone all evening and dwell upon the past.

Hailey chose a midnight-blue silk organza blouse she'd purchased two years ago and never worn. It was sleeveless with three folds of material draping into a softly plunging neckline. With her white silk pencil-slim skirt and collarless belted jacket to match, she'd look tailored yet chic. She pinned her hair in a soft coil on top of her head and curled those forever reluctant wisps of hair around her face. Just as she bent to strap a navy kid sandal on her foot, the doorbell rang. She snatched up her purse and the remaining sandal and raced down the stairs.

When she opened the door, Stephen stepped back and then leaned over into the bushes and pulled out a bouquet of red roses.

"Look what I found just lying here in the shrubs!" he said exuberantly, handing them to her as she stuck her remaining shoe on her foot.

"Stephen! I never expected anything . . . but . . . thank you!" she said and gasped, accepting the fragrant blooms. "Come in while I put these in some water."

He followed her into the kitchen while she filled a vase with water and arranged the flowers. She noticed Stephen poking around, and it was something she hadn't expected of him. "Would you like a drink?" she asked casually.

"No," he answered absentmindedly, wandering into the living room. "This is a lovely place you have." He came back and leaned against the doorjamb and smiled at her. "It suits you."

"Really? How's that?" she asked, placing the last rose in the vase and turning toward him.

"It's soft."

Hailey didn't miss the sparkle in his eyes whenever he looked at her. "Is that a compliment, I hope?" she asked as he stepped back and let her pass into the dining area, where she placed the vase on the parquet table.

"It is. I meant it was a nice place to come home to." Then he abruptly cleared his throat in that funny manner he had and said just as quickly, "We'd better get going. I don't like to be too late, even though it is fashionable."

Hailey thought she must not have heard him correctly. "Stephen, I doubt I've ever known when you've been on time, not even tonight."

"I try. Really, I do," he said, noting her skeptical look as she picked up her purse and flicked out the lights.


A "swankienda," as Stephen explained and as Hailey was about to learn, was a noted Houston columnist's term for an expensive, usually well over million-dollar home occupied by the city's famous celebrity couples.

River Oaks was the primary enclave of such estates, with Memorial a close runner-up. Stephen pointed out the homes of Ima Hogg and Oveta Culp Hobby, and John Connally's former home. Naturally, Stephen defended and praised this shrine to dignity and stability for, though his own house was small and not at all like the manor houses she was seeing, he too was a River Oaks resident. Hailey told Stephen she'd been here only once, to the Farrells', but she hadn't realized how large the area was at the time. She noted his surprise at the mention of the Farrells' name but was so occupied with the sights about her that she dismissed it.

When they drove up to the River Oaks address of Mr. and Mrs. Anthony Gregson, Hailey could well understand why a new word had been coined for such a home. The impressive French manor house looked as if it had been plucked off the banks of the Seine, for it was baronial in size and stature. It was three stories tall and was nearly encased by massive oaks with long, twisted limbs. The grounds were ingeniously lit by green-silver spots, which cast an aura of never-ending moonglow over the grounds. The driveway was jammed with expensive sports cars and Rolls-Royces, and Stephen teased about his eccentric Volvo. An elderly Mexican servant greeted them and as they entered through nine-foot-high carved doors, Stephen told Hailey more about what she could expect from the evening.

It was *de rigueur* that parties given by the owners of swankiendas be attended by Hollywood movie stars, writers, producers, politicians, artists and other owners of swankiendas. Such gatherings were never missed by the press. All these affairs were not necessarily outrageously sumptuous or expensive, but they were executed with flair, and Stephen never missed one.

These, then, were Stephen's friends. He was their resident artist. And as Hailey was soon to discover, he fed on their adulation as much as they drank in his notoriety. Hailey found that he was the darling of every notable hostess in town. They had barely entered the spacious living room when four of these ladies descended upon him like butterflies.

Hailey was nudged aside as his admirers entreated him to give them details about his latest project. He described a series of bronze sculptures he'd been commissioned to make by a wealthy New York socialite, whose acquaintance they all had in common. Somehow, Hailey had the distinct impression that she was watching a television interview. Stephen's ability to create suspense as he spoke was not only intriguing, but also charming. Hailey, not knowing anyone, felt terribly conspicuous; she clutched her handbag as if it were her escort. Surreptitiously, she let her eyes scan the room.

Clusters of casually though expensively dressed people were absorbed in conversation, and thus far she hadn't been able to discern the host and the hostess. Just then a slender woman not more than ten years older than Hailey walked toward her with an athleticlike gait. When the woman smiled, her teeth appeared iridescent against her sun-bronzed skin. She wore a sleeveless hand-painted cotton dress that revealed sinewy arms, toned by morning sets of tennis and afternoons of swimming. Her brown eyes were riveted on Stephen and his entourage. As she came up beside him, he spied her and accepted her exuberant embrace.

"Sylvia! How enchanting you look tonight," he said as he broke away from her and she laughed huskily. Too many cigarettes, Hailey thought.

"You know, Stephen, that's why I invite you to my parties. You're the only man I know whose lies I believe."

"Nonsense. I've never told you an untruth. It's not in my nature," he said, smiling wickedly.

"Bullshit, honey. All men lie. It's just a matter of picking one who is the most believable or at least who lies more sweetly than the rest."

"That doesn't make any sense," Stephen bantered.

"Sure it does, honey, think about it." As they were speaking the "butterflies" fluttered away, deferring to the power of their hostess.

Just when she thought Stephen had completely forgotten about her, she heard him say, "Sylvia, I want you to meet Hailey James."

He grabbed her elbow and pulled her closer. "Hailey, this is Sylvia Gregson, our hostess."

"How are you, Hailey?" Sylvia asked, and then not waiting for Hailey to respond, she said, "Stephen tells me that you're a fellow artist. I think that's admirable to have such talent. What medium do you enjoy most, Hailey?"

"Oils, mostly. I—" She couldn't finish her explanation, for Stephen interrupted her. She kept her smile intact even though she was annoyed at his putting words into her mouth. She felt like a child.

"Yes, Hailey had a portrait of hers shown at L'Artiste du Monde a few months ago at their opening."

"Why, that's wonderful, Hailey. I'm so happy for you. That's certainly an accomplishment."

"It was all Stephen's doing, actually. He arranged for the owners to see my work, unbeknownst to me." Hailey glanced at Stephen's self-satisfied expression. She felt as if she'd fallen into some sort of verbal entrapment. Had Stephen only his own ego in mind when he'd asked her to accompany him here tonight? Then she chided herself for being suspicious and ungrateful.

"Oh, Stephen, you're such a sly one. But I can see why you would encourage her. Talent and beauty all rolled into one." Sylvia nudged him with her elbow and winked at him.

Hailey felt as if she were a display item. It was a feeling she'd grown to know over the years and she was beginning to bristle.

"Sylvia, where's Tony? I want to introduce Hailey to him."

"There he is! Tony!" she called across the room to a tall, debonair man in white slacks and navy blazer. He smiled and nodded, then excused himself from his companions and walked toward them. "Tony, darling, meet Stephen's new protégée, Hailey James."

"Hailey," he said and shook her hand. "Glad you could make it, Stephen. It wouldn't be the same without you."

Hailey watched Stephen intently as he basked in the approval of his host as if he were sunning himself on the Riviera. He loved this limelight, she thought. Even more —he needed it. Why hadn't she seen that before? Hailey mumbled some response as Sylvia and Tony left them to themselves.

Stephen led her across the room to a long slate-covered bar, where the bartender handed them their drinks. The bar looked like a liquor store, and the multitude of glassware was enough to put Neiman-Marcus to shame!

While she sipped her drink, Hailey's eyes scanned the room and the one beyond. There was no division between the formal and more casual areas, save for a difference in area rugs atop the highly polished parquet floor. Antique french occasional chairs were blended with sectional sofas around the traditional fireplace in the living room. The second living area overlooked a series of sliding glass doors that opened onto a lovingly tended terrace, which was ringed with potted geraniums. Not a single bloom was past its prime. At once, Hailey's regard for Sylvia grew, for she'd been able to overcome the foreboding exterior of this house by creating an inviting and hospitable interior.

They drifted around the room, stopping to talk with everyone. By the end of the evening, Hailey was astounded that she had met a novelist, a senator, a heart surgeon, a real-estate magnate and two concert pianists. It had been a long time since she'd experienced such stimulating conversation.

When Stephen told her it was nearly midnight, she could hardly believe it. They thanked their host and hostess, and Stephen promised to bring Hailey to their annual Labor Day barbecue.

Stephen had just closed the car door behind Hailey and was walking around the back of the car when they heard the roar of a motor, then screeching tires as a sports car pulled to an abrupt and timely halt, for the driver had nearly smashed into the back of Stephen's car.

Hailey peered out the back window at the chocolate brown and tan vintage 1953 MG. Its wire-rimmed wheels, chrome grille and abundant adornments gleamed in the outdoor lighting. The convertible top was down and in the passenger's seat, Hailey spied what she thought was the most beautiful woman she had ever seen.

She was calmly running a brush through her long, dark hair. Hailey couldn't see her male companion that well, for he was opening the door for the woman. She wore a slinky white silk street-length dress that accentuated her well-endowed willowy figure. The dress was undoubtedly a Halston, Hailey thought as she viewed its simple, well-tailored lines. She must be a model, she thought.

The man was tall and wide-shouldered and his dark hair was thick and precision-cut. He had a dark moustache above his full, sensuous lips. He was dressed in the only western clothes she'd seen all evening. As the duo bounded up the steps and stopped beneath the coach lamps, she could see he wore a leather vest with simple tooling, a plaid cotton shirt and . . . blue jeans! Why, he even wore two-toned cowboy boots and carried a black felt hat! When the man grasped the woman and pulled her next to him and kissed her hungrily, Hailey was embarrassed but couldn't look away.

Surely they must have the wrong address! But when the door opened, she saw Sylvia welcome them both with embraces.

Stephen was cursing when he started the car. "That son-of-a-bitch nearly killed me! If I hadn't jumped out of the way . . ." he fumed.

"I know! Do you know who he is?"

"Never saw him before in my life. But I'll tell you one thing: He's an asshole!"

Hailey nodded but didn't say anything. An asshole. Or reckless. Or impertinent. Maybe all three. She certainly didn't know anyone who arrived at a party when it was almost over. But she had to admit one thing: Whoever he was, he made a dramatic entrance!

## Chapter Sixteen

HAILEY couldn't concentrate on her work. In the fall they were to have a special showing, and Leonard had told her to consider the theme she would use. But what should it be? African art? All sculpture? A certain period? A collection of one man's work? It seemed an insurmountable request.

She kept remembering when Stephen had walked her to her door after the Gregsons' party. It was an awkward moment for them both. She knew he expected her to invite him in for a drink. He had turned to leave and then spun around and quickly pulled her into his arms. She'd been so startled she couldn't remember when she'd finally closed her eyes. Had it been before or after she'd put her arms around him? Or maybe it was when she'd found she was kissing him back. It had been so long since she'd been kissed like that, all mouth and tongue and hands everywhere, that she'd forgotten she could feel like that. All that bottled-up sexual need had nearly overpowered her. For a moment she swore she'd been unconscious. It must have been then that Stephen had asked to come inside and she'd refused, saying it was too soon. Or some dumb thing like that.

But he had agreed with her and left, saying he would call her the next day. She hadn't slept all night, she was too confused, too tense and too excited. She had wanted him and she was frightened of the feeling. Had it been just sex? What did she want from him? And he of her?

She was a novice at this 1980s-style dating. In college there was the protection of the sorority house or parents. This was so different and so scary.

Her courtship rules were as old as the Dead Sea Scrolls and just about as useless. Being suddenly single required not only contemplation but also courage. There was no virginity to protect, nor worries about unwanted pregnancy. How did one overhaul the old rules? From her observations, there was now little connection between sex and love.

She couldn't imagine having a string of lovers, nor was she so romantic or idealistic as to think there was someone out there waiting just for her. There were no Mr. Rights.

The stress of the past year and the avalanche of changes she'd survived had consumed all her energy and thoughts. She wasn't sure why she was concerned with having a man in her future. She'd just gotten out of that situation. Was it Stephen or simply his persistent presence in her life that caused these observations? Or was she being too romantic after all? She doubted if it were even possible for two people to live and grow together.

It was obvious to her that Stephen didn't really care about her. It was a week after their date and he hadn't called her as he had said. Did he ever have any intention of following through? Why did he say anything at all?

She knew her behavior was ridiculous. Stephen was a busy man with his own life to lead, but she resented his involving her in his life. Or was she inviting him into hers? God! All these questions were getting her nowhere.

Two women came in and inquired about the painting of the stampeding mustangs in the window. Hailey explained a few details about the artist, and when she turned around, she was startled to see Stephen watching her.

"I'll be with you in a moment," she said to him, taking in his longing gaze. Then he winked at her and pretended to browse.

One of the women purchased the painting and made arrangements for its delivery. They left chattering excitedly about the most suitable location for their purchase.

Stephen watched them leave and said, "Personally, I think they should hang it in the bathroom."

"Tacky, Stephen. It's a good piece of work. As a matter of fact, I like it a lot."

"I didn't say I didn't like it. After all, where else would they get to see it more than in the bathroom?" He chuckled.

"Interesting analysis. I'll have to think about that for a while." He was looking at her almost hungrily. It was a look she knew, but it seemed misplaced on Stephen. Until just recently she'd thought of him only as a friend, a brother. Now she found herself scrutinizing him. Why had he taken such an interest in her . . . as a person, as an artist? What the hell was he doing here, running around the edges of her life? She should just tell him to go away, but then he moved closer to her and put his hands on her shoulders. He peered into her eyes as he toyed with a lock of her hair. She had the distinct impression he was restraining himself, for she felt his hands tremble slightly, and when he spoke, his voice was low and breathy.

"I've got a couple of propositions for you," he said and laughed lightly. "That didn't sound right, did it?"

"No, it didn't."

"I have an invitation to an art exhibition this weekend that I thought you might like. It's Rose Van Vranken's sculpture. Her work has been on exhibit at the American embassy in Costa Rica. She has fabulous bronzes. And then there's the Western Heritage Show in a few weeks. . . . Hailey? You're a million miles away."

"Hmmm?" she answered, still wondering what he really wanted from her. She was conscious of his warmth, standing this close to him. "What were you saying?"

"About the exhibit. Would you like to go?"

"I'd love to," she said, pondering the wisdom of throwing away her resolve to purge herself of him. She managed a more lighthearted tone. "You're being quite formal about this."

"I thought about what you said—about my always just assuming you would want to go out with me. What you're witnessing, lovely lady, is my reformation. I'll pick you up

Saturday night about seven?" His inflection rose at the last moment, turning his demand into a question.

"Fine," she said. He bent forward and kissed her. She knew he wanted her, yet he abruptly pulled away from her and started to leave.

"Stephen, one question before you leave. Why didn't you call when you said you would?"

He looked back over his shoulder and said, "My phone was out of order. How does that sound?"

"Flimsy. You'll have to do better than that."

"I'll try," he answered and he was gone.

Stephen seemed more mysterious to her every time she saw him. She knew him less now than she did when they first met.

# Chapter Seventeen

SATURDAY night in Houston was an attitude rather than any veneration of preestablished customs. When Hailey thought of Boston she remembered hushed voices in theater lobbies, and venerable restaurants. New York was brilliant Broadway and posh late-night dinners. But in Houston, rowdiness swept through the town at sundown like tumbleweed. Every bar, theater, dance hall and restaurant was booked up and there were waiting lines everywhere. With half the city in cowboy hats and pickups and the other in Cadillacs and diamonds, she kept wondering where she fit in. Or were they all one and the same—the dream and its culmination?

As she flipped her radio to KIKK and listened to the country and western strains of Boz Scaggs fill her bedroom, she dressed for the Western Heritage Show.

In the past weeks Hailey had found herself spinning through the cream of Houston's society, and always on Stephen's arm. Invitations to parties, theater and art openings engulfed them. Dom Perignon flowed like the Rio Grande. Had she been an ardent epicurean she could have found no fault with the gourmet delicacies she had enjoyed. The open and bottomless purses of their hosts never ceased to amaze her. A spirit of abandon pervaded the air and she found it increasingly difficult to keep her feet on the ground. A surrealistic aura hovered over the scene of herself amid these people, who had dubbed her their newest protégée; wondrously the requests for her paintings mounted, and a professional public-relations agent would not have served her better than Stephen.

She wondered if he fancied himself Henry Higgins to her Eliza Doolittle. Increasingly, he made suggestions— just like Mike—as to what she should wear, and if she didn't own the correct attire, he purchased it for her, which was how the black silk Halston dress had come into her possession.

Hailey wondered if there was something about her that compelled men to want to dress her. Stephen was more subtle in his approach than Mike had been, but Stephen was trying to manipulate her just the same. Both men were alike in that respect. The exception was that this time Hailey was aware of the problem, and consequently she kept a humorous view when Stephen had said, "How would it look in the papers if you wore anything less than an original?"

She had to agree, for the flashing of cameras was now a familiar experience. She was stunned the first time she'd seen her name in the society columns. The two lines were engraved in her mind. "This town's Stephen Ainsley, Design Media exec and noted artist and collector, was an 'item' last night at Jimmy's 2600 . . . the breathtaking, and we've discovered talented artist, on his arm was Hailey James."

That had been the first of many. Stephen had said they had studded the night like two stars and clowningly had called her "Hailey's Comet," predicting that their brilliance would never fade. That was the closest he'd ever come to revealing his "intentions."

Within the context of coming to find herself, Hailey realized that she didn't want commitment from Stephen, and somehow her actions or body language had communicated this to him. She realized that Stephen's shadow was no more appealing than Mike's. She was becoming her own person—a mixture of artist, mother and working woman with a dash of socialite. She loved everything she was doing and would not give up any part of it. She was no longer "just" a corporate wife; nor would she allow herself to focus on only one aspect of her life. She wasn't a misfit or a hermit. She was Hailey, and that's all she wanted to be.

She smiled at her reflection as she straightened the perilously thin straps of the simple black dress. The lines remolded her into a perfect silhouette. She let her thick hair fall in waves past her shoulders and she wore no jewelry save sapphire studs in her ears. They had been her mother's and would go to Kim on her sixteenth birthday.

At this thought, Hailey's mind traveled to Boston, and she wondered what Sonja was thinking tonight, this eve of the children's departure. At their insistence and Sonja's too, she had allowed them to extend their vacation by almost another month. When they had spoken on the phone Hailey had sensed that there was something Sonja wanted to discuss. But Hailey had been at work and a customer had just come in and she was forced to cut the call short. In fact, Hailey had feared further reprimands from her mother and hung up to avoid more guilt.

The last weeks without Joey and Kim had seemed like centuries. She was so excited about their coming home that the art auction had lost its thrill for her.

During her time alone, Hailey had formed some rules. Until she was more sure of herself and her future, she decided that she would not expose her children to any of the men she might date, and that included Stephen. Perhaps she was being overly protective, but there was no reason for Joey and Kim to become attached to anyone who was not a real part of their lives. And she also didn't want a man using her children for reasons of his own, either. Her way might not be the best, but it was hers alone.

At that moment the doorbell rang and startled her out of her thoughts. She slowly descended the stairs, satisfied with the turn her life had taken.


The Western Heritage Show was held at the Shamrock Hilton, Houston's first landmark hotel. It was the fabulously expensive dream of Glenn McCarthy, a Texas oil wildcatter who opened it on St. Patrick's Day in 1949. It boasted the "world's largest swimming pool" and for decades the Shamrock and its Cork Club were the scene of numerous outlandish antics of Houston's beautiful people.

A collection of cars ringed the circular drive in front like royal carriages. Every woman present was exquisitely coiffed and lavished with Cartier and Tiffany jewels. Expensive perfume filled the air. The shoes were Charles Jourdan, Maud Frizon and Botticelli. Mauve handpainted voiles, delicate ice cream shades of apricot, lemon and lime chiffons and soft, shimmering summer taffetas in brilliant jewel tones swished past her. Many of the gowns were designer originals. Ruffled Oscar de la Rentas, Dior silks and sequined Bob Mackie ensembles made their way through the crowded lobby and into the Astroturfed arena in the Grand Ballroom.

One ensemble in particular caught Hailey's eye. A shimmering henna-colored silk organza "raja coat" edged in copper beading flowed past the knees of a pair of apricot pants that were cinched with a bronze leather belt. When the brunette turned around, nearly all her bare midriff was exposed. Hailey thought she recognized the beautiful woman. Yes! The man with her was the one she'd seen that night at the Gregsons' party; the one who drove so recklessly. She watched as they were instantly surrounded by a large group of people. Hailey wondered what it would be like to be so beautiful.

Stephen took Hailey's hand and she looked up into his quiet, soft brown eyes and smiled.

Nearly a thousand people strolled through the exhibit hall to the music of the Light Crust Doughboys playing "Let Me Waltz Across Texas with You." On display were twenty-five quarter horses and twenty-seven Santa Gertrudis bulls, heifers, pairs and babies. The extravaganza had lasted for two days, but tonight was the night of the sale.

Some of the West's biggest and wealthiest ranches and art galleries had sent their representatives for the festivities.

Hailey, still stunned at seeing snorting racehorses displayed along with priceless western art, found herself being nearly dragged by an impatient Stephen. He said something about being late for dinner and the auction due to her dawdling in the exhibit hall.

As dinner was being served, the auctioneer stripped off his tuxedo jacket, peered down at them and began the business of raising money. His triple-tongued incantations began immediately as pretty girls dressed in tuxedos marched the first quarter horse in front of the well-heeled audience. As the bidding progressed, Stephen pointed out his favorite pieces of art, such as Clark Hulings' Mexican marketplace painting called "Kaleidoscope." Hailey admired Gordon Snidow's "Sam and Cow Boss," which was a painting of a middle-aged cowboy and his dog. There was a still life, "Yellow Rose of Texas" by William Acheff, that she and Stephen both liked.

At midnight the audience was informed that the Santa Gertrudis cattle had brought $621,500 and the quarter horses' sale tallied $871,500; but it had been the art lovers who had spent the greatest amount: $2,539,400!

The staggering amounts made Hailey wonder just how she could take advantage of her position at the gallery to capitalize on this big business of art. The evening gave her an entirely new insight into art collectors in Houston. Ordinarily, she would have expected them to purchase Monets, Van Dykes and Picassos. But this was strictly western art sold to lovers of the West and art.

The auction over, the patrons dispersed. Stephen stopped to talk with numerous acquaintances as they found their way back to the lobby. There were several verbal invitations for parties afterward, but Hailey was quick to decline, and when she did so, she noticed Stephen's disapproving look, but he remained silent and offered his apologies. They waited for the valet to bring their car and as they drove away, Hailey waited for his reprimand, but there was none. He remained in light spirits all the way to her house. When he walked her to the door, Hailey was expecting his usual kiss and was surprised and a bit nervous when he asked if he could come in for a while.

"Just for a quick drink. After all, this is the earliest I've ever brought you home," he said with an impish grin.

"I don't see any harm in it," she replied and let him unlock the door. She flicked on the lights, kicked off her shoes and went to the kitchen to mix him a Scotch and water. She poured a glass of wine for herself.

"Stephen, the only reason I wanted to be home early is because the children are coming home tomorrow and I have some special things I want to get done for them before they arrive. You do understand that, don't you? I had a marvelous time and wouldn't have missed it for the world. Thank you," she said as he accepted the drink, took her hand and led her to the living room. They sat on the sofa.

"I enjoyed it, too. Especially the company." He lifted his glass. "To you, beautiful lady," he said and drank deeply as she watched him. Then she sipped her wine. She toyed with the base of the glass, not understanding her own apprehension.

"You don't want me here, do you?" he asked bluntly.

"Why, no! Of course not. I mean, you'll always be welcome here . . . It's just that . . . well . . . After Joey and Kim come home . . ." God! She was having a hard time with this.

"You don't want me to see them, do you?"

She gave him a laser look. "No, I don't think so. I don't mean to sound cold. After all, they *have* met you."

"But that was just at the gallery opening and this is a different situation altogether. If I came over now, they would see me as your date, your man—possibly as a new father figure."

"I didn't say that."

"I know, but you thought it. You don't want that, I can tell."

"And do you?"

"I'm asking you. But I can tell from the look on your face that I shouldn't. So let's just drop it."

"All right," she agreed, feeling a vast distance between them.

Stephen placed his drink on the coffee table and held her hand. "Hailey," he said, looking down at her fingertips, then caressing them. He lifted his head and peered at her. "You're like Cinderella. Did you know that?"

Her laugh was nervous, but she started to warm again. "How do you figure that?"

"You just are. You've been hidden away behind the walls in your house for years. And now, suddenly, a whole new world, a new life has been laid at your feet."

"And when does it turn midnight?" she asked, watching the lights dance in his eyes.

"Never, not for you, anyway."

"And Prince Charming . . ." She had said it impetuously, not knowing now if she wanted the answer to that question.

He cleared his throat and looked away and she thought . . . no . . . she *did* see tears in his eyes, but they were dry when he turned back to her. "I think that . . ." He hesitated, trying to keep his voice even. "I think more than any man before or after me, I will have the most influence on your life. More like the godmother, in my case the godfather, and not the prince." He mumbled his last words very quickly and then picked up his drink and swallowed deeply. Hailey wondered if she had heard him correctly. He looked at his watch and stood abruptly.

"Look, I'm not going to keep you up all night. You've got a busy day tomorrow and so do I."

He took her hand and walked down the hallway to the door. This time he slowly took her in his arms and let his eyes roam her face as if he were memorizing every inch. His lips were cool when he kissed her, and his arms drew her in closer and closer. She sensed that something was wrong. His arms released her and he took her face in his hands, rubbing his thumbs along her cheeks. He was holding back. She half expected him to pick her up in his arms and carry her up to bed, but he didn't. He kissed her nose and ever so slowly her eyelids, forehead and finally her cheeks. Once more he pulled her to his chest. He hugged her so tightly she thought her ribs would be crushed. Then he reluctantly released her.

"I'll call you at work on Monday," he said and then

caught her look of total disbelief. "I promise!" he exclaimed. "Now you get some rest."

"Okay, I will," she said, opening the door.

"Good-bye, Hailey," he said and walked away.

"Bye," she said and watched until he disappeared from the halo of lamplight above. She closed the door and locked it. Her hand seemed as if it were frozen to the doorknob. Something wasn't right. She had half a mind to call him back and ask him about it. She felt an intense sense of sorrow, of loss, as if he were saying good-bye forever. His kiss had the taste of finality about it.

"Impossible!" He promised to call on Monday. He had never promised anything before. She was just being melodramatic, she told herself as she mounted the stairs to her room.

# Chapter Eighteen

JOEY and Kim sat in the front seat of the car, excitedly relating every incident of their vacation. Hailey tried to piece it together as days, times and locales were poured into a massive hodgepodge by her two little magpies. Sonja had arranged tennis and golf lessons for Joey and he'd loved them. Sonja's time with Kim was quietly spent in discussion, mainly about Hailey. Sonja sent a letter for Hailey which she promised to read when they got home.

Hailey was elated now that the children were home again, though she found herself not listening to some of the things they were saying; she had to keep resisting the impulse to reach over and hug them.

When they reached the house it took three trips to unload their baggage. Hailey thought they had brought back half of Boston! One suitcase was filled with things Sonja had sent for Hailey, and both children had numerous new T-shirts, games and souvenirs from just about every historical monument and house in the city.

Hailey helped them to their rooms, and as they unpacked she went to her room to read Sonja's letter, which was attached to the top of a beribboned shoe box. She pulled off the ribbon and excitedly ripped the envelope open.

Dearest Hailey,
    Upon finishing this letter I want you to call me for I

very much want to talk to you, but only after you have read this. I wish I could tell you all this in person, but that's impossible because of the distance and the circumstances.

The first week that Kim was here, I'm afraid I deluged the poor child with a million and one questions about you, though I said nothing you would disapprove of. I suppose I was searching for answers that can never be found. Truthfully, I had enormous difficulty in understanding this divorce. I kept wondering if I had failed you somehow, somewhere in the past, and I realized that I had. But my failure was recent, for I had not trusted you, a grown woman, to know your own mind. I realized that I was placing conditions of all kinds upon my love. That was very wrong of me, and I hope I can make up for that.

I came to all these realizations one day when Kim and I were in the attic browsing through all those old camel-back trunks of my mother's. You remember them, don't you? Anyway, among my wedding pictures I found a stack of poems I had written when I was in college. My mother had saved them all, including the magazines and periodicals in which I had been published. It was such a thrill to see those poems again. I had completely forgotten about them and the young woman who had written them.

You would have liked her, Hailey. She was courageous though terribly idealistic, as I suppose all youth are. She was very much a romantic woman, but she had something tangible she could call her own.

Before I met your father, I had dreams of becoming a poet. I wanted nothing more than to pursue learning and my talent. I wanted to be the best I could be and had nearly compiled an entire book of poetry and probably would have pursued its publication more forcefully had it not been for Austin.

From the first instant I saw him, I knew that he was the one I wanted. I know that young people don't believe in such things today, but for me, it was wonderful. I never wanted anything more than to be near him. I still wish it could be that way. I miss him a great deal, but I have learned to go on with my life.

I have put undue pressure on you through these years, trying to make you fill the void he left, and that was unfair of me. I think my greatest disappointment or shock was in discovering that you had never been truly in love with Mike. You spent all your married life away from him and you never complained. I should have seen it then. I would have become a screaming shrew but you didn't, and that was because it wasn't the same for you.

I can see why you need this career and how lucky you are that it revolves around the art world. You have something of your own making. It's a wonderful accomplishment and I'm proud of you. You have more determination than I had. Please don't abandon your dreams, Hailey. There are so many times that I wish I hadn't, for I will always wonder what my life would have been like if I'd pursued my poetry.

Take care of those adorable children. It meant a lot to me that you allowed them to stay for another month. Please call soon.

Love,
Mother

P.S. Look inside the box.

Hailey reread the letter and finally her tears flowed. Hands shaking, she opened the box.

"Mother's poems!" she said, unfolding one after another and wiping away her tears. She couldn't read them fast enough! They *were* sentimental and idealistic, but they revealed tremendous insight. Few were morose and all were well written. There was an October 1936 issue of *Atlantic Monthly* and a *New Yorker* dated December 1935. The corners of the appropriate pages had been turned down, and Hailey opened to them immediately.

"She's so good! She should never have let her writing die like that!"

Hailey put the shoe box aside and grasped the telephone

next to her bed, her fingers punching out her mother's number. Hailey's heart was beating wildly. She didn't know what to say first . . . and if she stopped now to plan her words . . . no, that wouldn't be good at all. Fifth ring. Sixth. The receiver was picked up.

"Mother, Mother, it's me!" she said, feeling her throat grow small.

"Hailey! You read my letter?"

"Yes, I did and the poems, too. Mother, they're so good . . ."

"Did you really like them?"

"Of course I did! Mother, it's not too late, you know." Hailey's words were tumbling out so fast she barely gave her mother a chance to respond.

"No, it's not. That's what I wanted to talk to you about. Hailey, can you ever forgive me for being so blind?"

"What are you talking about? You don't need to apologize for anything. It was a normal reaction. After all, I hadn't given you any warning about what was happening. But . . . you'll never know how much this means to me . . . just knowing you understand. I just didn't want you to hate me."

"Hailey, I could never do that. I love you, you're my daughter. Actually, I should thank you."

"Why on earth would you need to thank me for anything? All I've done is cause you pain."

"Don't say that—it's not true! No, Hailey, you've made me see a lot of things about myself and more importantly about my relationship with you. And that's the most important part."

"Yes, I guess it is. Mother, I want you to do something for me."

"What's that?"

"Please start writing again. These poems shouldn't be lost somewhere in an old shoe box. There must be some way you could get them published. Maybe one of Father's colleagues . . ."

"I suppose I could." Sonja seemed uncertain.

"Then ask around! Mother, I'm serious. At least think about it, okay?" Hailey pleaded.

"All right, I will." Her voice sounded more assured, determined.

Hailey thanked God for answering her prayers. Sonja had come back to her and she felt as if the whole world were right.

"I'll try to call you next weekend unless I can manage a few minutes to get a letter off to you."

"Oh, that would be great! I'll talk to you then. Bye, Mother. I love you," she said, hoping she would hear the same response.

"Good-bye, dear. I love you, too." Sonja hung up.

Hailey replaced the receiver, lovingly running her fingertips over it, this link to her past and her children's future. Hailey thought of Austin then and wished she had been able to reconcile with him. A smile crept over her face. No, she didn't need to hear Austin's words of forgiveness. She felt them. She just knew somehow that Austin was very pleased with her at this moment.

She leaned back on the pillows and listened to the familiar voices of her children as they giggled and argued. She felt she truly had peace of mind and heart.

The sales in the Galleria store for the first six months of its inception were unsatisfactory to Barrett. To Hailey, they were deplorable, for she took them as a direct reflection of her marketing ability. Now she was determined to change that. The Western Heritage Show had taught her two valuable lessons—that Texans were not only capable of but also anxious to spend a great deal of money on western and Indian art and that her gallery was missing this market by a mile. Selling Texans on Texas was not a difficult job, for they cherished their heritage as did no other region in America.

That morning she called every gallery in the city. As she had suspected, the galleries doing the largest sales volume were those that specialized in western art and bronzes. She jotted down notes and kept her figures in two columns: "European" and "Regional" were the headings. She realized that the more exclusive galleries stocked European art. Their sales were slow, but they were well-respected galleries. Texans viewed European art in various galleries, but they bought western art. With the near mania for Texas chic sweeping the East Coast, she wanted to strike out for the tourist trade. She worked up an ad for *Houstonian* and *Houston Home and Garden* magazines, thinking this might help sway Leonard to her side.

Immersed as she was in her new project, she was constantly aware that Stephen had not telephoned her as he'd promised. She passed it off, thinking he was just busy, until it was time to leave for the day. She locked the store and left, realizing he had broken the only promise he had ever made to her. She was angry and disappointed. She had expected more from him.

For the rest of the week Hailey worked on her portraits and presentation. And she waited. Stephen never called, but she kept telling herself it wasn't unusual. Today was the first time she had ever called him, but the receptionist at Design Media must have been new or a temporary because she had said that there was no one there by that name. Hailey didn't have his home phone number, and the operator told her it was unlisted. She felt like a fool.

The weekend passed, a mélange of shopping for school clothes for Joey and Kim, an Astros baseball game and long nights while she worked at her easel. And still the phone didn't ring.

By Wednesday she had arranged a meeting with Leonard to present her suggestions for the autumn collection. She sat across from him at his desk and took out her files.

"What I am proposing is an experiment for L'Artiste because it deviates drastically from our established marketing concepts. What prompted me to pursue this idea was your statement that L'Artiste was a business and not a museum. I want to change the status of the Galleria store from that of a museum, as it is now, to a lucrative business. I want to sell Western and Indian art *exclusively*." She placed heavy emphasis on her last word and then went on. "I've got the sales figures here for the past four months. My sales are half what this store does. You've been in this location for many years, have referrals and you're established. My customers are walk-ins, natives and tourists. I'm not asking to scrap my current inventory completely, but I do want to give this my best effort."

"For how long?" he asked as he picked up the sales charts she'd drawn up.

"Sixty days. That would give me some indication of what I can do with this."

"Well, I'm all for raising the sales. But Hailey, I must warn you we have always had cowpoke art available."

"I know, but the gallery has never pushed it. Not hard-sell, anyway. Is it worth the risk?"

"The Galleria has a different clientele. I know I haven't spent enough time over there and I should have. I've just been so busy with other aspects of this business. You've put a lot of thought into all this. Do you have anything in particular you want to see in that store?"

"I have a detailed list I've compiled for initial inventory." She handed him the sheet, listing specific prints and oils and where they could obtain them.

He laughed and leaned back in his chair, still looking over the list. "You didn't miss a trick, did you. It shows you believe in what you're doing. It looks great. Some of these artists we have, just not on display. I'll give it to Barrett. Frankly, I'm not sure he'll approve." Leonard paused and looked directly at her. "He put a lot of thought, time and energy into what went into that store. Even its inception was more his idea than mine and he's been quite insistent on the caliber of what we've stocked. He's been planning a very different showing, and as you know he's made another buying trip to New York. His ideas work well at this store, but at the Galleria I see many shortcomings."

"This is as much a test for me as it is for the store. If this fails then the only conclusion I can draw is that the poor sales are due to the salesperson. Then all of this falls on my shoulders."

Leonard eyed her. "That's too strong a stand. The store is very new, too, and that has something to do with it. But I think this is worth the gamble. I'll let you know before the week is out. Fair enough?"

"That's fine with me." She stood up but hesitated. "There's something else I wanted to ask."

"What's that?"

"Not long ago you said you would train me to make client calls. Have you abandoned the idea?"

"No. As a matter of fact, I'd like to get you started very soon. Could you meet me for a five-o'clock appointment tomorrow?"

"Of course!"

"Good. Have Agatha give you the address. I'll see you then. Good night, Hailey."

"Good night and thank you, Leonard."

He smiled. "Thank *you*."

Hailey was restless that night and couldn't sleep. All she could think about was Stephen. She was angry at him for breaking his promise. When she hadn't been able to reach him, she worried about him, fearing something had happened to him or that he might be ill. Then she berated herself for being concerned when he clearly didn't respect her feelings at all. She glanced at the clock. Two-thirty. She had to get some rest.

Suddenly the phone rang, startling her.

"I'm sorry to wake you, Hailey," Stephen said.

She sighed with relief. "It's okay. I couldn't sleep anyway," she said and flipped on the lamp. "What's happened? Why didn't you call me? You said you would."

"I know. I did that on purpose." His voice was pained.

"Why? What did I do?" She instantly regretted asking him. She felt cold and sensed the dread in his voice. She didn't want to hear this. She should hang up but her hand froze and she listened.

"Hailey, I feel you deserve an explanation."

"I'm listening," she answered; her breath caught in her throat.

"I've spent the last week tying up some loose ends here. I've been offered a grant to do research work on sculpture. It's a wonderful opportunity for me . . ."

"Stephen! I'm so pleased for you. That's fantastic." She knew she should feel relieved but she feared the lowered intonation of his voice. "When do you start? Where will you be working?"

"Hailey . . ." His pause was too long, she thought. "The work is at the Sorbonne in Paris. I'll be leaving in the morning."

"Paris?" She was in shock. She must not have heard him correctly. "I don't understand . . . I thought . . ."

"That's why I felt I should be gentleman enough to tell you. I've taken the coward's way out all this time. I've known for quite a while. I should have told you before this, but I found I couldn't face you. Hailey, I love you. You must know that. But it just wasn't meant to be. I wish you happiness; you deserve the best. I'm just not it."

"Stephen, for God's sake! Don't do this!"

"Hailey, don't make it any harder for me than it already is. I'll always love you . . . but I have to go . . ." His voice cracked and the line went dead.

Stunned by his words, Hailey sat frozen as tears streamed down her cheeks. "Why, Stephen? Why are you doing this? Why?" she whispered through her sobs, but there was no answer.

# BOOK II

---

## *Rex*

# Chapter Nineteen

REX COWERT was a yesteryear name, conjuring romantic visions of the western cowboy—fist-slinging, hard-drinking and reckless. In reality, Rex had spent the majority of his thirty years living down the image and proving to the world that he had breeding and a brain. Which was not to say that he had never been drunk nor in a barroom brawl. There had been plenty of that, especially when he'd been younger.

Rex's ancestors immigrated to America from England two decades before the Civil War, when his father's family owned a vast and productive plantation called River Bend, just outside Baton Rouge. The mansion boasted Italian marble floors, French chandeliers and Persian carpets. It was a massive, eight-columned structure with the entire third floor dedicated as a ballroom for extravagant parties that were often frequented by statesmen, senators and other dignitaries.

The Cowert family had been and still were God-fearing, Bible-reading people who adhered to the work ethic and the inherent goodness of man. They were conservative, believing in states' rights and suspicious of any politician offering something for nothing. They were not flamboyant people who only displayed their wealth for appearances' sake, though there was a love of luxuries—well-bred steeds and later, fast and fancy cars. However, these were purchased only for personal satisfaction. They were, on the whole, a quiet and unassuming family, but when angered or cheated their revenge was swift and sure. When necessity demanded they could be cold and calculating, but they were honest and fair in the end.

Strong in body and spirit, they had been the kind of pioneers who had built America. The Cowert men above all cherished their God, their family and their land. Even in the worst of times, they believed in themselves and always found a way to turn the tables in their favor.

They were an openly affectionate clan, feeling no embarrassment in their need for the love they gave freely to each other. Through the generations, not a single Cowert male had ever married for reasons other than love. Each one could sentimentally and accurately recount the day he had met his lady love. They were proud of their women, who were always beautiful, for Cowert men possessed a discriminating and demanding eye. These refined and intelligent women were cherished to the point of adoration and pampered lavishly when times were good. During the lean and strife-torn years, they remained loyal to their men, encouraging them with soft words. Their courage and strength matched that of their husbands, so the offspring were injected with a double dose.

The Cowert sons and daughters displayed all the robustness, curiosity and impatience that only youth knows. Their parents allowed them the freedom to discover their individuality at early ages. They put forth equal amounts of energy and exuberance into both work and play. In their teen years many wild oats were sown, and when they finally did "settle down," there was no remorse over an experience never tried, for they had done it all. By the time each had reached their twenties, they had discovered much of the realities of life, oftentimes the hard way. But they learned from their mistakes and didn't repeat them.

The Cowerts, in true southern tradition, not only loved the land, but also were obsessed with it. They fought for it, scraped their living from it and built an empire on it. And they lost it.

After the Civil War, between the scourge of the Reconstruction government and the plague of scalawags and

176

carpetbaggers, River Bend was lost because of back taxes. The Cowerts later moved to East Texas and began anew. Farming and cattle ranching prospered again as Rex's grandfather built the new River Bend even larger than the first.

Rex's mother, a magnolia blossom of a woman, tiny and soft, was born and raised in New Orleans. The only daughter of a prominent surgeon at Oshner Clinic, she had been quietly reared and expectantly pampered. Her parents had been thrilled with her marriage to John Cowert.

Rex had been her first son. There had been three more sons to follow, all stillborn, the last taking her with him. She had been too frail to endure the rapid succession of difficult pregnancies and had hemorrhaged to death while John stood at her bedside bellowing at the doctors and nurses who knew nothing could be done. Now there was only Rex to carry on the work and the Cowert name, for his father had never remarried.

Rex had only been six years old when he rode on horseback with his grandfather from one edge of the ranch to the other. The journey had taken the better part of two days. His grandfather had promised him that all he could see would one day be his. He made Rex kneel in the dirt, scoop it with his hands and smell it.

"This is life, boy; this land. Nobody will ever take the land away from us and there's only so much of it to go around. You remember that, son."

Rex had remembered. He remembered, too, that in certain places on the ranch, a slick, black, pungent liquid seeped through the layers of rock and clay and dirt. It was the same oil that had made Rex's grandfather very, very rich.

Alex Cowert owned a large part of Rusk County in East Texas. In October 1930, C. M. "Dad" Joiner, a persistent wildcatter, struck oil on what was to be the richest oil field to date in Rusk County. In a matter of days the brush- and pine-studded section of East Texas was host to a stampede of wild-eyed speculators. Alex had seen it coming and had a seventy-two-hour jump on the city slickers who faked a country air to make a sale. Alex was a country boy and neighbor to the small farmers and ranchers located around the gusher. Sunken in the depth of the Depression, the farmers were grateful for the ready cash and, above all, they trusted the Cowerts. Alex purchased the prime leases, and as time went by, John, then in his late teens, was not above winning a small lease or two in a poker game.

To their credit, Alex and John never forgot these men nor their families through the years that passed. If a man was willing to work, John gave him a job either at the ranch or at the oil company he ran hand in hand with his father. John never believed in charity for himself or for others. "Handouts break a man's spirit," he told Rex. "Don't take from anyone that you don't give something back in return." John adhered to that philosophy and applied it to the land itself, investing a large part of himself in River Bend.

True to his Cowert blood, Rex was a dreamer. His father and grandfather had struggled to build their empire, to which Rex never believed he was rightly entitled. He was not content to be the crown prince. Rex wanted more. He wanted to do it all, just as they had, by himself. He was rebellious, impatient, somewhat of a loner and a schemer. He was a hustler with a fluid, silver tongue that could talk a rattlesnake out of its skin.

There were two distinct differences between Rex and the generations of Cowerts before him. The first was that nearly all the men had fallen in love and married in or about their eighteenth year. Rex had never come even remotely close to love, though he'd known many girls, most of whom were interested in the Cowert wealth or simply attracted to him sexually. He had never met anyone who wanted him only for himself or who could be faithful to him. As the years passed, he erected a sturdy wall around his heart to protect him from the kind of hurt his forefathers hadn't known. Though he wouldn't admit it, even to himself, he still kept hoping—and searching. He kept leaning on his father's words: "When you do meet her, the one you couldn't live without, you'll know. It will be like the sky falling in all around you. That's the way it was for your mama and me, and you'll find it, son."

Rex knew it was an overly romantic notion, but his father had never been wrong.

The second thing that set Rex apart was that he was the first Cowert to attend college. It was an accomplishment his father had been proud of. But during Rex's junior year at Tulane, he could stand the wait no longer. There was money out there just waiting to be made, and he was stuck between the pages of Greek mythology and chemistry. Impetuously, he packed his bags, quit school and drove home in his green Mustang convertible to tell his father and grandfather of his plans.

The explosion that night had been greater than the 1902 eruption of the famed man-made Spindletop oil well. The cussing, neck-grabbing, pleading and bellowing that night shook the very timbers of River Bend. When Rex finally stormed away from his father's house, the front door never again hung properly on its hinges, and his tires left permanent marks on the red brick drive. Rex Cowert was headed for Houston, where he was certain he would make his own fortune and name.

After six months in the city, his idealism rotted away like an old mesquite tree trunk, and down to his last five-dollar bill, he quit his job as a used-car salesman. The owner had never paid Rex his commissions, using the back pay as Rex's incentive to stay on.

Rex then went to work as a roustabout on an offshore oil rig in the gulf. A roustabout was simply a "gopher" who was required to do odd jobs. The more specialized position was that of a roughneck, who did the actual labor of the drilling. Roustabouts did the majority of the manual labor on the rig, and like Rex, most were inexperienced and therefore were the most prone to accidents. Luckily, the company Rex worked for required Red Cross and rig safety courses for everyone.

The pay was good and there was plenty of overtime, so his paychecks were substantial. There were five rousta-bouts on this rig, drilling from a Gulf Oil platform. All were about the same age, the eldest being twenty-one. He was the only one who was not married. They took their orders from the crane and driller operators, whose primary concern was their safety. Safe drilling practices were mandatory, for the lives of everyone depended on the conscientiousness of every other person aboard.

Each man was required to wear a fire-resistant suit, which was simultaneously a blessing and a hindrance. Between the blazing coastal sun and the protective suit, Rex felt like a boiled crayfish. Like all the men, Rex had a life jacket stowed in his cabin, but the current this far out in the gulf, over one hundred twenty-five miles, was no match for an ordinary man. Should he ever find himself swirling in the water, his only hope was to get to another platform or pray for a quick rescue. Looking down from the platform, Rex had seen schools of playful dolphins, but he'd also seen sharks.

Mother Nature seemed to be working against these men. Once, while Rex was working on the rig, a tropical depression had moved over them. They'd been awakened in the middle of the night, scrambling for their life jackets. They were silent, but their dismal thoughts thundered against the winds that whipped around them. They had all been warned never to jump over the side. The surface of the gulf was a minimum of seventy feet below the drilling floor, and hitting the water from that height would be like landing on concrete. A broken back was the least amount of bodily damage they could expect. Luckily, the killing gale that night had passed them over before it had been necessary to run to the red Whitaker escape capsule. The men had all been instructed to belt themselves in properly and close the tight-fitting door which allowed the capsule to remain buoyant even in the worst of storms.

Rex's days on the rig were twelve to fourteen hours long. The work was rigorous, the joys were few. Monotony, boredom and nausea haunted him his first months, but he was determined to earn the kind of money he needed. This time he wouldn't give up; he would learn all he could about drilling and the workings of large oil companies. As his attitude improved, so did his days.

Drilling for oil in the middle of lapis lazuli–colored waters was fantastically more sophisticated than when his father operated four-foot-high land rigs in East Texas. But the fundamental principle was the same: Punch a hole in the earth and hope this time you've struck oil or gas.

During the evenings, when the other roustabouts and roughnecks played cards, read or ate to conquer the endless boredom that plagued life on the rig, Rex made friends with the Gulf Oil company man, Jerry Helstrom.

Jerry was responsible for the multimillion-dollar project and for the safety of all the men. At night they would lean against the railing around the open-grid-floored deck watching the water lap the structure's support legs far below. Sometimes they would watch an offshoreman's fireworks display—an ignited metal-basketful of garbage flung over the side by one of the cranes; the garbage would blaze against the black onyx sky.

Jerry recognized Rex's intense desire for knowledge of the finer points in drilling. He taught Rex how to monitor the dials, gas and pressure readouts and footage drilled and then how to record the figures in relation to time. Together they would examine the cuttings scooped out of the mud. These cuttings were dislodged rock fragments. They searched for any presence of hydrocarbons and tiny bits of fossil, which would indicate the stratum the drill bit had penetrated. It was a long and arduous process.

Considering it would be over a year before production would be completed, Rex decided he couldn't spend that much time out here where his only link to civilization was a nauseating ten-hour trip in a company speedboat.

On the rig there was no telephone, lousy reception on television, no liquor and no women. Once a week the men were taken back to shore to see their families and friends. For Rex it was a wasteful time in a bar hoping to pick up a girl to spend the night with. With his gleaming emerald eyes beaming out from his handsome, deeply tanned face and a thick shock of dark hair waving down over his forehead, he was seldom refused. His days on the rig had developed his arm and back muscles, and unlike the other men, he hadn't succumbed to killing time with food. His belly was flat, and his flesh had turned rock-hard along his rib cage. He stood nearly six feet tall, even taller when he wore his handmade boots. This was a time of impermanence in his life, this job, and he felt nothing for the girls who sidled up to him as he drank a long neck beer. They were there for only one thing and so was he. Actually, he thought, they did each other a favor, relieving their sexual tensions.

The weekend over and back on the rig, he and his buddies boasted of their exploits, but secretly he wondered if this was all there would ever be for him. After a year on the rig, Rex believed the time had finally come for him to move on. At the end of the month, Rex quit his job, enough money saved to get started in business now, hitched a ride on a diesel rig and once again was Houston bound.

In 1974 the recession was deepening across the country. Especially hard hit was building. Major housing projects, high-rise condominiums and apartment complexes were going bankrupt. In all the major cities were tales of woe. Coastal resort areas targeted for expansion had only deserted, uncompleted frames strewn along the shoreline like unwanted seashells. Interest rates were soaring and so was the inflation rate. The automakers in Detroit shut down manufacturing plants, as did much northern industry. Retail business was off and savings were down. The Arab oil embargo had sent fuel prices skyrocketing. Bad weather, drought and crop failures had stifled food production all over the world. The dollar devalued, the cost of living soared and the only thing booming was the Watergate crisis.

Optimism and confidence were not things one carried around in a leather briefcase. But Rex Cowert did. While driving one day in his newly purchased used Chevrolet, he found a parcel of land for sale just past Dairy Ashford between old Katy Road and Memorial Drive, north of Westheimer. He took down the phone number on the homemade "For Sale" sign. Rex made some discreet inquiries about the area, and that night he called the owner of the property, David Oates.

Mr. Oates told him he was asking eight thousand

dollars for the four acres of soggy ground. Rex offered him four thousand cash and told him he would deliver the money in the morning. David Oates agreed to the offer almost immediately, confirming Rex's information that the man was in some sort of personal financial bind. The following morning the papers were drawn up, title and deed were transferred and both men left thinking the other a complete fool.

For six months Rex studied both real estate and oil. These were the two industries he would use to make his base for future holdings. He went to work as a commercial real-estate agent for a small, successful firm. His commissions paid his rent, gas, food and supported his penchant for handmade leather boots, vests and belts. From his first days in the city, Rex's luck gathered strength and drew important clients to him like a magnet. His soft East Texas accent, mingled with his innate respect for people, regardless of position or top-heavy financial balance sheets, brought him social invitations from all the "right" people. He did not consciously seek them out, but more often than not, his Saturday nights were spent in the finest Houston homes.

His was the kind of spirit that made Houston what it was—a city in the midst of a mosquito-infested marsh where logic declared there should be no city. Instinctively, Rex knew this was the only place on earth that could support his undiminishable hope. Leaning upon illogical gut feelings, he subdivided the land he bought and promptly found a developer who bought it for fifty thousand dollars. He parlayed that money into one investment after another.

He bought more land, always with the idea of selling it for commercial development. Always six months to a year ahead of the developers, he built a reputation, limited as it was, for being the man to watch. When Rex Cowert leaped, there were dozens of men, far wealthier than he, who followed suit. He made himself—and them—all rich!

By the time he was thirty, he owned a real-estate and development company. He built industrial parks, commercial retail strip centers, and opulent high-rise condominiums. It was in one of the penthouse suites in one of these condos he had built himself that he made his home. His offices were just down the street near the Galleria. He lived, worked and played in the midst of the "magic circle," with all the luster, excitement and glamour that name conjured. He attended the opening nights of every ballet, symphony and play that came to the Alley or Tower theaters and Jones Hall. Though his workdays often numbered seven a week and his office hours never ended at five, he still made time to enjoy life.

Though his apartment was tastefully furnished and he had spared himself no amenities, his real extravagances were his cars. He owned three: a burgundy Ferrari, a black Silverado pickup and a brown and tan replica of a 1953 MG. They were his pride and joy, and many a Sunday afternoon he would drive to Memorial Park, stop underneath the shadiest oak he could find and painstakingly wax every inch of his car. Never trusting upkeep of his cars to anyone but himself, he kept them in perfect condition. Besides, those Sundays in the park kept him busy and made the loneliest day of the week more bearable.

He had plenty of friends he could have called and there was no lack of calls from women inviting him to spend the day with them. Due to some quirk in his upbringing, he told himself, he was unable to accept. Sundays were still sacrosanct to him, somehow belonging to families—the kind that came with fried chicken dinners, old silverware and smiling children. They should be spent with someone special. And for Rex, there was no one special. He decided he must have some character flaw, for he had never found anyone with whom he could be truly comfortable, never himself. Caught between his money and his success-laden notoriety, he was held in a web of his own making. There were Saturday night girls, wearing Daddy's diamonds, who wanted him for an ornamental escort, and Wednesday evening women who wanted only his youthful body with no questions asked. He had had plenty of time to look around, and he didn't like what he saw. And worse, he wasn't very proud of the calluses his heart had acquired.

For nearly a year, Rex had been dating Pamela Richland. At the mere thought of her, his blood surged. Pamela was an unbelievably gorgeous woman. There was not a blemish, nor freckle, nor bulge nor clump of cellulite on her body. Her skin, that tawny, golden, healthy velvet reminiscent of Neapolitan beauties, glowed without the aid of cosmetics. Her lips were naturally cherry pink, full and sensuous. She had thickly lashed eyes, black and shiny as onyx pearls. With long, sleek legs, narrow hips and full, round breasts, she had the kind of body whose picture appeared on the centerfold of *Playboy* or *Penthouse* magazines.

Every article of clothing she owned—the scandalously low-cut silk dresses, the too-small cashmere sweaters, and the clinging designer jeans and slacks—was purchased with an extremely critical eye. They were all outrageously expensive, all classics that she wore with a queenly dignity that won her the respect of all her admirers.

Pamela's background was similar to his in that both their fathers were self-made. Once while spending a weekend at Walden on Lake Conroe north of Houston, Pamela told Rex about her father.

In Pamela's estimation, he was the shrewdest business-man in the city of Houston, probably in all of Texas. But he hadn't always been rich. It was not until she was five years old that he began to make it big. That had been when her mother had run off with another man.

Harry Richland had made nothing of himself, being content solely with his beautiful wife, adoring baby daughter and a boring, middle-class rut of a job as a broker at Merrill Lynch. Arlette Richland had dreams of diamonds, furs and chauffeur-driven limousines. By the age of twenty-eight, they were as close to the reality of her life as a Disney cartoon.

When a handsome investor from New York came to Houston to buy land for the purpose of drilling oil, Harry invited him to his home for dinner. A week later, when the investor left, land leases in hand, he had packed Arlette with him.

Pamela hadn't seen her mother since, but from that day on, her father preached nothing but the almighty power of money and oil, and he set out to get some for himself. Never speculative, always investigating each project to the "nth" degree, his pace was slow but steady and very sure. There was no luck involved in his investments, for they were calculated and well founded. Harry believed that anything left to chance was just as apt to turn sour as it was to pay off. And pay off his did, so that now, in his fifty-fifth year, he was well respected, rich and powerful; and he was still in love with Arlette. He'd finally become the kind of man she had wanted, and it did him no good. He was as miserable now as he'd been the day Arlette had taken off.

Pamela had told Rex then that she wasn't sure she believed in love. She told him that she had learned from her parents' mistakes. And Rex had to admit she was not only more sophisticated, but also more intelligent and worldly than Harry Richland could ever dream of being. Pamela believed in relationships between equally matched people. Together, she said, they were the perfect blend of money, looks, sociability and potential. At the time, Rex had believed her statement to be conceited. But Pamela was bluntly honest and unnervingly realistic.

Rex was too experienced and tinged with enough cynicism to believe any longer in John Cowert's ideal of romantic love. No, Pamela was right. Love was something that belonged in another place and another time.

# Chapter Twenty

HAILEY had spent months trying to understand why Stephen had left her so abruptly. She told herself the inexplicable tears she shed were only from the pressures at work, but deep inside she knew they were for Stephen. She had trusted and believed in him. Sometimes, when he had merely held her hand, she'd felt so much at peace, as if everything in the world were right. Now her days and nights seemed barren. There were no longer peaks of excitement, only dull, vacant hours that never seemed to end. He had been her confidant, fulfilling a need no one else could.

He had been a blend of romance, friendship, fun and authoritative intelligence. She had come to depend on him and had asked him for guidance and advice. What had she done to fail him, and worse, how would she make it through the days without him? She had to admit she cared a great deal about him. He had told her he loved her! What reason did he have to leave? She had to face the fact that now she was left with painful tears and could only hope to let it die somehow, as he had so *easily* done.

Why had he taken over her life when he knew all along he would walk away? Had he planned it—the leaving—right from the beginning?

Sometimes she found herself actually jumping with hope when the phone rang, still needing to hear his voice. And then once again she found herself plummeted back to reality. She would never hear from him again.

He'd told her he would influence her life more than any other man before or after him. How right he had been! So much had changed for her. Even though there had always been that nagging suspicion in her brain that told her not to trust him, that didn't lessen the pain of a lost friend.

Of one thing she was sure: She would never know what really happened. The only intelligent course was to bury it and go on with her life. Somehow she had done just that. She revamped her thinking and reset her priorities. She had her children, her talent and her job. They were enough to fill anyone's life. Her days were so full that by midnight she fell exhausted into bed, knowing she had but a few hours' reprieve until the cycle began again. Packing lunches and doing household chores and laundry at six in the morning, and then off to work until five, arriving home, fixing dinner, helping with homework during her few precious hours with Joey and Kim; and then she would paint until she could barely focus and ultimately was overcome by sleep.

Two weekends a month, Mike hurriedly picked up the children. He usually came and went in a rush, not saying much to Hailey. She followed his lead. It was obviously still too painful for him to discuss anything but the children. Sometimes it seemed strange not to give him a quick kiss good-bye, as she had done for so many years, but he was so tense that she dared not even touch him.

As far as Joey and Kim were concerned, these weekends were exciting reprieves from the chores and mundane life with their mother. She knew she was fortunate, in that they never went through the stages of pitting one parent against the other. Hailey had to work harder than Mike; the children understood that and most times were more than willing to help her. They were all growing, and it was a good feeling. Hailey's diligence had paid off in the form of a good salary at work, and the fees for her portraits were piling up at the bank. She still had invitations to parties and she accepted only from those with whom she had become friends. She attended the parties alone, which increased her mystique with the columnists.

In the past months she had assumed the responsibility

of designing corporate displays. Leonard had discovered there were times when her presence was more to his advantage outside the store. Today was one of those days. She had an eleven-thirty appointment at Cowert, Inc., to plan an appropriate supplement to the owner's existing office collection. Leonard had informed her that Mr. Cowert desired something more eclectic than the pure western look he'd already achieved. Armed with a smattering of prints and information, she drove to the South Post Oak address Leonard had jotted down for her.

He was standing with his back to her, next to the secretary's desk, barking orders into the receiver of the phone. He had one hand shoved into the back pocket of his jeans, tapping his leather boot against the thick, camel-colored carpet. His brown and tan plaid shirt was shot with gold threads, and over it he wore a soft tan leather vest. His brown hair glistened in the fluorescent light as he quickly looked toward the ceiling. The secretary, nonplussed at the obscene language with which he punctuated his statements, kept handing him small square memos, which he promptly read, crumpled up and tossed into the wastepaper basket.

Hailey quietly shut the door behind her but kept her distance until he slammed the receiver down, at which point she jumped with a start.

"Goddamned son-of-a-bitch," he sneered, and without turning around, he stalked into his office and slammed the door.

Hailey blinked three times and smiled wanly as she approached the secretary. "Hello," she said, walking through the almost visible blue haze the man's anger had left behind. "I'm Hailey James and I have an appointment with Mr. Cowert."

The girl checked her appointment book and then looked up. "I'm sorry, I don't see anything here with your name . . ."

"Perhaps it was made under L'Artiste du Monde. It's concerning the art selections for this office," Hailey explained. "Is Mr. Cowert in?"

"That," she answered, nodding toward the still-reverberating door, "was Mr. Cowert."

"Really?" Hailey asked, incredulously looking over to the door.

"Yes, really. Ah! I do see your gallery's name here. Just a second and I'll see if he's free." She picked up the phone, announced Hailey and then hung up. "Go right in. He'll see you now."

"Is it safe?"

"I doubt it," the girl said and laughed.

Hailey tapped on the door and heard him answer her knock with the appropriate, "Come in."

He stood up and walked around the desk, his hand outstretched. "How do you do? I'm Rex Cowert."

Hailey took his hand, and the moment his flesh touched hers, she had the uncanny feeling that she'd met him someplace before. She remembered shaking his hand and muttering something, then she sat in a chair opposite him as he began a detached explanation of what he wanted.

He felt the offices too Texan. He needed a change. Pacing about the room, he stated that he wanted to rid himself of such tacky though sentimental adornments as the piece of tanned leather hanging on the wall, and the Texas longhorns. The Remington would stay, but that was all. Perhaps he could bring in more color. It was so common, his tan leather upholstery, camel carpeting and paneled walls. He wanted something drastic. He wanted a miracle.

Hailey watched him as his green eyes darted about the room. He hadn't yet really seen her, he was so involved in his explanations. From the discarded pile of memories in the back of her mind, the vision of him nearly running Stephen over with his brown and tan MG that night at the Gregsons' spiraled to the forefront.

"You almost killed him, you know," she blurted out, not realizing she had voiced her thoughts aloud.

He stopped dead center of the room and stared at her as if she were totally insane. "What in the hell are you talking about?"

Hailey wanted to sink farther into the chair, she was so

embarrassed, but she went on. "My date. You almost ran him over one night at the Gregsons', last summer."

He was unconvinced. "I don't remember it."

"You drove a tan sports car, convertible type. Your wife is a tall brunette. She wore a white dress and you were dressed much like you are now, but with a hat in your hand."

Now he was definitely intrigued. "Not my wife. That was Pam. Where were you? I didn't see you at the party."

"We were just leaving. The party was over when you arrived," she said in her best reprimanding tones.

*"Touché . . . Miss . . ."*

"James," she reminded him. "I'm surprised I didn't see you again at some of their other parties."

"They're more friends of Pam's than mine, actually. Do you and your friend see them often? The Gregsons, I mean?" Rex moved closer to her and sat on the edge of the desk, one leg still planted firmly on the floor. As he spoke he leaned closer. She was beautiful, all that moonbeam-colored hair and eyes as blue as the sea. She sat so stiffly, as if she feared he would pounce on her at any minute. She appealed to him. She was smiling at him and he saw something he hadn't seen since he'd left East Texas: trusting honesty. She wasn't hiding a thing, as if she'd stuck herself out there in the world, knowing she might be hurt but willing to take the chance.

"I don't see them as often as I did when Stephen used to take me . . ."

"You and Stephen . . . you . . . don't see him anymore?" His emerald eyes flickered, she thought, as he leaned even closer and his voice grew softer and more fluid, as if it were running over water-smoothed stones.

"No, not at all," she answered. What was she doing? This was a business appointment and here they were discussing personal details of their lives.

"Hmmm. Have lunch with me. Please?" he asked, his smile caressing her and exiling her objections.

"But . . . the paintings. I've brought some samples . . ." She was hesitant, struggling to regain her business façade. She wished he would stop looking at her like that.

It wasn't the hungry, lecherous drool she'd seen so much of in the past year. It was like cool summer rain, refreshing and brand-new. She was entering virgin territory and she felt her fingers turn icy as her fears wrestled with her impulsive nature.

"We'll discuss it over a glass of wine and a steak?" he said, glancing at her lithe body. "Maybe a spinach salad, on second thought. You don't look much like the steak type."

She laughed and her tension eased, but only a little. "I'm not, but what made you say that?"

"You're too thin to be steak and potatoes type," and he laughed, too.

He picked up her briefcase and took her hand as she stood. It was a soft hand and warm except for the very ends of her fingers. She was nervous. That was good, he thought while she walked in front of him as they left the office and entered the corridor. She glided like a spread-winged bird over the pines; she even smelled different somehow, though he thought the perfume a familiar one. It was just that on her, everything was different, and that intrigued him more.

Hailey couldn't see him, standing behind her as he was, but she could feel him all around her. She half expected his arms to cover her shoulders like a warm shawl as they waited for the elevator. She felt like an idiot thinking such things. She had never in her life reacted like this to anyone. She must stop! Then she wondered what it would feel like to have him hold her. Not tightly, not one of those bone-crushing bear hugs, but more like cradling. He stood next to her and she felt his arm as it brushed past her to depress the elevator button again. He was the impatient type, she surmised. She took a chance and looked at him. He was staring at her with such intensity she couldn't drag herself away from him. She wanted to say something. A cliché about the weather would have been handy, but none came to mind. If she would have smiled just then, it would have been forced and phony. He didn't smile either, but he kept sucking her into the maelstrom of emotions from which she'd only recently rescued herself.

The elevator door sprang open, shattering the moment. Hailey was relieved as she stepped forward. She was acting like a teenager. Where was her composure? She had better find it fast or he would think she wanted to have lunch in his apartment!

"Now that you've seen the offices, have you got anything specific in mind as to what I can do to make it more appealing?"

"Dynamite might be the quickest solution," Hailey joked and at once thought her statement ill timed, but he took it good-naturedly. "Do you want my honest opinion?"

"That's what I'm paying you for, aren't I?"

"And handsomely, too, I might add," she said airily. "I think you should keep it much the way it is. You wouldn't look good amid abstracts or French Impressionists, unless you felt comfortable with them. I think with a new arrangement, better lighting and a few additional, maybe more colorful prints, you won't need anything more. What's wrong with western art?" she asked, her inflection implying that he was unpatriotic for requesting this overhaul.

"Not a damned thing. I like it. Love it, in fact, if it's good."

"Then you should have it. And you will. I'll work something up that will give you the sensation of change but the reassurance of familiarity."

"You know what, Miss James?"

"What's that, Mr. Cowert?"

"You've just described how I feel about you," he said as the doors opened and he grabbed her hand and they rushed out of the elevator to his Ferrari, which was parked in front of the building.

Hailey sat up all night smiling and humming to herself. She was as keyed up as a five-year-old who'd been to a birthday party. Rex had taken her to Ninfa's for lunch and they ordered everything off the menu. Authentic Mexican food had been a revelation to her, for the broiled ribs, boiled shrimp and marinated vegetables were exquisitely prepared. She was glad they hadn't drowned everything in jalapeño peppers. Rex had talked a mile a minute, barely taking time to eat. Mostly she had just listened. He'd given her his life story in disconnected pieces that she tried to puzzle together, but there were too many gaps. But then, she thought, just how much could be crammed into an hour and a half?

Precisely just why she'd had such a marvelous time bewildered her. A good deal of the time he had talked only business, a subject she detested. Her lunches with Stephen had been in more romantic, less crowded places and yet, with Rex, she had felt as if they had been all alone, made invisible to others by some secret they shared. It was all so unsettling and because her attraction to him was so powerful, she couldn't trust it, nor herself. This inexplicable giddiness she experienced when she thought of him was either infatuation or sexual need. Probably both. Maybe that's just what she needed right now, a lover. She wondered if she could handle one of those affairs where they both knew it would end in a few months or, if you were lucky, a year. She well knew that was all that was left today, interludes in which they knew the ending before they began.

"Why bother? What's the point of getting involved?" she asked herself as she cleaned her brush of the last vestiges of yellow paint. The logical answer was that there was no purpose. She had already been through all the heartache one person could stand, and she wasn't about to set herself up for more pain. That was being just plain stupid. She had finally gotten her life into some semblance of order. There was no room for Rex Cowert in her life.

# Chapter Twenty-one

HAILEY had been at her desk for exactly fifteen minutes when he called.

"Hailey, this is Rex," he said in that drawl that slurred the consonants and sounded unnervingly sensual.

Caught off guard, she held her breath and didn't react instantly. "Hi," was all she could manage. Now what did he want? she thought.

"I was wondering if you, er . . . if you had anything in particular in mind for my offices. Maybe something there in the gallery I could see," he said.

"Why, yes, I do, Rex. I was going to put some things together this morning. You could see them this afternoon if you like."

"That'll be fine." He paused. "I was also wondering if you'd like to have dinner with me this evening," he asked.

Silence. Hailey's instincts told her not to tempt fate. "I don't think that's possible."

"You've already made plans?"

"Sort of. I promised my children I'd take them to McDonald's for supper."

"Children? You're kidding! How many?"

"Two. A boy and a girl. I've been putting in some late hours, and tonight was my night off. I needed a break."

"Yeah, I know the feeling. Say! How would it be if I took you all to McDonald's?" he said, pleased with his suggestion. He just had to see her one more time.

"No!" she responded a bit too quickly and too ada-mantly.

"Hey! I'm not going to kidnap them or something," he said.

"I'm sorry. It's not that. It's just that my private life is my private life. Sacred territory." She hoped he would understand that Joey and Kim had to be protected.

"I see," he said. His voice had dropped and fallen away. The pause at the other end disturbed her more than she cared to admit. He didn't understand. There was some-thing wrong. Why was his opinion so important to her? He *was* just a client.

"Rex, do you still want to see these paintings today?"

"Not today. I'm pretty tied up. Tomorrow is better. I'll be there after my three-o'clock appointment. How would that be?"

"That's fine. I'll see you then," she said. He mumbled a vacant good-bye and hung up.

Hailey stared at the dead receiver. Who did he think he was, anyway? She wasn't about to give him a blueprint of her personal life. Obviously, the fact that she had two children categorized her into a group of untouchables. It was probably just as well. A man like that was only looking for a quick fling and she wanted no part of it.

Now that she thought about it, he had seemed just a little too good to be true, the fancy cars and his dancing emerald eyes and little-boyish look. It was best she keep this relationship strictly business.

Rex was miffed at Hailey's businesslike attitude toward him over the phone. And then there was that little scenario about her private life. He wondered if she really had any children, or if this was her way of brushing him off. Maybe all he was to her was the commission on the damn paintings she was selling him. Before he had a chance to contemplate it any longer, his secretary buzzed him.

"Yes," he said.

"Miss Richland is here to see you, sir."

"Send her in," he replied, his smile growing wide again.

Pamela! At least she wouldn't shunt him off like last month's invoice.

She glided into the office dressed in a burgundy silk dress that outlined her shapely thighs when she walked. Her raven-black hair fell down her back and she wore gold leaf-shaped earrings and a matching necklace. Her eyes smoldered when she smiled at him.

"Hello, baby doll," he said, taking her in his arms and kissing her. "What brings you here this early in the day?"

"Before you made a jillion appointments I thought I would see if you were free for dinner, luv. It'll be my treat. I'm cooking," she purred and ran her hands down his back.

"Sounds very inviting, but I . . ."

She placed two well-manicured fingers against his lips to stop his protests. "What if I threw in soft music, romantic candlelight, French champagne, filet mignon . . ."

He laughed. "Okay, okay. I give in. I'd love to. What time?"

"Eight?"

"That's super. I'll see you then," he said and started to turn back to his desk.

She quickly pulled him to herself and kissed him long and hard. Her hands ran down his back as she pressed her hips into his. She crushed her full breasts to his chest and moaned with pleasure.

"Pamela," he said, almost breathless, "if you don't stop this, I'll never get any work done and dinner will have to be lunch!"

"Hmmm," her eyes widened. "I do like the way you think."

He put his hands on her shoulders and turned her around. "Now out with you, woman," he said, gently pushing her forward. Just as she reached the door he said, "Say, baby, do you want me to bring anything?"

"Just your toothbrush," she replied, blew him a kiss and was gone.

Hailey assembled a color lithograph, "The Wood Gatherers," by Earl Bliss. It was one of her favorites, with its snow scene of Crow Indians, tepees and horses. She thought its vitality, strength and yet dreamlike quality would appeal to Rex. As she worked, relating paintings to the personality of the purchaser, it was impossible not to try to dissect the enigma of Rex Cowert. She sensed somehow that most western art, with its tendency to realism, was not enough for Rex. She chose Mike Scovel's portrait of John Wayne's physiognomy hovering over a western scene. Surrealistic work would be perfect. A Bob Pack bronze deer, another fantasy-filled Earl Bliss and two American Indian art oils whose theme was the spiritual world rounded out the collection. With the Frederic Remingtons and Charles M. Russells he already owned, he would now have a collection he could display with pride.

When Rex arrived nearly at closing time, she had spent the entire day thinking of no one but him. Her smile was genuine and warm.

He stood just inside the doorway, gazing at her. He moved toward her as if he were being pulled by an undertow. She looked like a Victorian china doll with her hair wrapped in a soft knot on the top of her head and a halo of tiny silver wisps surrounding her face. The blouse she wore was an almost transparent vanilla cream crepe with a high ruffle at the neck, and she wore a cornflower-blue ribbon around the base of her throat. Its long sleeves ended in ruffles that covered a third of her hand, and her skirt was a slim brown linen that buttoned up the front. The long workday had erased the majority of her makeup, and she looked as if she had just stepped from the shower. When she spoke and said "hello" his gambler's instinct told him to play out the hand.

"I've got everything displayed in the office," she said, never taking her eyes from him. She delayed a moment and then she walked into the glass-partitioned area, where she turned on the spotlights. He pretended to study the items, all the while knowing they were exactly what he wanted. The bronze was only twenty inches long, ten inches wide and sixteen inches high, but displayed on the Plexiglas stand, it overpowered him. He wanted them all.

"You've done extremely well, Hailey. I expected to pick maybe one or two things. But they're all terrific! How did you know what I'd want? I mean . . . this is incredible! If I'd had them commissioned myself, I couldn't have expressed my needs better."

"Why, thank you," she said, a bit overwhelmed by his compliment. "I just tried to fit the different works to your personality."

"Ah! Am I that readable?" His eyes wandered back to her.

"No, you aren't." Her voice trailed. "In fact, you are quite complex and intriguing . . ." She didn't want to say all this. It just came out. She seemed unable to stop herself. She knew she must be blushing, and that made her even angrier at herself.

"It sounds as if you like me." He was testing the water before he stuck his foot in.

"I never said I didn't . . ." Then she remembered the phone call and his hesitancy. "Rex, I hope you didn't take what I said about my life with my children personally."

"Shouldn't I have? Oh, that's right. What is it? Your ground rules don't include letting your men meet your kids."

"Mr. Cowert," Hailey said, blushing furiously, "our lack of communication is causing us both some consternation. I'll be honest with you. There are no 'men.' I've just been divorced and I'm trying to keep the children on an even keel. And I don't want to expose them to any men but their father. They don't need to know every time I have a date. I don't want them to become attached to someone who is eventually going to walk away from them. And me."

"You've got it all figured out, don't you?" he said, his sarcasm singeing his words.

"Wouldn't you feel the same if you had two lives to protect?"

"Yes, I guess I would," he said after thinking about it for a moment. "But answer one question."

"Sure," she said, noticing he took a few steps closer to her.

"You don't believe in love, do you?"

"Of course I do. I love my children . . ." she was saying, but he interrupted her again.

"No. I mean the kind between a man and a woman."

"I don't know. I've never fallen in love with anyone."

"But you were married," he blurted out and then realized how his naïveté had surfaced. Or maybe it was just that she was so beautiful and kind that he couldn't imagine someone like this going through life without love.

"I know . . ." Hailey felt her guilt fly around inside her like bats in a cage.

He could see pain wash away her color. "I've never been in love, either. Sometimes I think it was invented by the record companies to make money."

She looked at him, this person who was studying her like a jeweler. He seemed to know her inner workings at a glance. How could he do that? Beyond his handsome face, past the lean and muscular physique, who was he? "I guess we've both been leaning on our cryptic eye a bit heavily, haven't we?"

He laughed. "I think so. Listen, since I can't take you out tonight, how about tomorrow night?"

"I don't know. I've got a lot of work to do this week . . ."

"Let's be honest. Do you want to go out with me at all?"

"Yes! I do. It's just that I've got to think of Joey and Kim first," she explained.

"Okay. Now that we've established that, you pick the day," he said, crossing his arms over his chest as if he'd just given her a challenge he knew she wouldn't refuse.

"Saturday is my only free night, and the children will be with their father all weekend. You probably already have plans for Saturday, don't you?"

"Nothing I can't get out of. Saturday it is. How about eight o'clock?"

"Wonderful. That'll give me time to change after work."

"You work Saturdays, too?" he asked disbelievingly.

"Yes, most of them, anyway. I have to earn my living just like everybody else. Speaking of work, when should we deliver these paintings?"

"Early next week, and then I want you to arrange them

for me," he said and winked at her. "That way I get to see you one more time. Tell your boss to bill me for your time."

"Oh, don't worry about that! He will!" She laughed and then suddenly remembered the time. "Oh, my gosh! I forgot how late it was. I've got to pick up Joey and Kim at the day-care center. They charge me for being late. You don't mind if we cut this short, do you?"

"Yes, I do, but that's all right. I'll see you Saturday. I'll give you a call later on this week," he said, and then he took her hand and kissed it and she felt a tickle as his moustache brushed across her skin. "Bye, Hailey."

He turned around and walked away with a swagger and adjusted his black felt cowboy hat. She resisted the impulse to call him back. "Go with us tonight," she wanted to say. But her damn logic superseded her desire to be with him . . . just for a little while longer.

# Chapter Twenty-two

DURING the remaining days of the week, Rex called Hailey every morning just as she arrived at work and always before she left for the day. They talked about their days, their nights, work, her children and he always told her that he missed her. She didn't tell him she thought about him. She was wary of his intrusion into her life, but at the same time she was conscious of her desire to be with him. The ambivalence she felt concerned her. Rex was the kind of man who would have been the hero in one of her mother's fairy tales. He couldn't possibly be real! She was not going to allow herself to depend on anyone. She had come close to being romantically involved with Stephen, and look at the emotional turmoil that had caused! She could have fun with Rex, but she would keep him at arm's length and proceed with ultimate caution, she told herself.

Protestations to the contrary, Hailey found that waiting for Saturday night to arrive was like sitting at a railroad crossing waiting for the slow cattle and freight cars to pass.

Hailey ripped the cleaner's bag away from the teal-colored silk dress she would wear. It was simple, with a mandarin collar, buttons down the front, self-belt and long, widely cuffed sleeves. She wore her hair down and curled over her shoulders. She fastened one side of her hair behind her ear with a mother-of-pearl comb and wore no other jewelry besides two pearl studs in her ears. She had half an hour to put on her makeup, so she ran naked downstairs and poured a glass of white wine to calm her nerves. This was just dinner, after all, not one of the parties that she and Stephen had frequented. She was going to have a good time, she told herself, and she would keep up her guard.

She had just finished applying brown eyeshadow and mascara when the doorbell rang. "Impossible," she said, checking the clock radio on her nightstand. "He's early!" She snatched up a silver satin robe and rushed down the stairs, tying the sash as she went. She threw the door open.

He was leaning on one outstretched arm against the doorjamb, his sports jacket flung over his shoulder. The open collar of his plaid shirt revealed a tan chest, and his amused smile was meant to entice her. "I know I'm early, but I couldn't wait." His emerald eyes inspected her from the tip of her head to the pink-frosted polish she had just applied to her toenails. "I like what you're wearing," he said huskily.

Hailey stepped back to avoid the compelling force of him. "Come in and I'll finish dressing," she answered quickly.

"Thanks," he said as he shut the door. "You go ahead, baby," he said as she nervously turned toward the stairs. "Hey! Baby, you got a beer? I could sure use one." His eyes twinkled.

"Sure. Help yourself. There's some in the 'fridge."

"I'll find it," he said, lazily letting his eyes travel over the length of her.

Hailey's knees were shaking as she mounted the stairs and stepped into her dress. Her fingers fumbled over the buttons, but she finally accomplished the awesome task. God! What was the matter with her? She swallowed a big gulp of wine, glanced in the mirror and realized she had forgotten the rest of her makeup. Too late. He'd already seen her. She swished on some blusher and a tiny bit of lip gloss. She didn't want to waste five seconds that she could be spending with Rex. She started out of the room and then nearly forgot her shoes. She picked them up and then went downstairs.

He was sitting on the couch looking at a stack of snapshots she'd taken of Joey and Kim.

"Boy! That was fast!" he said when she entered the room. "I figured you'd be up there for at least an hour."

"I'd rather be with you," she said, wondering what possessed her to say these things. She must have looked very foolish standing there struggling with her feelings.

"I'm glad you did. I feel the same way. Besides, you're already gorgeous. You don't need to do anything more," he said, standing up and coming over to stand in front of her. He touched her hair, gingerly at first. It was soft, like corn silk, no hair spray. "Your kids are beautiful. They look just like you. Especially the color of their hair. Sometime, when you trust me enough, maybe you'll let me meet them," he said, wistfully letting his hand sink into the folds and waves of her hair.

"We'll see . . ." she replied. He knew how she felt about that subject and she let it drop. She didn't want to start the evening on a bad note. "Are you ready to go?"

"Sure. I'll just take my beer with me. Okay?"

She nodded and he put his arm around her shoulder as they walked to the door. "Aren't you going to put your shoes on?" he asked with a grin.

"Huh? Oh," she chuckled tensely. "I . . . I almost forgot."

"That's okay, baby. It happens to the best of us. You didn't tell me you were the absentminded type."

"I'm not . . . normally."

"Oh," he replied with a knowing and pleased smile.


They dined at the Rivoli, where Rex knew the *maître d'* and the wine steward personally. They sat in a corner, ostensibly to be as inconspicuous as possible. Through wine, snails, veal marsala and cappuccino, Rex and Hailey spoke in hushed tones, their heads so close together their foreheads nearly touched. Rex held her hand almost all evening, often pulling it to his lips and kissing both the back of it and her palm. Once as they were finishing their coffee and waiting for the Courvoisier he had ordered, his lips lingered over her index finger taking her fingertips into his mouth, and when he did so, he closed his eyes.

They clinked the rims of their brandy balloons and he toasted her beauty. His eyes burned into her over the rim of his glass and she found it impossible to look away. When the waiter brought the bill, she glanced around the restaurant and spied one of the reporters who had followed her comings and goings during those days with Stephen. He winked at her, letting her know that on Monday morning she would see her name in print again.

Unnerved, feeling like a hunted felon, she turned to Rex. "Could we leave soon?" she asked anxiously.

"Sure. What's wrong?" he asked, investigating her dismayed expression.

"Nothing. I'd . . . well . . . Where are we going?" she asked, not paying attention to her words as her eyes cut back to the reporter who was still watching them.

"You'll see," he said, leaving a large tip for the excellent service. He took her hand and they left.

They drove to the Galleria and parked the car near Lord & Taylor's. As he opened the door for her, she asked, "What are we doing here?"

"Dancing, baby. You do dance, don't you?"

"I think so. It's been a while. I'm pretty rusty."

"You'll muddle through." He took her hand and they ran up the stairs and down the corridors to the Galleria Plaza Hotel. The elevators deposited them on the top floor, where Annabelle's overlooked the Magic Circle. The dance floor was immense, with strips of tiny red lights between the wooden parquet blocks. An overhead fog machine immersed the disco dancers in a thick haze. Rex quickly ordered two drinks and pulled a reluctant Hailey to the center of the mirrored dance area. It didn't take her long to follow his steps. He was the perfect partner, using his strong arms to lead her, and his hands to signal his next move. As Hailey watched him she thought, "John Travolta could take lessons!" There wasn't a dance step he didn't know.

But when they danced the first slow dance, that was when Rex and Hailey had the floor almost to themselves. His dips were so low that Hailey's hair brushed the floor. She kept her feet next to his, their legs nearly intertwined as they twirled and spun across the floor. When he stopped to sway his hips from left to right, she followed his every move.

"I've danced with a lot of girls, but you've got a natural rhythm," he said. As they danced, they talked with their eyes, and their bodies kept time to the music. There was no set plan they followed; just feeling the music was all they knew.

She was the most sensual woman he'd ever known; it radiated from her every pore. This was heaven, dancing with her—holding her; he wanted to crush her close to his chest. From the moment he had first seen her, he had wanted to hold her, and this had been his excuse to have the opportunity. He couldn't let this end.

"You were made for me, you know," he said, hoping the statement didn't sound like some line out of a "B" movie.

"Is that so? How do you know that?"

"God told me," he replied and gently pulled her head toward him and let it rest on his shoulder. He put both arms around her and kissed her neck.

He certainly had an original approach, she thought, feeling the tingle his lips caused. She wondered how many women had heard it and what his success ratio was. Damn! She wished he wouldn't hold her so close!

As the song ended they quickly spun around the floor one last time and then he bent her backward until she thought she would surely fall, but his arms held her steady.

He pulled her up to him and smiled.

"Let's have a drink. I could use one," he said, wiping the sweat from his brow.

They sat in a curved red banquette next to the window so they could see the city lights. "See that tall building over there?" He pointed to the northeast, toward Memorial Drive. Hailey nodded. "That's where I live. It's a better view from there because you can see downtown, too."

"I don't believe you," she answered, unable to imagine anything more beautiful than this.

"Ah-ha! A doubting Thomas! I'll show you, young lady!" He tossed a ten-dollar bill on the table and once again grabbed her hand and they were off.

Before Hailey knew what had happened, she was standing in the foyer to Rex Cowert's apartment. Penthouses had always conjured visions of opulence and sophistication. In the case of bachelors they were dens of iniquity, where drunken orgies were held. But this realm of rustic Victoriana had been totally unexpected.

The walls of the entry and the large living and dining rooms were covered in a natural grass cloth. A solid cream rug widely banded in deep navy rested atop the dark-stained plank flooring. In front of the flagstone fireplace sat two rolled-arm sofas covered in a cream and navy cotton print, and between them was an unusual coffee table whose base was a huge tree trunk. Its hundred years of "rings" were dramatically displayed through the clear oval glass top. Above the fireplace hung three antique shotguns. Glass windows wrapped around the room, and the wooden slat blinds had been lifted to display the impressive cityscape below.

Hailey was instantly drawn to the view and stood in wonder as Rex prepared two drinks at his copper-topped bar. She was commenting on the view of Buffalo Bayou and Memorial Drive when he came and stood beside her.

"You're right, it is a better view from here," she said, taking the drink from his hand.

"I thought you might like it. You know, New York City seen from this high is like being inside a meteor shower, there are so many concentrated lights. Chicago has the lakefront and then there's the Hollywood Hills, with its glittering stars and lights. But Houston . . . it's different. It's still brand-new, relatively speaking, and to me it holds the promise of youth."

Hailey watched him as he surveyed the sights outside the window like a proud father. "You really love this city, don't you?"

He looked back at her and smiled. "I sure do, baby. When I look out there, I know how my granddaddy felt when he set to building River Bend. Guess it must be the pioneer in my blood." He chuckled lightly but his eyes were deadly serious.

"What's River Bend?" she asked, sipping her Kahlua.

"That's my family's home in East Texas. I don't get back as often as I'd like, but we're pretty close . . . at least we are now."

"Weren't you always close?" she asked.

"Oh, a few years back we had a difference of opinion, you might say. My daddy didn't approve of the way I was living my life. He sort of had his own plans for me. We didn't see eye to eye for the better part of two years. But everything has been resolved now."

"I'm glad. I guess it's just as hard on our parents as it is on us when there's a misunderstanding," she said, ruefully looking down at her glass.

"You sound as if you speak from experience," he replied, lifting her chin with his forefinger. "I hope your rift with your parents is over."

"There's just my mother. My father died just before I left for college. But I think Sonja and I are mending. She seems to understand me better now."

"I'm glad for you, too," he answered, but still her former lightheartedness hadn't returned. "Say! How would you like a tour of my ranch in the sky here?"

"Is that what you call this?"

"That was my idea, but I didn't do such a good job."

"I wouldn't say that. I like it. It's very comfortable, homey." She saw his eyebrows crunch together with a hurt look. "That was a compliment. I would have been disappointed if you'd had tons of stereo equipment, sleek sofas and dimmer switches on all the lights."

Rex nearly broke out in a howl. "Yeah! I get your point. This isn't a typical bachelor's pad, is it?"

"Thank God! Not that kind of bachelor, anyway," and Hailey laughed with him.

As they walked toward the dining area, she thought how good it was to be here with him. She wasn't in the least bit afraid, though she should have been. It was the first time she'd ever been in a man's apartment. It was the notion that frightened her, but not Rex himself. Somehow she knew that if she turned around and asked him to take her home this instant, he would do it without argument. She hoped she wasn't just being naïve again!

"This table and chairs was my grandmother's. I started with them and built everything else around them. I guess that's why I like Victorian so much. Oak tables like this are hard to come by."

"It's beautiful," she commented, observing that the Tiffany lamp hanging above the table was not a reproduction. The adjacent kitchen was large enough to eat in, though in its center was simply a chopping block. Above the ranch oak cabinets with leaded-glass insert door panels were baskets of ferns and ivy. From the kitchen they went to a small library/music room that housed an upright piano and at least a half-dozen guitars and stacks of sheet music. Hailey twirled around to face him.

"Do you play both?"

"Sure do. I'll have to write a song for you sometime," he said. "You're the kind of woman who inspires a songwriter." His voice had lowered an octave and they were standing so close that Hailey thought he would surely feel her pulse quicken. He took her drink and placed it along with his on the bookshelf. He cupped her face in his hands and looked deeply into her eyes. "I liked it when we were dancing."

"I did, too," she whispered and took a step backward. Her commitment not to get involved was drowning in her feelings for him. She wanted to know what it would be like to feel his full, sensual lips against hers, but she checked herself and remained cool.

His fingers caressed the column of her throat, memorizing the smooth, soft skin beneath his touch. He found it unbelievably difficult not to play with her hair. He was fascinated by it. He wanted to kiss it, comb it with his fingers, and he wondered what it would be like to have that silvery veil draped across his bare chest. Without realizing it, he had drawn her close and nuzzled his face between the crook of her neck and the shower of her hair. It was like being snowblind, all that white softness. She shivered.

"Are you cold?" he asked, pulling away from her but keeping his hands on her waist.

"No. Well, maybe just a little," she said, glad that he had released her. She could control her thoughts better when they weren't quite so close.

"I'll build a fire. Would you like that?" he asked as he peered into her eyes. He wished she wouldn't look at him like that. He sensed that she was a strong woman, but that innocent look in her eyes compelled him to protect her.

"That sounds like a good idea. Mind if I help?"

"This is nothing against your capabilities, but I build the fires around here," he said as they started down the hall to the living room. He drew some kindling out of a wooden basket and placed three large logs on top.

"You're not one of those, are you?" she asked, curling her legs underneath her on the sofa. He took off his jacket and flung it over the back of the sofa.

"One of what?" he asked, turning on the gas lighter.

"Those male egotists. 'This is my job, that kind of work is your job.' You know, like that?" she teased.

"What's that? A nice way of saying I'm a male chauvinist pig?" he asked, still fumbling with the kindling.

"Naw, what I'm talking about is at least a step up." She chuckled under her breath.

He couldn't seem to find a match that would stay lit long enough to ignite the gas starter. Finally, blue flames shot up the chimney.

"I should have stayed in the Boy Scouts longer." He edged back to the sofa and sat next to her and put his arm around her and drew her toward him. "Listen, anybody who has that much trouble starting a fire would never dare have an ego problem."

She looked up at him and said, "Lost cause?"

"Exactly." He smiled and kissed her forehead.

They watched as the flames soared, crackled and then found a steady rhythm. From where she sat in the crimson shadows, Hailey could see the city lights against the midnight-blue sky. She had the eerie sensation that no life before had ever existed for her. She shouldn't get too carried away with the moment, she told herself again. She was just vulnerable and she should never let herself think that she was anything special to him. He must have had hundreds of women, most of them far more sophisticated than she. She must and she *would* keep her guard up. She felt better now that she had reinforced her convictions.

"If I made hot chocolate, would you drink some?" he asked her.

"You're kidding! Hot chocolate?"

"I know, it doesn't sound very suave, but I like it. How about some marshmallows on top?" he asked, his eyes growing playful. "If I had a candy cane, I'd throw that in, too. But I guess we'll just have to wait for Christmas for those."

"You like peppermint candy, too?" she asked, thinking of Joey and the perpetual sticky mouth he always had during the holidays.

"Yeah. What's the matter with that?"

"Oh, nothing."

"Anyway, this year I'm going to have my tree packed with 'em. And popcorn and cookies, too." He looked at her. "What are you laughing at?" he asked, noticing her smile of delight.

"I just never met a man who got that involved in Christmas decorating. I mean, I do, but then I have children . . ."

"Damn, woman! You mean to tell me that only people with kids can enjoy all the 'stuff' of holidays? Talk about biased! I'll match my tree against yours any day. Bet?" he said, sticking his hand out.

"It's a bet. You're on! And no cheating. You have to do all the work yourself. No going into Neiman-Marcus and just buying the whole thing already made up."

"Deal. Let's see . . . that gives us each three weeks to get busy. And on Christmas Eve we'll do the judging."

"Okay," she said and laughed. "Who's going to be the judge?"

"I will, of course!"

"That's not fair!" she retorted.

"I know. I'm a male chauvinist, remember?" He laughed and then got up and pulled her to her feet. "Let's make that hot chocolate."

They walked to the kitchen, where he poured two mugs of milk, stirred in chocolate syrup, put a marshmallow on top and placed them in the microwave oven. Then he stood back and waited with self-gratification on his lips.

"You call that hot chocolate?"

"How else do you make it?"

"From scratch. Real cocoa, sugar and milk cooked on the stove and poured over the marshmallow until it melts," she said, relying on her mother's recipe.

"Terrific. Next time you make it."

"Okay, I will," she said as he handed her the mug and she sipped from it. Still, it was good and warmed her throat.

Once again they sat by the fire, comfortable in the company of each other. Their conversation had ceased. Rex stoked the fire, and the flames lathered the room in a filmy glow.

Hailey was playing tug-of-war with her emotions. She was suspicious of his intentions. Any fool knew that this kind of reaction to a man was just chemistry—nothing permanent and couldn't be trusted. Maybe all he wanted was a lover. Maybe if she just went to bed with him, he would leave her alone and she could go on with her neatly ordered life.

Her eyes were locked on the fire ballet when she felt him watching her. He moved like a panther—sleek, sensual and aggressive. He wanted something from her, his body movements told her that; but it was the others—the birthday-wishful glances, the fatherlike assurance in his voice and the possessive and adoring caress of his hands—that bewildered her.

She didn't want to be another notch on his gunslinger belt, but worse, she didn't want to be a few weeks' frolic for him; her heart, not her body, the prize atop the glass mountain. She shouldn't stay here, letting him pin up photostats of himself in her head. She chastised herself for being a victim of romance, which was, after all, just make-believe, scene-setting. Any idiot knew that. But when he sat next to her as he was, not pushing her, only forcing her to believe in her mother's fairy tales, she was oh, so willing to cast her arrows into the air.

"Excuse me for just a minute," he said. He rose, careful that they did not touch, and left the room. He returned with a six-string guitar.

Hailey straightened up, not seeking the luxury of the back of the sofa. He strummed the chords and turned the keys until the instrument was properly tuned. He played a bittersweet love ballad, the words to which he said he'd written a long time ago.

She liked the song. It was one of those bleeding poems that made her sad yet calm, for to have put so much of himself on paper for display required courage and enormous caring. She knew that he was only playing this song as a stall tactic, not that he was baiting the trap, for she didn't feel like prey. She worried about her feelings even more. He obviously wanted her to see this side of himself, which common sense declared he should never do. But why? What gave him that outlaw's sense of the freebooter? She found herself winging toward him, circling around him but not coming to rest.

The song over, he put the guitar to the side and as his face turned back toward her, she impulsively bent forward and kissed him lightly, almost chastely, on his mouth.

It was a sisterly kiss, uncommitted. He felt an urgency to bolt and run, but the satin-soft lights in her eyes bound him to her. Her hand rested on his arm possessively, betraying the tentative smile on her lips. Her eyelids fell as her face moved forward, filling his scope of vision.

When their lips met this time, he sprinkled hers with tiny kisses like falling flower petals. Both her hands grasped his shoulders, not pulling him toward her, but rather securing him lest he go away. His hands on her neck, he pressed his lips full against her mouth. When his tongue delved into the interior of her mouth, she moaned. He was lost and as he pulled her closer, he didn't give a damn anymore. Her kiss was passionate and burning and her arms clung to him as if he were her savior.

He raised himself up on his knee and slipping his arms around her, effortlessly lifted her. She didn't protest and yet the look in her eyes, nearly childlike in its blind trust, made his heart surge.

She nuzzled her face into his neck as he carried her to the bedroom.

They stood beside the brass bed touching, discovering and memorizing, somehow knowing the urgency they felt was foolhardy. Buttons opened, zippers peeled apart and a waterfall of clothes fell like lengths of silk. Rex eased Hailey onto the forest-green velvet comforter that covered his bed. Her hair spread like an angel's wings against an evergreen thicket. Her eyes shone through the dimly lit room and descended into his soul, igniting an eternal flame. His lips rolled across and down her throat like pearls, smooth and cool and precious. She touched the top of his head gently, as if to protect him.

Rex cradled her in his arms as he nestled his face in her hair once more and traced the shell-like outline of her ear with his tongue. His hand rested on her ribs, just under her breast where he could, being that close to her heart, feel her heartbeat. A lazy spiritual peace circled around them on cat's paws as if daring its spell to be broken. As he kissed her again, he felt the exciting dance of her fingertips on his back, shoulders and spine, all the way to his buttocks. Desperate need for her now compelled him to drink thirstily of the taste of her; her mouth, nipples and belly. His tongue darted and romped over the velvety terrain of her. Not an inch of her did he leave unexplored.

There were no sharp planes or cliffs, nor rock-hard muscles, to Hailey. She was soft and inviting and when he moved back to the pillow of her breast he felt her hands still strumming his arms and legs and back, not in abandonment but in reverence. She created an excitement in him he'd never known, and were he to stop at this very moment, he knew neither of them would feel cheated. But he did want all of her, and when he entered her, a soft, slick stroking began, like promises spoken aloud.

Like mist rising, her ecstasy grew and overpowered them both. Now wanting, needing and craving more of her and from her, he met her in the glen. Lingering only briefly by a tranquil lagoon, they mounted winged steeds and galloped, then raced; they quickened their dizzying speed and finally they found themselves drowning in each other.

Hailey had never experienced such incomparable fulfillment before. Joy spiraled down her cheeks, and Rex lifted his head to drink her tears.

"I'm sorry. God, I'm sorry, Hailey. I don't want you to cry."

"No, please don't be sorry about anything," she whispered. His arms held her like a vise, and her eyes misted again. He started to move away from her.

"No!" she said urgently. "Stay inside me. Please don't go, not yet."

"It's so good with you, Hailey. It's so much better when . . . there're feelings."

"I know," she said, a sense of doom invading her thoughts. She was falling in love with him and she didn't know what to do. It wasn't just sexual need and it wasn't some indecipherable female need to belong to a man. It was Rex himself. He seemed to be all around her—that unfocused shadow from her past, the breathless courage of the present and the sparkling promise of tomorrow. She was no longer afraid of him; if anything, it was her lack of fear that disquieted her. She knew that if he cast her out the door this minute, she'd never feel this way about any man, ever again.

"Don't leave, not tonight. I want you here when I wake up. Please say you'll stay with me," he said, his green eyes destroying what fears she had left.

"I won't go anywhere unless you send me away," she said, caressing his face. She adored the touch of him, the way the very ends of her fingers tingled as her skin met his. It was as if they'd been burned and frozen all at once. His skin was smooth, not dry and leathery, the way most men's skin was. But Rex wasn't most men, he wasn't afraid or terrified into meaningless boasting. She could see it in his eyes, that blazing generosity so fearless that he'd offered it to her without demanding anything of her.

"I'll never do that," he said, the moonlight catching a wicked grin on his face.

"Rex?" She said his name and then felt him growing strong and hard inside her. She matched the devilish glint in his eyes.

"Isn't this proof enough that I want you to stay?" he asked, his voice a husky, sensual whisper that fell into her ear and teased her brain. She felt her nipples harden without his touch. Her eyes rolled back in her head and she felt him raise himself up on his elbows. With each plunge she craved more, her hips rising until she'd locked her legs around him. She was so wet in her desire for him that she thought her body had been ignited. Sweat broke out over the entire expanse of him and it trickled down his face and fell onto her breasts.

He pushed her legs down and rolled onto his back, taking her with him. Hailey's eyes flew open and then she smiled wantonly at him.

"Your turn to do the work, baby," he said in those tones that tickled her nerves like the fluttering of bees' wings. He pulled at her full breast and drew it into his mouth. He sucked and teased and nibbled so exquisitely she almost begged him to stop, but this was too divine ever to end. She rotated on top of him, breathing so heavily she was embarrassed about the degree of her desire.

With no warning, her moans scurried into a scream. Her arms and legs were quivering and he knew she couldn't hold herself up much longer. He rolled her over onto her stomach, spreading her legs apart with his knee; he filled his hands with her breasts and let his face fall into the veil of her hair. Still hard and eager inside her, he stroked her slowly. Each time he went deeper until he was certain he had lost himself. Every time she moaned, his pulse quickened. He was careening down a mountain and there, when he landed in utter sexual fulfillment, Hailey was holding him.

Rex gathered her up in his arms like a child in need of protection. Her hair curled around his fingers, bejeweling them like silver rings. Sleep threatened to overtake them but for now only hovered above them. He pulled her legs between his and locked her next to him, her head resting on his shoulder. Rex fought to stay awake, but the rhythmic sounds of his own breathing lulled him to sleep.

She felt him slip away from her as his muscles went lax and his lungs filled and emptied at a steady pace. She wanted to kiss him, wake him up and talk with him. "Spend some time with me," she said as she started to ease away from him, thinking he would sleep better without her wrapped around him the way she was. Her movement had been almost imperceptible, but he jerked and his arm unconsciously tightened around her shoulder. When Hailey fell asleep, a Dresden doll smile decorated her lips.

# Chapter Twenty-three

REX pulled the spun-sugar tangle of hair from Hailey's face, and suddenly he wished he were a bandit out of the Old West so he could lay claim to her. God! He couldn't stand the idea of another man even touching her. Her skin was flushed and soft, like a perfectly ripened peach.

"So goddamned beautiful," he said aloud, marveling at her beauty.

Her eyelids fluttered and opened and she saw him looking at her.

"I heard that. Are you always going to wake me with obscenities, Mr. Cowert?" she said, stretching her arms over her head and peering at him through sleepy eyes.

"I didn't mean to wake you, darlin'," he mumbled, lowering his mouth to hers. She kissed him quickly and started to wrestle out of his arms.

"I haven't brushed my teeth yet!" she protested as he pulled her back onto the sheets and pinned her arms down.

"Neither have I, so we're even," he argued, kissing her over and over until she couldn't get her breath. Abruptly he stopped and hugged her tightly. "You feel so good, I don't want to let you up. Not just yet, anyway."

She kissed his ear and smoothed his rumpled hair with her fingers. She liked the feel of him snuggled deep in the crook of her neck like this. His knotty, once-callused hands were smooth as he stroked her arm and down the side of her ribs and waist. He wasn't going to make love to her, she could tell, at least not sexually. But this—this adoration of her, not just her body, thrilled her. She needed him and she only hoped he needed her too.

His stubble of early-morning beard scratched her cheek when he moved his head, and she chuckled under her breath, but he didn't miss it.

"What's so funny?"

"We are," she replied blissfully. "Have you got a robe I could wear?" she asked.

"Sure, but what for?"

"Huh? Oh, I thought I'd fix breakfast. Aren't you hungry? I'm starving! What do you usually eat? No, wait! Don't tell me. Steak, eggs, biscuits, honey, coffee, fruit . . ."

"Whoa! Hold on! I'm not a lumberjack, you know," he said and laughed. "Why don't you surprise me?" he said, folding his arms behind his head as he watched her walk naked to his closet and fumble around for his brown velour robe. The shoulders hit her just above the elbows and she looked like a little girl playing dress-up. Her hair was still a tumble of silver, much like a slot machine that had just paid off. He smiled at her and she blushed! He couldn't believe it! Was this the same woman who had made endless, passionate love to him last night? She tied the belt around her slender waist and went to the bathroom. He heard her brushing her teeth, the toilet flush and then she emerged.

"I'll go rustle up some grub," she teased as she walked past the bed. He snatched her hand and pulled her to the edge of the bed.

"Give me some sugar before you leave," he said lightly.

She leaned down, expecting him to pull her onto the bed again, but he only accepted her gift. As she moved away he touched her cheek. "I'll be out in a minute to help you."

"Okay," she said and left the room.

A few moments later, he could hear her humming as she moved around in the kitchen. Pots and pans clamored and clanged. "Ooff," he muttered, "she found *that* cabinet," thinking of how he'd tossed his assortment of odd utensils in one place with gypsy-like abandon. But in a moment she was singing again and he could smell bacon frying. He tossed the covers aside and went to shower and shave.

Hailey was bending over, inspecting the browning biscuits, when he crept up behind her and caught her around the waist. She giggled and closed the door. He turned her around to face him. Though she smiled at him, gossamer veils shadowed the intense blue of her eyes he'd known before. Something had changed between them. What was she thinking? She wasn't fighting his embrace, he thought; in fact, she reveled in it. What could be wrong?

"You look like you belong here, dressed like you are, in my robe," he said.

Her eyes suddenly filled with tears, a reaction he never expected. "I . . . I know. I feel like I *do* belong here somehow."

"Well, what's wrong with that?" he asked huskily, bending down to kiss her neck.

"Nothing, it's just that I . . . oh, never mind," she replied and tried to turn away from him, but Rex would have none of it. He held her closer and forced her to look directly at him.

"You're afraid of me, aren't you?"

"Yes. I mean . . . not exactly. Oh, damn! I don't know what I mean," she answered, exasperatedly wishing he would just let her go. God! Why shouldn't she be scared? She was falling in love with him, and if she told him, he'd just laugh at her and then shut her out of his life. Wasn't that what men did these days? Men like Rex didn't need someone like her. Besides, nobody believed in love anymore; even she doubted its existence. But these powerful feelings, the ones that went beyond passion, superseded caring . . . How could this be happening to her?

Rex read her thoughts as clearly as if they'd been handed to him on a computer printout. His tension eased and he breathed easier. He kissed her forehead. "What are you doing in May?"

Hailey thought he'd missed a beat somewhere. Maybe he just wanted to change the subject. "Why?"

"I thought we'd get married in May. It's a nice time of

year. Not too hot, not much rain. What do you think?" His smile was curiously serene, as if he had her right where he wanted her.

"I think you're crazy! I just got unmarried! Besides, nobody proposes after only a week!"

"Sure they do! I did. Look at it this way, baby. May is a long way off. That should give you plenty of time to think about it. But you'll marry me," he said with that cocksure sparkle in his eyes she'd come to know already.

"We'll see . . ." she said. She wanted to say "yes" over and over again. She wished she trusted herself to be so sure. And how in the world could she trust him? This had to be some new ploy, a new line. She couldn't figure out why he would even bother with her. Things like this just didn't happen, except in the movies. Weren't they supposed to have years of getting to know each other and slowly fall in love? She had never been this confused.

"I sound like I'm nuts, don't I?"

"Yes, a little. But maybe no more so than I am," she said hesitantly.

"That's because you know as well as I do that you were meant for me. I can see it in your eyes. You're just afraid to say it aloud, that's all. But that's okay. I know it's too soon for you. And I've had the luxury of looking around for a very long time. I do know what I want."

"Rex, I don't know what to say, except that I'm afraid. You do frighten me, you know. You're rushing everything so fast I don't know what to believe or what's happening. I've never felt like this before," she said and watched as his smile burned in his eyes. They were erecting rope bridges between them, but would they be able to strengthen them and connect their lives forever? It seemed an impossibility. "I know I want to be with you. And it's so strange—as if you've always been there somehow and now I've finally found you. Is it too romantic to say that?" she asked, suddenly listening to her logical side, which persisted in condemning this foolish affair.

"Hailey, don't think it," he said, reading the inscription of her thoughts on her face. "Love knows no logic. I'll give

222

you all the time you want to be sure. I can tell you one thing: Crazier things than this happen every day," he said and then took her chin between his thumb and finger and pulled her lips to his. It was a tender caressing, his mouth as it covered hers. There was no urgency, only a seal on his promise to bide his time.

## Chapter Twenty-four

THEY had spent the rest of the day together, talking, learning about each other, their families, past experiences, all those tales that new lovers spin as if the successes and mistakes had belonged to someone else. They had driven through the rain to Brennan's and ate a late lunch on the patio seated beneath a huge umbrella, where they were oblivious to the weather, immersed only in each other. Rex held Hailey's hand all day, not content enough to be with her without the reassurance of her touch. He kept thinking of how it was going to be when he would have to take her home and he'd be without her again.

The children were due home at seven, she told him, and a reluctant Rex finally left her doorstep at quarter till. Joey and Kim had gone camping and horseback riding with Mike all weekend and were exhausted and hungry when they came dragging in. She fixed them a light supper while they bathed off the Galveston sand and horse smells. By nine o'clock both were sound asleep.

Hailey retreated to her easel to finish her portrait of Sylvia Gregson. Luckily, Hailey had only one other painting to complete before Christmas. As the days grew more hectic, she would need her extra time to devote to Joey and Kim and their own family preparations.

She examined the work she had done on this portrait, commissioned by Tony as a surprise for Sylvia. Now that she had painted them both, she was coming to know them better. She wished she could be there on Christmas when they exchanged two identical gifts. She marveled at their oneness, their ability to know the other's wants and needs.

She gave the portrait one last appraisal. It was very good. She improved with each project; her hand was more steady and conveyed more emotion to her subjects. She was particularly proud of this piece. And she knew her next would be just a little bit better.

Her commissions were beginning to accumulate in the bank: her security, and she had painstakingly saved every penny. Her salary at work supported them adequately, but then, her wants were few. She promised herself the luxury of hiring a cleaning service once a month. Maybe even twice. That would be her Christmas present to herself, but other than that, she and the children were happy, healthy and surviving.

This was how she had believed the rest of her life would be—this reasonably normal, structured world, where she would watch her children grow and where her work would sustain them, and her art would fulfill her. But tonight, as she stood back and looked at Sylvia Gregson's portrait, she was aware that a startling alteration had occurred. Rex.

In the minute span of one week, he had brought about the most cataclysmic change, and now nothing would be the same again.

Why was so much happening so quickly in her life when there had been so little before? Whatever the reason, she was glad for the reality of Rex.

Even now, when she had come so far, he made her want to believe in all those ideals she had passed and forgotten. It was treacherous terrain, this kind of loving. The children were gone for almost two months during the summer, and at the time she thought it impossible to miss anyone any more than that. But tonight, as she prepared for bed, slipping a lace-edged dusty rose nightgown over her head, she almost ached just to hear the sound of Rex's voice. As she lay beneath the covers and turned out the light, she forced herself not to succumb to this infatuation. It would be so easy not to believe this was love. Such thinking kept her security walls tidily intact.

She had just closed her eyes when the telephone rang. Her hand shot out immediately, stilling its commotion so as not to awaken Joey and Kim.

"Hello," she said drowsily, expecting it to be Janet or her mother.

"I just called to say that I miss you." His distinctive drawl poured into her ear and drew a smile on her face.

"I miss you, too. More than I thought I would." Had she said that?

"This isn't going to work, you know," he said accusingly.

"What isn't?" she asked, sitting up again in bed, flumping the pillows behind her back, ready to defend herself.

"I can't sleep without you here," he said sulkily.

"Well, you've done it for all these years, surely it can't be all that important," she ventured.

"But you know as well as I do that everything has changed now."

"Yes . . . I do . . ." she confessed.

"You sound as if you don't want to admit it."

"I don't." She wanted to squelch his persistence and yet she drank in his every word. Reassurance, how she craved it! Why did she allow ambivalence to ride her back like this?

"See, that's why I want to be with you now at times like this."

"What are you talking about?" she intervened hurriedly.

"Times when you start to doubt me and yourself. Don't do it, Hailey, there's no reason for it."

"There isn't?"

"No. I want to show you a place where you've never been, a place where you can feel free enough to love."

"You're so sure." She marveled at his conviction about her.

"Damn sure. I never thought it would happen to me, either. But it has and now I want you to be as certain as I am. Listen"—he paused—"I'm not going to keep you up all night. I promised I would give you time and I'm not an Indian giver, baby."

"You really mean that, don't you?"

"Yep. Sure do. Sweet dreams. God keep you, darlin'. I'll talk to you tomorrow. Okay?"

"Okay. Good night, Rex."

"'Night, my love."

He had sounded so close just then, as if she could feel him laying his hands on her, holding her. A tear trickled down her cheek as she exhaled.

She punched out seven numbers as rapidly as her fingers could fly across the dial. It rang twice and was picked up.

"Janet? Janet! Oh, I didn't mean to wake you. But I did, didn't I? I'm sorry." Hailey was rattled and it was revealed in her voice.

Janet was struggling to wake up enough to comprehend what was happening. "Is something wrong? What time is it, anyway?"

"Huh? Oh, it's uh"—she looked over at the digital clock—"it's one twenty-seven."

"My God! It must be awful! Are you all right? It's not Joey? Or Kim?" Janet finally grasped the scene. Hailey had never telephoned this late at night.

"No, it's not them. It's me. I need to talk to you, but not tonight. As soon as the bus leaves in the morning, I'm heading for your house. We'll have a couple minutes at least before I have to go to work. Okay?"

"Sure, sweetie. Are you sure you're all right tonight? You don't want me to come over now?"

"No. No. Get some sleep. I'll see you tomorrow."

"Okay, if you say so. Bye." Janet hung up.

Hailey replaced the receiver. She needed Janet's objective ear, even though she knew Janet wouldn't be able to give her any answers. She turned out the light and prayed for morning to arrive.

Hailey rushed through the front doorway, not waiting for Janet to answer the doorbell. Hailey was out of breath and leaned against the door, regrouping when Janet came in.

Janet eyed her suspiciously. Hailey looked well, even more rested than she was. But Hailey had the look of an errant teenager about her.

"Janet, I'm in trouble!"

"Oh, shit. I knew it! Okay, how bad and what kind? Money?" Hailey was shaking her head back and forth, still not catching her breath. "Then there's only one thing it could be. It's a man, right?"

"Yes," Hailey nodded, but the worried grimace that crumpled her face caused Janet decidedly more concern.

How bad could it be? Janet thought. Was he married? "Come in and I'll get us some coffee. Then you can give me the whole story," Janet said as they walked into the kitchen and Hailey sat at the table. "Now, listen, if your mother didn't tell you about the facts of life—birds and bees stuff—there's not much I can tell you . . ."

"Oh, Janet, be serious!" Hailey cried in desperation.

"You're not pregnant, then?" Janet taunted, thinking Hailey could use some joviality.

"No, it's worse than that. I'm in love," Hailey said, as if she were reading her own obituary.

"Is he married?"

"No, of course not."

"Well, you never can be too careful these days. Guys have all kinds of tricks to cover it up. Secret apartments away from home, the whole bit. He's not a traveling salesman or something like that?"

"No. He owns his own business," Hailey replied, rejecting Janet's hypothesis.

"Ah! The enterprising type. What's his name?"

"Rex. Rex Cowert," Hailey said, finally settling down and sipping her coffee.

"Not *the* Rex Cowert?" Janet's voice escalated in recognition of the man.

"You know him?"

"Never met him. I just remember reading his name a few paragraphs before yours in the society columns. It was a neat name. Did you meet him at one of those parties?"

Janet was now intrigued, yet ever ready to take Hailey's side.

"No. I met him through work," Hailey said with all the dignity the situation could warrant.

"This must be serious." Janet appraised the situation, witnessing the earnest expression in Hailey's eyes.

"It is! I wouldn't be here if it weren't."

"So, what's he done?"

"The absolute worst. He asked me to marry him," Hailey said dejectedly.

Janet howled. "You've got to be kidding! One of Houston's walking wonder boys has asked you to marry him and you think it's trouble?" Janet replied with exaggerated patience. "Hailey, listen to me. Do you really love him?"

"Yes, I think I do, and that's what scares me."

"Why? It's perfectly natural! It happens every day . . . I think. Some people aren't so lucky."

"But I've known him only a week!"

"Hey! If you want me to refute this whole situation on those grounds, you've come to the wrong place. I knew Dan only two weeks and we were married."

"Less than that, to be accurate," Hailey reminded her.

"Don't nit-pick," Janet said in a remote voice.

"But you don't understand. I've never been in love!" Hailey retorted.

"Don't knock it, there's always a first time. Besides, that's not what worries you, anyway. Isn't all this turmoil you're feeling over the fact that you think it's too soon after the divorce?" Janet accused.

"I guess I do," Hailey reluctantly agreed.

"Did you ever think that it just may be about time? You've spent the last ten years basically alone, even though you were married. I think all this happened because you were ready for it. Did you ever think of it like that, huh?" Janet pressed her impatiently.

"Not that way, no."

"Well, do . . ." More thoughtfully, she said, "You know, this could be the most perfect time in your life for this to happen. You're flying high on your job, your painting and all the other good things. There's absolutely no wrong reason for this to happen to you. You aren't looking for financial support and you already feel great about yourself. That's why I don't look too worried about it."

"Yeah, you don't."

"It looks to me like you really are in love with him. Five years from now you might latch onto somebody for all the wrong reasons—the children, money, loneliness. But now the only thing you are missing and always have missed is love."

"So what do I do?"

"Let it flow and see what happens. You don't need to test anything. Fate always has a way of doing that for you," Janet counseled but still Hailey looked unconvinced. "Hailey, just what do you want me to say? I haven't met the man. He has to have a lot of good qualities or you wouldn't be attracted to him, much less feel the way you do. Maybe he'll turn out to be the biggest bastard on earth."

"I know you're right. I'm just overwhelmed by what's happened."

"Just take it day by day. That's all life is really, when you get down to it. And don't ask for miracles, especially of yourself. Okay?"

"Okay. I feel better just talking to you about it."

"That's what I'm here for . . . to listen."

"Thanks. I've taken enough of your time and I've got to get to work," Hailey said, rising and gulping her coffee.

"Call me and let me know what's going on."

"I will. See you later." She bent and hugged Janet and let herself out.

Janet stared at the cold coffee at the bottom of her cup.

"I hope you'll be all right, my friend." Janet hadn't met him, but she had read about him and she knew one thing: He had a list of women a mile long. If she were in Hailey's position, she would be scared too. There were plenty of twisted egotists around, guys who got their kicks out of having women fall in love with them and then they would drop the girls cold. And Janet thought the description fit this Rex. "Whoever you are, Rex, I hope I'm wrong about you."

# Chapter Twenty-five

THE Christmas retail season was full upon them and Hailey found herself deluged at work. She never left the gallery before seven, and many nights she was there until nine if Leonard or Barrett couldn't take over for her. These were days she had wanted to spend with Joey and Kim, but unfortunately she didn't get home until nine-thirty. Janet had been a godsend. She picked up the children from school every day and kept them until Hailey got off work. Hailey didn't know what she would have done without Janet. While the holidays meant more hours at the gallery for Hailey, Rex's business slacked off during this period.

While Rex was willing and eager to attend the many parties he'd been invited to, all Hailey could think about was sleep. They finally had compromised: He attended them alone until nine, when he would meet her just as she left, at least for a few moments before she dashed off to Janet's house. Sometimes he brought her lunch when he could break away and she couldn't. He couldn't understand why her employer didn't hire someone part-time to give Hailey a rest, but she had explained to him that Barrett told her he had tremendous confidence in her ability and knew she could handle any situation. Rex thought she'd taken the compliment too blindly. As far as he could tell, Barrett was taking advantage of her.

Rex had expertly extracted a promise from Hailey to spend every Saturday night with him, and when the children were with their father, she was to spend the weekend at his apartment. Hailey had wangled a Saturday off by going through Leonard and not Barrett. The Farrells were having a Christmas party at their ranch at Magnolia in Montgomery County, and neither Rex nor Hailey would have dared miss it.

It was not a large ranch, actually more of a weekend hideaway, but as they left the main road, driving through the whitewashed gates, Hailey fell in love with the ranch. The ranch house was an excellent example of turn-of-the-century Texas Victorian. Its wide verandas swept around the house with intricately detailed gingerbread work. The Farrells had extravagantly decorated both the interior and the exterior for the holidays. Pine cone wreaths and garlands graced both the front and back doors. The walkway and front porches were outlined in Mexican pots filled with enormous red poinsettias. Filling a huge bay window in the living room was a twelve-foot-tall Christmas tree whose circumference almost equaled its height. Mrs. Farrell later told Hailey there were over eighty strings of lights and more than fifteen hundred ornaments from all over the world. She personally decorated the tree each year, and Hailey could well understand why it took over six days!

Hailey was surprised at this house, its every corner filled with country antiques, family photographs and memorabilia. Its rustic interior of wood floor covered with Navaho and Yea rugs, old brick fireplaces and thick, ancient beams was worlds apart from the Farrells' mansion in River Oaks. However, Rex informed her the dichotomy was not unusual for wealthy Texans. In the backyard stretched a forty-foot swimming pool surrounded by redwood decking. Numerous tables had been set up—each one covered in a red checked cloth with sprigs of holly and fresh fir woven around antique red lanterns as a centerpiece.

Off to the right were half a dozen ranch hands in butcher aprons, basting dinner—a whole steer! Black iron pots suspended over hickory fires held ranch beans and

Texas chili. The tantalizing aroma made Hailey's stomach growl.

Once the nearly one hundred guests had arrived, it was announced that a colt-breaking contest would be held, and the prize was a five-ounce gold nugget. Upon hearing the news, the younger men whooped and hollered and tossed their hats into the air. The entire crowd dashed toward the corral to get a good seat.

Rex grabbed Hailey's waist and hoisted her onto the top of the fence.

"Now, you just sit tight, darlin', and I'm going to win that gold nugget for you!"

Hailey's mouth gaped as she looked at the kicking, snorting Thoroughbred and then back to Rex's crackling emerald eyes. "Rex, I don't need a gold nugget . . ."

"But I want you to have it," he said, kissing her palm.

"It . . . it looks too dangerous," she said as she looked at the menacing horse again.

"Those little baby horses? Shit, honey. I was riding horses before I could walk. Have some faith," he said as he patted her thigh before heading for the opposite side of the corral, where the rest of the men were pinning numbers to each other's backs.

Hailey watched as one man after another tried his luck with a fresh colt, all without success. One man had been skilled enough to get the bridle on, but that was all. Finally, after the fifth man gave up and raced out of the corral, the colt fast on his heels, it was Rex's turn.

From the moment he walked forward, assurance and confidence in his steps, everyone could tell that he was not a city boy out for an afternoon of frolic as the others had been. He was a real cowboy. Rex circled the spooked four-year-old colt, speaking to it in low, melodious tones, constantly following its eyes. Rex made certain he was never out of the colt's frame of vision, thus reassuring the animal and establishing trust.

Rex took out his lasso, and in the flash of an eye he had slipped it over the colt's head. Still talking, Rex moved in closer, exerting pressure until the horse would give. Then he slipped on the bridle and followed the same process. He

235

rubbed the horse's neck. cooed to him and readied them both for his next task, the placement of the blanket. Rex pampered the horse, wooing him as he finally placed the saddle on the colt's back. He checked the bridle and tested the stirrups before finally easing on.

Every cowboy knows that a colt never dreams of being tamed. When the colt began bucking and snorting, Rex followed his lead. When the horse got nervous, so did Rex. When the animal would give and calm down, Rex followed suit.

Always quiet and gentle, Rex became the colt's ally. Never did he push the animal or try to display mastery, for that was not the point. Cowboy and horse became one and the same as Rex proudly rode the colt around the corral.

Rex dismounted, then petted and rubbed the horse's neck one last time, still talking to him like a close friend.

The guests were cheering as Rex was handed the gold nugget. He jubilantly placed it in Hailey's palm, lifted her off the fence, took her in his arms and kissed her long and passionately in front of the entire crowd, who yelled and whistled for their hero and his lady.

The excitement died down enough for all to hear the clanging call to supper. "Chow's on!" the head cook bellowed to the approaching guests. The sun set early during the last days of autumn, and Rex went to the truck to get his sheepskin-lined suede jacket for Hailey while she went through the chow line and filled their plates.

She struck up a conversation with the couple behind her in line and they invited her and Rex, when he came back, to sit at their table. Once seated, Hailey lost track of time as she joined in the conversation. Realizing she had almost finished her meal and Rex hadn't returned, her dinner companions suggested she find Rex so they could have dessert and coffee together.

Hailey worked her way through the sea of cars parked on the Farrells' front yard. It was difficult to see with the sun down; the only light was from the windows of the house. Finally, she saw him standing next to his Silverado and was about to call to him, but then she noticed there was someone with him.

She was tall, wearing jeans, an Eisenhower suede jacket and a western hat. Her dark hair nearly reached the middle of her back with her head bent back like that. Someone flicked on an upstairs light in the house and then Hailey could see them clearly. It was Pamela, and she was hungrily kissing Rex!

Hailey almost tumbled over, her legs twisted around each other as she spun around and rushed back to the brightly lit party area by the pool. She clutched her stomach, hoping she wouldn't throw up. She knew she must have looked deathly pale when she seated herself once again at the table. She didn't dare pick up her fork. Her hands were shaking so much she would probably stab herself with it!

Fool! she thought. How could I have been so stupid and blind to have fallen for his lines like that? "What are you doing in May?" he'd asked her. She'd really set herself up for this one. She should have stuck to her promise to herself to be cautious. She was so mad at herself. And they had to drive all the way back to Houston together!

What was she going to do? Not just tonight, but tomorrow and all those days to come? It had all been a mirage, an illusion. She had believed only what she wanted to hear and not the truth. Well, she knew it now! And there was no going back to what it had once been. It was over.

Trust. Ha! she thought. There was no such thing as trust or love. She wasn't going to let him or anyone else do this to her again. She'd had it! Had it with all the Stephens and Rexes in the world.

The picture in her mind of Rex and Pamela in each other's arms was in wide-screen CinemaScope. It wrapped around her, crushing the breath out of her.

He was teasing and joking heartily about being late when he reached the table, placing his jacket over her shoulders. The others smiled wanly, conveying their disdain for his negligence. But true to his nature, he won them over with his charm.

He could feel it; Hailey's change in mood was like a Panhandle blizzard, forceful and frigid. He had to get her away and find out the reason for it.

Sensing the tension between them, their dinner companions excused themselves and left. Hailey's elbows locked. If she could just let go of the chair, sip her coffee and act as if nothing had happened.

"Hailey, I think all the excitement this afternoon was too much for me. I don't feel much like eating. Would you be terribly disappointed if we left?"

"No, that's fine, Rex," she replied quietly.

He left to thank the Farrells. She should, too, but she couldn't face anyone right now. She would send them a card in the morning. Her mind was a carousel out of control. Anger flashed a fury of blinding lights in her eyes and she couldn't focus. She was glad they were leaving; she wanted to be safe again, locked away behind the doors in her house.

She desperately needed a harbor and she knew where it had always been. Her children loved her. They would bolster her. She would get more money, too, lots of it to protect her from this debilitating feeling of dependency she was prone to at the moment. She would show Rex she could take care of herself. She didn't need anyone, especially him! She would cultivate the mystique the columnists loved and she would increase the price of her portraits. She would make more money than Rex could ever dream of. She would break away from him. Her strength was in herself, the only person worthy of her trust.

It was Rex's strong hand she felt on her arm as he helped her up from the chair. It was Rex who supported her weight until they reached his truck. She hugged herself, trying to warm up while he got in, started the engine and turned on the heater.

Hailey listened as her heart kept rhythm with the mechanical drum of the engine while they drove back to Houston. The blood at her temples was pounding.

Rex was aware of her suspicious, furtive glances, for

they twisted into his brain like corkscrews. How would he get her to open up to him? Her rage was directed at him, for had it been someone else, she would have been spewing over by now.

Hailey felt she couldn't blame him for succumbing to Pamela. How could she ever try to win him from someone that utterly beautiful? Pamela had everything she wanted: perfect body, fabulous face, money, social standing and Rex. Hailey was aware that she was jealous of Pamela. Who wouldn't be?

Hailey had been such a fool to be swept away by Rex's lies! She had believed them all, including the story about his oak table belonging to his grandmother—a quaint, cozy tale to color the deception. He probably bought it at Evelyn Wilson's on Main Street along with all his other antiques. Who did he think he was? He had Pamela. Wasn't that enough? Why did he want to hurt and humiliate Hailey by playing all these games?

Hailey seemed detached, far away from him, and yet he could feel her rage. She'd always had moments of uncertainty about him. But now, this—this bloodbath of silent shrieking—he couldn't stand it any longer.

"Hailey, tell me what's wrong. Please," he pleaded, not knowing what his next move would be.

"Nothing. Why should anything be wrong?" she answered coldly.

"I know you well enough to know that you're upset about something."

"You don't know me at all! And I just wish I'd kept it that way!" Her words stung his face like ice pellets.

"Don't say that!" he shouted and reached for her hand.

She snatched it back and shoved both her fists into the jacket pockets. Hailey's shoulders were hunched, burying her neck into the jacket. Her cheeks flamed and he could see the sparkle of hysterical tears sliding down her cheeks.

"I hate you!" she hissed to herself. She thought she hadn't said it aloud. It was one of those reverberating, howling thoughts that had voiced itself on its own power.

"That does it!" Rex slammed on the brakes and turned

the truck to the shoulder of the road and skidded; gravel flew and tires screeched, nearly hurling them into the ravine below.

"You're a maniac! Now you want to kill me!" she screamed, beating at his chest as he tried to pull her into his arms.

"Hailey, for God's sake, shut up! Shut up and listen to me!"

She pounced on him like an animal. Her arms flew at him, wanting to hurt him for deceiving her—using her! Though many of her blows found their mark, none was powerful enough to inflict pain. Finally, she wore herself down enough for him to grab both her hands and pin them behind her back, forcing her to face him.

"Are you quite through?"

She was sobbing so hard she felt as if the wind had been knocked out of her. Her tears, sweat and running nose left her face drenched. She sniffed and tried to blow the matted locks of hair away from her mouth. "Take me home," she said.

"No. Not until we get this straightened out. But"—he sighed with relief—"I'm glad you finally got it all out of your system."

"All what? I don't know what you're talking about," she replied, rescuing her dignity and slipping her mask of control over her exposed emotions.

"You're mad as hell at me about something . . . I don't know what . . . and you won't even give me a chance to defend myself."

"Of course I'm mad at you. You were driving like a lunatic. We could have been killed!" she screamed again, remembering the looming danger of the steep precipice below.

"Well, we weren't," he said, his own indignation at this farcical bantering crackling around his words. He pinned her arms even tighter and through clenched teeth he said, "Now you tell me, or I'll keep you here like this all night if I have to."

Hailey could only stare at him. She had to get away from him before she lost her control. "Let me go, Rex. I won't fight you anymore," she said coolly, her calm a soft promise.

"Tell me, damn it!" he snarled and yanked her even closer so she could see nothing but his angry green eyes.

"What do you want from me? I just don't understand you at all," she said, tears of pain brimming in her eyes. She couldn't hold back any longer and she turned on him again. "You're just playing some twisted game with me! I won't let you use me, Rex. I'm not stupid! I know about people like you. You're just like Stephen!"

"Stephen Ainsley? For Christ's sake, how can you compare me to that faggot?"

"Faggot!" she screamed. "How dare you use that—"

"Oh, excuse me," he said slyly. "I suppose 'bisexual' is a fairer word. So I fail to see what he has to do with us."

Hailey blinked away her tears, trying to clear the fog in her brain. Stephen was bisexual? She let the words sink in. Of course! His association with Leonard and Barrett—and that would explain his prolonged absences and lack of explanations when he returned to her. He did love her just as he'd said. He hadn't lied to her at all. How torn he must have been! And how naïve she'd been not to have seen it. Stephen had no choice but to leave her. Everything made sense to her now.

Rex's hands were still gripping her arms, hurting her. At least Stephen had good reasons to leave her. Rex was a true bastard.

"Hailey, you have to trust me. I love you . . ."

"That's a crock!" she stormed. "You don't love me! I saw you! Yes, I did. What kind of devil are you? Do you tell Pamela you love her too?"

"Pamela?" He looked confused and then it hit him like a bullet. He eased away from her and relinquished her arms. "You saw her at the party . . ." he ventured, a lump in his throat.

"Of course I did!" Hailey spit the accusation at him. "How long did you think you could play me along? Both of us? I feel sorry for her, being sucked in by you. You're vile, Rex . . ." Hailey couldn't stop herself.

Rex had half a mind to start the engine and just leave,

letting Hailey think whatever she wanted. She didn't trust him at all, even though he told her he loved her. But then, how much trust could one expect after only a month? The mood she was in now, she wouldn't believe him now either. He clutched the steering wheel and suddenly felt overwhelmingly empty. "I do love you, Hailey."

It was a child's whimper. Hailey's lungs expelled the hate and anger she had been feeling. His head dangled on his chest as if his neck were broken. She watched as her fingers crawled over his shoulder and touched his hair. She was helpless and though she fought it, she was in love with him.

"I do believe you. I wish I didn't, it would be so much easier that way," she whispered.

"Hailey, you've got to understand. Pamela came driving up just as I had gotten my jacket. She jumped out of her car the minute she saw me. She didn't know I was going to be there or that I was seeing you, but she does now. You must have seen her kissing me before we talked about our situation."

"I must have," she interrupted.

"Well, don't worry about it anymore. I don't have any feelings for Pamela. She was never more than just a friend." He looked at Hailey with trepidation. It was a flimsy story, but it was the truth. "Hailey, I would never do anything to lose you. Christ! I don't even have you yet! Why would I botch it all up?"

"I don't know. I don't understand any of this, you or me. Especially me."

"What are you saying?"

"I think I've finally managed to destroy the last of my brain cells, because I do believe you. I don't want to. I wish I could just walk away from you and it wouldn't hurt at all, but I can't. God! I'm so messed up!"

"No you aren't, honey," he said and gingerly put his arm around her and she melted into him like wax. "Don't give up on me, please. And don't ever talk about leaving me. I can take a lot, I'm pretty strong, but I need you."

Hailey was crying again, but she kept her face sheltered in his neck. "I need you, too," she admitted and felt his arms tighten around her. She was throwing the dice again, she knew, but she would risk it to be with him. He kissed her ears and cheeks and mouth, letting relief and joy flood his body.

"I promise I'll never hurt you," he said and she nodded in affirmation, her fingers wiping her tears away. "Sit here next to me so I can hold you on the way home."

"Okay," she said as he started the engine.

"And don't you ever go any farther away from me than this, woman," he scolded playfully. "This is where you belong. Beside me."

She curled into him, her heart smiling again and hoping she was doing the right thing.


Rex pulled the Silverado to a halt in front of Janet's house, where Hailey had left Joey and Kim. He had agreed to drop her off so the children wouldn't see him, and Hailey would drive them to her house alone. Rex had already decided to follow them, just to make sure they were safe, but he knew it unwise to tell Hailey of his plans. He left his lights on and the engine running as he helped Hailey out of the truck. He had just kissed her and promised to call her before she went to sleep, when Janet came running out of the house, her long hair flying and her arms waving in panic.

"Hailey! Hailey! I tried to call you at the Farrells' but you'd already left. I'm so glad you're here now!" Janet was out of breath and her eyes were frantic.

"What is it?" Hailey asked.

"It's Joey. He's been throwing up off and on all day. I don't know anything about these children's illnesses. He told me that he was sick once yesterday at school but didn't tell you because he didn't want you to worry. Dan called the doctor and he said it was just the flu and if he got a temperature to give him some aspirin. Well, he did. So Dan left to get some at the drugstore. But even since he's been gone, the fever has risen to almost a hundred and four. I was just about to call the doctor again when you pulled up."

"Where is he?" Rex asked, his voice calm yet concerned.

"In my bedroom, at the top of the stairs."

Rex rushed toward the house and bolted up the stairs with Janet and Hailey directly behind him. Stealthily, he opened the door. Hailey pushed past him and went to the side of the bed. She laid her hand on Joey's forehead; he was burning up.

Rex turned to Janet. "Get his things and Kim, too. Hailey, get a blanket to cover him in the truck. We'll take him home. We'll call the doctor again when we get home." Rex slipped his arms under the sweat-soaked boy. His lips were parched, and Rex told Hailey to put a wet cloth on his mouth. Hailey carefully placed a thin wool blanket over him, and Rex pulled the boy closer to his chest.

Janet met them at the bottom of the stairs with a sleepy Kim, who didn't comprehend what was going on.

Kim sat between her mother and Rex and they stretched Joey across their laps. Kim placed her head on Hailey's shoulder and fell asleep. Janet kept fussing guiltily with the blanket. Hailey leaned down to hug her.

"Janet, don't worry. Little boys get fevers all the time. Once the aspirin takes effect, it'll drop."

"What do you think it is?"

"Probably the flu, like the doctor said, or a strep throat. He always gets a high fever with strep. He'll be fine. Don't worry."

"Okay." Janet was unsure. "Call me!" she demanded.

"I will, promise," Hailey said, and Janet waved to them as they sped away.

Hailey put Kim to bed.

Rex had pulled all the covers off Hailey's bed, laid Joey down and begun wiping his body with some rubbing alcohol he had found in the bathroom when Hailey came in with the thermometer.

Joey kept slipping from one dimension to another, never establishing residence in either. Though he mumbled in his sleep, Hailey managed to take his temperature.

"It's still one hundred and four," she announced to Rex, who then put more effort into his meticulous method of alcohol bathing. He didn't miss an inch of the silver-

244

haired boy. Gently he rolled him onto his stomach and made wide swipes at his back and legs and covered the soles of his feet and between his toes.

When he carefully rolled him back, Hailey placed a cool, damp cloth on Joey's forehead. In the bright lamplight his cheeks seemed more aflame than ever.

"Get the aspirin and more rubbing alcohol if you have it." Hailey rushed out of the room, and when she came back, Rex was on the telephone.

"That's right, Doctor, my son has a temperature of a hundred and four. We've been bathing him with alcohol, but it's not helping. How soon can you see him? That's not good enough. What do we do next? Yes." He paused, earnestly nodding in understanding of the instructions the doctor was giving him. "I'll call you if there's any change one way or the other."

Rex hung up the receiver and looked at Hailey, accelerated concern filling his face. "I wanted to take him to the emergency room, but the doctor said he was very busy. I guess a child's fever doesn't sound all that terrible to him. He did say that such fevers were not unusual in smaller children, but in Joey's case it's due to an electrolyte imbalance from dehydration. Anyway, he gave me instructions for ice sheets and ice baths if the aspirin and alcohol don't work, but I'll bet my last dollar we won't have to do that."

Hailey could only nod her head as she kept her eyes locked on Joey.

Rex patted her shoulder. "He's going to be fine." He smiled confidently at her. He went to the bathroom, where he crushed two aspirin into a small amount of water. He sat on the edge of the bed, lifted Joey's head and held the glass to his lips, letting the liquid trickle into his mouth. Joey winced at the bitter aspirin and moaned. With the last drops, he finally opened his eyes and appeared cognizant.

"Mom?" His voice was raspy with pain and disorientation.

"I'm right here, sweetheart," she answered reassuringly. "Can I get you something?"

"Thirsty. I'm thirsty. A Coke, please," he said weakly. Rex handed Hailey the alcohol-soaked washcloth.

"I'll go get it. You stay here with him," he said and left the room.

"I'm feeling much better now, Mom. Is that the doctor? When did we come home? Oh! You didn't forget the model I was working on at Janet's, did you?" His words were rattled off in rapid-fire succession. Joey sat up, his eyes darting around like a trapped animal. "Where is he, huh, Mom? I feel better. I really do. Can I have some ice cream?" He tried to get up, but Hailey held him to the bed.

"Joey! Slow down. You shouldn't get up. If you really want that ice cream, I'll get you some."

"I don't want any!" he shrieked at her. Suddenly he began kicking his legs and beating at the sheets with his hands. "Stop them! Mommy! Mommy! Kill them! Hurry!"

Rex heard Joey's screams and rushed up the stairs three at a time; he halted in the doorway.

Hailey was trying to hold Joey down and still him. She looked at Rex, her eyes pleading and frightened. Joey kept screaming about imagined fire ants that were crawling over him. He tried to slap at them but only stung his own flesh in the process. Impressions of his own handprints sprouted on his fever-flushed skin.

Kim came running into the room, awakened by the sounds of Joey's cries. "Mom! Is he all right?" she asked hesitantly, her eyes wandering up to Rex. He nodded at her, and her mouth gaped in bewildered disbelief at this stranger's presence. She would ask questions later. She assumed that this was the man who'd been at Janet's house tonight. It had all been dreamlike to her at the time. Not until now did she truly realize that there really had been a man with her mother.

"He's going to be all right. Kim, hold his legs still but not too tightly; let him kick a little. It'll just panic him if he's restrained too much."

"What's he doing, Mom? Has he gone crazy?"

"No. No, honey. It's just hallucinations," Hailey replied, thinking it impossible for anyone to refer to this awful pitching and agony Joey was going through as "just."

Kim wished she could be calm like her mother, but she was frightened.

Rex bolted back down the stairs and flung open the freezer door. After precious moments lost rustling around in the pantry, he found a plastic garbage bag. He filled it with the entire contents of the ice bin. He rushed back upstairs, tying a knot in the end of the bag as he went. The doctor had warned him of the hallucinations, but if he had known they would occur with such lightning speed, he would have had the sheets ready. This was an improvisation; he hoped it would work. He grabbed the top sheet he'd hastily tossed on the floor and wrapped it around the ice-filled bag.

Kim watched him as he worked with the bag. She could see desperation in his haste to help Joey, and this frightened her even more. She looked down at her brother. Sweat stood in beads on his upper lip and trickled down the sides of his face.

Rex was kneeling on the other side of Joey, holding the bag, which he'd now formed into an elongated blanket. Hailey spoke to Joey in soothing tones. She smoothed his damp hair away from his hot forehead.

The convulsions slowed and he didn't fight them as much. His screams ebbed to whimpers, with longer pauses between them. Rex was careful not to allow the full weight of the ice to descend on the boy. He held his own body rigid and his muscles trembled as the minutes grouped together, becoming half an hour; three quarters of an hour; an hour.

Hailey took Joey's temperature now that he had calmed down. It was down to 103.8. A drop, but not much. Rex felt that he could stop holding his breath, but only for a second.

Hailey repeated the alcohol bath and kept an icy cloth on Joey's forehead. She looked at Rex as if he had all the answers.

"Go fill the bathtub with cold water," he instructed Hailey.

"I'll do it," Kim answered quickly, glad to be able to make herself useful.

Rex's eyes flashed back to Hailey. "I'll put the ice in the tub and then we'll soak the sheets in it. Then we'll spread them on top of him. If that doesn't do it, we'll have to immerse him in the tub. Agreed?"

"Yes."

"How full do you want this tub?" Kim said, poking her head around the corner.

"Halfway," Rex answered her.

"Then it's ready," she said.

"That's real good, honey, thanks," Rex replied. He backed off the bed, tore at the sheet covering the bag and untied the bag. He poured the half-melted ice and remaining cubes into the water, then dipped the sheet in and wrung it out. He and Hailey stretched it out over Joey. Hailey knelt and pressed the cool cotton sheet against Joey's skin, and when she did she felt his fever heat pierce the cotton fibers. Rex spoon-fed the Coke into Joey's mouth. Finally he awakened and drank more.

"More," Joey said, finishing the glassful.

"I'll get you some, Joey," Kim replied and rushed from the room. She returned shortly with two glasses, one of apple juice and one of Coke. He quickly drank them both.

"That should make you feel better," Hailey said, placing her hand on his forehead. He was notably cooler. She beamed at Joey and then at Rex. "I think it's down."

"Here, check it," Rex said. Joey stared at Rex, his eyes revealing a thousand unspoken questions. Rex knew that as soon as the thermometer was out of Joey's mouth, the interrogation would begin. When Hailey withdrew the thermometer, Joey's face broke into a broad grin and he laughed airily.

"You all look like you're watching a monster movie on TV! You should see your faces!" He chuckled, covering his mouth with his hand.

The tension disintegrated among Hailey, Rex and Kim as they looked from one to the other.

"You *were* scary!" Kim exclaimed.

Hailey read the thermometer. It was down almost two degrees, and for the first time in those suspenseful hours, she believed it would keep on dropping. Joey was still thirsty, and that was a good sign. Joey's eyes were on Rex as he sipped more Coke, which Kim had brought to him.

"Did you take my mom to the party?" Joey asked, his innocence and honesty sparkling in his voice.

"Yes, I did. I'm Rex Cowert. Glad to meet you," Rex said, offering his hand to the boy.

"Hi," he said and paused, glancing furtively at his mother. "Are you in love with my mom?" Joey blurted out unexpectedly and giggled at the stunned faces of the two adults facing him.

"Joey! You shouldn't ask such things. It's none of your business!" Hailey scolded, but both Rex and Joey could see her embarrassment.

"I most certainly am!" Rex answered emphatically.

Joey's grin was wide, but Kim gasped in disbelief. "And I think it's very much your business." He turned to Hailey. "I'm not trying to usurp your authority. I just think he should know the truth."

Unsure of the wisdom of this line of discussion, Hailey said, "I think that Joey should get some rest." Hailey wanted to change the subject altogether.

"Aw, Mom! Can't I stay up a little longer? I feel better, honest."

"You need rest. Look at you—you can hardly keep your eyes open as it is," she said, observing his drooping eyelids. "And you," she turned to Kim, "most definitely should be in bed."

"But what if Joey needs something?" she protested, obviously quite intrigued by this strange man who so openly broadcast his feelings for her mother.

Hailey, wise to her daughter's ploy, said, "Then I'll get it for him. But you go to bed."

"Oh, okay," she said, her exasperation portrayed in her best theatrics. She hugged her mother and said, "Good night, Mr. Cowert."

"Good night, Kim," he said. She reluctantly left the room, still watching Rex.

Hailey gave Joey more aspirin and a last drink of water before she and Rex left him.

They sat on the sofa, Rex's arm around Hailey's shoulder.

"I'm sorry, Hailey," he whispered.

"For what?"

"I know you didn't want me to meet them, much less say what I did up there to Joey. Can you forgive me?"

"Actually, I was about to thank you for all you did for us. I guess I wasn't being very realistic at all. Sooner or later you would have met them anyway. I'm just sorry it had to be like this."

"I'm not," he said reassuringly. "In a way, it was good for all of us," he mused.

"How do you figure that?"

"Because. I know this will sound selfish, but it's the first time in years I felt needed. I know you could have handled everything by yourself and probably have many times in the past. But even if just for one moment you felt a fraction more secure just because I was here, then it was worth it. And I think you did feel that way. I could sense it."

"How is it you know so much?" she asked with amused reflection. "That's exactly how I did feel. It's pretty unnerving to know I'm so readable."

"Yeah," he snickered playfully. "I think I'll just go on letting you believe that, too."

"Why?"

"It gives me an edge, and I think I'm going to need it," he said.

Hailey laid her head on his shoulder, finally allowing herself to relax, but Rex didn't miss the way her eyes kept glancing upward.

"He's going to be all right. We'll go back up and check on him in a little while. But he's fine. We all are," he said in untroubled tones that soothed her brain.

"Yes," she reflected, "we are."

"You know what I'd like?"

"Hmmm. What?"

"I'd like to take you and Kim and Joey to River Bend for Christmas. I'd like you to meet my family. Granddaddy would love having us there. It can be pretty lonely for him during the holidays. He's got all kinds of homemade ornaments he whittled himself. And Daddy makes the eggnog from scratch. We could all go horseback riding, maybe even a hayride. And Bertha, she's the cook, she makes all kinds of baked things for Christmas. She's got these gooey cinnamon rolls just smothered in pecans, and a smoked turkey . . ."

Hailey watched as Rex's eyes danced with anticipation. "All right! All right! You've convinced me. We'll go."

Rex hugged her tightly. "You mean it?"

"Yes, I do."

"Thanks, darlin'. It would mean a lot to me."

"Rex?"

"Hmmm?"

"You've wanted to go home for the holidays all this time, haven't you?"

"Yes," he confessed. "Until I met you, that is. I just wanted to be where you were. This would make it all perfect. I'll call Daddy tomorrow and tell him the good news."

"I think the children would enjoy being on a real ranch. They've never seen one," she said.

"Hailey?"

"Yes, Rex."

"Does this mean we can call off our tree-decorating bet?"

Hailey couldn't keep from laughing. "You coward, you got out of that one pretty easily, didn't you?"

"Yeah, I did, didn't I?"

"Well, I still have to have a tree. It just wouldn't be Christmas without one of my own."

"Well, I don't know about that, but I do know that I can't imagine any holiday or any other day without you."

"Rex?"

"What, baby?"

"I'm glad."

"Me, too," he said and kissed her tenderly.

# Chapter Twenty-six

REX had stayed with Hailey all night, the hours marked by periodic inspections of Joey to monitor his improvement. Hailey had made coffee and fried doughnuts to break the monotony. They had talked and held each other and shared more of themselves. Rex could feel her inching closer to a commitment. She was no longer afraid of his knowing the children. Through the day's crisis, they had grown closer.

Rex took pride in that base that Hailey afforded him for now, more than ever in his life, he needed someone to believe in him. He needed something other than his own gut impulses, for he was about to embark on the most challenging of his business ventures. At eight-thirty the next morning he would sign the papers that would either make or break him.

Rex believed that until 1985, perhaps 1986 at the outside, it was possible for small natural-gas and oil companies to make it big in the energy field. His pioneer spirit, chained to a dream of his own River Bend, urged him to make the break with the development company he had founded and risk it all on one exploit. He was well aware of the huge risks, but Rex had that feeling, the one that had always pressed on him, telling him to try it. He never had so much to lose before, nor so much to gain.

Rex's friend from his Tulane years, Chess McAllister, a huge, burly country boy with sweet-talking ways and an uncanny stockpile of luck, was involved in drilling for oil and gas near Lafayette, Louisiana. Chess had approached Rex last spring about backing him. Chess owned the leases for a wide stretch of land where almost anything with a sharp end stuck in the ground would produce oil. Chess had purchased his rigs, hired crews and now halfway through the drilling had run short of funds. He needed a loan from Rex of $750,000. The total of his own assets, once all the loans and mortgages were paid off, just barely totaled that figure, Rex knew. And even then he would have to sell two of his cars and most of his antiques.

Rex asked Chess why he hadn't struck oil yet. Chess had no answer, only that everyone else had and he frankly couldn't understand it. Before Rex gave Chess an answer, he spent over a month investigating the leases, Chess's financial position, his past business ventures and the potential should the wells come in.

When Rex had reviewed the final figures and recommendations, he had been astounded. The forty-five projected wells, once they were all into production, would net $380,000 per month and somewhere in the vicinity of $7 million to $10 million annually. He immediately picked up the phone and arranged a helicopter flight to see Chess in Louisiana.

Rex flew directly to the oil field and landed thirty yards from the spot where Chess was working with the few men who had remained loyal to him. Rex informed him of the good news, and the two agreed to have the papers drawn up. On that day Remac Oil and Gas Company was born. The split was 49 percent for Chess and 51 percent for Rex, for without Rex's aid, Chess had nothing.

Rex spent half the following week in Lafayette meeting with Chess and the attorneys, and at every available moment, Rex was out in the field, investigating. He needed reassurance that his decision had been solid. He knew too many men who had put everything on the line and lost it. A millionaire one day, a pauper the next. In fact, there were more stories of hard luck than success. He felt uneasy only because his gamble was so large this time, he kept reminding himself. He still had commitments to keep in Houston until after the new year, but after that he would need to spend as much time as possible in Lafayette. Chess projected they would strike oil in mid-January, late in the month at worst.

Chess's unswerving conviction that he had a winner bolstered Rex's confidence, even though Rex knew the investment was wise. He wouldn't have hocked everything but his guitar and his grandmother's oak table if he hadn't thought they would make it. Chess himself had nearly as much to lose as Rex. Whichever way it went, they were in this together.

Eventually Rex knew he would have to tell Hailey, especially since he would be in Lafayette most of January, but the time wasn't right. At least not yet.

## Chapter Twenty-seven

REX and Hailey stood arguing outside the Galleria. He wanted to go Christmas shopping and she had promised Sylvia that they would stop by for drinks. This was not Sylvia's splashiest party that season; that would come later. Tonight would be quiet, only a few friends, and Hailey felt like a reprieve from all the hustle in and around the Galleria.

"Let's start right now," Rex said. "We'll compromise. You go shopping with me and then I'll go to Sylvia and Tony's with you. Take it or leave it," he said sternly.

Hailey burst into laughter. "I wish you could see yourself. You know damn well you've won."

"What's the matter with that?"

"Nothing. But I'll agree only on one condition: I make the hot chocolate when we go home."

"Deal."

"Okay, that's settled. Now, where's your list?"

"Come again? What list?"

"Christmas list! Who are you buying what for?"

"I don't have a list."

"You're kidding! That's un-American. Everybody has a list."

"I don't. I haven't that many people to buy for. Just my granddaddy, Daddy, you, Joey and Kim."

"That's it?"

"Yep."

"What about your friends? Your special ones?"

"Oh, I've already taken care of that. The company sends out a hundred and fifty fruitcakes to clients and acquaintances. I just give the list to my secretary," he stated, proud of his efficiency and forethought.

Hailey shoved her arm through his. "Come on. Let's get started," she said and laughed as they strolled through the Galleria doorway.

At the Sam Houston Bookstore, Rex purchased two novels, the racy, escapist variety, for his grandfather, and the newest best-selling formula on how to make a million dollars for his father, who collected them all—as joke books.

At Frost Brothers he purchased two shirts for himself, an annual tradition. He always took them home, wrapped them carefully and gave them to himself, he told her.

At Cartier's he chose a gold chain bracelet with tiny emerald baguettes for Kim. Hailey was opposed to the idea of precious jewelry for her daughter, but she was relieved that it was not overly expensive.

By the time they reached Neiman-Marcus, Rex was imbued with the spirit of the season. He bought two-pound boxes of Godiva chocolates for everyone, boxed dainty petits fours and cookies for all three households and large sacks of pistachio nuts.

In the toy department he was immediately drawn to a five-lane, fully lighted electric race car set. When he realized he could purchase separate cars, he knew he would have to test them all. Rex grabbed the pistols that operated the cars. The Pantera was the fastest, but the Trans-Am was nearly as quick on the turns.

"Hey! This is great! Come on, baby. Let's see how good you are behind the wheel," he urged her.

"Oh, Rex, I don't think . . ."

"Don't be a spoilsport. Here, I'll let you have the Pantera."

"Oh, all right!" she relented, taking the hand grip and pressing the lever. The Pantera raced ahead. But after two laps, Rex had overtaken her car and laughed heartily with his victory.

"We've got to get this for Joey. He'll love it!"

"I'm sure he will, but I have the sneaking suspicion that you're buying this just for yourself," she surmised, shuffling her bundles in her arms.

"I never said I wasn't," he admitted sheepishly as they took one of the enormous boxes off the shelf. "I guess that about does it."

"Are you sure? I don't want to miss anything."

"Not unless you have something you want to get."

"No, I did my shopping a month ago. It's all on layaway."

"Ah! A born budgeter. Commendable, sweetheart, but not very exciting. Don't you miss some of the excitement and the spirit doing it that way?"

"Not in the least. There were no crowds to fight, plenty of merchandise to choose from and I didn't get a single headache," she said airily as they walked out into the crisp night air.

Tiny clear lights were strung through the bare branches of potted oak trees and looked like iridescent spider webs. If only there could have been a light fluttering of snow-flakes, the big flat ones that look more like goose down, she thought, then the evening would have perfectly matched her mood.

While Rex unlocked the car, she looked up to the sky, half expecting the earnestly wished-for snow, but instead she saw only giant, bright stars, those special lights so big and luminous that one can only view in the Deep South. They were both in such a mirthful frame of mind that Hailey pondered the wisdom of attending Sylvia's party.

Stopping at home, Hailey dressed with the speed of a quick-change artist. She wore a pewter-gray crepe cocktail dress with a high, collarless neckline and long sleeves. It wasn't until she bent to adjust the strap of one of her matching satin high-heeled shoes that Rex noticed the dress was nearly backless. His approving smile danced in his mischievous eyes and before she straightened, he thrust his arms around her waist and sprinkled a row of kisses from her neck to the base of her spine. The sea of goose bumps that sprouted on her skin encouraged his

259

belief that this party was ill timed. He would much rather have stayed at home with Hailey.

"I wish I hadn't promised Sylvia we would come," she said, feeling his hands press against her abdomen, causing her knees to give ever so slightly.

"Me, too, but I have an idea," he said, placing his lips next to her ear. "We'll form a pact. When I give you the high sign, you feign illness; a headache. And then we'll leave, but it can't be any later than midnight. That'll give us two hours there, which is plenty of time to make our obligation."

"It's a deal. But not a headache, that's too transparent. An upset stomach. If they push for us to stay, then it's diarrhea."

"Ugh! That's awful."

"Exactly. It's also something everybody understands, and they'll always urge you to leave, afraid you might have the flu, and nobody, but nobody, wants to catch it. The bubonic plague couldn't get such good results."

"Hailey, you're terrible."

"I know," she said and giggled.


Sylvia Gregson adored Christmas parties, especially when she was the hostess. In her estimation there was no such thing as an impromptu or small gathering. What she lacked in numbers she made up for in lavish decor and sumptuous food and drink. Tonight was strictly cocktails, but the array of hors d'oeuvres was extensive and precisely planned to tease the palate of the most serious dieter and the most discriminating gourmet. The *pâté* was Alsatian, avocados were stuffed with marinated lobster, and an enormous glass platter held oysters on the half shell. In the center of the table was a pyramid of crushed ice jammed with boiled and seasoned crab claws and shrimp.

Sylvia was enough of a traditionalist to opt for red and green decorations, which were becoming increasingly obsolete as her friends searched out unusual and outlandish color schemes. Everything from fuchsia and canary to pink and baby blue were the choices of the holiday designers, who reaped enormous profits from their wealthy clients.

This year Sylvia had spent a small fortune on red roses and baby's breath. Her centerpieces, garlands and thickly branched Christmas tree were decorated solely with the blooms. The mingled fragrances of pine, rose and burning bayberry candles greeted the guests as they passed through the front doorway.

When Hailey and Rex arrived, an hour late, the party was in full swing. Many of the guests had been to previous parties. There were thirty guests, Hailey ventured, most of whom ambled about the house inspecting the decorations. Even the bathrooms had baskets of roses, pine and baby's breath, she had heard a woman say, as Rex came back handing her a glass of champagne.

Rex's hand rested lightly yet possessively on Hailey's waist while they conversed with a young attorney and his wife. Rex had met the man several times over the past three years during the negotiations on the high-rise he'd built, but this was the first they had met socially. Both shared a love of horses and quickly the men were engaged in a friendly dispute over the benefits of breeding and raising Thoroughbreds for profit.

Realizing that their argument would not be settled soon, Hailey politely excused herself and headed for the bathroom, which was located at the end of the entry hall.

Pamela spied them the moment they walked through the front doorway. She had known almost to the minute when they would arrive, for she had followed Rex all evening. In fact, for the past week, she had lived the life of a private detective, watching his every move, noting the hour he left work, where he went, at what time he met Hailey and exactly how much time they spent together. She had even gone so far as to rent a Chevrolet to render herself less visible.

Monday night, Hailey had worked until nine o'clock, at which time Rex met her at the Houston Oaks entrance to the Galleria. They spoke for eleven minutes. Rex then followed her out to Fleetwood, where they spent fourteen minutes inside a French façade house and later emerged with two children.

Pamela then followed them to Hailey's town house, where Rex remained until eleven-thirty, when he left and drove straight home. Only two nights did Pamela watch his penthouse all night, struggling more with her own impulse to pay him a visit than with the belief that he would go somewhere else. He had remained at home. This pattern was unbroken all week except for Wednesday night, when Hailey worked only until six-thirty and they took the little boy and girl to the Old San Francisco Steak House for dinner. Again, Rex left Hailey's house at exactly eleven-thirty.

Pamela formulated her plan with the facts available to her. Unfortunately for her, it was apparent that Rex saw Hailey every day. She couldn't lie about him having spent an off-night with her. However, since Rex and Hailey were creatures of an already established routine, Pamela would use that one quirk and manipulate it to her advantage. After being Rex's No. 1 choice for so long, she knew enough about him and his dating stratagems to implement various personality traits and idiosyncracies into her scheme. Using such tactics, her story would virtually chime with the truth. Pamela's almond-shaped eyes glowed with menace.

Undetected, she observed Hailey as she walked to the bathroom. A more perfect opportunity would not present itself all evening, Pamela thought. Just as Hailey was about to shut the door, Pamela surreptitiously dashed to the hallway and caught the knob before the door had fully closed. In the flash of an eye she slipped inside, shut and locked the door and then leaned back on it, smiling maliciously at a stunned Hailey, who immediately backed away from the gorgeous brunette. Hailey recognized her instantly, of course, but she was so confused by Pamela's actions that she said nothing.

Pamela, knowing that her hatred and jealousy of Hailey must undoubtedly show in her expression, blithely turned toward the mirror, pretending to inspect her makeup.

"I hope you don't mind my rushing in here, but I felt I

just had to talk to you about something that's vital to both of us," Pamela mewed with just enough sincerity to thwart Hailey's attention away from the peculiar circumstances.

"What could we possibly . . ." Hailey began, but Pamela wouldn't let her finish.

"I know what you're going to say," Pamela said, thrusting her hand up as if to wave off Hailey's opposition. "But the answer is . . . plenty." She took a shallow breath, punctuating the gesture with a reassuring smile. "I have always believed that we women should stick together in situations like this."

Hailey, a trifle dazed by Pamela's meaning, was reluctant to say anything and merely allowed Pamela to continue.

"I understand from some of my friends that Rex is seeing you on, er, a rather steady basis."

"Why, yes, he is, but I don't see what that has to do with you."

"Actually, not that much, since I'm not all that serious about him. Oh, don't get me wrong. He's a great guy and we've had a lot of laughs together. We have a lot in common, our upbringing and all, I mean," Pamela explained with wide, honest-looking eyes; eyes that spewed concern for Hailey without a trace of selfishness.

"Then what does all this have to do with me? Especially since you aren't dating Rex anymore?" Hailey retorted defensively.

"What? Who told you that?"

"Why . . . Rex did," Hailey replied so innocently and trustingly that Pamela wanted to clap her hands in glee. Hailey was falling right into her trap.

"Listen, Hailey. Men will say or do anything to get what they want. The truth of the matter is that I see him regularly."

Pamela watched satisfyingly as Hailey's face went ashen. Had the blonde not been leaning against the vanity, Pamela thought surely her knees would have buckled beneath her. She was tempted to give the girl a glass of water, but thought better of it. Such a gesture might be too melodramatic. Besides, she rather enjoyed watching Hailey endure this torture. Serves her right, Pamela thought deliciously.

"Did you ever bother to ask Rex what he does after he leaves your house at eleven-thirty every night?"

"Why, how did you know what time he leaves?" Hailey asked incredulously.

"How do you think? Because from approximately midnight until morning he is with me. Rex doesn't keep the same hours as most men," Pamela said, fully enjoying herself. "I know this must all be a shock to you. Why! You can imagine how I felt when I first heard about your involvement with him. I felt like a fool, and that's got to be how you're feeling now. It's written all over your face. Believe me, it's not pleasant knowing that you've been duped, taken advantage of." Pamela played out the words, utilizing phrases that would cut Hailey to the quick.

"He told me he loved me and I believed him. He . . . he asked me to marry him . . . and he's been so wonderful with the children . . . telling them how we were all going to be a family," Hailey whispered her thoughts aloud. Her hands were sweating and her stomach churned.

"Yes. He *is* convincing, isn't he? I should know. I just wanted you to know the truth about him, Hailey. It won't be long before he drops you for somebody else. Oh, it won't be me, I can guarantee that! I've learned my lesson, but there will always be another woman. Rex keeps a string of them following him around. And he'll be just as coldhearted to them as he was to *us*." She placed heavy emphasis on the "us" as she noted the near panic now veiling Hailey's deep blue eyes.

"You have to understand about Rex. He has absolutely no need for a commitment. He has everything a man could want. There're hundreds of women just itching to get into bed with him, and knowing Rex's sexual appetites the way I do, they'll all make it!"

Pamela loved this. She'd known with her very first words to Hailey that the blonde didn't really trust Rex, and that had been her wedge. Hailey was obviously not sophisticated enough to believe in open relationships, nor was she strong enough to fight back as long as Pamela kept hurling these charges about Rex at her. At this point, Pamela could have told her that Rex was the son of Satan and she would have believed it. That's where Rex's own past had worked against him. Why not use the truth to further her own means? Distorted truths were always more reliable than overt lies.

"I realize that you have to make your own decisions about yourself and Rex. I just wanted you to know that I won't be a threat to you anymore. I've found out the hard way what it's like to be taken in by him. I value myself and my feelings more than that. Don't worry about me, I'm going to be just fine, especially now that I've found out the *truth*." Pamela reached over and patted Hailey's icy hand in the warmest display of caring she could muster. "Good luck, dear. You'll need it," Pamela said as she ceremoniously turned to leave. "I'll be leaving the party immediately. No sense in giving the gossips fodder for the morning columns, is there?"

"No . . ." Hailey agreed wanly.

"Good-bye, Hailey," Pamela replied and vanished like a cold vapor.

Hailey's throat was so tightly constricted she thought she would choke. Who was telling the truth, Rex or Pamela? Even Janet had said that Rex had lots of women, a fact he never once denied. Why would he want her then? She was a divorcée, over thirty, with two children. How could he give it all up and be faithful to her? How long before he found someone else? A month? A year?

Hailey knew that some men were so immersed in themselves that all they sought were conquests. There were men who could not meet the challenge of fidelity, so insecure were they that they believed themselves worthy of nothing more than fleeting affairs.

What kind of man was she in love with? She had been foolish to believe and trust him thus far. Did he intend to marry her and keep others, like Pamela, on the side, until she, his wife, became the joke of all their friends? She could never stomach the pity she would see on their faces—the women he had approached, the men who knew from his boasting. When would she stop it, for it was her decision? Pamela, at least, had been right about that much.

She glanced in the mirror. Her eyes were bone dry with no luster; only determination sparkled at the edges. She knew what she must do. She'd had to make so many big, overpowering, life-affecting decisions in such a short period of time. But this one . . . she wasn't so all-fired sure she was right. When she turned the doorknob, her hand was shaking.

# Chapter Twenty-eight

REX spent three days mentally stomping over the events of the last hours with Hailey. It made no sense to him, he thought as he dangled the brandy glass between his fingers. They had gone shopping and she had been nearly effervescent, she was so happy. She sparkled with holiday gaiety at the Gregsons' party, though he did think she had tired somewhat shortly after their arrival, for her voice had sounded strained at moments. Not so much when they were in the company of others, but when left alone, she'd appeared aloof. He'd thought it simply part of her "act" to feign illness so they could leave early, but once outside the house, she'd asked him to take her home, breaking her promise to spend the weekend with him. She told him she'd been caught in her own lie, for she actually felt as if she did have the flu. Her pasty color made him believe her.

And now here he was, alone again, his weekend turned to ashes where he had dreamed all week of being with Hailey—holding her, making love to her and praying she would finally relent and marry him. Hell! he thought as he ran his fingers through his hair, he even missed Joey and Kim!

He called her every fifteen minutes all day Saturday and Sunday, but there was no answer. She had even turned the answering machine off. Something was drastically wrong. Today he'd called her at work and she'd put him on hold and never came back. If he hadn't been swamped with meetings and appointments, he would have gone right over and demanded an explanation. In fact, he'd almost done just that, but she had left early, telling Barrett she didn't feel well. Maybe she really did have the flu.

A nagging suspicion in the back of his mind told him that wasn't the answer either. She was clearly avoiding him and he decided it was up to him to find the reasons for it. As far as he could tell he hadn't done anything she could possibly misconstrue. Unless, perhaps, she felt he was pushing her too hard. Now that he had met Joey and Kim due to unforeseen circumstances, maybe she wanted to break the bonds he was forming with them. But if that was the reason, why was she afraid just to tell him so? He would back off, hard as that might be for him. If that's what she wanted, he would comply.

Sitting here weighing pros and cons was getting him nowhere. He checked his watch. Eight o'clock. She was probably getting the children into bed now and then she would be alone, so they could talk. If they didn't have this out face to face, he would go on forever trying to catch this elusive woman. He put down his drink and picked up his sheepskin-lined jacket and headed for the garage. He'd take the Silverado, for he would need a peace offering to break the ice and he had the perfect gift in mind.

Hailey sat numbly on the couch, staring vacantly at the stack of Christmas cards she needed to address. She had no energy, no incentive to think about or participate in anything connected to the holidays. She thought by now she would have been completely cried out, but it seemed that there was nothing whatsoever to celebrate. She thought surely by now she could have gathered enough strength to call to cancel the rest of her social engagements for the month. But she hadn't. She couldn't face anyone in her state of mind. She could function well at work and was able to keep up a good front for the children, but when the sun went down, she felt ripped apart inside. The scene with Pamela had been bad enough, but it was worse each time she replayed it. Pamela's words haunted her and kept needling at her brain. Her whole world seemed to be crumbling down. The final blow had come today at work, when Barrett had called her into his office.

"Hailey, I was just going over the books now that we're nearing the end of the year, and I have a memo here from Leonard stating that you haven't given us your check for the finder's fee on your portraits. I know of twelve that we contracted here. Were there any others?"

"Why, yes, only a few. But they were on referrals. Surely I don't have to pay the fee on those," she asked.

"I thought it was clearly understood that you would. Doesn't your contract state that?" he replied in business-like tones.

"Not that I know of," she said flatly, her eyes narrowing suspiciously.

"I'll have to look at it again. Perhaps I was wrong," he said sweetly. "At any rate, here's the final tally," he said, handing her an invoice with her balance due typed at the bottom, and it was signed by Leonard.

She gasped. "Thirty-six hundred dollars! Barrett, there's been some incredible mistake here!" she retorted. Her nerves coupled with sleepless nights had left her strung to the limit. She was unable to focus on the blurry page.

"Oh, no mistake. That's it. Twelve paintings at three hundred each. That's fifty percent of the price you were paid, providing you did charge them all six hundred dollars. You didn't raise the price and not tell me, did you, Hailey?" he asked condescendingly.

Hailey was on the verge of explosion. "Fifty percent! Where did you come up with that figure? We agreed on five percent, and that's what my contract states."

"What? There's been some terrible mixup. The company copies clearly state fifty. How can this be?"

"I don't know," Hailey huffed. "Do you have a copy of the contract?"

"Of course, right here, uh, let me see. Where did I put that folder?" he mumbled to himself as he shuffled frantically through the stacks of paper on his desk. "Ah, here it is," he said, holding it up triumphantly.

Hailey quickly snatched it out of his hand. Her eyes zeroed in on the percentage. In bold black type it was proclaimed: 50 percent.

"Really, Hailey. Don't you think you're making too much of this? After all, this was what we agreed upon," he said indignantly as if she had challenged his integrity, and Barrett was suitably disturbed and defensive.

"I remember signing a five-percent contract," Hailey replied, tightly gripping her anger. "I can't believe Leonard would have proposed this . . . but I can see that he did." Hailey felt as if she'd been betrayed. "How could Gerald have missed it?" she mumbled to herself.

"I can see this has upset you. Why don't you take the rest of the day off. You don't need to pay the money right away, if that helps. I'm sorry there has been some error on your contract and that you've been under some misconception about these minor details."

"Yes . . . maybe that would be best," she said faintly. "I could use some time to sort this out."

"You do that, Hailey. And I'll see you tomorrow," he replied. Still stunned she turned mechanically and left the store.


Once Hailey had arrived at home she immediately called Gerald's office, only to learn he was in Vail for the holidays skiing and not expected to return until after New Year's. She then called Leonard at the Montrose gallery, but he was out and Agatha said he would not return again before closing. She promised to have him call her in the morning.

How could everything have disintegrated so quickly? She was dangerously close to losing her job. Half of all the money she'd earned, those long, exhausting nights at the easel, was about to be swept away. She had lost Rex—if he had ever been hers to lose—but worst of all, she was virtually devoid of self-esteem. She hadn't managed a single facet of her life with any intelligence whatsoever.

She could have handled the argument with Barrett over

270

the money if she'd felt secure about Rex and his love for her. Even if she lost her job, she could get another one. But now, without Rex, everything took on those thick, black outlines and garbled words that nightmares were made of. How long would it take to forget him? At least a thousand times she'd started to phone him to ask to see him. Deep inside she knew it would be easier to let him go now, before they became any more involved.

Tears stung her eyes. God! When would she stop this? She drew her knees up, wrapped her arms around them and laid her head on them. She had to get Rex out of her system.

Just then the doorbell rang. Hailey had half a notion to ignore it, but when it rang two more times in quick succession, she finally rose and trudged to the door. She looked through the peephole. It was Rex! Convictions, better judgment, vows to herself never to see him again and all of Pamela's words were burned on a pyre in those split seconds while she fumbled with the lock. The door flew open.

"Hailey, please . . ." he started to say, when he pulled her into his arms and kissed her face over and over, tasting the remains of salty tears. She had been crying and not just a little, but a lot, for her eyes were red and swollen. He pressed her into him. She was sobbing.

"Hailey, what is it? What have I done?" he asked, her arms growing tighter around his neck.

"Oh, Rex. I love you. I love you. What am I going to do?" she cried.

"About what, baby?" he said, easing her backward into the house and closing the door behind him.

"About me. I've been trying so hard to stop it and I can't."

"Stop what?"

"Being in love with you!"

"Jesus Christ! Don't do that, baby!" He tried to laugh to lift her spirits, but he felt his feet sinking right through the floor. "Why would you ever think something like that?"

Hailey remained silent but was finally able to stem her

tears. She knew she could never tell him about Pamela because she was in love with Rex and if she tried to discredit Pamela in any way, it would only make her look like a shrew, not simply the injured party. After all, even though Rex said he didn't love Pamela, she was his choice once and Hailey would never accuse him of poor taste or bad judgment. The problem was not between Rex and Pamela at all. This was Hailey's battle to win. Pamela wanted Rex all to herself or else she wouldn't be fighting so hard for him. Pamela had been the one who was playing mind games with her, not Rex.

As she looked up into his eyes filled with unburied love and openness, she knew instinctively she could trust him. Maybe it would have been easier if she had known him longer. After all, love was blind, but she had been so miserable the past three days without him that she was willing to try again, trust in herself again. Perhaps that was the true dilemma. At this moment, with all these crises mounting, believing in herself was not easy. She wondered if she had ever made a right decision in her life.

"Everything has gone wrong," she finally said.

"It can't be all that bad. Do you want to talk about it?"

"I'm not sure. I don't see what good it would do."

"Well, I sure as hell do!" he fumed, his anger and hurt at her avoidance of him commanding his words. "You've refused to talk to me for days, even putting me on goddamned hold at work, and now when I finally see you—at my initiative, I might add—you tell me you want to stop loving me. Not that you have, or could, just that you want to. So what the shit is going on with you, woman?" His jaw ground back and forth as he searched her face for an answer. His grip on her arm was firm but not rough. He was insistent.

"For starters, I think I'm about to lose my job, my boss is trying to weasel thirty-six hundred dollars out of me, I can't find my attorney, it's Christmas and my bills are stacking up and I can't even find a Christmas tree for my children. Why on earth would you want someone like me . . ." It was all pouring out of her like a flood, and she almost let it slip about Pamela.

"Wait a minute, wait a dad-gum minute. Let's take this one by one. What's this about the money?" Rex asked, trying to put some order to everything.

"I have to pay the gallery a finder's fee for the portraits I do. I signed a contract that states a five-percent fee. I was so sure I had done all this intelligently. I was so proud of myself. Now Barrett says it's fifty percent, and that's what his copies do say. I saw them with my own eyes, but mine state five percent. Why would he do such a thing?"

"I have an idea. Can I see a copy of your contract?"

"I just had it out to check it. It's upstairs. I'll go get it for you," she said and scurried up the stairs and returned in moments. Rex was seated at the kitchen table, an open beer in hand.

As soon as he read it he could see that it was impossible for someone to get away with this. Blatant illegal alteration of a contract like this was meant to frighten Hailey. It wasn't the money, he thought. Perhaps someone wanted her to quit. But why? Once her attorney was contacted, he would undoubtedly verify Rex's suspicions.

"How long have you known Leonard and Barrett?"

"Not quite a year. Just since I went to work for them."

"What's your attorney's name?"

"Gerald Harrison. I've got his card over here by the phone," she said and then handed it to him.

"Hailey, I want you to understand, you don't have to do this. But I think I can get this cleared up, if you'll let me. Legally, you're covered. They can't do anything to you."

"What are you going to do?"

"I'm just going to investigate this a little farther. Tomorrow, when you go to work, tell them that you'll have the money in full before New Year's. You could tell them it's in a certificate of deposit at the bank and you don't want to lose your interest. They'll buy that. Then just go about your business as usual. Okay?"

"Okay. But how do you plan to investigate?"

"With a private detective. Leave it to me."

Hailey's hands were balled into fists and he could see her rage building. "God! I've been so stupid!"

"No, you haven't. You handled everything perfectly. It's

just that I think this thing goes a little deeper. My guess is that someone is out to nail you for some reason. Perhaps Barrett thinks he can make a little money on the side. It's a small-time con game he's playing, but there's always the chance it could be a lot more than that. We need some background information on both Leonard and Barrett. If they're in this together, you aren't going to want to work for them anymore, are you?"

"No," she answered with resignation. "But then what will I do? I have to feed my family."

"You can go to work for me," he said, holding her hand.

"Doing what?"

"Right now, I don't know." He pondered the wisdom of telling her about Chess and the oil. Maybe it was just as good a time as any. "I can take care of you, Hailey."

"Sure you can. You have lots of money. But I can take care of myself, you know," she said indignantly.

"I never said you couldn't. You've proved that to me and yourself. And I didn't mean it like that, not derogatorily, anyway. What I meant was that together we make a pretty strong team."

"Yes, I guess we do," she replied, letting her smile come from within her eyes. "You know, it's really strange, but it feels . . . I don't know . . . reassuring, maybe, to have you there to help me. It's like a new brand of confidence I didn't have before."

"Maybe it's trusting yourself and your judgment enough to rely on me," he observed.

"Yes, maybe it is."

"Hailey, there's something I need to talk to you about," he said, looking down at their intertwined fingers.

"This sounds very serious."

"It is." He paused. "I think that I should tell you that in January I won't be around very much. I have to go to Louisiana on business."

"How long will you be gone?" she asked, remembering how lonely just three days without him had been.

"Three weeks, a month. Maybe longer."

"Why so long?"

"I've invested quite heavily in an oil company with a

friend of mine. In fact, if the wells don't come in, we may have to live on your income until I can get started again." His laugh was stilted, and instantly Hailey realized what he was saying.

"I'm sure you wouldn't have done it if you didn't think you could make money, but even if you don't, you'll find something else. As long as we have each other we can do anything."

He kissed her hand and then gently tugged on her arm, pulling her out of her chair and onto his lap. He hugged her as she snuggled her face into his neck. "We're going to make it, baby, you just wait and see," he whispered.

"I believe you," she said.

"I hope so," he said as they held each other in silence. Then suddenly he started pushing her out of his lap. "Get up," he ordered urgently.

"What's the matter?"

"I forgot something. It's out in the truck. Just to prove to you that I do intend to take care of you," he said, pulling his keys out of his pocket. He headed for the door. "Hold the door open for me when I get back."

"Rex? What are you doing?" she asked, confused at the sudden change in his mood.

"You'll see," he said and left.

In a few minutes he returned, dragging a lushly branched seven-foot Douglas fir tree.

"My tree! You brought me a tree!" she said, excitedly inspecting the soft needles.

"Yeah, beats roses, doesn't it?" he joked as he pulled it down the hallway to the living room.

"It sure does!" she said and then noted his dilemma as he looked around the room.

"Hailey, I'm surprised at you! You haven't even rearranged the furniture yet. Where are you going to put this thing?"

"By the window. Here, let's move the sofa to an angle," she said, grasping the arm of the sofa and pulling it toward her. "I've got a stand in the storage closet and all the decorations and lights."

Rex was laughing when he took her into his arms.

"That's what I love about you, baby, you really get into these things. Sometimes you're just like a little girl."

"Is that bad?" she asked, running her fingertips over his lips.

"Huh-uh. Because I know you're all woman. All I'd ever want." He let his lips savor the taste of hers.

Hailey molded her body into his, wanting this moment to last forever. Everything with the world had been made right again. When they were together like this there were no Pamelas or Barretts or oil wells. They were right for each other and that's all that mattered to her. His hands caressed her back eagerly, building the fire he had started in her.

"Rex," she said as he planted tiny kisses on her neck, "don't go home tonight. Stay here with me," she said and then he held her face with his hands and peered deeply into her eyes.

"Are you sure?"

"Yes, I'm sure. I don't want you to go away."

"I won't do that, I promise. I'll never leave you, Hailey. I love you too much," he said and kissed her again, more hungrily than before. And then abruptly he started laughing. "Woman, if we keep this up, we'll never get that tree decorated, and I think it would be neat to surprise Joey and Kim with it in the morning. What do you think?"

"I think that as usual, you're right. I'll get that stand," she said, breaking away from him. She went out between the french doors and returned in a few minutes.

Hailey held the tree while Rex affixed the screws through the trunk and together they strung the multicolored lights. Hailey pulled out box after box of glass ornaments. Two hours later, they stood back and inspected their handiwork.

"Needs candy canes, doesn't it?" he asked.

"It sure does. But I guess we'll just have to wait until morning to buy some," she said, looking up into his eyes.

"How about we worry about it then?" he replied huskily and bent down and unplugged the lights. He put his arm around her waist and walked her down the hallway. When they reached the stairs, he swept her up in his arms and carried her upstairs.

"Everybody needs a little romance, don't you think?" he teased in a low whisper.

"Oh, yes!" she answered as he closed the bedroom door with his foot and gently laid her on the bed.

As he gazed deeply into her eyes, he said, "I hope no one ever shares this bed with you except me."

"There never has been anyone else and there never will be," she promised, putting her arms around his neck and drawing him closer to her.

He touched her face, letting his fingers trace the slope of her nose and lips. His kiss, gentle and sweet at first, grew more passionate as he felt her hands pull at his shirt. She unbuttoned it very slowly, relishing every moment she put him off. He heard rather than felt his jeans zipper open. He kicked off his boots and socks without moving away from her.

"Aren't you the clever one?" she teased, surprised at his deft disrobing.

"Now it's your turn," he said, groaning as his fingers touched the neckline zipper of her caftan. He pulled it open and found she was naked beneath it. His lips fell upon her breasts, devouring the honeyed delicacy of her nipples. It seemed like centuries since he had made love to her and he wondered how he could ever last more than a day without her. Her willingness to give him all her love thrilled and excited him more than he believed possible. He wanted her more now than he had the last time.

They sank into each other, their bodies uniting amid ecstatic sighs. Stroking slowly and cautiously tender, he interspersed his rhythm with quick, unexpected thrusts that drove her to moan out loud. Rotating, then thrusting, meeting and falling away from each other, her passion grew by the second. He released her hips and played with her breasts, massaging, pulling, almost pinching and watched her head push back farther into the pillows while he relentlessly stroked her. Her eyelids were tightly shut and he knew she would scream at any moment. Her panting quickened and suddenly she held her breath. Instantly he covered her mouth with his, swallowing her climactic cry. Her fingernails dug into the skin on his buttocks and drove him to an explosion of his own. And this time her mouth drank his groans of pleasure.

"Oh, God . . . I love you, Hailey," he whispered. "Say you'll marry me. I can't stand this anymore. I need to be with you."

"I need you, too. I don't like it when you aren't here," she said as he rolled over and held her next to him. His hand slid tenderly up and down her side and then he hugged her again. "I want to spend my life with you. I think from the first day we met, I knew; I don't know how, but I did. This is probably dumb to say, but somehow I know we were fated," he said. "I've just had a tough time convincing you of that."

"Not anymore."

"What . . . what are you saying?" he asked, lifting her face to his so he could read the thoughts in her eyes.

"I'll marry you," she replied quietly.

He sighed with relief. "I'll make you happy, I promise. Damn! You've made me so happy already," he burst with hope. He kissed her over and over. "Are you sure?"

"Very sure."

"Good. That's settled," he said matter-of-factly. "Now the question is when?"

"In May, like you said."

"But that's five months away!" he exclaimed.

"What's wrong with that?"

"Plenty. How about April? Eastertime! That's it! Think about what a beautiful time of year that would be!"

"You're trying to sell me a bill of goods," she teased, watching his dejected look as she taunted him. "But . . ." She watched. He was holding his breath. "April is nice, too. April sounds fine."

"Early April," he pushed. "Maybe March would be better . . ."

"Rex! Will you stop it? Mid-March and that's it! No earlier," she said and giggled.

"Not Valentine's Day?"

"No," she said adamantly but couldn't stifle her laugh. "Rex, why don't you just tell me when you want to get married so we can stop all this foolishness."

"Good idea. Get up. Let's go," he said, jumping out of bed and tugging on her arm.

"What for? Where are we going?"

"To get married . . . tonight, of course."

"Not until May!" Her eyes narrowed.

He slithered back into bed and covered them both and pulled her next to him again and ran his fingers through her hair until she started to fall asleep. Her breathing became slow and measured. Just as she was about to fall into unconsciousness, he whispered, "Mid-March."

When they fell asleep, they were both smiling.

# Chapter Twenty-nine

REX had his investigator's report and a copy of Hailey's contract in his briefcase when he arrived at Leonard's office at the appointed hour. He was ushered in by Agatha.

"Mr. Cowert. How do you do?" Leonard said politely, shaking Rex's hand. "You said on the telephone that this was urgent. I'm quite pressed for time, the holidays and all, you understand. Won't you have a seat, please?" he said.

"I understand quite fully. I'm as equally pressed for time, Mr. Sims," Rex said as he seated himself across the desk from Leonard. "I understand there has been a dispute between Hailey and your associate, Mr. Anderson, over her finder's fee for her portraits. I told Hailey I would intervene on her behalf. What I've discovered is enlightening, to say the least."

Leonard leaned forward, still cautious but intrigued by what Rex was saying. "I wasn't aware of any dispute, but go on . . ."

"I assumed that was the case. In short, Mr. Sims, the documents in your files have been altered. Once you check it against this copy of Hailey's contract—I think you will agree with me." He paused to watch Leonard's reaction to this information.

"I haven't informed Hailey of the extent of my investigations because they are of interest only to you. As a businessman, I thought you should be the sole recipient of this report. You can deal with the problem in whatever manner you see fit. To put it bluntly, there is a viper in your nest. Mr. Anderson is nothing more than a con man and has been embezzling and stealing both money and stock from the gallery. Somehow, Hailey got caught in the crossfire or perhaps he felt she would eventually discover his scheme. At any rate, he wanted her out of the way. I think you will see this once you have read my report. Hailey has a lot of respect for you, and I hope it hasn't been unwarranted."

Rex placed the file on the desk as Leonard rose.

"I'll look it over at once," Leonard replied, "and I'll make my own conclusions. Good day, Mr. Cowert," Leonard said icily.

Rex couldn't blame him for his wariness. After all it was his judgment of character that was on the line as much as his business. No one likes being told he'd made an error. But Leonard impressed Rex as a fair man.

"Good-bye, Mr. Sims," Rex replied and left, hoping that he'd been correct in his appraisal of Leonard's integrity.

During the last week before Christmas, Rex and Hailey fulfilled their long-standing invitations to the splashiest parties in the city. Rex joked that by New Year's he would have completely worn out his narrow-lapeled tuxedo and would need to have a new one tailored. Hailey thought half seriously that a fortune could be made in a "rent a Dior" business. This season the evening clothes were more romantic, with ruffles, lace, sequins and beading even on the Halstons. And they were expensive. Somehow she had made it through it all with a copy of a black lace St. Laurent she had purchased at Loehmann's for just under two hundred dollars, and a black satin dirndl skirt with matching camisole and black sequined jacket. There was a three-year-old black crepe sheath, barely used, however, that she often wore with a matching shawl.

She purposefully chose black for all her evening clothes. It enhanced the silver color of her hair and she hoped that since all her clothes were the same color, everyone would have to think long and hard as to whether they had actually seen that particular dress before, or if they only *thought* they had.

It wasn't like her to be this overly concerned with the labels in the back of her dresses. Something in her relationship with some of the people they associated with had altered drastically and for no apparent reason. Perhaps she had been too easily accepted by them in the beginning. Maybe now she was simply a fading fad, her portraits now passé. She was beginning to feel that she needed to win them back.

What had she done to fall into disfavor, if that's what this actually was? Ever since that night at Sylvia's and the confrontation with Pamela, Hailey had noticed at all the parties a distinct iciness, a forced politeness except for Sylvia and Tony and a few others. At first Hailey thought she'd only imagined it all and she was reluctant to mention anything to Rex. Men always thought women took such things too seriously, saying they were too sensitive. It was Christmas, she told herself, everyone was on edge, tense from their own hectic schedules. Admittedly, her life was bulging at the seams trying to juggle Rex, the children, work and all the holiday obligations they had. It was understandable, she surmised, and too, perhaps after the holidays, everything would fall back into place and return to normal.

The night before they were to leave for River Bend, they had been invited to a dinner given by a group of five couples, including the Gregsons, who had extended the invitation to them. It was to be held at the River Oaks Country Club.

That night Hailey wore the black silk Halston Stephen had given her. She couldn't help but think about him now. It seemed so long ago now, as if it were part of another world. He had been right that he was the one to change her world more than any other man. He had given her the courage to find her talent and use it. And sadly, she had never had the chance to thank him, but somehow he must know by now how grateful she was. Her bitterness had died and she understood now how much he had cared about her.

And now there was Rex, who had given her love and completed the miracle. She was wonderfully blessed and she wondered sometimes why she had been singled out for it all.

She slipped on a high-heeled black satin shoe. Her purse was black, beaded and borrowed from Janet. A final spritz of Oscar de la Renta perfume made her feel extravagant.

The children were to spend the night with Janet and Dan. When Janet had told her that the four of them would go caroling that night, Hailey nearly tossed all her plans aside. It sounded wonderful, but she knew if she'd said anything about it to Rex, he would gladly have traded the tux for his guitar. However, several of Rex's financial backers would be attending the party and he had been adamant about seeing them on friendly ground now that Remac Oil and Gas Company was his mainstay. Already he had lost touch with several friends once the development company had been sold and he wanted them all to see firsthand that he was not abandoning them or Houston.

The country club, which sat at the end of River Oaks' most impressive row of mansions, loomed over its subjects with as much splendor as Buckingham Palace. The arrival of the guests was as impressive a spectacle as the party itself. Streams of Rolls-Royces, Bentleys, Mercedes and Cadillacs deposited their owners at the front door. Into this group of motorized royalty roared Rex's Silverado, the only pickup in the group.

Hailey sensed something ominous all evening, and even now, as they entered the plush country club, social haven of the superrich, the chill she experienced was real, not imagined.

They were halfway through the reception line when she caught the flash of Pamela's smile out of the corner of her eye. Hailey couldn't help thinking that there still might be something between Rex and Pamela. She hadn't openly confronted Hailey again, but suspicion gnawed at Hailey constantly. No matter where they went—a party, the theater, the ballet—Pamela was *always* there. What else was she to think? She had heard of men carrying on other affairs like this. Besides, a man would have to be made of stone not to be attracted to Pamela. None of the women in the room came close to Pamela's beauty. And worst of all, Hailey knew Pamela most definitely hadn't given up on Rex.

They finished greeting their hosts and were immediately served champagne. Hailey bolted hers down and asked Rex for another. He stared at her quizzically but made no comment. He had left her only for a matter of moments when Pamela wandered past with Sylvia. Pamela purposefully steered Sylvia within Hailey's earshot.

"If I were Hailey I wouldn't be caught dead in that same dress again. She has absolutely no taste whatsoever. I should think she'd need to cultivate a little mystery if she wants to keep Rex around. Why he hangs onto that pale little girl, I'll never know."

Then Hailey heard Sylvia's distinctive voice. "He probably feels like most of us, that Hailey is a talented and intelligent woman, not to mention a few other things I doubt you'd know anything about. She has qualities that can't be found in a damn clothes closet!" Sylvia stalked off, never realizing how close Hailey stood to her.

Hailey then turned to face Pamela. Her eyes burned with hatred as she glared at Hailey. Suddenly, nonplussed, Pamela glided off to capture the arm of a handsome man who had been signaling to her from across the room.

Just then Rex returned, oblivious to anything or anyone but Hailey. He kissed her cheek and then moved his mouth to her ear and said, "Do you know I love you more than anything in this world?"

Hailey smiled triumphantly. "I hope so, because I'm very much in love with you."

Rex beamed as he looked at her, put his hand on her waist and steered her toward a quartet of men, whispering to her that at one time they had been investors in one of his industrial parks. Just as they walked up, Rex cheerily greeted them all. Their faces turned stony and they each made excuses for the dispersal of the clique. Hailey was more prepared for the plaster smiles that openly snubbed them than Rex was. Only she saw the hurt in his eyes, for he successfully masked his shock from the others. Had she not been witness to the scene, she never would have guessed what had taken place.

The orchestra was playing "Misty," and Rex took Hailey's hand and silently led her to the dance floor. With her held securely in his arms they slowly made their way around the floor, Rex stopping to chat with acquaintances. Polite smiles and stilted compliments spun around them, as if in tune to the music. Hailey's stomach churned. Not once had she ever felt like this, and the oddest part was that most of the thinly coated hostility was directed toward Rex.

The music ended and everyone drifted off to their tables. Hailey found their name cards at a round linen-covered table near the window. Rex aided her with her chair just as Sylvia and Tony arrived and sat next to them.

Hailey couldn't stand the tension any longer. She was worried that Pamela might have been up to her tricks again and she wanted to stop it before it went any farther. She asked Rex to order her some champagne.

"Sylvia, would you care to go to the powder room with me before dinner is served?"

Sylvia started to decline, but she caught the imploring look in Hailey's eyes. "Sure."

They walked into the hall and sought a small alcove with a yellow damask-covered love seat. "Let's go over there," Hailey said, nudging Sylvia in the right direction.

"Okay, you got me out of there, now what's wrong?"

"I was hoping you could tell me. For the past few weeks everyone in the crowd has been treating me as if I had the plague. I know Pamela has been using every opportunity to get her digs in. I'm fully aware that lately she's been saying she's engaged to Rex. He hasn't heard it yet, but he will."

"Hailey, dear heart, I do think you're being a bit paranoid. No one could give two cents what Pamela is doing, except you, of course. It's *your* business, not theirs. I agree with you that she can be a pain in the ass; she does have a talent for stirring up trouble." Sylvia spoke with finality but Hailey could tell she was holding something back.

"Something is wrong, though. I can see it in your face. If it isn't Pamela, what is it?"

Sylvia sighed deeply. "All I know is that Tony told me some of the men are apprehensive about Rex now that he's finalized the sale on all his holdings. They feel that he's sold them out. Selfish as it is, they know that they could have made more money in the years to come if he hadn't done it. But Rex had cleverly retained control as far as his decision making went and they had no say-so in the matter. They think he's packing it all up, turning his back on them and the city. Some have said that his luck has turned, but I don't think so and neither does Tony."

"No wonder Rex was adamant about our being here tonight! He never told me how serious the situation was. You're right not to believe any of that gossip, and I thank you for your loyalty to us. Rex would never give up on Houston or the people here," she said staunchly.

"I believe that too," Sylvia agreed. Then more light-heartedly she said, "Let's not worry about all that tonight. Now, come on. Let's go enjoy dinner. Maybe I can manage to gain another five pounds," she said and laughed.

As they returned to the dining room, Hailey knew that in time Rex's associates would realize that he hadn't discarded them at all. He had told her that he fully intended to reinvest his profits back into Houston and possibly resurrect the development company *if* the wells came in. Hailey also knew that for the sake of her family and the life she was trying to build with Rex, she would have to be the one to confront the menacing Pamela, and the sooner, the better.

## Chapter Thirty

THE Silverado was overflowing with suitcases, boxes full of wrapped gifts, Rex's guitar and Hailey's sketch pads. As they rode Rex led them all in Christmas carols, persistently confusing the lyrics to "The First Noël" with the music to "It Came upon a Midnight Clear." It was the twenty-second of December and Leonard had closed the gallery a day early due, he said, to his own plans for Christmas in Acapulco. Rex wondered secretly if he'd needed the time to deal with Barrett.

It was almost eleven o'clock and both Joey and Kim were barely able to stay awake. Joey was sitting on Hailey's lap, his chin bobbing on his chest. He would jerk his head up, his eyes open, and then his eyelids would slowly fall again. Kim leaned against Rex's shoulder and as soon as he took his hand off the wheel and put his arm around her, she slumped down into his lap, fast asleep.

The night was cold and the sky, a transparent ebony, was dotted with shining stars. Scattered along the highway were small country homes, outlined in lights, always with a Christmas tree in a front window. Under the makeup of night shadows their crumbling paint and rickety structures were camouflaged and each appeared magically transformed.

Leaving the highway, they traveled for ten miles until they came to a whitewashed fence that ran along the side of the road. Another five miles ensued, then they slowed just as they reached a highly arched gate with a swinging plate with "RIVER BEND" emblazoned in the wood.

Rex stopped the truck and let the headlights shine on the gateway. "This is it, baby. We're home," he said proudly.

The driveway, he explained, was three quarters of a mile long and each brick had been hand-laid by his grandfather. A mass of tall southern pines cut off virtually all the moonlight. As they drew closer, Hailey's jaw dropped. She thought she had seen every conceivable mansion known to man in River Oaks, but this!

In both size and grandeur, it was palatial. Eight Ionic columns supported the Southern Colonial mansion not only in front but also along the sides, creating a wraparound terrace on the first floor. The entire second floor had a railed balcony above the lower terrace. The roof was a modified pitched mansard, with beveled glass dormer windows jutting out, indicating a third floor. On either side of the ten-foot-wide double front doors were three black-shuttered sets of french doors that opened onto the terrace. The second-floor window treatments matched the symmetry of the first floor. And through every window poured a flood of light, bathing both the mansion and the surrounding grounds. Three huge, twisting oaks shaded the front drive and the newly clipped lawn. The formal landscaping was precisely balanced so as not to detract from the architecture. A five-car garage, to the left, was recessed somewhat. Rex explained that it had once been a carriage house at the turn of the century, when the house was built, and still held full servants' quarters.

Rex had never said much about River Bend, only that it was a large ranch and that they still drilled for oil on the land. She had been expectantly nervous about meeting his father and grandfather for the first time. Rex hadn't wanted to discuss it much, telling her only that they would love her and the children instantly.

But now she wasn't so sure. The mansion was intimidating to say the least, and she was quite leery of meeting two men, widowers who would undoubtedly try to talk Rex out of marrying her. After all, they had been without a woman's influence in their lives for years and it seemed only natural that they would want Rex back at River Bend—alone.

Rex had told her that when he had called his father, he'd only told him he was bringing his lady friend and her two children. His father had asked no questions and Rex had offered no explanation. This perplexed her and made her wonder if some of their fences were unmended.

Rex parked the Silverado at the front door and as Hailey woke the children, Rex blew the horn twice. The doors to the mansion opened and a tall man, much taller than Rex with thick wavy silver hair, was advancing toward them, his muscular arms outstretched in greeting.

"Rex!" his voice boomed in the night and seemed to clear away the last cloud. They stood hugging and slapping each other's backs.

Hailey thought she had never seen such joyous smiles. Then between the night shadows and the incandescent light in the doorway slipped the slightly stooped frame of an elderly man who leaned patiently on a gold-handled black cane. Hailey couldn't see his face, but his thick white hair sparkled in the light from the coach lamps above. "Grandfather," she whispered, a chill of wonder coursing her back. He moved closer to the exuberant Rex, who had finally noticed him.

"Granddaddy," Rex said with respect and love graveling his voice. Rex jumped the two steps to his grandfather, then walked tentatively toward the elderly man. They nearly matched eye to eye in height and frame. The old man dropped his cane and hugged Rex even more forcefully than John Cowert had, his emotions, not his physical strength, surging through his body. Hailey could see that both the old man and Rex were tremendously moved by the reunion. They were speaking to each other in whispers, and finally Rex bent down and handed the cane back to his grandfather. The old man was disappointed to use the inanimate object once again rather than Rex's arm for support.

Joey and Kim watched the reunion through sleepy eyes but were now fully awake.

Kim looked over at Hailey. "Mom? Is that Rex's grand-father?" Just then Rex came back to the truck and heard Kim's question.

"It sure is, honey," Rex said, taking her hand and helping her out of the truck. "And this is my father, John Cowert."

John moved closer and extended his hand to Kim.

"Daddy, this is Kim," Rex said.

"How do you do, sir?" Kim said politely and a bit too formally, but Hailey breathed a sigh of relief.

"Very well, missy. Welcome to River Bend," John said.

Joey, not to be overlooked, quickly scrambled out of Hailey's lap and jumped out of the truck. "Hi! I'm Joey. Are you gonna be my grandfather?" he blurted out in typical Joey fashion.

Hailey thought she couldn't crawl back to Houston fast enough.

Rex burst out laughing along with his father. John rumpled Joey's silver hair. "Why, I don't know about that, son. But with hair like that you sure look like you could be my grandson," he teased, but Hailey noticed the curious glance John flashed at Rex, who had his arms possessively around Kim's shoulders.

Hailey unlocked the door and walked around the truck. "I apologize for my son's, er, unusual greeting," she said, offering her hand to John.

"Daddy, this is Hailey," Rex said proudly.

"No need to apologize," John answered graciously. "A man should always speak his mind."

Rex took Hailey's hand and ceremoniously led her up the steps to where his grandfather was waiting. She felt as if she were being presented at court. The eldest Cowert even in his late years possessed a magnetic aura that instantly commanded respect and awe.

"Hailey, this is my granddaddy, Alex Cowert."

"I'm so pleased to meet you, Hailey, and your two young 'uns," he drawled in deep tones conjuring all the charm and illusion of a landed southern gentleman. "I'm mighty glad you all could spend Christmas with us," he said, taking Hailey's hand and kissing it and as he straightened back up, he grinned mischievously at her.

"I can certainly see where Rex inherits his charm," Hailey said, winking at Alex. "Thank you for the invitation. I just hope we won't cause too much confusion."

"Nonsense! This is a big house. It could use some livening up!" He chuckled.

"Hey, Mom!" Joey said, "I think you forgot my suitcase!"

"Excuse me," she said and left Rex and Alex in order to help Joey.

Alex leaned next to Rex and said, "I think you had better nab this one quick, boy. I think she's pretty taken with me. I just might steal her away from you."

"You'd be the only man I'd let take her and even then you'd have a fight on your hands," Rex teased and patted Alex's shoulder and then went to help unload the truck.

John, Kim and Joey carried the suitcases inside while Rex and Hailey brought the gifts, being careful the children didn't see their names on the tags. They all tromped into the foyer, John stating that Raymond, the butler, would put everything away in the morning.

Once inside, the children stopped dead in their tracks, their eyes investigating the double set of curved staircases soaring up to the second-floor landing. The spindles were painted white, as was all the molding and woodwork, and the stairs were carpeted in an unusual Aubusson in pastels of blue, cream, rose and yellow. The walls of the rotundalike foyer were papered in a pale blue-and-white-stripe Colonial paper. A larger matching Aubusson carpet covered the center of the foyer. Overhead, a huge antique brass and glass globe held six candle-shaped lights. Two antique rococo mirrors hung opposite each other on the walls, and opening off the foyer were four sets of eight-foot-tall hand-carved double doors. Later they would explore what lay behind those doors.

Joey placed his suitcase on the white marble floor and put his hands on his hips. "Which one is the kids' staircase?"

"Joey!" Kim cried once again, mortified at her brother's persistent questions.

Alex laughed and said, "I think I'll have a brandy in the library while you all get settled," and he went between the doors just ahead and to the right.

"Well, Grandpa," Joey said, looking up at John in anticipation, "which one do we take?"

"I'll tell you what, Joey, you pick one and then we'll go see what's up there."

"Okay. But then what's on the other side?" Joey asked.

"I guess you'll never know," John replied, amused with the mystery he was creating.

"The one on the left," Kim said. Joey looked at her.

"Yeah, the left one," Joey replied, relieved his sister had taken the decision upon herself. Besides, he thought, that way he could still find out what was on the right side, since Kim had picked the left. He smiled at John.

John knew exactly what Joey was thinking and he chuckled under his breath. "Let's go then."

They gathered up their overnight bags, John leading the way and Joey asking a million questions before they reached the landing.

Hailey watched them as they disappeared from view. "Rex, are you still sure this was a good idea? I mean, Joey can be quite a handful, and your father isn't used to . . ."

"Quit worrying, would you, please? Daddy loves every minute of this." Rex put his arms around Hailey. "I think he better get used to Joey, since he *will* be his grandfather, very soon," he said and kissed her. He pulled her closer, savoring every moment, until he heard his grandfather.

"Eh, hem! Pssst!" Alex had poked his head around the door and was motioning to them. "Come join me by the fire," he said.

"All right," Rex said, and he and Hailey entered the library.

Hailey had been prepared for a cozy paneled room smelling of tobacco and leather, but this massive expanse of a room had been totally unexpected! One-foot-square D'Hanis tiles covered the floor, and the walls were of Austin limestone. The slatted wood ceiling, which was eighteen feet high, like the rest of the house was made of materials from all over Central and West Texas. There were no windows in the room, only massive wood doors from Mexico. They encompassed almost one entire wall, and when opened, Rex said, it was as if there were no wall at all. The fireplace was enormous, the roaring fire filling the room with warmth and light. Above it hung a whip, a Winchester rifle, a twisted cane and a Confederate saber. They were all family heirlooms, Rex said.

Flanking the fireplace were two rough cedar gun cases filled with priceless rifles and pearl-handled pistols. Two walls of floor-to-ceiling shelves held the Cowerts' awesome collection of books on everything from art and music, drama and poetry to history, biographies and fiction. Four ornate columns from Oaxaca, Mexico, guarded the corners of the room and each was topped with Mexican baroque gilt capitals. Two sofas, covered in a surprising oriental motif cotton of cream and reds and blues, flanked the fireplace, and between them was a square oak coffee table Rex's father had made himself. A long rectangular writing desk was the only other furniture. A small sea captain's chest held Alex's cache of aged Napoleon brandy and Kentucky bourbon.

"This is a beautiful room, Alex," Hailey said, warming herself by the fire. "It's so unusual for a library."

"You mean it's as big as all outdoors," the old man said. "I planned it that way. I can't stand cramped little rooms. That's why River Bend is big. I always did need lots of breathing room." He handed Hailey a small glass of sherry. "I hope you like it. It was Alecia's favorite," he said, his voice growing wistful at the mention of his wife's name.

"How long ago did she pass away? If it's not too painful for me to ask," Hailey said.

"No, of course not. I like to talk about her. It keeps her with me. It's been about ten years now. It seems like a hundred sometimes. I sit here in the evenings and talk to her about my day. I know she can hear me, and sometimes I can feel her presence and she helps guide me. Lots of folks around here think I've gone loco, but I don't pay them much mind," he said, easing himself into a corner of a sofa and placing his cane on the coffee table.

"I wouldn't pay any attention to what other people say," Hailey replied and looked down into her sherry. "Too often we allow the opinions of others to cloud our vision. I think we're all better off sometimes when we listen with our hearts." She looked up to see Rex and Alex both watching her with intense concentration.

They smiled at her and once again she was struck by how similar they were in appearance. Alex's green eyes were just as clear and full of vitality as Rex's and they both possessed an impish grin that embellished their faces with a fascinating blend of larceny and vulnerability. Hailey could well understand why Rex's break with his family was so tumultuous. She sipped her sherry slowly. It was excellent, sweet and not too dry, the kind of sherry she liked. "It's very good," she said.

Alex beamed. "I made it myself. Old family recipe."

"Granddaddy makes all kinds of good things," Rex stated.

"Sure do, and all of 'em have booze. No recipe is worth its salt without booze," Alex said and laughed. "I've always said that, haven't I, Rex?"

"That's true," Rex replied, placing his hand on his grandfather's knee.

Hailey sensed that they needed some time alone. "I think I should go upstairs and see that the children are in bed. They may keep John up all night," she said, placing her sherry on the coffee table.

"I'll be up in a while and show you to your room," Rex said.

"Good night, Grandfather," Hailey said and bent down and kissed Alex's cheek.

The old man smiled and as Hailey walked away his chest was puffed out just slightly more than before and his shoulders were squared. "Sweet dreams, Hailey," Alex said and watched until she was out of the room. "You see that, son? Just like I told you. She's after me!"

"I think you just might be right about that, Granddaddy. I'd better keep on my toes."

Hailey could hear the children's giggles two doors away, so she stealthily approached the room, peeking around the door. Joey and Kim appeared even more diminutive on the mammoth sea-blue-covered canopy bed. They sat Indian style, already in their pajamas, listening with rapt expressions to every word John was saying.

"And tomorrow morning—early, mind you—we'll go out into the woods with an ax and cut down our own tree."

Hailey opened the door and it creaked just enough to catch their attention.

"Mom, did you hear that?" Kim exclaimed. "We're gonna get a real forest tree for Christmas and Grandpa grew them all by himself!"

"That sounds wonderful," she said, sitting next to Kim. "Is it all right if I come along, too?"

"Certainly," John said. "We can use plenty of extra muscle."

"And we're going to make all the decorations ourselves. We used to make cookie ornaments, didn't we, Mom?" Joey asked.

"Yes, we did. Only you usually eat them all before Christmas arrives!" she said, poking him in the stomach.

"We'll put you in charge of the cookies, then," John said. "I suspect that if we have all this work to do tomorrow, there are two people here who need to get some sleep," John said, eyeing the children.

"I agree," Hailey said, rising and pulling the covers down. She kissed them both and started to walk away with John when Joey said:

"Grandpa? Can I have a hug?"

"You sure can, son," John said and hugged him tightly.

"Me, too?" Kim asked.

"Yes, you, too," and he bent to kiss her.

Kim whispered, "I sure like your beds you have here. They're so big! I bet we could all fit in this one!"

"I think we probably could," he agreed. Just as John left

297

the room, he flipped out the light. "God bless," he said, taking one last long look.

As they walked down the stairs, Hailey said, "Thank you for getting them ready for bed. I should have been there to help you."

"I rather enjoyed it, having them all to myself for a while. They're both good people. You've done a fine job raising them," he said sincerely.

"I hope I have. Sometimes I'm not quite so sure," she said, thinking of Joey's persistent directness.

"You have," he replied confidently.

Once Alex and John had retired for the night, Rex took Hailey up the stairs to his old room. He opened the door and turned on the light. A serene blend of neutral tones had been used to decorate the room. From the white-on-white carved carpeting to the beige linen-covered walls and draperies to the muted tan and beige plaid cotton that hung from the square-canopied bed, there was not a harsh tone to be seen. Three overstuffed chairs were covered in a textured off-white linen, and two skirted tables on either side of the king-size bed were covered in white silk and topped with round pieces of glass. A massive dark mahogany armoire, the only piece of cabinetry in the room, sat majestically between two french doors.

"This is the only room that doesn't have an antique bed and some fond piece of family history to go with it," Rex explained, placing Hailey's suitcase on the thickly padded bench at the foot of the bed.

"It's so peaceful. A real retreat."

"I'm glad you like it. I only wish I could sleep here with you tonight, but I can't."

"I understand," she said.

"The bath is through that door, and I'll be across the hall. Granddaddy is at the end of the hall."

"And your father?"

"Across from Joey and Kim. He'll hear them if they wake up and need anything. Oh, I think I should warn you, breakfast is at six in the morning."

"That's not all that early for me," she said with mock indignation.

"Well, it is for me! I'd just as soon sleep until ten!" Then he took her into his arms. "It's been some week, hasn't it?"

"Yes, it has," she said, stifling a yawn. "I guess I'm more tired than I thought."

"Kiss me good and long, baby. It's gotta last till morning." Rex's tongue teased and taunted her, making her more aware than ever how much she wanted him. And tonight he would have to sleep across the hall! she thought.

"I love you. Good night, darlin'," he said and left the room.

Hailey stood in the middle of the room thinking how strange it was that when Rex was with her the room seemed so full and alive and once the door had clicked shut, the echoes reverberated in her mind, as if she were in a multichambered cavern. God! She was becoming too dependent upon him. Where was her strength? Soon he would be going to Lafayette and she wouldn't see him for days on end. Maybe even weeks. How would she ever handle it?

"I'll do it! Somehow, some way I just have to, that's all!" she said to herself.

She opened her suitcase and pulled out a pale mauve negligee and a deeper mauve robe with scallop-edged collar and lapel. She opened the door to the bathroom.

"My God!" she exclaimed in astonishment, "don't these people believe in anything small?"

Both the floor and walls were covered in tiny blue-and-white mosaic tiles. The tub was elevated two steps and was large enough for two people. The pedestal washbasin and all the fixtures were originals of the house. The faucets were white china with handpainted blue forget-me-nots. One large gilt-framed mirror hung over the basin, its silvered glass now wavy, and it distorted her features when she gazed into it. Overhead hung a baroque bronze and crystal six-branch chandelier. Adjacent to the basin stood a Louis XV *bombé* chest with geometric marquetry paneling and rococo brass fixtures. Inside its drawers were stacks of fluffy royal blue towels and dainty openworked linen fingertip towels.

Hailey filled the tub with hot water and added some jasmine bath salts from a milk glass container and soaped her arms and legs with a large sponge. There was so much room in the tub and the water was so silky, she almost fell asleep. After drying off, she slipped the nightgown on and donned her robe. She turned down the covers, flicked off the lamp and nestled between the thick goose-down quilt and fine linen sheets.

Hailey was poised somewhere on the thin edge of sleep when she dreamed that Rex was standing over her. He kissed her ear and crawled into bed alongside her. He pulled her up to him, lying back to belly like spoons, his hand on her breast, his face buried in her silver mane. His familiar breathing patterns lulled her over the precipice into subconsciousness; she was at peace, the dream comforting her.

Rex, not realizing she was asleep, whispered, "I can't even sleep without you, baby. I wonder what that means?"

# Chapter Thirty-one

WHEN Hailey and Rex entered the kitchen the next
morning they were greeted by both Raymond and
Bertha, the middle-aged black couple who had lived and
worked at River Bend all their lives, as had their parents
and a few assorted cousins and friends.

Bertha was as skinny now as she had been when she
was fourteen. The years of baking, cooking and running
the household had only grayed her hair and increased the
volume of her voice when she barked orders to the maids
and, of course, Raymond. Raymond, a husky, good-
natured man, was standing behind Bertha while she was
busily frying sausages and scrambling eggs.

"Raymond, if you don't take your hands off me this
minute, there ain't nobody gonna have breakfast!"

"Aw, Bertha, honey, I was jest funnin'," he drawled and
backed away, spying Rex standing in the doorway as he
did so.

"Mr. Rex! It shore is good to see you!" Raymond's smile
was wide as he shook Rex's hand and slapped him affectionately on the back.

"Good to see you, Raymond. I'm glad to see you're still
supervising the kitchen help," Rex said and chuckled.

"Help! Humph! Now, you see here, Mr. Rex. We all know
who runs this here house, don't we?" Bertha teased as Rex
went over and gave her a big hug. "How y'all doin', baby?"
she said and let him go. "You sure you been eatin' right?
You look a mite thinner to me."

"Look who's talking, Miss Scrawny," Rex bantered.

"You jest hush up. I never get a chance to fatten up, everybody always around botherin' me," she said, poking her spatula at Raymond.

"Bertha, Raymond, I want you to meet Hailey."

"Hello," Hailey said, shaking their hands and smiling at them both.

"We was wonderin' when you all were gonna git down here. Yer young 'uns has been up since dawn. Sweet as sugar, that pair!" Bertha said. "And hungry, too. They already had doughnuts with Mr. John and now they're waitin' for their big breakfast."

"Why, thank you for looking after them. I hope they haven't caused you any extra work," Hailey said.

"No trouble at all. They've been makin' all kinds of plans for this mornin'. If they do all they want, they're gonna need plenty of nourishment," Bertha said and laughed.

"I think we'd better see what's going on, don't you, Hailey?" Rex said.

"Yes, I do. Where are they?"

"In the dining room," Raymond said.

"It was nice meeting you," Hailey said as Rex put his arm around her waist and led her through the doorway.

"Glad to have you all home," Bertha said and then turned to Raymond. "What do you think?"

"I think we're gonna have a house full at River Bend again."

"It's about time," Bertha replied staunchly.


The dining room, Hailey discovered, was like all the rooms so far: massive and elegantly appointed. An oriental vine-and-magnolia-blossom handpainted wall covering in soft blue and silver wrapped around the room. Suspended from the ceiling were two twelve-branch Waterford chandeliers that glittered in the early-morning sun. The table, a double-pedestal long oval of buffed and waxed cherry wood, was surrounded by high-backed cream silk-covered fully upholstered chairs. At each end were two large Chippendale wing chairs in matching fabric which looked like they belonged more in the living room than in the dining room.

At the far end of the table sat Alex, with Joey and Kim on either side. The chairs were so huge, all she could see were the children's heads hovering above the gleaming silverware and gold-banded white china.

"Good morning, Mom!" Kim said and lifted her hand to wave at her mother as if they were valleys apart in distance. "Isn't this fancy?" Kim's smile was so broad, Hailey wondered where her cheeks had gone.

"And this is just for breakfast!" Joey chimed. "I can't wait for supper!"

"Oh, Joey, all you think about is food," Kim reprimanded him.

"I do not! I think about the Christmas tree I'm gonna cut down and all those presents I'm gonna get," he said, greedily rubbing his hands together.

Alex was roaring with laughter. "We've been having a big conference here. I think you two better get in on this before you find yourselves with more work to do than you bargained for."

"Like what?" Hailey said, sitting down next to Kim.

"Gosh, Mom! We have this whole house to decorate. And all the baking to do. Bertha said she's only half done and we'd have to help. And there's firewood the men have to chop, and the tree . . ." She was rattling off the list as if she were the mistress of River Bend.

"It does sound like a lot."

"Yeah, it is. And Grandpa Alex has the worst job, don't you, Grandpa?" Joey asked.

"What's that job, Granddaddy, as if I didn't know?" Rex asked, sipping his coffee.

"Supervisor! It takes a lot of organization to get this place moving," Alex replied and winked at his grandson.

"Ah! I knew it. Well, what's first on the agenda?"

"The tree, of course!" Kim said, stunned that Rex would possibly consider anything else. "Grandpa John went to get the horses already. We're gonna have to be ready the minute he comes back. He said so," Kim said, lifting a tall-stemmed crystal glass of orange juice to her lips, trying to accomplish the maneuver without mishap. She was successful.

John came strolling in at that moment, dressed in jeans, sheepskin jacket and cowboy hat. He took off his deerskin gloves. "Well, everything is ready whenever you are! The horses are saddled and I've got plenty of hatchets and a makeshift sled to bring it back on."

"Oh, boy!" Joey exclaimed. "Let's go!"

"You sit right down and finish your breakfast," Alex grumbled. "John, you're just as bad as these young 'uns. That tree isn't going anywhere. You sit and have some coffee until they finish eating."

John sat opposite his father as Raymond served Rex and Hailey their plates of potatoes, sausages, eggs and coffee cake. Joey was bolting down his food and chewing as fast as his jaws would allow. Everyone at the table watched him until he proudly put his fork down. He looked up at all the faces staring at him. He sheepishly blotted his mouth with the linen napkin and very politely said, "May I be excused now?"

Hailey looked at him sternly, hoping her amusement didn't show. "Yes, you may."

"I'll get my jacket," he said, getting up and struggling with the heavy chair, which proved to be a better match for him. He squeezed out between the table and chair and then stopped at John's chair. "I'll be right back. Don't go without me!" he whispered.

"I won't, son," John replied and patted Joey's hand.

"Can I be excused, Mom? I want to go, too."

"What about the baking we need to do?"

"Oh, yeah," she said, disappointed at her mother's answer. "Maybe after we get the tree?"

"Kim, don't forget a hat and gloves. It's pretty cold this morning."

Kim's face brightened. "Right!" And she raced off to her room.

Rex finished his eggs and gulped down his coffee. "I guess I'd better get my things, if I'm going, too." He leaned over and kissed Hailey. "Don't worry, sweetheart. Daddy and I will bring you back the biggest tree you ever saw. I guarantee it."

"I'll hold you to that," she teased and watched him leave.

John finished his coffee, surreptitiously eyeing the expressions on Hailey's and Rex's faces. He mentally marked down his findings and added them to his observations and made his judgments.

In a matter of moments Rex returned with the children, and along with John they were off to their adventure.

Alex looked over at Hailey standing at the french doors watching the quartet ride off on horseback toward the woods. He drank the last of his coffee and replaced the cup. "Days begin early at River Bend, don't they?"

"I don't mind. I have to be up early every day to get the children off to school and do the housework before I leave."

"And where do you go?"

"I work at an art gallery in Houston."

"Really? That's very interesting. I've got a small collection of Icarts up in my room. Would you care to see my etchings, my dear?" he asked, his bushy eyebrows raised in jovial devilishness.

"What kind of proposal is this?" she teased.

"The only kind I know. Indecent!" he guffawed and began to rise. Hailey helped him with his chair and then took his arm as they mounted the stairs.

The paneled walls of his room were studded with the provocative etchings of Jazz Age ladies as depicted by Louis Icart. The most valuable were the nudes, which now commanded prices of over five thousand dollars, Alex said. But during the thirties they hadn't sold that well in the United States. The majority were sensuously attired models in negligees. They were a fabulous blend of Art Deco and Impressionism, the kind of work Hailey liked. Alex proudly explained each print and conveyed the story surrounding its acquisition. His eyes twinkled in merriment and Hailey well understood Rex's purchase of the bawdy novels for his grandfather. As she listened to him

speak of days past and his accomplishments, Alex won her
heart just as surely as Rex had.

The activity that took place that day was a hundredfold
more than River Bend had seen in over a decade.
Raymond had instructed two of the ranch hands to gather
fir and pine branches and pine cones for the making of
garlands and wreaths. While Bertha and the day help,
Cindy and Jane, baked breads, pies, cakes and cookies,
boiled shrimp and cooked oyster stew, Hailey was immersed in fashioning garlands that she wove along the
staircase banister. At the points where she gathered the
garlands up, creating a deep swag, she affixed clusters of
pine cones, lemons and apples and then topped it all with a
huge pineapple. Two matching green wreaths decorated
with apples and pine cones and big red satin bows hung on
the front doors when Rex, John and the children returned
with a twelve-foot fir tree. It took every adult in the house,
plus Alex's supervision, to position and brace the tree.
While Rex and John strung the lights, the children
retreated to the kitchen to decorate the cutout cookies
Bertha had made. Alex patiently strung cranberries and
popcorn while Rex retrieved the boxes of wooden ornaments from the attic.

When the florist arrived with a van of white and red
poinsettias and table arrangements of evergreens and
white chrysanthemums, Hailey decided they were much
too sparse. She added lemons stuck to long sticks and
inserted them in the arrangements along with small pine
cones and clusters of holiday nuts in the shell.

By nightfall the living room's white marble fireplace
crackled with the fire from newly chopped wood. The tree,
an imposing delight of fantasy, rested in the far corner
between two sets of white louvered french doors. The
adults rested on the three rose silk camel-back sofas while
Joey and Kim, lying on their stomachs, chins resting in
their hands, looked in awe at their handiwork.

Joey was fascinated by the wooden soldiers, both Confederate and Union, the tiny horses and bugles. Kim
preferred the angels, choirboys and wooden snowflakes.

Joey reached up and snatched a cookie off a low-lying branch, took a bite and handed it to his sister.

"These are the best ornaments," Joey said proudly, and Kim nodded in agreement.

Bertha and Raymond served an informal bowl of oyster stew and crackers to everyone, followed by a rich lemon chess pie for dessert. Before they finished their pie, both Joey and Kim fell asleep under the tree. Rex carried Kim upstairs while John wiped Joey's sticky mouth and likewise carried him to bed.

When Rex returned, Hailey was asleep on a slumbering Alex's shoulder.

"Hailey, come on, sweetheart. I'll walk you upstairs," Rex whispered, trying not to disturb his grandfather.

"Huh?" she said sleepily. "Is it that late?"

"Late enough," he said and put his arm around her. Once in her bedroom she sat on the edge of the bed and yawned. He knelt on the floor next to her.

"Are you going to sleep with me again tonight?" she asked, placing her hand tenderly on his head and running her fingers through his hair.

"Yes, I will, but not yet. I want to talk to Daddy for a while."

"Okay. You know, last night I thought I was dreaming, but you were really there, weren't you?"

"Yes, I was, baby. But I'll have to leave again early in the morning, like I did today."

"That's okay. I just like to have you close to me," she said as he put his hand on the back of her neck and pulled her head down to meet his lips.

"I know what you mean. You get some sleep and I'll be up later."

"Good night," she said as he stopped by the door, took one last look, blew her a kiss and was gone.

Rex sat by the fire, swirling his cognac in a crystal brandy balloon when John walked in.

"I think we wore them all out, son, including your granddaddy."

"Yes, sir. I believe you're right," Rex replied as his

father sat on the sofa opposite him. "I poured you a cognac." Rex handed him a glass from the silver tray on the library table behind him.

"Thanks," John said and sipped it slowly, letting the expensive liquor flow down his throat. "It was a good day, wasn't it, son?"

"Sure was, Daddy," Rex answered. There still remained a hesitancy between Rex and his father. Rex was afraid John was going to ask him to move back to River Bend, and then they would argue again, the holidays would be ruined and nothing would be accomplished. Rex wondered how he would ever be able to explain his involvement in Remac Oil and Gas. River Bend was a part of his past, a cool retreat from the pressure-packed city life he led. But River Bend was his grandfather's land and his father's achievement.

"When are you going to make a decision, son?" John asked bluntly.

God! Rex thought. I'm too tired. I don't want to go into that; not now. "About what?" Rex hedged.

"Hailey, of course! What else could be more important? She's in love with you, you know."

"I know. I love her, too."

"Then why don't you marry her? What are you waiting for?"

"Because she thinks it's too soon. She wants to wait until May. I think I've talked her into moving it up to March, but I'm not sure she will do that."

"You can't fool me, son. If *you* really wanted to marry her now, you would have done it. There's something else that bothers you, isn't there?"

"Yes," Rex said, leaning back. "I want everything to be just perfect for us, and right now I'm afraid isn't the time to get married."

"There's an old saying that I think holds a lot of truth. 'There's never a right or a wrong time to get married.' That is, providing, of course, that you do love her."

John was testing Rex. Something wasn't right, that was for sure, but as to just what it was, he wondered if Rex would feel comfortable confiding in him.

"I do. It happened just the way you said it would, Daddy. I knew she was the woman for me almost from the moment I met her. I fought my feelings, but only for a few days. It was uncanny. And Hailey said it was the same for her. It's just that . . . God! I don't know how to say this. But right now, I couldn't support her and the children."

"What?" John was truly concerned now. He knew his son's assets almost to the penny. "You must have had a hell of a setback!"

"Not exactly. But I have sold everything in order to invest in Remac Oil and Gas."

"Never heard of it."

"I know. It's mine. 'Re' is for Rex, and 'Mac' is for Chess McAllister. You remember him. He and I formed the company and we're drilling on a stretch of land near Lafayette."

"You haven't struck yet, I take it."

"Not yet. I'm confident we will, though."

"Tarnation, Rex! I know good and damn well you wouldn't have gone ahead with this venture if you couldn't make any money with it. I know that area down there in Lafayette pretty well. There's plenty of oil, and even if you did pick up a piece of totally dry land, that still has nothing to do with your happiness. Good God! If I haven't taught you that much by now, I guess I really have failed you."

"Daddy, you've never failed me."

"Yes, I did. I was wrong when I wanted you to live the life I'd planned for you. It was only inevitable you would leave. I know you're sitting there waiting for me to beg you to come back to River Bend. Well, I'm not going to do it. I can't make you do anything. If you ever decide this is what you want, it'll be here, but in the meantime I see you wantin' this woman and you're still fightin' yourself. That's all there is to it, and it's wrong! Even your granddaddy can see how strong the love is between you. That's what lights up this house. There aren't many people in the world who experience a real passion for each other. I was damn lucky. Your mama and me, we had something . . . she was the finest woman God ever created. I could never marry again unless I found that special feeling I had for her. I won't settle for second best. Maybe I'm crazy, but that's just the way I am."

"It's a good way to be," Rex mused.

"Hailey impresses me as the kind who would stick by you."

"I think she will, too. She knows about the oil. I guess it's just my insecurity because I want to feel that I can take care of her."

"Bullheadedness, I call it," John retorted.

Rex laughed and took a deep swallow of his cognac. "I guess it is, isn't it?"

"You wait right here. I'll be back in a minute," John said and quickly rose and left the room. He returned in a few moments with a tiny velvet drawstring sack.

"What have you got there?" Rex inquired, leaning forward.

"These were your mama's. I thought maybe you'd like to give them to Hailey for Christmas," he said, handing the sack to Rex.

Rex pulled the strings and emptied the contents into his hand. Two familiar platinum bands of diamonds tumbled out.

"I gave one to your mama when we announced our engagement, and the other on our wedding day. She always did love those rings the best, even though there were other rings I gave her."

"I remember. I guess we think along the same lines. You see, I bought Hailey a ring. I've got it with me," he said, reaching into his jeans pocket. "It wasn't very expensive. I don't have much money these days." He handed the ring to his father.

"I think it's real pretty," John said, inspecting the oval sapphire surrounded by tiny diamond chips. "It's very sentimental, chosen in true Cowert tradition. I like it."

"Yeah," Rex said wistfully. "I like it, too."

"So will she, son. It comes from the heart, not the back pocket," John said and was convinced that his son had made the right choice in so many things.

# Chapter Thirty-two

REX and his father had talked until daybreak. It was Bertha's rumbling around in the kitchen that alerted them to the hour. The aroma of fresh, hot coffee beckoned them to the kitchen. They were sitting in rush-seated pine chairs when Joey and Kim came scrambling in.

"Merry Christmas Eve, Rex," Kim said, giving Rex a hug and kiss. He pulled her onto his lap.

"How did you sleep last night?"

"Good," Joey said, his eyes inspecting the enormous pecan coffee ring Bertha had just pulled out of the oven.

"Well, are you two ready for Santa Claus to come tonight?" John asked.

Kim couldn't hide her irritation. "Oh, Grandpa, there's no such thing as Santa Claus! Everybody knows that!" she said with every ounce of a ten-year-old's sophistication.

"Oh, I see!" John replied, his eyes wide. "You're one of those!"

"What do you mean, 'one of those'?" she queried, her curiosity stung by his reaction.

"A disbeliever. You know what they say about disbelievers, don't you?"

"No. What?" Joey asked.

"They never get anything because they don't believe in anything to begin with."

"I believe in lots of things but not Santa Claus," Kim said.

"Why not?" John bantered.

"I never saw him."

"Okay, let me ask you this. Do you believe in God?"

"Of course!" Kim replied staunchly.

"Did you ever see him?"

"Well . . . no . . ."

"You see? There you go." John put his cup down, satisfied with the confused look that clouded Kim's eyes. Joey scoured his sister's face with a reproachful glance. "Santa Claus has come here every year. Maybe he comes only because I believe in him," John replied blithely, rose and walked out of the room.

Joey tugged on Rex's arm. "You think maybe he's right?"

"My daddy is always right. Only once did I think he was wrong, but he wasn't. He wanted the best for me and I was just too stubborn to listen to him. If I were you, I would at least give what he said some consideration." Rex noticed the glances the children exchanged.

"Sometimes Santa comes at different times of the year, especially for adults, I think."

"Aw! Come on!" Joey howled.

"It's true! I think Santa brought you and Kim to me. That's the most precious gift I ever got."

Kim gave Rex a hug. "I see what you mean. There really could be a Santa after all."

"I'm sure of it," Rex replied emphatically.

Christmas Eve at River Bend was just as busy as the previous day. Rex took the children horseback riding in the morning. John left in the pickup for hours, never disclosing his destination, and Alex was busy assembling his finest sherries and ports and preparing the eggnog they would all have that night when a few of the neighbors stopped by for the annual caroling around the tree. Hailey helped Bertha in the kitchen preparing hors d'oeuvres for that evening and most of the food for their dinner the following day. When there was a lull in the activities Hailey stole a few moments to retreat to her bedroom, never telling anyone her reason for her disappearance. She was quiet that day, immersed in remembrances of past holidays at home. She wondered if it was snowing in Boston and if Sonja had made Russian tea cakes this year.

Blessed with a few moments to herself, Hailey telephoned her mother. They chatted briefly about their holiday plans, and Hailey described River Bend and told her about John, Alex, Bertha and Raymond.

"Oh, Hailey, you sound so wonderfully happy. I don't think I've ever heard your voice quite like it is."

"Mother, this may sound crazy, but I don't think I've ever known what happiness was until now. I thought I did, but I had no idea!"

"That's all I ever wanted for you. When do I get to meet this man who has made such a change in your life?"

"Soon."

"Good. The sooner the better. Kiss the children for me and call me when you get back to the city. I want to hear all about your holiday," Sonja said. "Oh, I forgot to ask. Did my gifts arrive?"

"Yes, Mother, we brought them with us."

"If the sizes aren't right on the children's clothes, send them back and I'll return them. I took their measurements when they were here and I think they'll be fine."

"I'm sure they will, Mother. But if not, I'll let you know. Merry Christmas. I love you."

"Stay happy," Sonja said.

"I don't see how I can miss! Good-bye, Mother." Hailey replaced the ivory receiver on the french phone and laid back on the pillows. "No, I really can't miss."

Rex and the children replenished the firewood and practiced their carols, Rex playing the piano in the living room, and Joey plunking vital chords on the guitar. Only after much cajoling did Rex and Hailey get them bathed, shampooed and dressed in their party clothes.

Around four o'clock, longtime neighbors and friends began filtering into the mansion. Hailey wore a dark brown cowl-neck sweater and a long plaid wool skirt. Rex and his father wore their finest leather vests, plaid shirts and jeans. Only Alex dressed formally, in his traditional red velvet blazer and black wool slacks. It was an informal affair, with no particular format planned.

Alex greeted everyone at the door, and though he seemed to be leaning more heavily on his cane than usual, Hailey could tell that he was in his element. He must have adored entertaining on a lavish scale when he had been younger and his wife was alive. She could see now why River Bend was so large. A "few" neighbors turned out to be more than a hundred. Carolers clustered around the piano and when one pianist retired for more eggnog or wassail, another took his place.

Bertha kept the boiled shrimp coming and Hailey wondered where she had stored it all. There were crudités, homemade sausages, salmon mousse, marzipan, and lacy florentine cookies among the fourteen different varieties of sweets.

Rex proudly introduced Hailey as his fiancée, and Hailey never refuted it. A number of the guests had brought their cameras, and almost everyone had their picture taken by the Christmas tree, including Joey and Kim—more than once, Hailey noticed. They were having the time of their lives hamming it up for the cameras.

When the last guest had gone at nine-thirty, the children's energy clocks had run completely down. Hailey and Rex walked them up to bed, undressed them and covered them up.

After Rex closed the door he said, "How about helping me with the presents, Mrs. Claus."

"I'd love to, Mr. Claus," she replied and started to walk away. He grabbed her arm and pulled her back and leaned his body into hers.

"How about a kiss, Mrs. Claus," and before she could answer, his mouth was feasting upon hers with such intense passion, Hailey's mind blanked out everything. The tender yet forceful manner in which he held her seemed spiritual, somehow, causing tears to brim in her eyes. He was reluctant to release her. "I wish you knew how much I love you, Hailey. I know you aren't going to believe me when I say this, but I think that what we're doing is wrong."

"Don't say that! Nothing could be wrong. Not between us!" she protested, her heart pounding. What was he saying? He wanted to leave her? What?

"That's what I mean. God! It's all so mixed up inside me. It *is* right with us. It's good and so very fine. I don't like sneaking down the hall to be with you. For the first time since we arrived here, I realize now that this is wrong. We should be married. We're already married in our hearts and somehow. . . . Jesus! I can't believe I'm saying this, but what we're doing is like desecrating sacred ground. Do you know what I mean?" His eyes searched her face.

"Oh, yes, I do," she said, touching his cheek and letting her fingers travel down to his lips and trace their outline. He held her hand and kissed her fingers, drawing them into his mouth.

"What are we going to do?" she asked.

"Unfortunately, there is nothing we can do about it tonight. But I just wanted you to know how I feel." He wanted her to know that he loved her, but he still didn't feel right about not being able to support her. Maybe he was bullheaded, as his father said. He hoped Hailey loved him enough to wait.

Hailey knew what was on his mind. He didn't want to say that she was taking second place to business, and strangely she didn't feel as if she was. She was still uncertain about the logic in such intense emotions. Everything had happened so quickly for her and Rex that she was wary of it. Sometimes she thought she was experiencing a whole lifetime in a flash of light. God! If things would just slow down. More than anything, she wanted them to last. She wanted to be with Rex for the rest of her life, not just a few months. How much could she depend on fate to give her that wish?

Joey poked his head through the doorway. No one was in the hall, and the house was deathly silent. He could tell Bertha wasn't even up yet. He tiptoed across the hall and leaned his ear against the mahogany door. Again silence.

It was pitch black outside. It must still be nighttime, he thought as he went back to his bedroom. Wasn't morning ever going to come?

Kim was sitting straight up in bed. "Well?" Her eyes were huge ovals of anticipation.

"Everybody is still asleep."

"If we only knew what time it was!"

"Well, I'm not staying here!" he rallied and turned and opened the door and was not careful to stifle the noise of the door's closing. He stalked down the hallway and carefully opened the door to his mother's bedroom.

"Mom?" he whispered but shook her shoulder roughly.

"What?" she opened her eyes. "What's wrong?"

"Nothing, except that it's Christmas!"

"Oh, Joey, what time is it? Look over there on the clock."

He crawled over her to the night table. "Hey! It's almost six o'clock!" he said, relieved.

"Lucky for you! But everyone was up late last night cleaning up. Now, you just go back to bed and wait. When everyone else gets up, then we'll go downstairs. We don't know what they do here on Christmas morning."

"Open presents, I hope!"

"Maybe, Joey, they eat first or go to church," she warned.

"Oh, no," he said despondently.

Just then they heard a light tapping on the door. "Come in," Joey said.

It was Rex and Kim. "Good morning, sleepyhead," he said to Hailey. "I think Santa Claus has been and gone."

"All right!" Joey said, bounding out of bed.

"I'll get my robe and be right there," Hailey said.

"Okay. Come on, kids, let's get Granddaddy up," Rex said, taking their hands.

Hailey ran a quick brush through her hair, brushed her teeth and when she got to the landing, the entire family was waiting for her. Joey and Kim raced down the stairs and flung open the living-room doors. They stood frozen in the doorway, as if the breath had been knocked out of them.

Underneath the tree was a mountain of gifts. On either

side of the tree sat two saddles, one in deep burnished leather, the other a soft camel color. There were two sets of western hand-tooled boots with a western hat resting atop them, and two leather belts with large pewter buckles glistened in the glow of the colored Christmas lights.

Hailey threw Rex an accusing look, but he shook his head. "I didn't!" he whispered.

Alex lifted his cane and tapped Joey's bottom. "Well, don't just stand there, son. Get goin'."

The children were hesitant to approach the tree, fearing the mirage would vanish. Joey looked at the card bearing his name.

"It's from Santa!" he exclaimed and glanced at his sister, who was equally as bewildered.

Alex leaned down to inspect the saddles, and when he straightened he smiled and winked at John. Rex caught his grandfather's implication and nudged Hailey.

She crossed to John and hugged him. "Thank you, Dad," she whispered.

"Well, I don't know what for. I didn't do anything," he said, pretending no knowledge of the incident.

"Now, why on earth would Santa bring saddles to you two? You don't have horses in the city," Alex said.

"But .... couldn't we use them when we come to visit?" Kim replied.

"Sure you can!" John replied. "We'll store them in the carriage house with all the other gear."

Rex, sensing that his father's contrived intrigue was not over, walked to the french doors and peered outside. "Just as I suspected . . ." he said to himself. "Come see what I've found!"

The children rushed to his side and followed his gaze. There, tethered to the oak tree in front, were two ponies— one a golden palomino with a pink bow around its neck, and the other a black-and-white mustang with a blue ribbon.

"Horses! Real ones just for us!" Joey squealed and ran to the front door, with Kim right at his heels. In minutes they were across the drive and lovingly stroking the backs of their respective colts.

"I'd better get them back inside before they catch their death of cold," John said.

Rex stopped him with a huge hug. "Thanks just isn't enough, Daddy. But I think you know."

"I do. But my reasons were selfish. Did you see how big their eyes were?" John said and grinned.

"I sure did."

"That's why I did it," John said and left to get the children.

Hailey walked over to Rex and held him. "You Cowerts are such a special family. It's hard to decide which one I love the most."

Before Rex could reply, Alex broke in, "Well, I'm glad to hear it. That means I could still take her away from you, Rex."

Hailey laughed and leaned over and kissed Alex. "I hope he remembers that."

"I have something for you, Hailey. It's over there in that blue paper," he said, pointing his cane to a long, rectangular gift. "Open it up."

"All right, I will," she said as she peeled away the paper. "An Icart etching! Alex, are you sure you want to give me this? I mean, they're so important to you. I don't think I can . . ." Her eyes were wet with emotion.

"Of course you can. You're what's important to me, not the etching."

"Thank you," she said, smiling, as John and the children returned. They were all giggles and excited voices as they began wading through the gifts, opening some, handing others to the adults.

Rex received a case of Alex's homemade liquors and a watch from his father. Hailey had sketched charcoal portraits of both Alex and John and promised to do the oils later and have them framed. She explained she had worked on them nearly since their arrival and finished them just last night.

When all the gifts had been opened and the race car track was in full operation, John and Alex wandered out to the kitchen to check on breakfast.

Hailey sat on the edge of the sofa next to Rex, watching

the children playing on the floor. Rex looked up at the fireplace. "Baby, go over and get my stocking off the mantel, and yours, too. Let's see if Santa brought us any more."

"Greedy," she teased but rose and brought the stockings to him. He dumped his in his lap. "An orange, nuts and no candy! Santa must be on a health-food kick this year."

Hailey emptied hers and all that fell out was a wad of tissue. "If this is a piece of coal, I'll cry, I swear I will!" She unwrapped it. The sapphire and diamond ring gleamed at her. Her eyes lifted to Rex's in astonishment. He took her hand and slipped it on her finger, his eyes mesmerizing her.

"This makes it official, baby." His voice was low and fluid in that soothing, compelling tone he had.

He reached in his pocket and withdrew the two diamond bands. "You can't have these just yet, but they're your Christmas present from Daddy. They were my mother's and he wanted you to have them."

"Oh, they're beautiful, I love them," she said. "I'll be proud to wear them."

Rex's face drew nearer, his emerald eyes physically pulling her to him as he kissed her, sealing his promise.

Christmas Day had been quiet and peaceful, the most memorable one Hailey had known. The entire family had attended midmorning services at a quaint country church. The children had dressed in their new clothes; Sonja needn't have worried about the sizes, Hailey thought. When they returned they found Bertha and Raymond setting the table for the sumptuous afternoon feast.

Hickory-cured ham, smoked turkey, rice pilaf, candied yams, dressing, gravy, pecan pie and Alex's sherry left them all satisfied and tired.

Hailey would remember it all, every minute detail, she thought, as she sat in the Silverado as they drove away from River Bend. She took one last long look.

John was still waving, Alex standing next to him, leaning on his son's arm and not so much on his cane. Bertha and Raymond stood just below them on the front steps, their smiles still broad. Hailey whisked away a tiny tear. They were going back to Houston, back to reality and the problems they had left. This short reprieve had been more than just a rest. Rex was right. They were married in their hearts. She felt as much a part of his family as she was sure he felt a part of hers. Their lives were intermingled now, and Hailey felt stronger and more sure of the future and its promise than ever before in her life.

# Chapter Thirty-three

THE first of February brought constant rain and dismal, gray skies. It was as if the sun had died and refused to resurrect itself. The winter had been depressing and lonely for Hailey; her only respite had been Rex's visit two weeks earlier, when he had flown in for a three-day visit from Louisiana.

The drilling was slow and unproductive. Every day since the first of the year, Chess had persistently stated the well would come in. And every day the results had been the same: nothing. Rex's expectations were dwindling, Hailey could tell. When he had been with her, he refused to talk about the well, Chess or their boring days of hard work and the lonely nights he'd spent on a cot in Chess's poorly heated trailer. Rex called Hailey every night before she went to sleep, and the sound of his voice only made his absence more agonizing.

The very first week he'd been gone could only be described as torturous. After the blissfully joyous holidays, this sudden vacuum was almost more than she could stand. By the second week, she'd regained her lost appetite and was able to sleep at night. At the end of the third week, she had resigned herself to the fact that he wouldn't be returning at any time in the near future and forced herself to trudge mechanically through her days and empty nights. She threw herself into planning the spring showing and worked again on her portraits.

She had gone back to the gallery as soon as they returned to Houston, to find Leonard waiting for her at her desk. She approached him warily, for she had no knowledge of his encounter with Barrett. Rex had told her of his meeting with Leonard, but that had offered her no security.

Leonard told her that he had dissolved his partnership with Barrett after much consideration and further investigation of his own. Barrett had turned out to be a greedy egotist, and Leonard was glad to be rid of him. Hailey was shocked at what she heard, even though she had suspected Barrett of being underhanded. She was gratified to know that Leonard trusted her enough to tell her about the incident. That in itself said something about the working relationship they were building.

Leonard told Hailey that she would be the manager of the Galleria store and to some extent would assume Barrett's duties, while he would take on the rest. He would begin searching immediately for someone to man the Galleria store to free Hailey for her outside appointments. He warned her of the extra work she would have until they were better organized, but he compensated for it by giving her a substantial raise.

The mountains of paperwork were a blessing in disguise, for they kept her nights full, where there had once been Rex's smile, his playful teasing and his lovemaking. She tried to forget what it was like to have him hold her as she slept. She helped the children with their homework as always, and together they wrote to Rex every day. Joey and Kim still had their two weekends a month with Mike, and wondrously they loved Rex for himself without comparing him to Mike and taking anything away from their father.

When Mike rang the doorbell last Friday night, it was pouring rain and she'd asked him in and took his raincoat. Joey and Kim were still packing and they hadn't come down the stairs yet.

"You're looking well, Hailey," he said, his voice noncommittal, as was his expression.

"You do, too," she said, but that guilt crept over her.

"Joey's almost packed. It won't be long. How are you, Mike?"

His eyes brightened. "Great! I just got a promotion."

"That's wonderful, Mike. I'm really happy for you." She watched as he folded his arms across his chest.

"I've been working hard for it. It was a substantial raise, too. I'll be doing more traveling now."

"You always liked that, didn't you?"

"The travel? Of course! There were three other guys in contention for the job, but I beat them all out."

"The best man won, didn't he?" Hailey cleared her throat. His face seemed blank and she wondered if this was difficult for him. "How are you otherwise, Mike?" she asked. She guessed she still wondered if he hated her and how much he blamed her.

"Fine. You know, it's funny. In a lot of ways it doesn't seem much different at all. I'm still traveling and I don't spend much time in Houston. But then I never did spend any time at home. I do try to plan my weekends around the times when I see Joey and Kim. You know, that's another surprise."

"What is?"

"They've turned out to be neat kids. I guess I've gotten to know them better this past year than I ever have before."

"Yes, I guess you have."

"I never took the time to know them before. Or you, either. I meant it when I said you look good. Actually," he said, studying her face more intently, "you have a . . . a confidence, an aura about you I've never seen before."

"It shows that much?"

"Yes, it does. I'm glad you're happy, Hailey. You deserve it."

"Thanks, Mike, I . . ." She was interrupted by the banging suitcases against the banister.

"Hey! Dad! We're all ready!" Joey said, reaching the bottom step. He and Kim kissed Hailey.

"Bye, Mom. See you Sunday," Kim sang.

"Be sweet," Hailey replied, embracing Kim. Mike put on his raincoat, and Hailey helped him with it; her hand brushed his shoulder. He flinched and hastily tried to cover it up by fiddling with his collar.

"Good-bye, Hailey," he said and escorted the children to the car. Hailey closed the door. Strange, she had spent over ten years with Mike, and today was the closest they had ever come to real communication, futile as it was. There were still painful moments between them. It would probably always be that way. But they had both gone on and survived and made new lives. Mike had been right about one thing: She was confident now. She was lonely without Rex and she missed him, but she wasn't afraid anymore. No matter what happened in the future, she would face it without fear.

Rex's eyes were bleary from inspecting the mud washings. His nerves were about to break. He'd had four arguments with Chess this past week over inconsequentials—meaningless bickerings, and Rex chastised himself more than Chess's bellowing could ever do.

Rex felt guilty because he was going to miss Valentine's Day with Hailey when he had promised he would fly to Houston and take her out. However, he'd been as convinced as Chess that they were close to hitting oil. The men were weary and Rex was too. The indications were good, but he'd warned Chess if nothing happened by eight o'clock he was taking a helicopter to Houston at least for a day.

Chess finally agreed. Rex's temperament was always better after he had seen Hailey, and he knew Rex could use the break.

Chess was baffled. Every test they'd taken indicated this well would come in, but it was well over three weeks overdue.

Rex had called for the helicopter and was told no one would fly him to Houston because of the dense fog that covered the city. Hobby Airport had delayed all departures and advised against any flights. Severe thunderstorms were predicted for the Galveston area and as far north as Conroe. Only a misting, icy drizzle fell in and around Lafayette, and Rex was determined to fly.

He was in no mood for the hassles the pilot kept giving him. He ordered the pilot to offer an extra two hundred dollars to anyone who would fly the 'copter. The pilot, anxious to be rid of this stubborn fool Texan on the phone, turned to Andy Gilbert, a newly licensed green kid, and jokingly told him of Rex's offer.

Andy, deep in debt for the new car he'd just purchased, jumped at the offer, tossing all warnings about the fog and thunderstorms into the garbage can along with his cigarette butt.

Rex was informed the helicopter would meet him at the oil field in twenty minutes. Elated, Rex telephoned Hailey. It rang once.

"Hi, baby. What are you wearing?"

"Right now?" she asked, towel-drying her just shampooed hair. "Nothing. I just got out of the shower."

"Great! Keep it on," he laughed.

"Rex, would you please be serious. I miss you."

"I miss you. That's why I'm flying in tonight. Screw this oil shit. I want to see you. Make reservations at Tony's or any place you want. We'll do the town. Just you and me. Deal?"

"Yes, oh, yes! It's a deal! I'll be ready."

"Hailey?"

"Yes, Rex?"

"I love you, baby. I really do. You want to get married?"

"Yes!"

"When?"

"Tonight! Tomorrow! Now! I can't stand this any longer. If you go back to Louisiana, I'm going too."

"You're serious, aren't you?"

"You better believe it. This has been the longest winter of my life, and only because you aren't here."

"As soon as I get there we'll arrange everything. The license, whatever . . ." His voice was excited. "Do you want flowers or something? You don't want a big church wedding?"

"I want you! That's all! Now get off this phone and hurry up and get here," she pleaded.

"You won't change your mind?"

325

"No. I promise."

"I'll be right there!" He slammed down the receiver, not wanting to waste time with good-byes. The helicopter lifted off the ground, turned and headed west into the rain.

Hailey made no reservations. The last thing she wanted was to share Rex with a restaurant full of people. She promised to wake the children as soon as Rex arrived.

She defrosted two rib-eye steaks, made twice-baked potatoes, broccoli soufflé and chocolate mousse and then readied all the ingredients for a tossed salad.

She set the table with her best china and silver and placed Waterford goblets and champagne glasses on a cutwork Belgian linen tablecloth. She found two red candles and put them in silver candle holders. She chilled a bottle of champagne in a sterling ice bucket and waited.

She dressed in house pajamas of peach striped silk, curled her hair and let it fall in waves just the way Rex liked it. She placed the children's valentines to Rex on the table, her only centerpiece in lieu of flowers.

The minutes passed like hours. Never prone to premonitions, Hailey fought the chills that coursed her spine as the thunder boomed and the rain whipped the window-panes of the french doors. Everything was so good with her and Rex. They had found in each other a love that was tender, passionate and caring. It had all happened so quickly, and many times she had thought that it was too much, too soon.

"God brought you to me," he had said so many times. He had made her believe in miracles and gave her tomorrows a new meaning. He had shown her a world she had never known. "Oh, Rex. Where are you?"

# Chapter Thirty-four

HAILEY sat bolt upright on the sofa, tears streaming down her face for no reason at all. So he was a little late, she had told herself at eleven o'clock. At midnight she paced, wrung her hands and fought her churning stomach. At one o'clock her tension eased with the passing of the thunderstorm. She rationalized every detail. The rain slowed his flight. Maybe he couldn't rent a car. It could take an hour or more to go from Hobby to Memorial in this kind of weather. At two-thirty she turned on every light in the house and drank a glass of wine. Her hands were shaking by three o'clock. When the phone rang it seemed to rattle the windows, she thought.

"Yes," she answered, her skin icy.

"Miss James?"

"Yes."

"This is Dr. Edmunds at General Hospital. We have an accident victim here. A Rex Cowert. He asked me to call you."

"An accident?"

"Yes, ma'am," the doctor replied politely.

"How bad is he?"

"He's asking to see you," he stated flatly.

"Is he all right?" she screamed at the faceless informer on the other end of the phone.

"I'd get here as soon as possible, Miss James. I'll tell him you're coming." He didn't wait for an answer and hung up.

"Doctor! Doctor!" Hailey cried frantically. The line was blank. She hung up the phone.

"An accident. An accident. Rex has been in an accident," she repeated to herself, slowly making her mind understand. Her hands had stopped shaking. Wasn't that strange? she thought. She was very rigid. She was in shock but didn't realize it. She checked her purse. Keys. Money for parking. Yes. She needed those things.

She went upstairs. "I can't wear this. It's much too fancy. Yes. I'll wear slacks and a sweater," she repeated aloud so she would remember. She spritzed on Oscar de la Renta perfume. Rex always liked that one.

She woke Joey and Kim and helped them dress. She couldn't leave them alone in the house. She explained slowly and carefully what had happened, but they were too sleepy to understand. She left all the lights burning as they left the house.

There was little traffic at three in the morning. The children awakened and asked her questions. She answered them but couldn't remember what she said. Her hands were cold and seemed frozen to the steering wheel. She turned left off Fannin to the emergency room entrance at General Hospital.

There were some places on this earth that even God would not go, and one, she knew, was a charity hospital. When the muggers had tossed their victims into the sewers, and the rapists had left their prey for dead, and when the police knew the half-mutilated bodies of survivors of any kind of accident were beyond hope, they were sent to General. It had the finest trauma unit in the city, but she could not conquer her fears.

She parked the car, and with a child on either side of her she entered the crowded corridors. Aides, nurses and interns stood against the walls, drinking coffee and trying to stay awake. She went to the main desk and they directed her to emergency. She took the wrong turn twice and was lost. She asked questions and then had to double back.

A stretcher with a barefooted wino was in the hall. His

head was bloodied and his feet and coat were caked with mud. Hailey felt as if she'd descended into hell with the smells of blood, excrement, sweat and those thousands of hospital anesthetics and chemicals that can nauseate the strongest of constitutions.

The emergency room was packed with humans all in need of treatment. It was in such a state of disorder. The whole place was a mess, she thought. Why didn't they admit these people? Why were they so battered, those boys with the bruises and cuts on their faces and arms?

The obese black girl in a pink uniform refused Hailey admittance to the ward. She was not a member of the family, the girl said.

"I'm his fiancée. We were getting married tomorrow. Uh, no, I mean today."

"Sorry," the girl replied blankly.

"Where's Dr. Edmunds? Can't you page him? Please?" Hailey implored.

"Oh, all right!" The girl was clearly irritated at Hailey's persistence.

Hailey stood against the wall clutching Kim's hand and waited. Joey sat in a chair next to them, tapping his fingers on the metal arm. Ten minutes. Fifteen. Hailey wished she smoked. She could use a cigarette. Twenty minutes.

"Miss," the black girl beckoned to her, "take this slip in to the nurse. You have fifteen minutes. He's had exploratory surgery, but he's awake now."

"Oh, thank you. Thank you," Hailey said, grasping the yellow piece of paper in her hand. Joey and Kim were silent but followed her into a wide ward where the beds were lined up against the wall.

The first two beds were empty. In the third bed was a man covered in fresh and dried blood. His hair was matted to his head, and a sheet covered his abdomen and legs. He was propped up so she could see his swollen face; then she realized that his eye was gone. He must have been in a rough knife fight, she thought, for his arm was slashed open and three deep gashes oozed blood that covered his face and trickled down onto his chest. The sheets were smeared with blood, and she wondered why no one was caring for the unfortunate man.

Just another in the pile of rubble, she thought. Another statistic they would read about in the papers, though no name would be mentioned. He was like the numbered tags on the bodies in the city morgue. No one was here to visit him; no family, no friends. Was it like that for all these people? Had they no place to turn to except this hell?

She passed his bed, looking onto the next bed, where she recognized the wavy brown hair of the man lying with his back to her. Thank God! He was all right!

"Rex?" She said his name joyously as she approached him.

"Yeah, baby." The voice was slurred into a mushed drawl, but it was Rex's voice. Shocked, she suddenly realized it was not coming from the man in front of her but from the mangled human behind her!

She whirled around. From this side she could see it was he; one green eye winked at her. She rushed over to him. His mouth was caked with blood and dirt. She couldn't even tell if he had all his teeth. His lips were cut through the center and separated.

Hailey's heart raced, pounded and banged against her ribs. She went numb and icy cold, as if someone had siphoned all the blood from her body. She was going to vomit. Her head was spinning; she knew she would faint. She held the rails of the bed to stop her from falling. She was going to urinate; bile rose in her throat. She couldn't focus, everything was hazy. Panic and shock were stripping her insides.

The excruciating pain he'd experienced was relieved by heavy doses of drugs. Demerol and Percodan flowed in his veins, causing a numb sensation where his extremities seemed no longer to be part of his body. He felt as if he were only a head and a trunk.

Hailey's face turned a paste white and her lips were blue.

"Do I look that bad, baby?" He made a futile effort at the joke, for he winced with pain whenever he spoke.

"Don't talk. You look fine." Never had words been so difficult to find. There were IV tubes and a catheter attached to him.

He lifted his hand and she held it. Though he couldn't raise his arm, his grip was tight. A tear fell from his good eye. "I love you, baby," he moaned. "You . . . you won't leave me now that I'm not pretty anymore, will you?"

"No! No! Don't think such things. Just think about . . . getting well."

What strength she had left, she used to stem her tears. She couldn't let him see her crying. Her hands started shaking so forcefully she rattled the bed rail. Her knees were giving way. Why couldn't she stand? What was happening to her? She had to sit down.

"Kim, honey. Bring me a chair," she said weakly.

"Okay, Mom," Kim whispered blankly.

Rex could barely move his head. "Kim is here?" he asked.

"Yes. And so is Joey."

"Where? I can't see them."

Joey was pacing. If he kept moving he wouldn't throw up, he thought. Both children were as pale as she was. They came and stood next to Hailey.

"How y'all doin'?" he mumbled through his blood-caked lips.

"Fine," Joey replied wanly.

Hailey's eyes fleeted across the room. Where were the nurses? Why wasn't he being cared for? Why hadn't he been cleaned up? Just then she saw a young blond nurse walking through the room. Hailey found her strength and jumped off the chair and grabbed the girl's arm.

"Where's the doctor? I want to know Mr. Cowert's condition," she stated frantically.

"The doctor is busy. He can't see you now," she said curtly.

"Please. Please just wash him. Why hasn't he been washed?" Hailey was hysterical; her tears streamed down her face. "I'll do it myself if I have to! I know you're shorthanded."

"All right, Mrs. Cowert," she said, her voice softening as

she tried to calm Hailey. "I'll clean him up as soon as I deliver these X rays."

"Oh, thank you. Thank you," Hailey said and went back to hold Rex's hand.

"You shouldn't worry so much, darlin'. I'll be all right."

"Sure you will," she said, though she didn't believe her own words.

The nurse returned with a basin of soapy water and two cloths and began cleaning Rex's wounds. Rex slipped into unconsciousness. Thank God, Hailey thought, at least it wouldn't be so painful now.

"How long has he been here?" Hailey asked.

"Since about ten or so. I wasn't here when they brought him in. They just did exploratory, but the doctor hasn't told me what they found."

"Why didn't they stitch up his face? And his eye? My God! He's blind!"

"His eye is fine. It's just covered with blood."

Hailey was aghast as the nurse cleaned away inches of blood and dirt. There was a huge flap of skin from a deep cut perilously close to his eye.

The black girl from the front desk came in. "I'm sorry, miss. You're going to have to leave."

Hailey couldn't believe it. "I just got here! Couldn't I stay for just a little while?"

"I'm afraid not. Only members of the immediate family." The black girl's face was stone. She'd probably dealt with interfering friends and relatives for so long that she had become immune to their pleadings. Hailey was facing resistance in all its closed-minded magnitude.

"Very well," Hailey said and leaned down to kiss Rex. He didn't open his eye but he was awake.

"I'll be back, Rex, you get some rest," she whispered, and he squeezed her hand even tighter.

"Promise. Promise you won't leave me."

"I have to go for just a little while, but I'll be here in the hospital."

"Good. That's good. Just don't leave me." He fell asleep again.

Hailey grasped Joey's and Kim's hands and they left in

silence as they strode past the beds covered in soiled linens and the icy stares of the nurses at the desk who were besieged by patients standing in line for treatment. Her anger grew in proportion to the commotion around her. Now that dawn drew near, the emergency waiting area was more crammed with people than it had been less than an hour ago. Hailey followed the signs to the cafeteria. Once the children were fed, she called Janet.

"Oh, thank God you're home, Janet. I need you."

"Hailey, what's happened? You . . . you sound just awful."

"It's Rex. He's been in some accident. God! I don't know if it was a car or a plane or what. Nobody has any answers around here."

"Where are you? Where are the children? My God, I can't believe this! Is he going to be all right?"

"I don't know. I just don't know, and that's why I'm so frightened. I'm at General Hospital. The children are with me. Could you come down here?"

"Of course I will! You don't even have to ask."

"I don't know yet about Rex. He looks horrid and I can't find the doctor who called me . . ." Hailey wanted to cry but she just had to hold on until Janet arrived. Just that long . . . then she would take the next step. "Janet, I'm worried about Kim. I think she's in shock. She's so quiet. I just never thought it would be this bad, and I couldn't leave them at home in the middle of the night. I guess I didn't think about anything except getting here. The doctor made it sound as if Rex were going to die at any minute."

"Hailey, I'll be there as soon as I can. Just hang tight, okay?"

"Okay. I'll be in the cafeteria. And thanks." Hailey hung up and returned to the table, where the children sat finishing their breakfast. Joey had eaten all of his eggs plus half of Kim's pancakes. He was always ravenous when he was nervous. Kim was silent, much too silent. Hailey rubbed Kim's arm.

"Kim, honey, don't you want something to eat?"

"No, Mom. I'm not hungry." Finally tears broke

through the wall she had built around her emotions. "Rex is going to die!" she burst out.

"No, he isn't!" Hailey protested, all her anger swarming around her like Furies. "I won't let him!"

"You can't stop it, Mom. Even the doctors aren't helping him!" Kim howled.

The inadequate care he was getting was apparent even to a child! Hailey knew she had to do something. But what? She wasn't family. That was it! John! She had to contact John. He could do something!

"You wait here and watch out for Janet. I'm going to make a phone call." The children nodded in reply.

Hailey fumbled forever for a quarter, found one and dropped it in the pay phone, placing a collect call to River Bend. John answered and accepted the charges.

"Hailey? How are you? How's Joey? And Kim?"

"John, I don't know how to say this except to get right to it," she said, quickly ignoring his inquiries.

"Go on, girl," he said, alerted to the seriousness of the situation.

"Rex has been badly injured in an accident, John. How specific should I be about all this?"

"Very! I want all the details you can think of," he demanded.

"He's at General. I'm calling you from here. They won't let me see him because I'm not family. I did get fifteen minutes with him. I don't know how bad the injuries are. At first when I saw him I thought his eye was gone."

"My God!"

"But it's all right. His lips are split in half. I could see some teeth, but I don't know yet if they are all there. There are big gashes over the eye and in his cheek, three larger ones on his arm but no broken bones. I think. I'm not sure about that. He had exploratory surgery and even there I don't have any idea what they found. He's just lying on a bed in the emergency ward. He's not even in a room. I had to beg the nurse just to wash him!" Hailey was growing more hysterical with every word. "John, why aren't those cuts stitched up already? That should have been done hours ago! He's been here so long. I think these poor people take numbers when they come in and if they die while waiting in line, it's just too bad. It's awful here. Oh, I remembered that they do have an IV hooked up and a catheter . . . . He's . . . so weak." She couldn't stop the tears that slid down her cheeks, but she brushed them away with shaking fingers.

"I want him transferred to Methodist. I'll make some calls and fly in this morning. Hailey, you go home and wait for my call."

"I can't do that! I have to stay here in case he needs me!" she cried as her voice shattered across the telephone wires.

"All right. I'll contact you there at the hospital as soon as I get in."

"Thank you, John."

"Hailey?"

"Yes?"

"He's going to make it. I never met a Cowert yet they could keep down."

"I hope you're right. God, how I hope you're right!"

"I am. Trust me. See you soon."

"Bye," she mumbled wearily and hung up. She walked back to the cafeteria. "Trust me," John had said. "Give me a chance," Rex had said once. "Trust me. Trust me." They both had said the same thing. That had been one thing she had found the hardest to do. Trust Rex to love her and not be playing her for a fool. Trust John to be right. Trust in God, who was nowhere to be found in these noisy halls. Somehow, some way she had to pull herself through this.

She sat down and asked Joey to get her more coffee. Kim followed him just to keep her mind on something else.

Time seemed to stand still. It always did in moments of pain. Hailey's head was bent; her hair tumbled around her face and hid her from the world and it from her. She felt a hand on her shoulder.

"Hailey, I got here as fast as I could," Janet's voice said, but to Hailey it sounded far away.

She lifted her head; it weighed a hundred pounds, like dead weight, she thought. She touched Janet's hand and felt a sensation of pressure but not temperature, as if her nerve endings had been disconnected.

"I'm glad you're here," Hailey said.

"What happened?" Janet asked, seating herself in the chair next to Hailey.

"I still don't know. All anyone seems to know is that he was brought in around ten. Now that you're here, I intend to find out," Hailey said, her resolve bolstering her courage.

"I'll stay here with Joey and Kim," Janet said. "Once we get some answers, I'll take them home." Janet knew she could never convince Hailey to budge from the hospital. It was obvious Hailey hadn't slept or eaten, but now was not the time to act like a mother hen.

"Thanks. I don't know how long this will take. Oh! Could you call the school and tell them Joey and Kim won't be in today? Give them some excuse."

"For God's sake, don't worry about things like that. I'll handle it."

"All right. I'll be back in a while."

Hailey left and went directly to the emergency room again. The administrator, Angela Wright, an older, blond woman with deep lines in her caring face, was back on duty, and Hailey was able to obtain a sketchy explanation of the accident.

Andy, the pilot, had cleared their landing at Hobby and they were only minutes from the field. The bolt of lightning that struck the blades of the private helicopter came from nowhere. Sparks shot across the panel board, dials whizzed around inside their glass cases. The stick had jammed and the radio went dead. The helicopter nosedived toward the ground.

Andy had frozen in panic while Rex screamed at him to pull up. Rex had tried to pull his hands off the steering wheel, but the controls had jammed. Then the lights went out. Rex had yanked the column and flipped switches in vain. Andy had heard Rex cussing at him to get the plane up, saying that he wasn't ready to die yet. When the helicopter impacted with the earth, Rex had been thrown on top of Andy and into the dashboard. Andy started crying and snapped out of it in time to grab Rex and scramble out. Together they had gotten away from the helicopter before it burst into flames. The pilot had few injuries and had given a full statement to Angela and the police. He had been released hours ago.

At the thought of how close Rex had come to being burned to death, Hailey thought she would faint again. This time the nurse sat her down immediately and got her a glass of water.

The medical report was worse. Two hours after admittance Rex's breathing had been labored and he'd gone into shock. Five ribs on his left side were broken. His spleen had ruptured and during the exploratory he'd had a splenectomy. Hailey knew he wasn't being watched closely enough. So did Angela. Hailey was becoming increasingly aware of the hospital's overload of patients and limited staff.

Angela arranged for Hailey to stay with Rex. Just as Angela was walking back to her desk, where Hailey was waiting for her, a young nurse rushed up, whispered something to Angela and they both raced back to the emergency ward.

Hailey waited for over an hour for her to return. She kept trying to calm herself with the knowledge that she would at least be able to stay at Rex's side until John arrived. It was cold in the sparsely furnished office. The morning sun streamed through the wire-mesh-covered windows, creating chicken-wire shadows on the old linoleum floor. No amount of security precautions could stop the harpies that roamed these halls and carried their prey off to death, she thought.

When Angela walked in, Hailey knew then that the emergency she'd run off to had been Rex. "Is he still alive?" She was afraid even to ask.

"Yes, but he's in intensive care." Angela took a deep breath.

"Why?"

"His lung collapsed. They inserted a chest tube under local anesthetic, but he needs to be monitored for a while."

"I want to see him."

337

"I know you do, but it's really impossible. Intensive care has very strict rules. Even I couldn't help you out there. I will see if I can at least arrange to get you outside the room, but it'll take some time. Why don't you get something to eat? There's nothing you can do right now. Check back with me in an hour. I've got other patients . . ." Angela apologized.

"I know . . ." Hailey rose and thanked Angela and left. How much wasn't she saying? Doctors and nurses never told you the full extent of the problems. They were so damn protective, thinking they would spare the family more worry. There was nothing she could do. Nothing. God! Can there be anything worse than this helplessness I feel? she thought. She walked back to the cafeteria, where Janet was waiting. How many more hours until he was out of danger? What else would happen? Would he ever be normal again if he did live? How many miracles could she pray for?

## Chapter Thirty-five

EMPTY Styrofoam cups and an ashtray of Janet's
cigarette butts littered the table. Joey had fallen
asleep on Hailey's lap. Kim's head rested on her folded
arms on the table. Hailey had relayed the story to Janet.
The hour passed and Angela had not returned and no one
knew where she was. Stymied, they waited for another
hour.

Hailey grew more tense with each minute. Her mind
flashed over every moment she'd ever spent with Rex—
their first lunch, the song he sang to her the first time they
had made love, the way he had helped Joey through his
fever. Rex's smile loomed in front of her. She could hear
his words in the channels of her mind. She saw him riding
the Thoroughbred triumphantly around the corral and the
kiss he'd given her in front of all their friends. She had
never wanted to believe him, always anxious to think this
was just a dream. But their love was strong and powerful,
so much so that it had changed her entire life, her way of
thinking. "Too much, too soon," she had once thought.
God! Was that what it had all been about? Some twist of
fate? She knew fate was notorious for playing with human
lives, giving them a taste of heaven and then snatching it
all away. Goddamned Indian giver! she cursed.

Had they been given so much together only because it
was never meant to last a lifetime? "Never meant to be"?
How many times had she heard that phrase? Even said it
to herself? Changes she could endure, but to have her

future left in ashes . . . What lucky number had she drawn to deserve this? O God! Please don't take him from me!

Janet read Hailey's torment and knew she couldn't answer her questions. No one could. The scenario wasn't over yet and all Janet could do was offer Hailey her help and friendship. Right now, this was not the place for the children. Hailey needed some time to herself to do what she had to do. Janet wisely decided to take the children to her house. Later, Hailey agreed, she would call and keep her informed on any news they had of Rex.

Once Janet left, Hailey began scouring the halls for any sign of Angela. She had just walked out of Angela's office when John came rushing up to her.

"Hailey! There you are! I've been looking all over for you."

"John! Thank God you're here!" she said, embracing him, relief flooding her body.

"I've already seen him. I've got it cleared for you to go into intensive care. He's been calling for you."

"Let's hurry. I can't stand this much longer."

They rode a frustratingly slow elevator in silence. John ushered her down the hall to the waiting area, where he instructed her to wait for him while he spoke to the head nurse. Hailey nodded in agreement.

A gray-haired woman with eyes wrinkled by years of hard work gazed at Hailey. Pity and pain rang in her voice when she spoke.

"Is your husband here, too?" the woman said.

"Yes . . . well . . . no. My fiancé. We were going to be married today." Hailey gulped.

"I'm so sorry. My Alfred is here. His heart . . ." Her voice cracked and she couldn't finish her statement. She closed her eyes and forced herself to speak. "We've been married for thirty years and he's never been sick a day in his life and now this . . ." The woman's fright bled through her every pore.

"He'll be all right," Hailey said, hoping she could be of some comfort. "A man with that kind of constitution will surely make it."

The woman's smile came slowly but she seemed to drink in every ounce of hope anyone, even Hailey, could give her.

John returned. "Hailey, I have to fill out some papers, but I shouldn't be long. The nurse said you'll be able to see him shortly."

"Thank you, John."

"Just hang in there, it won't be long now," he said as he patted her shoulder.

"John, is he awake?"

"In and out, really. Once the crisis is over, we'll transfer him. I'll feel better when he's at Methodist."

"Okay," she said, and John left.

Hailey offered to get some coffee for the elderly woman, but she declined. Just then a doctor still in surgical greens approached them. He wore a surgical mask down now around his neck, and his cap was sweat-soaked. Hailey held her breath.

"Mrs. Jacobson?"

"Yes?" the woman replied tentatively, visibly holding her nerves intact.

"I'm sorry, we did all we could," he said softly.

Hailey could see the agony in his eyes. The green angel of death, she thought. Mrs. Jacobson's tears made no noise as they fell from her tired eyes.

"Won't you come with me, please?" he asked. She nodded as he put his arm around her to help her. He spoke quietly as he walked her down the hall, and as they disappeared, Hailey could hear the woman saying:

"Oh, thank you, Doctor. Thank you."

Thank you for what? Hailey's mind stormed. Thanks for letting him die? Thanks for leaving me all alone without the person I loved and who loved me? Why? Why? Hailey's head sank and she rested it on her hands, her elbows propped on her knees. How long until that doctor said the same to her? How long . . .

"Well, well, Miss James," Pamela's voice purred at her.

Hailey's head snapped up and her body jerked upright. It took her a brief moment to focus. "Pamela? What are you doing here?"

"Why shouldn't I be here? Don't you think I would want to be at my fiancé's side at a time like this?"

Anger, frustration and panic rushed through Hailey. She bolted to attention and stood eye to eye with Pamela, feeling the force of the brunette's hatred. Hailey's fists balled. She wanted to attack her. But as Pamela's eyes narrowed she could see that was just what Pamela wanted. Hailey's common sense and courage replaced her impulsiveness.

"I don't know how you found out . . ."

"I have my connections," Pamela said with that icy, superior tone she had so effectively cultivated.

"I'll bet! But they're pretty lousy ones, if you ask me."

"How's that?" Pamela placed her hands on her hips.

"They failed to inform you that Rex and I are engaged," she said, flashing her sapphire ring at Pamela.

"That cheap thing? Rex has better taste than that and can afford a lot more. You can't fool me," she spat.

"Pamela, I think you've been telling your lie so often even you believe it now."

"Is that so? Then explain why you haven't been allowed to see Rex and I have?" Pamela said triumphantly. She would drive this stupid blonde out of Rex's life yet.

"I don't know. But I'll tell you what I *do* know. Rex loves me and not you. All your conniving and scheming isn't going to do you any good. You wouldn't be fighting so hard and so viciously if you really had him. A man like Rex can't be bought or tricked into love. He knows what he wants. You might as well go home, Pamela. Go stalk new territory. This one is off limits."

Before Pamela could say another word, a nurse came rushing up. "Miss James?" she asked.

"Yes?" Hailey replied.

"Would you please come with me? Mr. Cowert is awake and he's very insistent about seeing you," she said.

Hailey walked away, her eyes focused on the ICU doors, all thoughts of Pamela pushed back into her brain, where they belonged with other discarded problems of the past.

Hailey donned a mask and green surgical gown. She pushed the door open. She stood over his bed and he lifted his hand and he held hers very tightly. Besides the IV and catheter tubes, he now had blood plasma and a chest tube. He was lying on a flat bed surrounded by a bevy of mechanical devices. The nurse had told Hailey he wouldn't need a respirator anymore and the chest tube would remain for a week, two at the most.

The doctor had finally stitched the gashes and cleaned away all the blood. He was terribly bruised, but when he opened his eyes and tried to smile, he had never looked quite so handsome.

Her eyes were brimming with tears of relief, thanksgiving and hope.

"What took you so long, baby?" he mumbled through the stitches in his lips. "I was afraid you had left me."

"I told you, Rex. I'll never leave you, and I keep my promises."

"I'm glad," he said and squeezed her hand.

# Epilogue

T HE crisis over, Rex was transferred to Methodist Hospital, as John had wanted. Though his recovery was swift, Rex's disposition was sour most days, for his mind was still on the unproductive wells in Louisiana. Chess had called daily to inquire about Rex's health, and always the report was the same: no sign of oil.

Rex was frustrated, thinking that if he were in Lafayette, he could make those wells produce. Many times he had scorned the nurses' help, wanting to do everything for himself much too soon. Hailey had brought flowers and plenty of candy to cheer him, but it did no good. He seemed to wallow in self-pity, and she had no idea how to cope with it all. She was so grateful that he was alive, but Rex was still impatient to get back to Chess and the field. About the only thing that made him happy was the marriage license they'd gotten.

Ten days had passed when the chest tube was removed, and that day when Hailey came to visit, he was sitting up in bed, his black eye now a smudgy yellow and brown. He winked at her.

"I like what you're wearing," he said mischievously as she bent over to kiss him. "But I'd like it better if you didn't have anything on at all."

"Hmmm," she said, grinning. "You must be getting better."

"I am. This has been a good day for me."

"It has? Why? Because the nurses haven't been riding roughshod over you today?"

"No. Besides, I haven't been all that terrible to live with. Have I?"

"I wouldn't answer that if my life depended on it. Suffice it to say that it's all a matter of opinion."

"Well, anyway," he said, his eyes twinkling, "guess who called me this morning?"

"I don't know, Rex. Who?" she humored him.

"Chess."

"What's so unusual about that?" she said and finally caught the excited gleam in his eyes. "Rex? You don't mean that . . ."

"I sure do, baby! The well came in just last night. Isn't that great?"

"Oh, Rex, that is good news. I'm so happy for you."

"For us, you mean. Everything is working out great over there, and not only that, but the doctor says I can go home in a couple of days. But only as long as there is someone there to take care of me. I told him not to worry. He kept insisting on a private nurse, but I told him we didn't need one. My wife was the only medicine I needed."

"Rex! How could you lie to him like that? We aren't married!"

"I didn't lie. I never lie!" He smiled broadly at her indignant expression.

Just then the door opened and a middle-aged man wearing a clerical collar approached them. "Mr. Cowert?" he asked.

Hailey leaned over and whispered to Rex, "Who's that?"

"The man who is going to make sure I stay honest," he said and chuckled. "All hospitals come equipped with a chaplain just for emergencies like this one." He turned to the minister and said, "I think you'd better hurry up, before she changes her mind."

346